Darkness Among the Stars
Book One: Defeated

by
S.D. McKee

Behler™
PUBLICATIONS
California

Behler Publications
California

Darkness Among the Stars
Book One: Defeated
A Behler Publications Book

Copyright © 2005 by S.D. McKee
Cover design by Sun Son – www.sunsondesigns.com
Initial design by Dave Kern and S.D. McKee

This is a work of fiction. Names, characters, places, and incidents either are the product of the author's imagination or are used fictitiously. Any resemblance to actual persons, living or dead, events, or locales is entirely coincidental.

Library of Congress Cataloging-in-Publication Data is available
Control Number: 2005921796

SECOND PRINTING

ISBN 1-933016-23-X
Published by Behler Publications, LLC
Lake Forest, California
www.behlerpublications.com

Manufactured in the United States of America

I would like to express my sincere gratitude to all those who made this book a reality. First, to the voices in my head for their comments and suggestions; to the wonderful folks at Behler Publications; to Garrett Lewis, who served as the guinea pig for my first draft; to my wife, who paid for the shock-therapy sessions that helped induce this story; to you, my readers. And, of course, to that one obsessive fan who will no doubt stalk me someday. You know who you are.

"The greatest threat to peace lies not in weapons or machines of war, but in the hearts and minds of those leaders who would persuade their followers to use them."

— *Rael Kashan*

Prologue

There was darkness, so much darkness that had consumed everything, save a small splinter of light that sneaked through unnoticed. Or perhaps the light had been noticed and the darkness simply didn't care. It was timeless and powerful after all, and the light was nothing more than a trivial speck, weak and insignificant. Or was it? The light gained in strength. Slowly but surely it brightened, waiting for precisely the right moment. It came. The light rose up and overpowered the darkness, defeating its ancient enemy after what had seemed like an eternity of waiting, hiding amongst the rapacious shadows. The door to the old starship had slid open.

The silhouette of a mysterious robed individual appeared, stepping into the pocket of commanding light. There he lingered until a small hovering orb moved into view above him, bathing him in a soft yellow light that remained after the door swished shut. His royal-blue robe shimmered in the silky radiance, looking unmistakably majestic. Yet his face was curiously veiled behind the shadows of the hood that draped his head and his arms were folded, pressing and partially obscuring a golden object against his chest. A chiseled ruby crest hung at his neck, clasping the two ends of his robe together, trembling ever so slightly as he walked.

The floating light followed, keeping the darkness at bay while revealing the individual's path as he walked through the gloomy metal passageway. His steps were awkward, almost painful, removing any ambiguity about his age. He approached a control panel that was covered in age-old dust and studied the archaic interface. Wiping it clean with one arm, the elderly figure looked over the console, examined it, as if waiting to recall its purpose and method of operation. He eventually tapped a few of the pressure-sensitive areas that were offset with a feeble red glow. Power began flowing through the ship, coursing through a labyrinth of wires and circuitry like blood transfused into a dying patient's veins. A quiet hum drifted across the musty air as the overhead lights flickered, struggling to illuminate the enormous vessel.

The sounds of shuffling footsteps resumed as the robed figure continued through the maze of corridors, walking a predetermined path. When he came upon what appeared to be an elevator, he stopped and pressed the access button, leaning his full weight against it as he rested. The distinct squeal-like hum of the approaching elevator drifted down through the sealed tube, growing louder as it heeded its beckoned call. The doors soon rustled open, though not completely. But the gap was sufficient enough for him to squeeze inside.

"Bridge access," he mumbled, sounding shaky in his old age.

"Access…granted," the muffled feminine voice of the computer responded, sounding old and tired as well.

Bouncing a little from lack of maintenance, the elevator struggled to ascend the high-rising tube. And once the end of the journey was reached, the elevator jerked to a screeching stop, allowing the doors to stutter open, though no wider than before. Out stepped the robed figure, shuffling across the metal mesh flooring of the cold, dark room. Electricity had failed to reach the bridge, leaving the heart of the ship ostensibly lifeless, save a ghostly yellow glow that radiated from the orbiting light.

Creeping up a set of steps, he approached a railed perch that overlooked both levels of the circular room and eased himself into the dusty chair. The vinyl covering was a little stiff, groaning almost as much as he did, yet the chair still maintained a degree of comfort. Taking his time to scan the bridge, he reminisced of days long gone, bringing a serene atmosphere to the room. And the more he slipped into fond recall, the more animated the bridge became, until his imagination had brought the room to life. He could hear the familiar voices of old friends and acquaintances, surrounding him in a warm embrace. The sounds of laughter and cheery conversations helped diminish the effects of the stale, chilling air.

"You had a good crew," he professed to the ship. "They served us both well."

Though spoken with sincerity, his remarks brought a sharp end to the tranquil sounds. Faint screams faded in from the shadows, growing louder with each pounding of his heartbeat. The elderly figure began to weep as the room was overrun with the calamitous sounds of war. The ship would not let him forget its dreadful past.

"I remember," he cried. "I have not forgotten the cataclysmic events that brought death to so many. How could I ever forget such a thing, such a terrible thing?"

The room quieted, leaving him alone, lamenting the past. Exhaling with a deep, bitter breath, he cast his eyes down at the peculiar device that rested in his lap. Gold plating was exquisitely molded around the many wondrous symbols that decorated the exterior of the creation, which vaguely resembled a book, though it had no pages. Such beautiful craftsmanship was certainly worthy of attention, but it was the striking centerpiece—a sparkling white crystal in the shape of a diamond—that had commanded the entirety of his gaze. He remained silent for a time, staring at the precious gemstone, which seemed to draw the troubles from his mind.

One of his veiled hands moved over the strange device causing a small, etched symbol in the upper-right corner to glisten with a blue radiance. Clearing his throat, he began to speak.

"My son, I leave these words for you today speaking as one of the Defeated, in the native tongue of our ancestors. You have become a wise and noble leader, respected and revered by our people. Your life and upbringing have prepared you well for the burdens of leadership, but it is your heritage, your blood that will make you a great and just ruler.

"I will soon travel beyond the veil of life, entering into the peace of those who have gone before me. I now entrust this most precious archive of our people to your care. It contains much of the history, knowledge, and insights of mankind. It also contains the teachings of Rael Kashan, that great and noble leader who shaped the destiny of our people through his suffering and sacrifice. Learn from his unparalleled wisdom and use it to illuminate your path. His spirit will be watching over you, bringing you comfort as he did for me in my times of heartache.

"The archive also bears record of the Great Awakening, when mankind's destiny was fully realized, establishing order during a time of dreadful chaos.

"And lastly, my son, I have included a full account of the Great War, based on my own recollections as well as the testimonies and memories of those who fought so bravely. But there are many whose voices will never be heard. So many precious lives were lost. The historical account of the Great War was recorded so the suffering of our people would never be forgotten. History must not be allowed to repeat itself—a burden that is now yours to bear.

"If your mother was still alive I know she would be proud, as am I, of what you have accomplished. I wish I could be there to hand over the mantle of leadership and authority myself, but I have already outlived the time allotted me. I cannot escape death any longer. Live with honor, Noble One, and remember that I will always be with you on the long, difficult journeys of your life.

"In death, I choose to be known as Jonathon Quinn. Remember me not as your leader or superior, but as your father and your friend. Goodbye, my son."

Waving his hand back the other way, he caused the illuminated symbol to dim and brought the recording to an end. He then draped his arms across the armrests of the chair and reflected on his previous words. His head grew heavy with fatigue and slumped with the passing time, with the fading of his life. Before long, he spoke again, sounding even shakier than before.

"I will listen to the full account, one last time, before I enter the great sleep."

Peering down at the centerpiece, it began to shine with an angelic glow, responding to him as if it knew his thoughts, as if he and the gemstone were one. His head drifted back against the chair and his eyes, which had witnessed so much suffering, so much wonder, gazed out into the blackness. He no longer feared the darkness, which had once stalked among the stars. He had been but a speck of light, yet he had risen up and defeated the shadows that had nearly consumed everything. But that was history, a terrible history, an unforgettable tale of the twilight of humanity.

The recorded history of the Great War began to play.

Chapter 1
Dawn of a New Age

"Good morning, Captain Quinn," the soft-spoken feminine computer voice chimed within Captain Jonathon Quinn's cozy quarters. "The time is 0700 hours on June 1st, 2271, Earth Standard Time. There are two messages waiting for you. Have a pleasant day."

The computer's morning wake-up call had proceeded right on schedule but it did little more than solicit a yawn from Jonathon. He was already up, having awakened prematurely from a restless night's slumber. Mounting anxiety and excitement over what was destined to become an historic day had occupied his thoughts and dreams all night.

"Computer, play back new messages," Jonathon instructed as he dressed in his dark, neatly pressed military uniform routinely left for him by the previous day's cleaning staff. Though onboard a warship, Jonathon's rank afforded him certain perks, not the least of which was to have his quarters tended to while the rest of the crew was duty-bound to look after their own clutter. And this was fortunate for Jonathon. Otherwise he might have to give himself a reprimand for lax tidiness.

A small monitor inset into one of the walls began to flicker and in popped the image of Admiral James Breckard with his slicked-back silver hair and a battle-worn face that had only been known to display two emotions: irritation and rage. "Good morning, Captain," his stern voice boomed, prompting Jonathon to stand at full attention and take notice of the recorded gaze of one of High Command's most prominent officers. "I suspect everything is ready for today's operation. As you know, this project is of the utmost importance to the Intrastellar Coalition of Planets. If anything goes wrong I will hold you personally responsible. Don't fail me, Captain."

The admiral's image disappeared abruptly from the monitor. As usual, his message was short and to the point.

"I think he's actually starting to warm up to me," Jonathon said sarcastically as he smoothed his uniform to regulation-stated perfection.

Standing before a full-length mirror, he inspected every inch of his appearance starting with his black leather boots on up to his red-trimmed jacket. Particularly close attention was paid to the various campaign ribbons and medals that decorated the right breast of his jacket. Though he was only thirty-four years old, Jonathon had already seen more than his share of action, ranging from minor engagements with pirates and corporate mercenaries to the bloody First Interplanetary War in 2267, a tragic piece of history that had shaped more military careers than merely his own.

As the video monitor flickered again, another familiar voice from High Command drifted across the recycled air, though it had a much friendlier tone.

"Hello, Jon," General Sean O'Connor greeted with a subtle Irish accent. The image of the stalwart, middle-aged marine had appeared on the monitor, proudly wearing a black beret that blended seamlessly with his wavy hair and short-trimmed beard that surprisingly had yet to display any signs of aging. And his face was relaxed and friendly, in sharp contrast to Admiral Breckard. "I'm assuming everyone's favorite, fun-loving admiral has already delivered his usual inspirational message," the general said with a smirk. "Don't mind him. He's relatively harmless. I think the Coalition keeps the admiral on the payroll strictly for PR reasons. What can I say? People love the old lunatic for his military service record. Let's just pray he doesn't ever get the idea in his head to go on a motivational speaking tour when he finally retires. I think the suicide rates are high enough as it is."

Jonathon chuckled.

After a brief pause, the smile on O'Connor's face dimmed. "I don't think I need to tell you how important this operation is, Jon. I'm sure you've heard plenty about that since you were first assigned to the job. Hell, this thing grew to mythical proportions within a week of being leaked across the data net. And now everything from the economy to morale is on the rebound system wide. Every major corporation's salivating over the prospects of interstellar space travel. We're on the verge of a new Golden Age, Jon, and it's about time. I just wanted to wish you good luck, not that you need it. You're a fine officer and certainly one of the best I've ever had the privilege of serving with. Well, you've got a busy schedule ahead of you, so I'll shut up now. Expect to see me at 1600 hours for the celebration. O'Connor out."

He's right, you know. Jonathon bounced a confident gaze and a reassuring smile off the handsome reflection staring back at him. *Blush all you want at his praise, but you are the right man for the job. Of course, there's always the possibility the whole operation will be upset by some whacked-out freak with a political agenda and a protest sign. They love getting their faces broadcast around the system and it'd be just my luck to have that happen while the admiral's breathing down my neck.*

Turning toward the L-shaped desk that suspended snugly in the corner, he grabbed his personal communicator from the desk's reflective black surface and slapped it against his right wrist. The segmented chrome wristband crumpled around his wrist and clicked as the two ends joined magnetically. Despite the sophisticated technology embedded within the small broadband communicator, it resembled nothing so much as a common watch. It even displayed the current time.

Reaching back down, he retrieved a golden picture frame that had been leaning in one corner of the desk. It preserved a tattered photograph of himself as a little boy sitting on the shoulders of his late adoptive father, who had raised him as his own son after discovering him abandoned along a deserted road when he was merely two years old. While gazing at the captured moment in time, a warm smile washed across Jonathon's face.

"It's going to be a good day today, Dad," he uttered softly to the photograph. "I wish you could be here to see the experiment. They say it's going to be quite a show. And you always did love to gaze at the stars."

Jonathon's attention lingered fondly in the past for a bit longer before he eased the picture back onto the desk, quickly surveying the room to see if he had forgotten anything. Feeling eager to start his shift, he snatched a compressed meal packet off the dresser and dashed out the doorway. His hurried footsteps echoed through the long metal hallway as he jogged toward the elevator.

"Good luck with everything, sir," a cheerful young recruit piped up while straightening his green-trimmed military jacket.

"Thanks, Ensign," Jonathon hollered back before he arrived at the elevator. "We'll take all the luck we can get."

After taking a bite of his breakfast, he tapped the elevator's access button a few times. The sealed doors retracted with a faint swishing sound, permitting him to step inside.

"Bridge access," he ordered.

"Access granted," the computer responded as the doors swished shut.

The elevator began its ascent to the bridge of the Intrastellar Coalition Starship *(ICS) Intimidator*, the largest, most powerful ship in the fleet and well deserving of its name. The *Intimidator's* service record in battle was impeccable, though it hadn't seen any significant military action since its instrumental role in crushing the Martian war machine during the brutal interplanetary conflict.

"It's show time," Jonathon mumbled to himself as the elevator halted its ascent, the doors sliding open. Out he stepped onto the rear balcony of the bridge, a sufficiently large circular room comprised of two levels, yet still managing to maintain a fluid, open-spaced environment. The architecture of the bridge was designed to reflect the chain of command, starting at the captain's chair—the highest point—descending to the lower command level where ten junior officers busily went about their duties.

Five senior command stations were located along the outer edge of the rear balcony—two along the portside section with three across the way. Each station had a glossy black finish with a pressure-sensitive surface that rose at an outward angle, providing efficient access to the color-coded command functions that were illuminated within. Officers could monitor their respective operations on the crisp flat-panel displays that jutted straight up from the back of each station.

The steel-mesh flooring of the rear balcony merged with the few steps that led up to the captain's platform. It was on this small platform that the captain's black-vinyl chair was located.

The central location of the platform provided an excellent vantage point from which the ship's operations could be overseen. Such a perch could also serve as a mechanism to feed a captain's ego, though Jonathon guarded against all such temptations.

An elevated walkway extended out from both sides of the rear balcony, curved along the perimeter of the room. The catwalk provided access to the forward balcony, which contained a pair of computer terminals and three state-of-the-art tactical display stations. The central station was currently active, utilizing the latest holographic technology to display a semitransparent yet photo-realistic projection of the moon, hovering mere inches above the surface of the display grid. Three-dimensional replicas of all ships traveling within lunar space were also on display. A green aura conveniently surrounded all commercial and civilian transports while a blue aura encircled the military vessels, reducing the odds of mis-identification.

Although the holograms were interesting to view, they were a poor substitute for seeing a real starship up close, as was obvious to anyone who peered out the sizeable windows arrayed along the forward half of the bridge. They looked like tinted-glass picture frames that had captured breathtaking snapshots of the moon and surrounding stars. Striking views of the *Intimidator's* kilometer-long, charcoal-gray hull could also be appreciated due to the bridge's elevated placement at the rear of the flagship. Such imagery made even the most vapid moments of command duty well worth the time.

Commander Paul Jensen jumped swiftly up from the captain's chair after noticing Jonathon's reflection in the window. But rather than acknowledging his captain's presence, Jensen remained in Jonathon's shadow, standing at ease but with a certain degree of tension. Although it wasn't against protocol to be on the captain's platform without permission, most captains considered it a sign of disrespect. Jensen had intended to return to his post before Jonathon arrived, before he was caught in one of his all-too-common displays of insolence—a gnawing byproduct of Jensen's self-inflicted frustration that mounted daily over his inability to leapfrog ahead of Jonathon in rank and praise.

And for better or worse, both men had been assigned to work together, despite Jensen's routine requests for a transfer to other high-profile assignments within the Military Protection Force (MPF). High Command had decided to keep him on the *Intimidator*, feeling that his straight-laced, by-the-book approach to the military would help balance Jonathon's more relaxed style of command.

"Good morning, Commander," said Jonathon, sounding a little annoyed. "I hope my chair was comfortable for you."

Jensen casually brushed one of his hands through his jet-black hair, which had been trimmed to a traditional military crew cut even though the tradition had died out two generations prior. Adjusting his red-trimmed jacket, he turned around and saluted. "Good morning, Captain," he replied, acting as if he had done nothing wrong.

"Give me the morning status report," Jonathon ordered while stepping to the side, creating a space that was wide enough for Jensen to move through yet restricted enough to make him feel uncomfortable when he squeezed by.

"We had one minor security incident at the Lunar Research Facility last night," recounted Jensen, scooting around the chair and avoiding eye contact until he stood at the rear of the platform. "A couple of tech thieves tried to sneak in. Thanks to Lieutenant Chang's security recommendations, however, they were immediately apprehended and have been taken to a holding cell for interrogation. As far as we can tell this was an isolated incident and nothing to worry about."

"Good. What else?"

"The supply shuttle is nearly finished with its transfer." Jensen handed his small datapad containing the transfer log to Jonathon before continuing. "As you'll see from the report, we received all of the supplies we requested as well as six personnel transfers."

"Very well, Commander. Notify the shuttle pilot that he can depart at his earliest convenience. And make sure the cargo's properly secured."

"Yes, sir."

Jensen proceeded toward the lower command level to speak with the ship's cargo officer while Jonathon sat down in the captain's chair and made himself comfortable. Sliding the datapad into the appropriate interface slot on the chair's right arm, he caused a thin touch-screen display console to rise out of the armrest and click into place. A faint hum followed as the console's black frame automatically expanded, stretching the luminous plastic screen to an adequate viewing size. Jonathon spent the next few minutes going over the latest information reports while finishing his meager breakfast. He was in his element and loving every minute of it.

Lieutenant Kate Hayes was sitting in the swiveling black chair that was permanently fixed to her portside command station. The affable communications officer was dressed in the standard dark uniform, but with navy-blue trim and two bronze bars on her collar, signifying her rank. She was currently glancing over the previous night's transmission logs while making a few adjustments to her shimmering brown hair, which had been pulled up into a bun, her hairstyle of choice for the day.

"Captain," she called out, "we're receiving a communication from the Lunar Research Facility."

"Put it through," Jonathon replied, turning his attention to the primary display screen that obscured the upper third of the forward window. The image of the aged but distinguished Dr. Alek Nazarov popped into view, framed by two quarter-sized display screens on either side. Even though he was a civilian, his position as Director of Scientific Advancements at the Lunar Research Facility allowed him to serve as de facto second in command over the pending operation. He answered only to Jonathon.

"Good morning, Captain," he hailed with a stubbornly persistent Russian accent. "I just wanted to give you a quick update and let you know that we've nearly completed our preparations for today's operation. In fact, we're proceeding with the equipment diagnostics as we speak."

"Very good, Doctor. The *Intimidator* will be moving into position momentarily, which puts us about right on schedule. But before you go, I do have one last matter to discuss with you."

"I'm listening," Dr. Nazarov responded, glancing down at his watch as if to persuade Jonathon to be short and to the point.

"It makes me a little nervous having so many mission-critical scientists in one location, given the importance of the operation."

"We've taken all the appropriate security measures, as you instructed, Captain," Dr. Nazarov interrupted in an irritated tone. He recognized and resented the direction the conversation was headed.

"That's good, Doctor, but I would still feel more comfortable if you could spare two or three of your team members to be transferred to my ship."

"Might I ask why?"

"If anything goes wrong down there, such as a communications failure, I want people at my disposal who can inform me about the details of the operation. We can properly monitor everything from the bridge of the *Intimidator* and a live video feed will be maintained at all times. You'll still be able to speak with them if you need to."

Dr. Nazarov's brow furrowed. "I object to this, Captain!" he growled. "It wasn't part of the original plan and it would be a significant inconvenience at this point."

Jonathon leaned forward in his chair, displaying his own irritated expression. "I understand that, Doctor, but it's also a direct order."

"As you wish, Captain," Dr. Nazarov snapped before terminating the video feed.

Jonathon shook his head and leaned back into his chair. *That man's ego never ceases to amaze me. His promotion's gone straight to his head.*

"Captain," said Jensen, "the supply shuttle has cleared the hangar bay and laid in a course back to the lunar colony."

Jonathon glanced down and nodded in acknowledgement before turning to face Lieutenant Darin Parker, who was quietly sketching a Destroyer-class warship on his palm-sized digital art pad. He had accurately recreated the long, slender design of the warship, the whole of which appeared as if it were one big weapon.

"Power up the engines, Lieutenant, and move us into orbit above the research facility."

"Yes, sir," the reserved Martian-born navigation officer replied as a big smile brought a splash of color to his youthful, pale face. His unusually pallid complexion was the result of life within the domes of Mars, unexposed to natural sunlight.

Turning his attention back to the display console on his chair, Jonathon finished reviewing the morning status report. The scrolling text that filled his console acquired a faint blur from the telltale vibrations that subtly roamed the bridge as the ship's powerful engines engaged. The day was off to a fairly routine start and the buzz of friendly conversations soon filled the room, helping Jonathon relax. Despite Jensen's objections, Jonathon had always allowed, even encouraged casual discussions between the officers while on duty. He felt it strengthened their working relationships, improving their ability to pull together in a crisis. But even though the environment was more relaxed than on most warships, Jonathon still maintained a sufficient degree of order.

"Captain," beckoned Kate, "the luxury cruiser *Starry Night* is requesting permission to enter lunar space and dock with the colony."

"Grant their request, Lieutenant, but instruct them to approach from the far side, away from the restricted zone above the research facility."

"Understood, sir, and while I have them on the comm should I book us a couple of tickets for the return trip?"

Jonathon chuckled. "I'm afraid not, Lieutenant. We'll be entertaining High Command this evening in the officers' dining hall, which should be about as much fun."

"Right. To them the *Intimidator* is a luxury cruiser."

Lieutenant Chuck "Dead Eye" Adams tapped the Micro Music Man earpiece that was hidden inside his right ear, against regulations. He swiveled his chair toward Jonathon, looking troubled. "We aren't all required to attend that little shindig, are we, sir?" he inquired.

Jonathon turned his head and glanced over at the young weapons officer, whose wrinkled forehead indicated his level of discomfort with the notion of mingling with officers from High

Command. An opportunity for amusement was ripe for the taking. "No, not everyone," he replied casually.

Dead Eye breathed a sigh of relief and interlocked his hands behind his completely shaved brown head. "Good, so can we—"

"But," Jonathon interrupted, looking rather serious, "Admiral Breckard has specifically requested your presence. I believe he mentioned something about wanting to fill a vacancy on his administrative staff. He wanted an officer who had spent time in the marines, someone that would appreciate the war stories he likes to share."

The lieutenant's eyes widened, though his mouth was glued shut. His mind was racing, trying to decide if Jonathon was serious. He had always thought Admiral Breckard was senile and he wouldn't put it past him to make such an odd request.

Kate was doing her best to refrain from laughing. She knew Jonathon well and recognized teasing when she saw it.

"Relax, Lieutenant," urged Jonathon, smiling at the unique expression on the nervous officer's face. "You don't have to attend the dinner."

Dead Eye exhaled with a deep breath. "Good one, sir," he admitted, sporting a sheepish grin. "You had me going there for a sec."

Though he always appreciated a good prank, Dead Eye generally preferred to be the one dishing it out. In many ways he hadn't yet outgrown the class clown persona from his childhood. And his jocular, sometimes reckless behavior had cost him dearly on at least one occasion, the most recent of which had resulted in the loss of an eye, the consequence of attempting to pull off a brazen stunt during a routine training exercise.

The common misconception among those that didn't know the lieutenant well was that his nickname of "Dead Eye" was derived from the fact that he had a bionic implant for his left eye. In actuality, his nickname referred to his deadly aim with almost every weapon at his disposal.

"Anyone who wishes to spend time at the lunar colony can do so tonight after you go off duty," Jonathon announced, much to the delight of his command staff. He turned his head toward Dead Eye before continuing. "Just make sure you behave yourselves down there."

Dead Eye looked around, pretending he didn't know why he was being singled out. "What? I'm a good boy."

"Right," Jonathon replied with a subdued smirk and a voice full of irony. His attention then shifted to Jensen. "High Command will be expecting to see you at the celebration tonight, Commander."

"I'm looking forward to it, Captain," Jensen replied, though the celebration aspect of the planned social function bore no real interest to him. He was focused solely on the opportunity to rub elbows with so many high-ranking officers, the greater portion of whom were known to favor individuals who were particularly gifted at stroking the egos of their superiors.

Jonathon nodded at the commander's response before turning his attention back to his console. With the morning status reports out of the way, he began brushing up on Dr. Nazarov's research data. While he wasn't required to have a full understanding of the technical details of the operation, he was naturally curious and had always enjoyed reading about the latest scientific discoveries.

Dead Eye reached over to the auxiliary weapons station and gave a friendly tug on the end of Lieutenant Li Chang's short ponytail, gaining his attention. "I've heard there's gonna be a freakin' huge party tonight in the lunar colony's entertainment dome. Between their bicentennial celebration and the festivities they're planning for after the operation, they're expectin' a massive turnout, which means plenty of ladies lookin' for a good time."

"I'm in," the strapping young lieutenant replied without hesitation. He enjoyed an energetic nightlife almost as much as Dead Eye, though serving as the *Intimidator's* chief of security had given him greater respect for law and order than his cohort had sometimes displayed.

"All right, but you've gotta stay away from the female population for at least the first ten minutes," Dead Eye continued. "They seem to be drawn to you like a moth to a flame. Don't ask me why, though. I'm obviously better looking and far more charming."

"If you're going to start having delusions of grandeur again, then I'll be forced to remind you about that little incident in the bar back on Earth Dock last month. How are your ribs, anyway? Still sore?"

"Man, that ain't funny. How was I supposed to know she was the Prime Minister's daughter? And I could've taken that gorilla she had for a bodyguard if he hadn't snuck up on me from behind like he did. Another two minutes and she would've left with me and had the time of her life."

"Uh, the way I remember it she threw her drink in your face within the first thirty seconds of your conversation, which set a new record, if I'm not mistaken. And you retaliated by throwing *your* drink in the face of her bodyguard, a strategy that still has me puzzled."

"There is something seriously wrong with your memory, Li."

Chang chuckled. "Getting back to the subject of the party, who else is going down with us?"

"A few of the guys from the armory and...hold on a sec." Dead Eye turned toward Parker and got his attention with a snap of his fingers. "You wanna go to the entertainment dome with us tonight? It should be a great time, man."

"I don't know," Parker began, feeling his anxiety inch higher from the notion of mingling with so many people in such a boisterous environment. "I think I might just do a little reading—"

"Oh come on," Dead Eye objected politely, making it his personal crusade to get Parker to come out of his shell for the evening. "You do that practically every night. It'll be nice to get out and stretch our legs a little. Nothin' bad's gonna happen, and there won't be another party like this for a long time."

"All right," Parker replied reluctantly. "Count me in." He still felt uneasy, but often he resented his shyness for the social anxiety it inflicted upon him, leaving him with a genuine desire to be more like his friends and colleagues. But changing the essence of his personality was easier said than done.

"Lieutenant Adams," called Jonathon, having paused from his scientific reading. "Activate our shields and bring the defensive grid online. I don't want to take any chances, given the recent mercenary activity in this sector."

"Yes, sir," Dead Eye replied. He began interacting with his command station, activating the ship's defensive systems with a few taps of his fingers. "Shields are up and the Rapid-Track-and-Attack system is coming online."

"That reminds me, Lieutenant," continued Jonathon, his hands interlocked, resting in his lap. "How did last night's weapons training go? Are we about done with this round of certifications?"

"It went really well. We had close to sixty people in the battle room, which was a pretty good turnout."

"Yeah," Chang added, "and that leaves just over one hundred crewmen that still need to renew their pulse-rifle certification. We should be able to finish certifying everyone by the middle of next week."

"I managed to pop in last night and watch most of the training," Jensen interjected, prompting Jonathon to swivel his chair in order to see the commander. "And I'd just like to add that the performance of both lieutenants was praiseworthy."

"Excellent work, men," remarked Jonathon, turning his head and glancing back at the two lieutenants.

"In fact," Jensen continued, "I believe Lieutenant Adams even managed to refrain from hitting on any of the female trainees for the duration of the entire session. His unusual display of restraint was commendable." Though someone else might have conveyed such comments in jest, Jensen stated them as matter of fact. He often masked his criticisms with a compliment in order to come across more friendly than he actually was.

"Oh, I don't like to move on the ladies when they're armed, Commander," Dead Eye quipped, sounding almost serious. "I have my safety to think about."

His comments provoked laughter from some of the officers. Jensen, however, simply rolled his eyes and waited for the laughs to die down before redirecting the conversation.

"On a side note, Captain," he said, "I put in a request for Specialist Tippits to diagnose the problems with our new targeting drone."

"I didn't realize it was malfunctioning," Jonathon replied.

"Yes, well, it has a rather nasty quirk of trying to stun me whenever I set foot inside the battle room." Jensen glared at Dead Eye after finishing his statement, feeling certain that he was responsible for the "malfunction."

"I see," said Jonathon, trying to keep a straight face. "Well I'm sure Specialist Tippits will be able to work his magic and fix the problem."

Turning back around, Jonathon sneaked a sideways glance at Dead Eye, projecting a restrained smile of amusement. Dead Eye accidentally let half of a chuckle burst free, then immediately cleared his throat, masking his amusement as a cough. He was trying his best to refrain from laughing openly, knowing full well that Jensen would view such an outburst as an admission of guilt.

"Captain," Parker called out, displaying a grin of his own, "the *Intimidator* is in position."

"Very good, Lieutenant. Adjust our orientation so the research facility can be seen clearly from the starboard windows."

"Yes, sir."

The *Intimidator* engaged its maneuvering thrusters and tilted to its starboard side. This made it possible for the research facility and test site to be viewed from the bridge. The ship's Dynamic Reactive Artificial Gravity (DRAG) field maintained a near-constant gravitational environment, preventing anyone from feeling the effects of the change in orientation and speed.

External sensors and cameras provided more detailed views of the moon's surface, but the digital images were no substitute for the magnificent view out the windows.

"Lieutenant Chang," said Jonathon, glancing over at the lieutenant.

"Sir?"

"Contact High Command and inform them that we're ready for the security net to be established around the moon. I don't want a single ship within one hundred klicks of our position."

"I'm on it," Chang acknowledged as he began interacting with his command console.

"Lieutenant Hayes, contact Dr. Nazarov and inform him that we're ready to receive the personnel transfer at his earliest convenience."

"Certainly, Captain. I'm sure he'll be thrilled to hear that."

Chapter 2
Ripple Effect

The Lunar Research Facility had been created by the former United States military in the mid-twenty-first century, shortly after the Third World War. The lunar compound had come under the jurisdiction of the United Nations (UN) a few years later, after the UN had been reorganized into a worldwide government and military federation. The UN utilized the lunar laboratories for research into projects that would accelerate mankind's expansion into the Solar System. After the Intrastellar Coalition of Planets (ICP) had been formed, jurisdiction was transferred once again and with it came a directive to accelerate humanity's expansion into the universe.

Architecturally speaking, the facility was an exuberant, honeycomb-patterned metallic dome with several supporting structures jutting out from its base. An adjacent landing pad allowed shuttles to ferry cargo and personnel to and from the facility as needed, though for basic necessities the lunar dome was self-sufficient, complete with living quarters. Most of the scientists who worked there also had a residence within the nearby colony, but they tended to spend more time at the research facility than their own homes, especially as of late.

The interior layout of the facility was rather sterile in appearance—white-tiled floors and gray walls and ceilings. Of course, research didn't require elaborate architecture or colorful interior design. The venue was famous for housing the latest in computer and scientific technology. Working there was every scientist's dream.

Two stone-faced soldiers stood motionless outside the doors to the Lunar Research Facility's main laboratory, providing added security. They were both dressed in black military fatigues and combat boots, with threatening twin-handled black pulse rifles gripped tightly in their hands.

Dr. Nazarov walked casually past the two guards without even looking up to acknowledge their presence. He was a relatively quiet man who kept mostly to himself, usually because he was preoccupied with his research. At the moment he was especially pensive, busily poring over the latest simulated results for the pending experiment while waiting for the equipment diagnostics to complete.

"Excellent," he mumbled to himself, his eyes still focused on his datapad while walking blindly through the entrance to the main laboratory.

Upon concluding his examination of the report, Dr. Nazarov tucked his datapad into one pocket of the beige jacket that draped his slim torso. He then tugged at the tattered brown clip-on bow tie that had been attached in a futile attempt at sartorial elegance. After removing it, he quickly unbuttoned the restrictive collar of his wrinkled white dress shirt and ran one finger along the inside to loosen it further. Looking relieved, as if a great weight had been removed from around his neck, he strolled forward, navigating around the armed guards and scientists that populated the spacious room.

"Alek, you're back," hailed Dr. Wayune Choam in his usual raspy voice. The elderly white-haired scientist of great repute hobbled toward his associate, tapping his oak cane against the floor with each awkward step. His standard-issue white laboratory coat was a tad wrinkled but he wore it proudly nonetheless, along with a golden lapel pin denoting his latest Nobel Prize. "How did the press conference go?"

"It went well enough," answered Dr. Nazarov, looking quite pleased with himself. "I even discovered an effective way to evade any questions that I didn't want to answer outright."

"Oh? And how was that?"

"Simple. I answered with the most complicated scientific gobbledegook I could think of. They hadn't a clue what I said but were too proud to admit it, so they'd wisely abandon any plans for follow-up questions and proceed to the next topic."

"You always were good at dealing with the press. Perhaps you should consider politics, eh?"

Both men chuckled at the suggestion as Dr. Nazarov sat down at the nearby computer station. Reaching across with one arm, he brushed aside the pile of datapads and empty foam coffee cups that had cluttered his workspace and partially obstructed its three-dimensional holographic display. A surge of auburn-tinted data flickered into view at and below his eye level. Using his index finger, he prodded a few of the symbol-encoded areas of the data display, triggering a changeover to a graphical user interface that was comprised of a series of overlapping, partially translucent red cubes, each filled with a queue of commands.

"Well, I have good news," Dr. Choam continued. "The equipment diagnostics have completed, without even the slightest hiccup in stability. And we have verified the synchronized data feeds to the military's secured network. Big Brother is now watching, as the old saying goes."

Dr. Nazarov nodded and said, "Good. I only need a few minutes to input some minor adjustments into the system, and then we should be ready to proceed."

Dr. Choam sat down in one of the adjacent padded chairs, groaning in discomfort.

"How are you feeling today?" Dr. Nazarov inquired, taking notice of the pained expression on his colleague's face.

"My muscles are tender and there's a small quantity of fluid in my lungs, but I'm otherwise okay. Fortunately, the excitement of the day's work has helped ease the pain somewhat."

He removed a white handkerchief from the front pocket of his coat and covered his mouth as he coughed, sounding congested.

"Did you go to the medical center last night?"

"Yes, but the diagnosis was the same. The disease doesn't appear to be going into remission."

"Are you—"

"Don't worry, Alek, I'm all right." The wrinkles surrounding Dr. Choam's mouth were pushed aside as a thin smile was forced into view. He was trying to appear optimistic, despite having progressed into the late stages of Kunzler's Disease—a rare but deadly illness that, along with a host of complications, causes degenerative failure of all vascular tissue within the body.

"I may be old," declared the ailing scientist, "but I've still got plenty of fight left in me."

"I don't think nurse Traeden would argue with that," Dr. Nazarov commented with a chuckle. "She still curses at the very mention of your name."

His remarks caused Dr. Choam to go into a fit of laughter interspersed with coughing.

Part of Dr. Nazarov wished that Dr. Choam would retire so that he no longer had to witness his friend's suffering. It wasn't easy watching a man die a little bit each day. But the better part of him was glad Dr. Choam chose to stay. His contributions and friendship had proved invaluable.

"The final corrections are in the system," stated Dr. Nazarov.

"Then it's time, old friend. Time to make history."

"You're right, Wayune. I'm just not certain if I should be excited or nervous about all of this."

"How about a compromise? Let's choose to be excited now so we can be nervous later when something goes wrong."

Chuckling, Dr. Nazarov patted his associate gently on the back and said, "Excellent suggestion."

"Dr. Nazarov is hailing you, Captain," announced Kate while glancing over at Jonathon, who was conversing with the two visiting scientists on the rear balcony.

"Put him through," Jonathon replied, turning to face the flickering main display screen.

"Hello again, Captain," chimed Dr. Nazarov, beaming with a prideful grin. "Ah, I see doctors Zhan and O'Neill have joined you."

"Hello, Dr. Nazarov," the two newly arrived visitors spoke in unison as they gave a little wave of acknowledgement toward their supervisor's image. They were still wearing their white lab coats, which provided a sharp contrast against the dark uniforms of their hosts.

"Everything's ready to proceed on our end," Dr. Nazarov continued. "We're eagerly awaiting the proper clearance from High Command."

Jonathon placed his hands firmly on the railing in front of him, leaned in a little toward the display screen and said, "Well then, Doctor, you'll be happy to know that we just received confirmation from High Command that Operation Giant Leap is a go. I've already entered my authorization code, so the honor of starting the countdown is all yours."

"Excellent, Captain, and thank you. We'll transfer your video feed to our primary screen where you'll be able to observe the entire lab. We'll also keep the connection active at all times, so if you need anything, simply speak up."

"That sounds fine, Doctor."

Jonathon turned his attention back toward his new guests.

"Where would you like us, Captain Quinn?" asked Dr. Zhan, speaking with a discernable Chinese accent. She was twisting the ends of her shoulder-length black hair, feeling nervous about her first visit to a warship.

Jonathon courteously pointed toward the forward balcony and declared, "You'll be able to monitor all aspects of the experiment from over there. But keep in mind that you're mainly here to provide assistance in the event of a problem."

"Oh, everything will go smoothly," Dr. Zhan boasted. "The micro wormholes we created in our previous simulations and laboratory experiments worked flawlessly. And while I recognize we're working on a much grander scale today, the outcome of this experiment won't be any different from the others."

Jonathon responded only with a polite smile, feeling amused with the young scientist's presumption. Though he had no formal scientific background and hadn't graduated summa cum laude from a prestigious research university, Jonathon seemed to have his feet better grounded in reality than Dr. Zhan did. Glancing sideways at Dr. O'Neill, he saw a gleam of amusement in the lanky scientist's eyes and a faint smile being held back. The elder scientist was well aware of the likelihood of failure for the bold experiment, having already calculated a mere thirty-eight-percent chance of success for the operation—well shy of a scientific sure bet.

"Woohoo!" Dead Eye cheered from his weapons station. "Operation Wild Ride is good to go."

Grinning in amusement, Jonathon turned to face the outspoken lieutenant. "Operation what?"

"Wild Ride, sir. I mean, I get the operation's whole Neil Armstrong, lunar landing connection, but why does the brass back at headquarters always have to come up with lame, inspirational names for the operations? I think mine sounds better, 'cause going through that wormhole would definitely be a freakin' wild experience."

Jensen shook his head at the lieutenant's words, considering them to be out of line, almost childish. But everyone else took the spirited remarks in the lighthearted context they were intended. Even the visiting scientists chuckled while strolling along the starboard catwalk.

"I'll be sure to tell High Command to contact you the next time they need a new project name, Lieutenant," said Jonathon, returning to the captain's chair.

"Why, I'd appreciate that, sir," Dead Eye replied in jest. He then tapped his right ear and reactivated his Micro Music Man earpiece, providing him with a private, energetic musical backdrop for the commencing experiment.

Once the command console on the captain's chair slid up, Jonathon began interacting with the pressure-sensitive display. The video feed from the research facility was transferred from the main display screen to one of the adjacent monitors, allowing a crisp image of the quantum gate to take center stage.

Both the left and right tactical stations were brought online as well, projecting holographic recreations of the lunar colony and the research facility. The central station still displayed a full projection of the moon, where a replica of the *Intimidator* was clearly visible, indicating its exact position above the research facility. Six Destroyer-class warships were also displayed, holding their positions in a wide circular perimeter around the *Intimidator*. The moon was under the watchful eye of the MPF.

Dr. Nazarov reached one hand up into his holographic interface and entered his authorization code, starting the ten-minute countdown timer. The larger-than-life main display terminal, mounted high on the wall along the back of the room, overlaid the video feed from the *Intimidator* with the countdown timer. Two identical screens, one on either side of the main terminal, displayed video feeds of the quantum gate from different perspectives.

"T-minus ten minutes," the computer's voice echoed through the room.

"Dr. Choam," called Dr. Nazarov, "please contact Dr. Kroger and instruct him to bring the first reactor core online."

"I've already spoken with Yohan," Dr. Choam replied as he hobbled toward his computer station, which was fitted with a more traditional touch-screen plasma monitor that was easier on his eyes. "The reactor should come online momentarily."

A low hum drifted through the enormous underground chamber of the Kroger-Stevens antimatter reactor—a heavily guarded sub-lunar compound that was located over two hundred kilometers from the Lunar Research Facility, due to the extremely hazardous nature of antimatter. One of the ten giant, spherical reactor cores had begun to power up as requested. The titanium-plated cores comprised the heart of the facility and were centralized in the chamber, with long magnetic tubes jutting out from their centers, connecting each core to the appropriate holding cells for its diametric fuel components. The containment fields within the prototype reactor cores had been engineered to control the explosive reactions, channeling the unrivaled energy up into the cylindrical power converters and out through the long stretch of buried conducting cables en route to the quantum gate.

Four black rods containing the potent antimatter fuel source were gradually lowered into the first magnetic holding cell while white fuel rods containing normal matter were simultaneously injected into their own holding cell at the opposite end of the chamber. Initially only a few grams of fuel would be released, but as more power was demanded from the reactor the rate of matter, antimatter consumption would increase dramatically. Once a reactor core reached full load, the adjacent core would come online. This process could continue until all ten cores were running at full capacity, generating more energy than mankind had ever harnessed. For the sake of simplicity and safety, however, the scope of the power requirements for this experiment had been constrained to only one reactor core.

"T-minus eight minutes," the computer announced.
"The reactor core is holding steady at one percent of capacity," an assistant shouted.
"Good," confirmed Dr. Nazarov. "I'm transferring power to the quantum gate now."

The Nazarov-Choam Quantum Gate was located approximately one hundred meters from the Lunar Research Facility in a heavily restricted, flat, wide-open area. A red-laser fence and twelve automated energy turrets enclosed the extensive radius of the test site, protecting the sensitive equipment from terrorists and tech thieves. Star fighter patrols from the MPF's lunar security force made routine sweeps over the area as well, enforcing the no-fly zone. Anyone attempting to gain access to the gate without authorization would be incinerated on the spot. The ICP wasn't shy about demonstrating their desire to protect their multi-billion-credit investment.

The quantum gate was a circular structure measuring five meters in diameter and had a deceptively simple appearance for such a complicated piece of technology that only a handful of scientists could comprehend. The glistening copper-toned ring itself was fashioned from several interlocking segments, each of which was composed of a thick, durable metal alloy designed to resist the intense gravitational fluctuations that were predicted to occur during the experiment. Additional support was provided at its base—a pyramid-shaped clamp that rose out of the ground, keeping the gate upright and immobile.

Having been designed on a limited scale for the initial operation, the quantum gate would only permit probes and small, unmanned drones to pass through. Eventually, however, the gate would be expanded by adding additional interlocking segments, forming a sufficiently large opening through which starships of any size could come and go at will.

Dozens of reinforced cameras and sensors were stationed in the area surrounding the quantum gate, mounted on small pedestals at every conceivable angle. The monitoring equipment would allow every aspect of the gate's operation to be observed and scrutinized.

Small white lights around the outer perimeter of the gate brightened in sequence as power flowed from the antimatter reactor into the gate's inner circuitry.

"T-minus six minutes."

"The quantum gate is now online," Dr. Choam broadcast to the group. "I have confirmation that the quantum wormhole has been isolated and suspended within the gate's stasis field. It's now primed for reorientation."

"The reactor core's holding steady at two percent of capacity," announced the assistant monitoring the power readout.

"Excellent," said Dr. Nazarov. "I'm bringing the celestial targeting system online and entering the coordinates of Polaris. Stand by."

Polaris, also known as the North Star, had been chosen for the first wormhole destination due in part to its popularity, particularly in ancient cultures and mythologies. Astronomers in the late twenty-first century had also discovered a planetary system orbiting Polaris. Their findings hinted at the possibility that the second planet in the system was suitable for colonization. This discovery made the Polaris system an even more tantalizing target for the operation.

Tiny emitters located all around the inside perimeter of the quantum gate popped open, releasing steady bursts of subatomic tachyon particles that irradiated the center of the gate in an invisible, pre-programmed pattern. This method of tachyon bombardment enabled the exit point of the suspended quantum wormhole to be adjusted, within a fixed degree of error.

"T-minus five minutes," the computer stated, right on cue.

"Reorientation complete," Dr. Choam reported without even looking up from his computer terminal. "The quantum wormhole is ready for aperture synchronization."

"The reactor core's still holding steady at two percent of capacity."

"I'm transferring power to the expansor guns now," said Dr. Nazarov.

Six compact antigraviton-beam emitters, more commonly known as expansor guns, were attached to block-shaped metal platforms in front of and behind the quantum gate. The long, transparent barrels of the dusky, sophisticated devices were angled toward the center of the gate at a cool thirty degrees. They would fire intersecting beams designed to create a reverse gravitational field as the antigravitons collided with the quantum wormhole, triggering a controlled expansion. Once the power feed was increased, the wormhole would, in theory, steadily expand to fill the interior of the quantum gate.

Repeated pulses of red light began propagating through the clear firing tubes as the expansor guns came online.

"T-minus four minutes."

"The expansor guns are online and charging," Dr. Choam announced to the group.

"The reactor core's holding steady at three percent of capacity," said the assistant monitoring the power readout.

"Good," Dr. Nazarov remarked. "I'm firing the synchronization lasers now."

Each expansor gun discharged a continuous thin, red laser through the center of the quantum gate, intersecting at the exact location of the suspended quantum wormhole.

"The expansor guns are synchronized and precisely on target," Dr. Choam declared confidently after reading the sensor report.

"T-minus three minutes," the computer interrupted.

"I'm powering up the ghost-radiation field now," Dr. Nazarov stated.

Over 250 gigawatts of power began flowing into the quantum gate as an invisible energy field known as ghost radiation enveloped the space within the ring. Ghost radiation functioned to stabilize the wormhole, preventing a premature collapse. The strength of the energy field was directly proportional to the size of the wormhole so that when the quantum wormhole began to expand, the ghost radiation would automatically draw more power from the reactor. At its full, designated size, the wormhole would cause the quantum gate to consume nearly one hundred percent of the reactor core's power output.

"T-minus two minutes."

"Ghost radiation active," Dr. Choam acknowledged. His attention then turned to the pair of display screens that relayed images of the quantum gate.

"The reactor core is holding steady at six percent of capacity," the assistant monitoring the power readout shouted, sounding more excited each time the energy output spiked.

"Everything's proceeding according to plan," Dr. Nazarov proclaimed proudly. "I'm powering up the first probe."

Four spherical sensor probes were stationed along small, steel launching platforms that had been fastened to the lunar surface a short distance from the quantum gate. The light-gray probes measured one meter in diameter and were covered with tiny maneuvering thrusters, imaging devices, scanners, and four solar-charging fuel packs—everything necessary for the exploration of a new star system. But they served another purpose, not purely functional. Plastered along every unused inch of their surface were the handwritten signatures of each scientist involved in the operation, commemorating their years of dedication, and, in a way, taking part of them along for the ride.

In order to maintain an active communication link across the 430 light years that would soon separate the probes from their creators, they were fitted with standard communications hardware that linked them with the ICP's Quantum Communications Hub. The Hub, as it was more commonly known, made use of the bizarre discovery of quantum entanglement, which states that when one entangled particle is altered, the other particle in the pair is simultaneously altered as well, regardless of the distance that separates them. As each new communications component was created, so was a uniquely entangled system of particles. Half of the particles were placed inside the component's core while the other half was added as a new node within the Earth-based Hub. This clever arrangement enabled each starship, probe, mining platform, and colony to experience clear, real-time communication from anywhere within the Solar System. And with the advent of interstellar space travel, the transmission would continue uninterrupted from anywhere in the universe.

Short bursts of yellow exhaust shot out of the side thrusters of one of the probes as its engine test fired.

"T-minus one minute."

An increasing number of scientists began to huddle together in front of the display screens that relayed video feeds of the quantum gate.

"Here we go, gentlemen," Dr. Nazarov proclaimed enthusiastically to his colleagues, all of whom had their eyes and hopes fixed on the live coverage.

"T-minus ten... nine... eight... seven... six... five... four... three...two...one."

"Firing the expansor guns now," Dr. Nazarov shouted. Reaching up with one hand, he touched the illuminated firing command.

The pulsating red lights within the firing tubes of the expansor guns began to increase in frequency as the emitters prepared to discharge. An initial antigraviton burst was unleashed, causing a lambent twinkling of white light to appear at the center of the quantum gate.

"I'm detecting a small vibration in the gate from gravitational eddies, but it appears to be within acceptable parameters," Dr. Choam called out to Dr. Nazarov.

"The reactor core has climbed to ten percent of capacity," one of the assistants reported.

"The quantum wormhole has begun to expand," declared Dr. Nazarov, his eyes wide with anticipation. "I'm increasing power to the expansor guns now."

The pulsating light within the firing tubes began to intensify, then unexpectedly turned solid red as a copious burst of antigravitons shot into the wormhole. A blinding flash of light erupted from the center of the gate as the wormhole expanded to full size in a fraction of a second, releasing a gravitational shock wave that thundered out from the test site, slamming into the research facility.

Screams of panic flooded the lab as the dome trembled, causing a few of the startled scientists to lose their balance and stumble over backwards. The lights in the room dimmed and flickered while poorly placed pieces of equipment slid off desks, crashing onto the floor, even causing a small electrical fire to break out in one location.

The tremors soon subsided, leaving the laboratory in an unsettled quiet. After assisting those people who had fallen, the cautious group began surveying the room, checking for damage. One of the soldiers noticed the fire, grabbed an extinguisher off the wall and doused the flames.

"What the hell happened?" Dr. Nazarov shouted, his face burning red with anger.

"The sensor readout indicates that a power surge occurred in the expansor guns seconds before they fired, sir," one of the laboratory assistants stated, looking perplexed by his discovery and nervous about having to report it. "Uh, they apparently fired at full strength."

"How? The diagnostics didn't detect any anomalous hardware."

"I don't know, sir," the assistant replied, shrugging his shoulders out of habit. His lackluster response served only to increase Dr. Nazarov's level of irritation.

"The reactor appears to be functioning," one of the scientists interjected. "In fact, the reactor core's holding steady at ninety-eight percent of capacity."

Dr. Choam approached Dr. Nazarov's computer station where they both frantically tried to bring the cameras and external sensors surrounding the quantum gate back online.

"Dr. Nazarov!" Jonathon's voice anxiously blared from the lab's main display terminal. "We detected massive seismic activity down there. Is everyone all right?"

"Yes, Captain. We're a little shaken up, but I don't believe anyone was harmed." Dr. Nazarov's eyes swept once around the room, quickly verifying his claim before resuming the conversation. "And there doesn't appear to be any structural damage to the research facility, but we're still investigating. We're also trying to bring the gate's external sensors back online, so at the moment we're unsure of the full extent of the damage at the test site. The epicenter of the quake seems to have originated from the quantum gate's location."

"Was the quantum gate destroyed?" Jonathon asked, his head heavy with anticipated disappointment.

"I don't believe so, Captain. The gate's internal sensors still seem to be functioning and we're showing that it's currently drawing power from the reactor. We're merely awaiting visual confirmation."

"Captain," interrupted Kate, "Admiral Breckard is demanding a status report. He doesn't sound too happy."

"He never does. Tell him to stand by."

"Some of the cameras and sensors are coming back online now, Captain," added Dr. Choam. "You should see the video feeds on your terminals...now."

A shallow, twenty-meter-wide circular crater had appeared around the quantum gate. The lunar depression had formed under the explosive gravitational forces that had been unleashed during the instantaneous expansion of the wormhole.

The gate itself appeared to be structurally sound, although part of the stabilizing clamp had buckled. But all six of the expansor guns had been crushed, as had several of the cameras and sensors. Two of the probes were also irreparably mangled, including the one that was preparing to launch. Nevertheless, floating eerily within the quantum gate was the open mouth of a wormhole. Strange ripples moved across the spatial distortion, followed by small flares of white light. It was like staring into a pond as the moonlight reflected off gentle, wind-blown waves. A new star system could clearly be seen within the gently oscillating boundaries of the wormhole.

The low rumbling of simultaneous conversations flooded the laboratory as the dismayed scientists discussed the damage they were observing. But once the test site's remaining cameras came back online, silence swept through the room, leaving everyone to stare in awe at the crisp images of the wormhole that decorated the two outer display screens. Such striking imagery complimented the astonished faces of Jonathon and his officers.

"Dr. Nazarov, is that what I think it is?" Jonathon called out, sounding guardedly optimistic. He was leaning forward in his chair, staring at the peculiar image of the wormhole on the main display screen of the bridge.

"Yes, Captain. We are indeed observing a fully expanded wormhole within the quantum gate. It appears that despite our little mishap, the initial phase of Operation Giant Leap is a success."

"Fascinating," Jonathon replied in a whisper. He took a moment to admire the spectacular view, then asked, "Are you certain the wormhole's stable?"

"I believe so, Captain, although stability is a relative term here. We've yet to fully master wormhole physics." Dr. Nazarov peered down at the latest status report before continuing. "We're not detecting any anomalies with the gate's operation on our end."

"Commander," said Jonathon, turning to face Jensen, "gather a damage report of the test site ASAP and forward it on to High Command."

"Yes, sir."

"Dr. Nazarov," one of the scientists interrupted, "I'm showing an unusually high concentration of radiation emanating from the wormhole's location."

"Is the wormhole radioactive?" inquired Jonathon, sounding surprised.

"No, Captain," Dr. Choam assured him. "The radiation must be coming from the other side of the wormhole. It's possible that our destination coordinates were a little off their mark, placing the exit point closer to Polaris than we had intended. Unfortunately, there is a certain degree of error with the celestial targeting system."

"I see. Well then, is it safe to proceed with the second phase? We're showing that two probes are still operational."

"Absolutely," Dr. Nazarov answered without hesitation. "There are a few minor fluctuations in the wormhole, but our readings indicate that it's operating within acceptable parameters. I strongly recommend that we proceed with the launch sequence for the first probe."

"What about the unmanned drone? Is it still functional?"

"Yes, Captain," confirmed Dr. Choam. "It's stationed on our landing pad, safely out of harm's way."

"Once the surveying probes have cleared the wormhole," Dr. Nazarov explained, "their automated guidance systems will course correct onto a proper trajectory for a sustained, low orbit of the second planet. At that point we will move to the third phase of the operation. The unmanned drone will shuttle the land rover through the wormhole and down to the surface of the planet to begin sampling its soil and plant life, if any."

"Hopefully," Dr. Choam interjected, beaming with excitement, "we'll be able to gather enough data between the probes and the rover to keep us busy for a month or two while we make the necessary repairs and upgrades to our equipment. If the planet proves to be as ideal as we think it is, the Coalition should be able to commence construction of a colonial outpost by the onset of the new year. It's all very exhilarating to think about."

"I share your enthusiasm, Doctor," said Jonathon with an equally radiant grin.

"Do we have your permission to launch the first probe?" Dr. Nazarov petitioned, sounding a little impatient, like a child waiting to open a long-awaited present.

"Well, all things considered it sounds as if it's safe to proceed with the operation. Go ahead and initiate the launch sequence."

"Now please be aware, Captain, that the probe will vanish briefly as it crosses the threshold of the wormhole. It must travel through the concealed spatial distortion, or tunnel, that is connecting our Solar System with the Polaris System. Once it is safely through we'll establish a video link."

"Understood."

"I'm starting the ten-second countdown sequence now."

Controlled bursts of yellow exhaust shot out of the side thrusters of one of the remaining probes as its engine test fired. Then came a spurt of energetic vibrations, like pre-show jitters as the probe's main fuel source ignited, releasing flickers of golden light between gaps in the launching platform and the cone-shaped main exhaust port that had kept the probe balanced upright. It was time for the small explorer to begin its journey. Lurching off its platform, the probe fired its maneuvering thrusters, adjusting its course to perfect alignment with an entry vector into the wormhole. And as the engine engaged at full burn, a flaring surge of exhaust sent the probe racing away and into the history books.

Iridescent flashes bounced across the wormhole as the probe penetrated its boundaries, disappearing into the darkened tunnel. The bizarre spatial distortion the probe traveled through was formed from exotic black matter that spiraled counterclockwise, twisting and churning against bolts of crimson energy that randomly shot through the tunnel. So violent were the forces in play that it appeared as if the fabric of space itself was on the verge of being torn apart. Yet the probe continued undaunted, passing through the eye of the perilous storm until it penetrated the wormhole's exit and popped back into normal space. Firing its maneuvering thrusters, the small voyager slowed its movements to a crawl in order to allow its optical lens to pan around and obtain a closer look at the new star system.

The static-interlaced video feed from the Polaris System started to come through on one of the lab's display screens, eliciting excited chatter from its audience.

"Astonishing," Dr. Nazarov exclaimed, his eyes immovable from the video feed. "Are you seeing this, Captain?"

"We certainly are, Doctor. We certainly are."

"The probe's systems are showing all-clear across the board," one of the scientists announced, barely able to take his eyes off the display screen long enough to check the probe's vitals.

"The wormhole also appears unaffected by the probe's passing," another scientist added. "Energy levels are continuing with a point-two degree of variance."

"Good," Dr. Choam replied. "Very good."

"Wayune, can we enhance the image to eliminate the static?" Dr. Nazarov asked.

"I'll try, Alek, but the intense radiation from Polaris may be difficult to filter. The shielding on the optical lens wasn't designed to handle these levels."

The image improved gradually, showing an amazing panorama of the Polaris System, despite the bursts of static that still came through on occasion—a minor annoyance at best to such a scientific milestone.

"Captain," interrupted Kate, "Admiral Breckard is complaining of technical problems with the video transmission. He says the relay from the probe has blacked out."

"The probe's signal is linked directly into the Hub," Dr. O'Neill interjected, turning partway around from his post. "So whatever technical difficulties High Command is having must be originating at their end, otherwise we would have lost the signal as well."

"Inform the admiral that he'll need to call in one of his engineers to diagnose the problem," Jonathon advised.

"Will do."

The probe's camera continued to rotate, relaying detailed views of Polaris, which was indeed exceptionally close to the wormhole. Then vistas of the first planet came on, orbiting the guiding star a little ways off in the distance, thereby forcing the probe to increase magnification. Upon closer examination the planet appeared to be a twin of Mercury—hot, barren, riddled with craters.

Igniting its engine once again, the probe fought against the star's strong gravitational pull. Away it crept into the system, struggling to distance itself from the fiery giant. And as the journey continued, the camera zoomed in toward the second planet, a mere speck in the distance. But that speck soon became a breathtaking spectacle, a bluish-green world with sprawling, discernable landmasses and swirling white clouds. The imagery was so peaceful, so alluring, yet it became gradually more astonishing upon closer examination. There, peeking out from beneath the clouds, were sporadically clustered patterns of lights, suggesting that intelligent life resided planetside. An array of large objects was also discovered in orbit around the planet, as if it had a natural ring. But further scrutiny showed the objects to be moving and in unnatural ways. They were enigmatic and would remain that way since the probe's powerful lens had reached the limit of its abilities.

Polaris continued to tug at the visiting piece of technology, which limped toward the second planet, expending precious fuel.

"Unbelievable," Dr. Nazarov exclaimed as the chatter in the room became louder. Though he was frustrated with the probe's diminished speed, he was still impressed with the images it was capturing—scenery that almost made him forget about the damage to the test site. Almost.

"Please correct me if I'm wrong," Jonathon's voice called out, sounding surprised, "but it appears as if the Polaris System is inhabited by some sort of alien society."

"Fascinating, isn't it, Captain? We always believed we weren't alone in the universe, but never in my wildest dreams did I anticipate establishing first contact during this operation."

"Now hold on, Doctor. We don't have authorization to do any such thing. Try to position the probe in orbit around the first planet and do not send any transmissions toward the aliens. Refrain from any further activity until I contact High Command and determine how the operation should proceed. The prospect of colonizing the second planet is obviously out of the question now. However, I do recognize that we have a unique scientific opportunity here and I want to make sure we go about this in the right way."

"Very well, Captain," conceded Dr. Nazarov.

"I'm detecting strong fluctuations in the wormhole," one of the scientists called out, sounding nervous, on the fine edge of panic. "I think it's destabilizing!"

Dr. Nazarov scowled at the sensor readout that hovered in front of his eyes. "He's right," he muttered to Dr. Choam. "It's behaving erratically."

"The wormhole's close proximity to Polaris is most likely the source of the problem," Dr. Choam hypothesized. "Perhaps if we—"

"What's going on?" Jonathon demanded.

"There were some fluctuations detected, Captain, but the situation isn't as bad as my impetuous colleague implied," Dr. Nazarov asserted. "I believe the internal sensors monitoring the wormhole's activity may have sustained damage, so I'm going to take them offline temporarily while I run a thorough diagnostic. The other sensor readings are within the predicted results, however, so there's no need for alarm. It's perfectly safe to continue."

Even though Dr. Nazarov's response should have calmed Jonathon's nerves, it didn't. But he couldn't terminate the operation on a gut feeling, especially since it would be impossible to initiate a second attempt at exploring the Polaris System until repairs had been made. So he made the logical decision to wait. "Very well, Doctor. I'll defer the judgment call to your expertise. But I ask that you exercise extreme caution. Now, please stand by."

Jonathon turned toward Kate and said, "Mute the communication link and contact High Command. Put the transmission through to my console."

"Certainly, Captain."

Dr. Choam's face was more wrinkled than usual as he stared suspiciously at Dr. Nazarov. "What are you doing, Alek?" he whispered. "Those sensors are fine."

"I won't give him the opportunity to terminate the operation," Dr. Nazarov grumbled under his breath. "Between the repairs we already have to make and the political nonsense we'll have to suffer through, it will take months before we get another shot at this. I've waited long enough for this day as it is and I'm letting the operation continue. We can't imprudently disregard an opportunity to establish contact with an extraterrestrial civilization. We're on the verge of the greatest achievement of our careers, Wayune. And besides, there's a chance the wormhole will stabilize on its own."

"And if it doesn't? There are a lot of unknowns here, Alek. What if the quantum gate is damaged in the process? It could set us back even further. It's an awfully big risk—"

"That I'm willing to take."

Dr. Nazarov's face began to relax as he forcefully calmed himself, trying to avoid an emotional escalation of the discussion. "You've got to trust me on this, old friend. Please."

Dr. Choam nodded in agreement, although he averted his eyes in shame. While he didn't approve of Dr. Nazarov's decision, he selfishly chose to go along with it nonetheless. With his health deteriorating, he wasn't sure he'd still be alive to witness a second attempt at the experiment. And for the moment, at least, that provided him with enough justification for his morally questionable decision.

The soft, grandmotherly visage of Admiral Jane Hughes, the presiding officer over High Command, faded in on Jonathon's display console. She looked deceptively harmless for someone who held such a powerful position. But those who had crossed her knew differently.

"What do you have to report, Captain?" she asked in her usual polite tone.

"An unexpected situation has developed with the operation, Admiral. We—"

"Look at the probe's video feed!" Jensen shouted, inadvertently interrupting Jonathon's conversation.

"One moment, Admiral."

Placing the communication link with High Command on hold, Jonathon shot a suspicious gaze up at the probe's video relay. One of the objects circling the alien planet was approaching with tremendous speed.

"Lieutenant Hayes, restore the audio link with the research facility."

"Done."

Sounds of excited conversations from within the research facility overflowed into the bridge once again.

"Dr. Nazarov, hold the probe where it is for a moment. Since we've intruded on their home territory, we'd better play it safe and let them make the next move."

"As you wish, Captain."

Static once again overlaid the probe's transmission, making it difficult to see the approaching object, yet no-one could avert their eyes from what they believed to be a technological wonder, a starship of an unknown alien intelligence. The large vessel was most peculiar in shape and design, with its midnight-blue surface shimmering sporadically against the light of Polaris, even nearly vanishing at times. It was unlike anything they had ever seen or imagined.

The static worsened.

"Wayune, can't we do anything about that static?" Dr. Nazarov complained, growing more irritated that the experiment seemed to be spiraling out of his control.

"The interference isn't coming from the star," Dr. Choam responded, having analyzed the sensor readings. "There's a distinct disruption pattern in the probe's optical system. I believe our transmission is deliberately being interrupted by whatever's approaching."

"I don't like this," Jonathon stated as his muscles tensed with nervous anticipation. Glancing at the alien vessel one more time, he heard a chorus of muffled whispers drift by him, almost through him, leaving a chilling, shuddersome sensation in their wake. He felt as if someone had sneaked up behind him, drawing uncomfortably close, so close in fact, that the hairs on the back of his neck stood on end. Snapping his head around, he glanced behind his chair but nobody was there. His command staff was all accounted for, sitting quiet, motionless, drawn to the enchanting video feed. So Jonathon turned his attention back to the overhead monitors, feeling even more uneasy. He sensed the imminent danger and his premonitions had never been wrong before. Never!

"Turn the probe around and bring it back through the wormhole," he ordered, almost yelled.

"Captain, please," Dr. Nazarov objected. "Let's refrain from making any rash decisions. The aliens may simply be trying to initiate contact. There's no reason to overreact."

At that moment, a bright flash of light enveloped the display terminals, followed by uninterrupted static.

"What just happened?" Jonathon demanded. The uncomfortable feeling in the pit of his stomach began to swell, providing him with the answer to his question before anyone else could respond.

"We've lost contact with the probe," Dr. Choam replied, his head sagging in disappointment.

"Please tell me that it's due to technical problems."

"It's highly probable the probe experienced a technical failure," Dr. Nazarov replied. He then glanced at Dr. Choam, who looked uncharacteristically perplexed at the current status of the operation.

Though he had seen eye to eye with his colleague on most occasions, Dr. Choam had found himself in an uncomfortable position. There was simply too much at stake for him to continue to go along with Dr. Nazarov's charade. And so, with a deep exhale of disappointment, he looked up at Jonathon's image and confessed, "Captain, I detected a significant energy spike before the transmission terminated. I believe the probe was destroyed and I *strongly* recommend we terminate—"

"We don't know anything for certain at this point, Captain," Dr. Nazarov argued sharply, seeking to put an end to any further discussion of aborting the operation. "It's imperative that we power up the second probe and verify the situation. We don't want to foolishly waste this unprecedented opportunity."

"No, Doctor," Jonathon rebutted. "What we need to do is close that wormhole. At this point it poses a grave security risk. Now shut it down!"

"Captain, you can't be serious. If we abort now we won't be able to—"

"I'm detecting strong vibrations from within the quantum gate," one of the scientists cautioned. "Something's wrong with the wormhole."

"You've got to do as he says, Alek," Dr. Choam pleaded, grabbing his supervisor, his friend by the arm. "There will be other opportunities."

"Shut it down now, Doctor, before I place you under arrest," demanded Jonathon. Every nerve in his body was taut as if he sensed that his life was in peril.

With their pulse rifles in hand, two soldiers standing near the right wall began advancing on Dr. Nazarov's central location. The stubborn scientist finally nodded in agreement, having reluctantly been forced to his senses. He attempted to initiate the shutdown sequence, but it was too late.

From within the quantum gate, chaotic ripples stormed across the fluid boundaries of the wormhole, followed by increasingly frequent pulses of light. The ground had come alive as well, shuddering with one seismic tremor after another. Suddenly, the wormhole's opening in the Polaris System started to shift, bouncing ever closer to Polaris before piercing straight to the center of the star. Tremendous quantities of nuclear material from within Polaris's core poured through the wormhole and violently exploded outward across the surface of the moon, detonating with the destructive force of several hydrogen bombs. It was the beginning of an unprecedented lunar catastrophe and one that might have consumed the moon itself, had the wormhole not collapsed when it did.

Having been stationed at ground zero, the research facility was utterly vaporized and the lives of every unsuspecting scientist, every soldier, were stolen away in an instant, leaving nothing behind, not even ashes. Stampeding on, the powerful shock wave quickly reached the bustling lunar colony, plunging it into chaos. The landing platforms that encircled the colony were uprooted and ripped apart, annihilating each of the commercial ships that were docked. And the six sprawling steel domes that comprised the heart of the colony gave way to the rampaging forces as well, shattering like so many wineglasses. Every man, woman, and child within the colony was incinerated before their terror-filled screams could escape their mouths. And the fate of those passengers still onboard the assortment of starships that had lingered in low orbit above the colony was no different.

The death scene ended with the destruction of the aging mining platforms that lay beyond the colony's outskirts. In the blink of an eye, an entire colony and all its inhabitants had been swept off the face of the molested moon.

Onboard the *Intimidator*, the once active terminals were dead and the projections of the research facility and lunar colony had vanished from the tactical displays. The horrified expression on Jonathon's face was brightly illuminated as he stared out the starboard window, watching in disbelief. For a brief moment it had appeared as if the moon was igniting into a second sun.

"Brace for impact!" he yelled to his command staff, dropping to one knee and grasping the railing beside his chair. Everyone promptly obeyed, as much out of fear as duty.

Reaching over with one hand, Jonathon slammed his fist down through the thin glass lid that covered the emergency alarm switch on the left armrest of his chair. His action brought a swift end to the tranquil atmosphere throughout the ship, replacing it with flashing red lights, piercing sirens, and the distinctive clanking sound of protective armor plating sliding down over every window and view port.

The shock wave radiated swiftly up from the moon's surface. And though its strength had dissipated somewhat, it still struck the *Intimidator* with tremendous force, igniting its shields in a dazzling display of sparkling yellow light as it shoved the flagship into a higher orbit.

Tempestuous vibrations stampeded through the ship, eliciting screams from its panicked crew and causing access vents to crash down to the floor, landing among the sparks that had erupted from several of the command stations. The fail-safes on the ship's reactor promptly kicked in, plunging the *Intimidator* into unquenchable darkness followed by palpable silence.

Having inadvertently smacked his mouth against the railing, Jonathon felt a few drops of blood trickle across his tongue. The bitter taste of his own mortality heightened his concern for his crew.

"Is everyone all right?" he called out.

"I'm all right, Captain," Jensen groaned from the darkness.

Reaching up with both arms, Jonathon grabbed the top railing and carefully pulled himself up from the floor, still unable to see the full extent of the damage within the pitch-black room.

"I've got a bruise or two, but I'll live," Dead Eye replied. "Thank God for the DRAG field or we would have splattered against the windows like a bunch of bugs."

"Amen to that," echoed Chang.

The other officers also responded, conveying their relatively unharmed states, which put some of Jonathon's worries at ease.

But new fears and questions soon crammed the vacant spots in his mind. There was nothing else he could think about, nothing else worth thinking about.

"What happened?" inquired Dead Eye.

"I'm not sure," said Jonathon. "Something triggered an explosion at the test site, but it couldn't have come from the quantum gate. That's just not possible, not with that kind of magnitude."

"Can we raise the blast shields on the windows to see how bad the damage is down there?" Chang asked.

"Not without power," Jensen interjected.

Just then, a soft red glow began brushing the darkness aside as the barely adequate overhead emergency lights received their ration of electricity from the ship's auxiliary energy cells. The command stations, however, remained dead.

Jonathon immediately scanned the room, examining every shocked and troubled face in order to confirm the wellbeing of his command staff with his own eyes. They were his first priority.

"Captain," beckoned Jensen, "I'm picking up the *Intimidator's* automated distress beacon on my datapad. It's a safe bet that all ships in the area have been alerted to our situation and standard protocol requires them to investigate and assist."

"Good," Jonathon replied before turning to face Kate. She was sitting beneath her command station, holding her knees snugly against her chest. Though she was no longer bracing herself against the impact, her body was still tense and her head was bowed, hiding whatever emotions her face disclosed. The sheer violence of the lunar catastrophe had brought back traumatic memories of her near-fatal encounter with mercenary star fighters during her service as an escort pilot. That incident had been a life changing experience that had persuaded her to opt for a less dangerous path through life. But life, it seemed, had other plans.

Jonathon walked toward her, crouched down, and carefully examined her physical condition. Through his eyes she seemed more fragile than the other officers, more in need of his attention.

"Are you okay?" he asked.

Kate raised her head and nodded, but just barely. She was too upset to utter a single word, but she didn't need to. Jonathon could read her body language and the horrified look in her eyes with perfect clarity. Gently placing his hand under her chin, he raised her head until their eyes made contact. "We're going to get through this, Kate. We'll survive."

"They're all dead, aren't they?" she asked in a quivering voice as a few tears broke free, gliding down the sides of her face. "The research facility, the colony, it's all gone, isn't it?"

"I don't know that for sure. I hope not."

"Captain," Jensen called out, "some of the crew have started reporting in over their wrist-comms."

"I need to go," said Jonathon, having turned his attention back to Kate for a moment.

"I know," she replied, trying to project her best soldier's face. "Go take care of the crew. I'll…I'll be fine."

She scooted out from under her command station and pulled herself up into her chair as Jonathon made his way back toward the commander.

"What's our status?"

"So far we've only received reports of minor injuries, mostly bumps and bruises."

"That's a relief. Any reports of damage to the ship?"

"None yet, but I'm certain we'll be in need of repairs."

"You're probably right. Fortunately, the auxiliary energy cells seem to be keeping the DRAG field charged. But if I'm not mistaken, their power output will only last for about twenty minutes or so. And once the artificial gravity goes offline it'll complicate the repairs. We need to get the reactor back up and running before that happens."

"What about the crew? Are you going to make an announcement?"

"Yeah," Jonathon uttered with a sigh. "I'd better take care of that right now."

His right arm seemed heavier than usual as he raised it and positioned his wrist-worn communicator a short distance from his mouth. Pressing down on the tiny activation button, he spoke a directive into the device. "Link to all personnel."

The communicator replied with a pair of beeps, signaling a successful link.

"This is Captain Quinn. There's been a tragic accident near the Lunar Research Facility. The shock wave from the explosion struck the *Intimidator* moments ago. We need to quickly assess and correct our current situation before we can begin assisting in any recovery effort on the moon.

"In keeping with standard emergency protocols, all personnel are required to report in to their supervisory officers, and those officers in turn must report to the command staff, ASAP. Check for wounded and contact sickbay if necessary. All personnel are also required to inspect their own quarters and duty stations for signs of damage. Report anything you find to Commander Jensen.

"I expect all engineers, including off-duty personnel, to assist with the repairs. Our top priority right now is the reactor. Get it back online as soon as possible.

"And remember, we're all in this together. Quinn out."

He pressed down on the tiny button again, severing the communication link.

"I'll gather all the information into a formal damage report," Jensen offered. Although he seemed to be void of emotion, he was as disheartened as the rest of the command staff. He simply chose not to display it, keeping his emotions bottled up as he often had.

"Thank you, Commander," Jonathon replied before turning his attention to his security chief.

"Lieutenant Chang."

"Sir?"

"Since you have ultraviolet security clearance, I want you to head down to the secured cargo hold and check for damage. I don't suspect there will be a problem, but I don't want to take any chances, given the nature of the cargo."

"I'm on it."

Chang rose to his feet and walked toward the emergency exit to the right of the elevator.

"And Lieutenant, have your security personnel make sweeps through their assigned decks to check on the crew and

ensure the situation stays under control. I don't have the patience
to deal with any troublemakers right now."

"Consider it done," Chang promised as he unlocked and
removed the circular escape hatch. A ladder was revealed,
descending into the dimly lit hallway below. Chang grabbed hold
of both sides of the ladder and prepared to descend hastily.

"Hey," said Dead Eye, catching Chang's attention. "Be
careful, man. I've heard…stories about what's in that cargo
hold."

Chang cracked a thin smile, though he did look a little
nervous. "Don't worry, I'll be all right." He then glanced over at
Parker and made a request of his own, "Keep him out of trouble
until I get back."

Parker donned the faintest of smiles and returned a single
nod, feeling even less talkative than usual. He had seen and
experienced a lot of bad things in his life, especially while living
on Mars. And no matter how detached he tried to force himself
to become, each tragic event imprisoned another small part of
him, recessing him further inside his shell of timidity. It'd most
likely take him a few weeks, if not months, to recover from the
day, which would soon be referred to as Black Thursday.

Jonathon took a step toward the edge of the rear balcony
and leaned against the railing, watching his command staff tend
to the situation as best they could.

"Captain," called Jensen, "our engineers have finally assessed
the damage to the ship's reactor."

"Go on," said Jonathon after a brief pause, his grip around
the railing clenching tighter. He appeared as if he was bracing
for another impact.

"They've reported that the main circuit board for the
manual override of the reactor's fail-safes has cracked.
Fortunately, that seems to be the full extent of the damage, to the
reactor at least. They've estimated, however, that it'll take
approximately forty-five minutes to make the necessary repairs,
possibly longer once the auxiliary power goes offline."

"Why so long?"

"The circuit board is apparently in a location that's difficult
to reach. They have to disassemble a few components in order to
get to it. I won't bother repeating the colorful language that

Specialist Tippits used to describe the reactor's design team and their mothers."

"Then I guess we have no choice but to wait it out. Let me know if they run into any other complications."

"Yes, sir."

Scanning the room once more, Jonathon took quick notice of the two visiting scientists. "Time to get some answers," he mumbled to himself as he made his way around the catwalk, toward the forward balcony.

Dr. Zhan was sitting on the floor with her head bowed into her cupped hands, weeping. And Dr. O'Neill was down on one knee beside her, trying to offer what little comfort he could while struggling with his own grief. He glanced up as Jonathon approached.

Crouching down near Dr. Zhan, Jonathon placed a sympathetic hand on her shoulder and said, "I'm sorry. I know you lost a lot of friends and colleagues down there but I still need your help. I need to make sense of all this and figure out what happened down there."

Dr. Zhan nodded and wiped the tears from her eyes before employing the assistance of both men in rising from the floor.

"Can either of you tell me exactly what went wrong? I thought the wormhole was stable."

"I'm still trying to makes sense of it all myself," Dr. O'Neill began, straightening his coat and posture, "but it appears that the sensors Dr. Nazarov shut down weren't malfunctioning. I believe the wormhole may have been unstable from the moment it was created."

"Dr. Nazarov didn't seem to think so," Jonathon responded pointedly.

"Well, the data wasn't correlating with his opinions."

"Curious," argued Jonathon, folding his arms and staring more intently at the elder scientist. "Then why didn't anyone speak up about it?"

"He is...was the director of the facility and he didn't like his decisions to be questioned. Besides, he was usually right."

Dr. O'Neill's response caused Jonathon's eyes to widen and intensify, as if he was ready to assault the man, though the thought hadn't actually crossed his mind. "Well he was obviously wrong in this case and the results were disastrous."

Dr. Zhan began crying again.

Jonathon angled his eyes downward, allowing his emotions to cool while he debated how to proceed. He didn't want to turn the conversation into a heated argument, nor did he want to assign blame. *High Command can sort this mess out. The most important thing right now is to just get the facts about what triggered the explosion.*

"Why was the wormhole so unstable?" Jonathon asked in a calmer tone, though the expression on his face had yet to relax.

"Well," Dr. O'Neill thought aloud, "either our coordinates for the wormhole destination were off or the celestial targeting system was in error. Either way, the wormhole opened too close to Polaris."

"Wormholes are sensitive distortions of space," Dr. Zhan explained in a shaky voice as she dried her tears. "And as such they are susceptible to other forces that affect space as well, including gravity."

"In theory," Dr. O'Neill continued, "the strong gravitational curvature of space around Polaris could interact with the wormhole, causing its tunnel to stretch along that curve. And as it continued to stretch it would become highly unstable and link to the strongest gravitational source in its proximity."

"The star's core," Dr. Zhan expounded. "The wormhole merged with Polaris's core."

Jonathon's jaw dropped at the shocking revelation. "You're telling me we pulled a stellar core through the wormhole?"

"Not all of it," Dr. O'Neill replied. "But a fairly significant amount of matter was transported. You've got to keep in mind, Captain, that the center of a star is composed of extremely dense nuclear material. Releasing even a small quantity into a low-gravity environment would have devastating consequences, as we have already witnessed."

"So the moon was basically nuked?"

"That's one way to put it, yes."

"We shouldn't only be worried about the moon," Dr. Zhan insisted.

"What do you mean?" Jonathon inquired, squinting suspiciously.

"The Polaris System was destroyed, along with whatever extraterrestrial race inhabited that planet."

Dr. Zhan broke into tears again and slumped back down to the floor.

Jonathon was stunned by the young scientist's remarks. "What's she talking about?" he demanded, hoping that she had misspoken.

"There's no question that Polaris was affected by the wormhole, Captain. You don't create a spatial anomaly in the center of a star without causing that star to become unstable. It's possible that nothing more than a small compression wave was emitted from the star's photosphere, causing no real harm other than introducing a little more radiation into the system, nothing that would be life threatening."

"Is that the most likely result of the accident?"

"Unfortunately, Captain, it is not."

Dr. O'Neill ran one hand through his thatch of thinning brown hair, looking uncomfortable with the information he was about to share.

"The most likely scenario is that the wormhole caused a temporary gravitational collapse of Polaris, due in part to the loss of core matter, but primarily due to the space-warping effects of the wormhole in such a high gravitational field. The only logical result from that collapse would be for Polaris to go supernova."

"All life within the system would be destroyed in mere hours," Dr. Zhan stated as she raised her head and looked up at Jonathon. Her eyes echoed the sorrow in her voice.

"This is unbelievable," Jonathon uttered, leaning back, almost falling against the window. He shut his eyes and the color faded from his face as the severity of the disturbing hypothesis sank in. Black Thursday was getting blacker by the minute.

"For what it's worth, I'm terribly sorry," professed Dr. O'Neill, hanging his head with regret and a hint of guilt. "We obviously should have taken more care in our experiment. Our arrogance proved costly."

Popping his head upright, Jonathon glared at the humbled scientist but remained quiet, looking as if he was about to say something he'd later regret. He finally looked away and shook his head. "I'm not your judge, Doctor," he said, unable to disguise a measure of contempt as he began walking back toward the rear balcony, moving without even the slightest bounce in his step.

Though the mood on the bridge was grim, Jonathon's face was the gravest of the group. Part of him wished the destruction had been caused by terrorists or even the aliens themselves. He was well conditioned to handle such war. Anger would have been permitted to flow freely through his veins as he ventured on a crusade to bring the "bad guy" to justice. But an accident—one that was most likely preventable—was much harder to cope with. The emotions had nowhere to be directed but inward.

How could I let this happen? That was the recurring question that haunted Jonathon as he dragged his feet up the steps to the captain's platform and plopped back into his chair. The silence around him should have been comforting, but it wasn't. It was lonely and accusatory, leaving him with his thoughts and the nauseous feeling in his stomach. He was wishing and praying for even the smallest amount of good news to come his way, anything that would spare his conscience from utter collapse.

Jogging down a barren corridor, Chang kept moving at a steady pace, working to complete his task expeditiously, as usual. But more than that, he felt that if he slowed down, reality would catch up with him and he'd end up dwelling on one aspect or another of the lunar accident. And so he pressed on, even picked up the pace a little. But as he rounded the next corner, he stumbled a bit and felt a temporary spurt of dizziness from the side effects of the *Intimidator's* weakening DRAG field.

A short distance further a faint clanging resonated through the shadows, blending with the stifled clicking sounds that bounced up from the floor as the magnetic soles of his boots kissed the metal ground with each step. Slowing a bit more, he listened closely. Upon recognizing the source of the sound, he sprinted to the end of the hallway and stopped at a sealed airlock.

With a loud bang, the rounded access wheel to the airlock's door turned, releasing the airtight seal. The heavy door hissed and creaked open, allowing a crack of vivid light to burst through. Chang stepped forward, took hold of the sturdy handle along the edge of the door, and tugged on it, assisting whoever was pushing on the other side. The door swung open, exposing the well-lit interior of an MPF shuttle, along with a few of its passengers.

"Commander James Mitchell of the *ICS Pathfinder* at your service," the tall, middle-aged officer at the forefront of the group stated in a friendly voice as he removed his right hand from the door and raised it in a salute. "How can I and my engineering entourage be of assistance?"

Feeling relieved that help had arrived, Chang returned the salute and smiled. "I'm Lieutenant Chang and it's good to see you and your men, sir. As you're well aware, our power is out, so the main priority is to get the reactor back online. And I'm guessing there'll be other repairs to make, but I can't give you any specifics right now. The captain's still gathering a damage report and any assistance you can provide would certainly be appreciated, Commander."

"Well now, Lieutenant, I can tell you that the exterior of the *Intimidator* appears to be structurally sound. Sure you lost a few laser turrets along your starboard hull, but all things considered I'd say that's no big deal at all. This ship can take quite a beating."

"That she can, Commander," affirmed Chang with a relieved chuckle.

"Well all right then, let's get down to business," Mitchell stated as he walked out into the hallway and stood next to Chang. "I've brought ten techies with me, all of whom are eager to get to work, but I want them back when you're done with them," he said with a smile.

"That's great, Commander. I'll escort your men down to the reactor. I was heading that direction anyway."

"Sounds fine. We've also brought a few spare generators to help keep your DRAG field charged. Losing gravity can be a real pain in the behind. I'll certainly never forget my first week onboard the *Pathfinder*. Now don't get me wrong, son, she's a real beauty of a ship. But taking control of a brand-spanking-new destroyer right out of the shipyards was an eye-opening experience. There were still a whole lotta kinks to be worked out with the electrical systems and within twenty-four hours of operation the *Pathfinder's* DRAG field went belly up. I swear they're getting worse with their quality control these days. Anyway, the entire system fried, sending sparks flying in all directions. It scared the bejeebers out of our chief technician and we were without gravity for three long days. It was a whopper of a pain to deal with, although I must admit the first night in the mess hall was a real hoot. They hadn't adjusted the dinner menu at all, serving all kinds of crazy stuff like soup. Can you imagine that? They actually figured people could eat soup in a Zero-G environment. Everyone's meals kept floating up and getting away from them. That night I finally figured out why it was called a mess hall. There was food all over the place and I couldn't help but have a great swell of pity for the poor soul that had to clean up that mess."

Having finally paused from his rambling, Mitchell turned toward his engineers who were still standing in the shuttle. "Well, come on, get moving. This fine lieutenant doesn't have all day."

One by one, blue-jumpsuit-wearing electrical and mechanical engineers stepped out into the hallway. They represented a wide range of expertise, as indicated by the compact toolboxes that hung from their left shoulders. Some of the toolkits had shiny crimson surfaces while others were dull and dented from frequent use. Three of the more physically fit men in the group also had ivory-black portable generators strapped to their backs. The devices were bulky, but not quite as heavy as they looked, though some of the engineers might have begged to differ.

"The comm system onboard this shuttle's also at your disposal," said Mitchell. "We've made an initial report to High Command, but there's a whole lotta information we aren't privy to. They're demanding that Captain Quinn speak with them immediately."

"I'll contact the captain and relay your message."

Chang cleared his throat, tensing slightly before continuing. "How bad is the damage to the lunar colony?"

Mitchell's pleasant countenance faded into the shadows of a grim expression. "It's a total loss, son."

Chang nodded solemnly in response. While news of the colony's loss was hard to take, the situation still seemed surreal to him. "Well, we'd better hurry down to the reactor," he suggested, abruptly changing subjects before reality had a chance to sink its teeth in.

"If you need anything else, Lieutenant, feel free to give me a holler," Mitchell continued, saluting and stepping back into the airlock. "I'll wait in the shuttle for your captain."

"Understood, Commander."

Chang motioned for the group to follow him to a nearby emergency access hatch. And as they gathered, he removed the rounded cover, exposing a long shaft that descended into the bowels of the ship. The visiting engineers began their single-file descent, giving Chang a spare moment to contact Jonathon before he joined them.

Raising his wrist-comm near his mouth, Chang established a link and said, "Captain, this is Lieutenant Chang. Come in, sir."

"Go ahead, Lieutenant."

"Commander Mitchell from the *Pathfinder* has docked a shuttle and brought over a complement of engineers to assist in the repairs."

"That's great news," declared Jonathon, sounding relieved, like a prisoner who had received a temporary stay of execution.

"He's also requesting your presence, sir. High Command is demanding to speak with you."

"I see," Jonathon replied, his voice reverting to a dejected tone. "Which airlock has he docked with?"

Chang glanced back and read the reflective orange markings painted above the opened airlock before responding. "Uh, he's at Beta Three."

"I'll be right down. Quinn out."

"Commander," called Jonathon, rising from his chair, "notify Specialist Tippits that a repair crew from the *Pathfinder* has docked and will be at his disposal shortly."

"Yes, sir. Is there anything else?"

"I'm heading down to the shuttle so I can contact High Command and brief them on the situation. You have the bridge until I return."

"Understood."

"Good luck," Kate called out, knowing full well that Jonathon was heading toward a tough confrontation with his superiors.

He knew it as well. It showed in his eyes and the sideways glance he lobbed to Kate before departing. He felt as if he should be preparing opening arguments for his court marshal rather than formulating the requested status report. With each step down the ladder, he felt his level of anxiety inching higher and he fought it, refusing to shrink from his responsibility. He would fulfill his duty, yet he couldn't help but dread having to stand before High Command and report the catastrophic failure of the operation— facts they already knew. They would want all of the gory details, but more importantly, they would want to know who was to blame. There were no accidents according to the military way of thinking. There was right and wrong, black and white, missed opportunities and mistakes, but no accidents. Someone would have to go down in history as the man responsible for Black Thursday and Jonathon could already hear his name being penned in.

Mitchell reclined in one of the two red-cushioned pilot's seats within the cozy cockpit of his shuttle. His arms were folded and he was staring out the forward window, whistling as he waited for Jonathon to arrive.

The small communications console embedded within the center of the light-gray control panel began beeping, prompting the relaxed officer to sit up and take notice. He casually reached over and activated the console, causing the image of Admiral Breckard to pop into view.

"Where is he?" Breckard growled.

"Who, sir?"

"Captain Quinn! Have you made contact with him yet?"

"Yes, sir, and I suspect he'll be here shortly. The *Pathfinder's* engineering team has begun—"

"I didn't ask about your engineers, Commander."

Turning his head to glance back through the cockpit's entrance, Mitchell checked to see if Jonathon had arrived, desiring to end his conversation with the abrasive admiral.

"Raise him on your communicator," Breckard demanded.

"Actually, sir, I think I hear someone coming right now. I'm going to place you on hold for just one second." Quickly suspending the communication link before Breckard had a chance to object, he stood up and exited the cockpit as Jonathon stepped inside the shuttle.

"Commander Mitchell, I presume," greeted Jonathon.

Mitchell smiled and saluted. "At your service, Captain. And might I say that it's an honor to meet you, sir. I only wish it could have been under better circumstances."

"Thank you, Commander. I also want to thank you for your assistance with my ship. The efforts of you and your crew are greatly appreciated."

"Happy to oblige. Oh, and I've got that old blowhard, Admiral Breckard, holding on the comm."

"Holding?" said Jonathon, his eyebrows raised. "You're a brave man, Commander. I know how much he hates that."

"Yeah," Mitchell replied with a roguish grin. "Well, I'll step out into the hallway so you can have some privacy. Holler if you need anything."

"Thanks."

Jonathon entered the cockpit and sat down in the portside pilot's seat. The flashing red indicator beside the communications console immediately consumed his attention. He paused to gather his thoughts, took a deep breath, and pressed the resume button.

Images of the ten senior officers that comprised High Command popped into view on the console. The grievous, and in some cases angry, expressions on their faces conveyed the overall somber mood of the group. They were all wearing their gold-trimmed military uniforms and sitting in a semicircle around their marble-surfaced conference table, which resided in the most exquisite room on the top floor of Earth Dock, their lofty perch among the stars. The orbital space station had originally been designed as a docking port and place of trade. But as was the way with politics, many influential figureheads had lobbied to gain control of the facility, expanding its purpose to serve their own and elevating themselves to a position where they could literally and figuratively look down on everyone. Earth Dock had become the most prominent symbol of bureaucracy within the Solar System.

"We've received the initial data regarding the disaster on the moon," Breckard stated furiously, his face molded to one of his classic expressions of anger. "The operation was a complete failure. How do you account for this, Captain?"

"Now hold on a second," General O'Connor intervened, glaring objectionably at Breckard. "Captain Quinn isn't on trial here. And might I remind everyone that we were all well aware of the risks involved with this operation when we agreed to put it in motion. Pandora's Box has already been opened, so let's just keep a cool head and gather the facts."

"Now," continued O'Connor, turning back toward Jonathon, "due to technical problems with the video transmission, we weren't able to gather much information surrounding the details that led up to the accident. We know of the incident that occurred during the countdown sequence, and we were able to visually confirm the creation of the wormhole, but other than that we're pretty much in the dark. Can you tell us exactly what went wrong?"

Jonathon cleared his throat and answered, "Unfortunately, sirs, the operation was plagued by one complication after the other, right from the start. And while we did succeed in opening a wormhole into the Polaris System, the destination coordinates were a bit off their mark. The wormhole's exit point was apparently perilously close to the star."

"Why is that significant, Captain?" inquired Admiral Hughes.

"Well, sir, we believe the wormhole's proximity to the star is what caused the accident. Dr. O'Neill and Dr. Zhan have theorized that—"

"Wait a minute," Admiral Hughes interrupted, looking rather perplexed. "Are you saying that some of the scientists survived? How is that possible?"

"Dr. O'Neill and Dr. Zhan were transferred to the *Intimidator* prior to initiation of the operation. They served as liaisons between Dr. Nazarov and myself."

"Excellent thinking, Captain," interjected O'Connor, nodding a gesture of approval. He was the only one to do so.

"Continue with your explanation, Captain," instructed Admiral Hughes in her usual collected demeanor.

"Both scientists have theorized that the gravity from the star caused the wormhole to become unstable. The exit point within the Polaris System somehow merged with the core of the star and that's what triggered the explosion at the test site."

"That's interesting," O'Connor began, "and it does seem to explain the magnitude of the blast. According to the sensor readings from the neighboring destroyers in your vicinity, the amount of energy released during the explosion was equivalent to approximately five Omega-class fusion bombs. Does that correlate with your own readings?"

"Unfortunately, General, our power was knocked out before we could properly assess the situation. However, based on the information from the scientists and my own first-hand witness of the explosion, I'd say that estimate is pretty accurate."

"I see," Admiral Hughes remarked. "And how much damage has the *Intimidator* sustained exactly?"

"We're still assessing, but we appear to be in reasonably good condition. Getting our reactor back online has been our biggest challenge. Everything else should be easily fixed, as far as I'm aware. I don't believe we've sustained any structural damage."

"Well, that's at least some good news out of all this. As I'm sure you're aware, Captain, we suffered heavy casualties today."

"Based on our most conservative estimates," Breckard interjected, "approximately two million people were killed, which was a higher population count than usual due to the lunar holiday and the celebration that was planned for this evening. The only people who survived this catastrophe were those who were stationed at the antimatter reactor. That provides me with very little comfort."

Jonathon averted his eyes from the console as the Admiral's report sunk in. Though he had already suspected the worst, the news was still difficult to hear.

The middle-aged and balding Vice Admiral Eberhard Kreider, the newest member of the group and the only token representative from Mars, felt obligated to ask a question. "Were there not any indications that such a terrible result was going to occur?" he asked with a German accent that still lingered from his youth.

"That's where the situation gets a little sticky," said Jonathon, squirming in his seat. "I believe the wormhole may have been unstable from the moment it was created. One of the scientists at the lunar facility had alerted us to fluctuations within the quantum gate, but Dr. Nazarov dismissed them. He even took the sensors offline, claiming they needed to be tested. The situation grew out of control from there."

"Captain, are you blaming Dr. Nazarov for this?" Breckard inquired in an irritated tone.

"I'm just saying that he may not have been as well prepared as we thought and I'd suggest that you speak with Dr. O'Neill and Dr. Zhan for yourselves, to probe the situation further." Jonathon paused for a moment before continuing. "I recognize, Admiral, that I share in the responsibility for this mess."

"Well, I think we have all the initial facts we need for our investigation," Admiral Hughes stated as she examined her datapad. "We expect to receive a copy of your sensor logs and video transmissions as soon as you're able to send them."

"Actually, sir," Jonathon interrupted, "there is one other matter to discuss."

"Go on, Captain."

"The probe that was sent through the wormhole didn't find an uninhabited system, as expected."

Jonathon's mind was racing. He'd been searching for a good way to explain the bigger problem, the greater catastrophe.

"Excuse me, Captain," Breckard interrupted with a puzzled look on his face. "Are you saying that the Polaris System is inhabited by some kind of alien race?"

"That's correct, sir."

The high-ranking officers conversed noisily with each other for a few minutes. After the room quieted again, Admiral Hughes addressed Jonathon.

"Was any contact made with these aliens?"

"Yes, Admiral, but we didn't initiate the contact. It was regarding this matter that I had attempted to contact you earlier, before the accident occurred." Jonathon tugged at his jacket collar with one of his fingers before continuing. "The aliens sent some sort of starship toward our probe."

"They're a space-faring race?" Vice Admiral Kreider asked, looking as if astonished that his own clever species hadn't cornered the market on space travel.

"Yes, sir. And judging from the initial images, they appeared to be highly advanced. They also didn't appreciate us nosing around in their backyard."

"What do you mean?" Breckard inquired, staring suspiciously at Jonathon.

"They destroyed our probe."

An animated discussion immediately broke out amongst the senior officers and continued for several minutes before the rumbling finally died down.

"Was there any further contact with the aliens?" Admiral Hughes asked.

"Do we have any reason to go on the defensive?" Breckard interrupted, feeling that his question was more to the point.

"No, sirs. The explosion at the quantum gate occurred shortly after the probe was destroyed. I also seriously doubt we'll ever see them again."

"Why do you say that?" asked O'Connor.

"How can I put this?" Jonathon mumbled to himself.

"Speak up, Captain," Breckard commanded.

"The Polaris System was most likely destroyed when the wormhole merged with the star," Jonathon stated without pausing to take a breath and without looking at the console.

The video transmission erupted with a thunderous debate among the high-ranking officers. The negative tone of their voices reflected their outrage at the grave, unexpected news.

"Are you telling me that we've annihilated another civilization?" Breckard exploded at Jonathon through the monitor.

Jonathon's head snapped to attention. "It's impossible to confirm, sir, but it appears that way." Small beads of sweat trickled down the sides of his face.

"How is that possible? Explain yourself, Captain," Admiral Hughes demanded, rivaling Breckard in her portrayal of anger.

"Doctors O'Neill and Zhan have both theorized that the wormhole caused the star to go supernova. If that's true, then the shock wave from the exploding star would have destroyed all life within the system and most likely the planets themselves."

"Calling this operation a failure would be a gross understatement!" Breckard yelled. The veins in his forehead had become far more pronounced than before. In fact, they were bulging to the point of bursting. He looked as if he wanted to reach through the monitor and strangle Jonathon.

"Captain," interrupted O'Connor, "we need some time to absorb this information and determine the appropriate course of action. We also need to speak with the scientists as soon as possible. Put them on a shuttle and send them back here for immediate debriefing."

"In the meantime, Captain, you are to get your affairs in order," Admiral Hughes instructed, having cooled her temper a little. "An emergency hearing has been scheduled for midday tomorrow and all Coalition cabinet members are expected to be in attendance. The hearing will attempt to determine the root causes and widespread consequences of the failed operation, which, as you have pointed out, are even more catastrophic than originally thought. You will, of course, be required to attend and testify at the hearing.

"We'd also like to meet with you in person, after the hearing has concluded. We need to...*discuss* your performance during the operation. We will permit you the dignity of retaining command of the *Intimidator* up until your departure. However, you are hereby ordered to delegate the responsibility of overseeing the ship's repairs and routine operations to Commander Jensen. He will take full command once you've departed. The ship is to remain in high lunar orbit until further notice."

"We expect to see you here within twenty-four hours, Captain," added Breckard, his statement sounding more like a threat than an order. He seemed almost pleased at Jonathon's predicament.

The video feed terminated.

Jonathon sat in stunned silence. Leaning forward, he buried his head in his hands as an overwhelming sense of grief seeped into his system. *This can't be happening. It was just supposed to be a simple experiment. It was supposed to change life for the better.*

After several long and quiet minutes had passed, he rose from the chair and exited the cockpit. Trudging out through the airlock and into the brightened hallway, he almost seemed unaware of the fact that the *Intimidator's* power had been restored.

"Good day, Commander," he mumbled, barely taking notice of the man.

Mitchell saluted out of respect and opened his mouth out of habit, but no words came out. There was simply nothing he could say to ease Jonathon's burdens so he opted to leave him alone with his thoughts.

With his footsteps echoing softly around him, Jonathon progressed toward the elevator at the end of the hallway, deliberately pacing himself. He eventually reached the sealed tube and pressed the access button, but the elevator didn't respond, so he slammed the button hard. The doors slid open.

"Living quarters, first floor," he snapped, stepping inside the vacant elevator. It promptly descended three decks, stopping at the first floor of the living-quarters section. Jonathon stepped out into the hallway, rubbing the sides of his head in an attempt to ease the stress-induced headache that had developed. A few of the lights flickered overhead, indicating that the repair crews had yet to inspect that area of the ship, having had more important matters to attend to first.

Approaching the door to his quarters, Jonathon smacked the back of his right hand against the small security pad that was attached to the adjacent wall. The subdermal microchip that had been implanted in his hand when he first joined the military transmitted his uniquely imprinted code. With a click and a swish, the door slid open, activating the lights within the small room.

As Jonathon stepped inside his quarters, his headache intensified into a full-blown migraine, warranting a groan of discomfort. He instinctively headed straight for the bathroom, punched his coded request for pain relief into the automated medicine dispenser, and popped a tiny but potent analgesic into his mouth, where it dissolved almost instantly.

The display monitor in his quarters activated.

"Please stand by for an emergency broadcast from the Prime Minister of Earth," a firm yet feminine voice announced, catching Jonathon's attention.

He strolled out of the bathroom and turned to face the monitor. The sober face of the distinguished statesman, with his ash-colored hair and dark, sorrowful eyes, floated into focus. Clearing his throat, he addressed his audience. "Citizens of the Earth and the Intrastellar Coalition of Planets: it is with a grieving heart that I come before you today to inform you of a tragic accident that has occurred on the moon. We—"

"End transmission," Jonathon ordered to the computer as he stepped back and collapsed onto his bed, feeling exhausted. His headache had started to dim, but was still pronounced.

"Computer," he mumbled while struggling to kick off each of his boots, "contact Lieutenant Hayes on the bridge, audio only."

"Request confirmed."

"What can I do for you, Captain?" asked Kate. She tried to sound calm and perfectly normal, but Jonathon heard a faint sniffle or two. Even so, her soft voice had lost none of its soothing effect, easing some of Jonathon's tension.

"I need you to put Dr. O'Neill and Dr. Zhan on a transport and send them to Earth Dock. High Command is expecting them."

"Easy enough. What else?"

"Tell Commander Jensen he can play captain until the replacement command staff arrives at the end of his shift. Make sure he transmits a copy of the recorded video link of the operation and a complete log of our sensor readings to High Command. And have him keep the ship in high lunar orbit until further notice."

"Will do. Can I help you with anything else?" She sounded as if she was hoping that Jonathon would make a particular request.

"No," Jonathon replied quietly, shifting into a more comfortable position atop his bed. "I'm not feeling well, so I'm just going to rest for a little while. But if any complications develop with the repairs, contact me immediately."

"I understand. If you want to talk, Jon, you know where to find me." Kate's soft voice soothed the last bit of tension from Jonathon's body.

"Thanks, Kate. I'll take you up on that offer tonight in your quarters, around 1700 hours. I'll pick up dinner from Murphy's and we can have a peaceful night, just the two of us."

"Roger that, Captain," she replied warmly. "Sleep tight."

The communication link terminated.

Jonathon's heavy eyelids gave in to the chemical forces that were tugging at them, bidding them shut. "Computer," he mumbled, "dim the lights and wake me up at 1600 hours. Record all non-priority transmissions."

"Request confirmed," the computer responded, apparently to itself. Jonathon was asleep.

Chapter 3
The Approaching Storm

Up until a few hundred years ago, before mankind took its first baby steps among the stars, the Solar System was a relatively quiet and boring corner of the cosmos. But it has since become littered with manmade trinkets and oddities, adding to the many bizarre wonders that make the universe so intriguing. And the most peculiar of them all was the *Jupiter III*, a lone dust-mining platform in high asynchronous orbit around Jupiter, hidden within the planet's system of rings.

Most reasonable corporate executives would never consider expanding beyond the safe boundaries of the asteroid belt's mining cluster. There was still an abundance of minerals to be tapped, enough to provide work for countless generations to come. But some individuals had to be different, had to push the envelope to the bleeding edge of insanity. Such was the case for the eccentric billionaires who ran the Hadlock Interplanetary Mining Corporation (HIMC). The *Jupiter III* was their property.

This unique mining station had been designed to collect and refine the dust particles and minute rock fragments that populated the giant planet's rings. For all intents and purposes, the *Jupiter III* was the equivalent of an oversized Dust Buster in space. Some people had even insisted that from the right angle and distance it resembled an antiquated industrial vacuum.

Two standard emergency escape transports were securely docked along either side of the station's elongated blocky frame and looked more like permanent fixtures than separate vessels, whereas the upper docking zone was reserved for corporate transports, one of which was making its final approach. Despite the latest advancements in starship-propulsion technology, it still took between one and two months to travel from the nearest docking ports to Jupiter, depending on the planetary alignments. It required a staggered caravan of corporate transports and cargo ships to help maintain a vital lifeline to the isolated station.

From a functional standpoint the *Jupiter III* was a mining platform and not a vessel, though it did have a starship propulsion system. The engines were simply limited to a specific purpose: to keep the station from entering synchronous orbit around Jupiter and becoming a gravity-bound slave to the king of planets. The *Jupiter III* was swimming upstream like a stubborn salmon, never gaining an inch of territory. Instead, it held its position, sweeping up the dusty contents of the rings as they rotated by, creating grooves that would one day be visible from Earth-based telescopes.

Probably the most peculiar aspect of the *Jupiter III* was that despite the billions of credits that had been spent on its construction and operation, it had virtually no checks or balances governing its personnel. The MPF's security patrols rarely strayed beyond the asteroid belt, so aside from the routine long-distance communications from corporate headquarters, the station's command staff was free to behave as they saw fit, and they did.

"The corporate transport is ready to dock, Commander," a frail young man reported as he interacted with the inadequate command console that stretched along the front wall of the compact, windowless control room. Waiting for further instructions, he glanced back at David Bruso, Chief Labor Commander (CLC) of the *Jupiter III*.

"It's about frigging time!" Bruso barked in his usual gruff voice. Despite the obvious similarities, his title was not a military distinction. Most of the workers on the mining platform begged to differ, however, based on the amount of power Bruso wielded and frequently abused.

With a deep moan, Bruso struggled to extract his obese body from the tattered leather chair that barely contained him. A smattering of stray crumbs from the day's super-sized breakfast fell from his coffee-stained shirt, adding to the layers of glop that already smothered the once shiny metal floor. Tossing his personal datapad back into the chair, he lumbered forward, shoving his overworked assistant out of the way.

"Get down there and help with the crew transfer," he growled. "We're already a day behind schedule, so don't screw anything else up."

"Yessir," the assistant replied with an edge of fearful relief. Even though he was exhausted, he was grateful for the opportunity to get away from his cruel boss and the foul stench that radiated from his unwashed body. He departed without hesitation.

Pressing one of the buttons on the rather primitive command console, Bruso caused the image on the central monitor to switch over to the mineral-processing center.

"Hey," he shouted into the small display screen.

A dust-covered worker wiped dark soot from his eyes, crept forward and peered at the commander. "What do you need, sir?" he asked in a timid, cautious manner.

"Where's Jaren? He's supposed to be on duty down there."

"I don't know. I haven't seen him."

"Well find him and tell him the transport's docked. He needs to get his lazy butt in gear and load the latest round of processed ore into the cargo hold. We're already behind schedule and I don't want any more delays. Got it?"

"Yes, sir," the worker responded nervously, his wide eyes beaming brightly.

As the video link terminated, Bruso started back to his chair, having strayed from it long enough to warrant a rest for his overburdened heart. Before he could sit down, however, the sensor terminal started beeping as a continuous stream of data came pouring in across its small, chipped screen.

"Now what?" he grumbled to himself, walking toward the far end of the command console.

Reaching over with his left hand, he held down the button that activated the PA system. "I need Richard Warren in the command center right now," he demanded in an amplified voice that echoed throughout the facility.

Turning his attention back to the unusual sensor readings, he resumed fiddling with the controls for the external cameras. An image of Jupiter's turbulent equator popped into view on one of the terminals.

"Nothing there," he mumbled while squinting at the colorful images on the screen. More shots of the gas giant came into view as he poked and prodded every button within reach. He'd had the requisite training on proper operation of the equipment, but his motto had always been, "Why do it yourself when you can bully other people into doing it for you?" His laziness had left him completely dependent on his enslaved support staff and if they ever managed to wake up and realize that fact, he'd most likely have a mutiny on his hands.

Warren came bursting into the control room with his tanned corporate jacket hanging partway off his lanky shoulders. As chief of security, Warren commanded a great deal of power in his own right, despite having a rather lengthy criminal record that should have automatically disqualified him from the job. By appointing Warren, Bruso had hoped to hinder the HIMC's efforts to maintain a watchful eye on the station and their profits. His plan worked.

"What's goin' on?" Warren gasped, struggling to catch his breath.

"Where've you been? We've got something weird going on outside."

"Move over," Warren snapped as he stepped toward the active display terminal. "It's probably just an energy spike in Jupiter's magnetic field, but let's take a peek anyway."

The cameras were reconfigured to lock onto the source of the energy readings and zoom in.

A twenty-meter-wide circular distortion in space had formed less than two kilometers from the station and parallel to Jupiter's rings. Sharp bursts of energy were spiraling away in vivid blue streaks from the perimeter of what appeared to be a wormhole, although it was of a different nature than the one that had been produced during Operation Giant Leap. The unnatural distortion was animated at first, but the energy discharges soon slowed before stopping altogether. Perfect stabilization had been achieved, despite the wormhole's close proximity to the massive planet, suggesting that whoever had created it possessed a keen understanding of the intricacies of cosmic gateways, much keener than mankind's scientific elite, who were like toddlers blundering through their understanding of the universe. Radiant flashes of light began arcing across the ominous opening as a dark object crept through.

"What is that?" Bruso asked, perturbed by the intriguing images on the terminal.

"Beats me. Maybe the Coalition's conducting one of their weird experiments out here."

"This close to our mining platform? I don't think so. Besides, didn't you hear? They botched their experiment earlier today and damn near took out half the moon."

"Well then, genius, what do you think it is?"

"How should I know? I'm no scientist."

"Shouldn't we contact corporate headquarters or the military or something?" Warren asked as he ran one of his hands through his thinning, slicked-back hair.

"Are you nuts? I don't want the military nosing around out here. They might find out about our little embezzling scheme."

"Then get headquarters on the comm and tell 'em what we saw."

"Yeah right. They'd assume we had Jovian Hallucination Syndrome and ship us off to that psycho ward on Mars."

"Well we've gotta do something," Warren squawked. "That thing out there's really starting to freak me out."

The sensor panel started beeping again, as did other control panels around the room. The camera feed on the small terminal switched to static, followed by a flickering of the overhead lights. Random power surges were harassing the entire facility.

"What's wrong with this piece of junk now?" Bruso hollered, smacking his fists against every cluster of buttons within reach.

"I don't know, but stop beating on the controls, you'll just make it worse. Something must be wrong with the reactor or—"

The room was suddenly plunged into darkness as the reactor mysteriously shut down. And to make matters worse, tremors began rumbling through the facility as Jupiter's gravitational field grabbed firm hold of the idle platform, tugging it slowly into orbit.

"Oh that's just frigging great," Bruso huffed, bracing himself against the command console.

"Calm down and grab one of the emergency lights."

Bruso felt his way around the thick darkness, probing for anything of use. His hands finally brushed across the wall-mounted cabinet that housed the emergency kit.

"Found 'em," he announced, tugging on the metal handle that hung from the hinged door. The cabinet creaked open, enabling the commander to retrieve one of the handheld emergency lights, although he also spilled most of the kit's contents down onto the floor, even caused a bottle of painkillers to shatter. But it was of little concern to him since someone else would be forced to clean up the mess.

"Turn it on," Warren called out from the darkness.

"What do you think I'm trying to do?"

Bruso repeatedly fat-fingered the activation button, but to no avail, so he smacked it once against the wall then tapped the button again. "The energy cells must be dead."

"Give it here," Warren demanded, grabbing at the darkness.

Before the exchange could take place, the small elliptical light flickered a few times, then stabilized, temporarily blinding Warren as it beamed straight into his eyes. The overhead lights reactivated as well, indicating that the reactor had came back online. When the engines kicked in, the *Jupiter III* jerked hard, sending Warren stumbling into Bruso, who made a large, soft target.

"Get off me," Bruso groaned, shoving Warren back a few steps.

With power flowing freely through the mining platform again, the two jumpy men quickly examined the images from the external cameras. Not only was the spatial distortion gone, but they couldn't detect any trace of the small craft that had eased through earlier.

Feeling less edgy, Bruso reached over and turned off the display terminal.

"What're you doing?" Warren asked, still noticeably upset.

"It's gone. There's nothing to worry about now. We'll just go back to business as usual and pretend that frigging light show never happened."

"What about the ship we saw coming out of that…hole? It didn't look right. There's no way that thing was manmade. It didn't even register on the radar or our sensors." Warren nervously brushed both hands through his hair, waiting for a remark or two from Bruso that would justify his own paranoia. But he didn't get any such remarks.

Bruso replied with a mocking laugh. "You're telling me you think little green men have dropped by to say hello?"

"Like you know what that thing was."

Grabbing a fistful of his shady associate's jacket, Bruso yanked him closer. "What thing?" he growled. "There's nothing out there and there never was. Do you understand what I'm saying?"

"Yeah, all right. I get it."

"Now get back to work and keep your mouth shut about all this."

Bruso released his hold on Warren, permitting him to storm out of the room.

Chapter 4
From Mourning to Night

"Good evening, Captain Quinn. The time is 1600 hours on June 1st, 2271, Earth Standard Time," the computer's voice chimed, awakening Jonathon from his therapeutic slumber. As the lights in his quarters brightened, he stared at the ceiling. All traces of his migraine were gone and the silence that lingered in the room was comforting, almost too comforting. For a moment everything seemed normal, as if he had awakened from nothing more than a bad dream.

"There are five messages waiting for you. Have a pleasant evening."

Jonathon groaned at the computer's announcement as reality began to sink back in. Swinging his legs over the side of the bed, he sat up. "Computer, play back new messages," he muttered, leaning forward and interlocking his fingers, his elbows resting on his knees, his head bowed a little.

The display monitor across from Jonathon flickered until the face of Dr. Margaret Whyte appeared, with her trim, curly black hair and penetrating eyes that magnified her uncanny ability to discern when someone was lying. And without a second's delay the middle-aged chief medical officer began speaking in a stern voice that mirrored the serious expression on her face. "Captain, it's almost 1400 hours and you've yet to pay me a visit. You know the military's policy on a mandatory mental wellness treatment that must take place shortly after any personal trauma or high-casualty incident. Nearly one half of the crew has already been treated and I expect to see you within the next hour."

Jonathon rolled his eyes in response to Dr. Whyte's message as it terminated. He didn't approve of the MPF's recent change in mental health policies, considering them to be a detriment to the strength of the military. He opined that their dependence on medication as the primary means of treating the emotional stresses that arise during military service would leave those whom it was designed to help desensitized to the cruel realities of life and incapable of making difficult decisions on their own. Jonathon still favored the classical mental conditioning system that used to be widely employed—the same rigorous training he had undergone when first promoted to commander. All recruits were put through a basic shakedown when they first signed up, but the real conditioning came with a command promotion. It was known as "Mental Hell" and it was the kind of experience that never leaves you, no matter how hard you might want to forget. Jonathon had survived the three-week ordeal and emerged a better officer because of it, but not everyone came through unscathed. Even Jensen had shown signs of severe strain during his training, emerging with what some of his fellow officers had claimed was a darker, more abrasive personality. The program was far from popular, yet it was High Command's way of weeding out the weak officers from the strong. But the days of weeding were gone and the weeds have since flourished.

Admiral Breckard's callous face was the next image to pop into view on the display monitor, prompting Jonathon to sit up at attention out of habit. The admiral spoke in his usual booming voice. "I wanted to express my utter disappointment—"

"Computer, terminate message," Jonathon called out hastily. He wasn't in the mood to receive another tongue thrashing from the admiral, not at that moment and probably never again. Besides, he derived a certain satisfaction from cutting Breckard off, even if it was only a recording.

Replacing the admiral's image was the soft, pleasant visage of Kate, bringing a faint yet inflating smile to Jonathon's face.

"I just got back from visiting sickbay and I wanted to remind you about dinner tonight," she said with a wink, sounding almost like her old self again. "Oh, and I'm also supposed to tell you to go see Dr. Whyte." Clearing her throat, Kate scowled comically and began speaking in a lower tone, trying to mimic the doctor. "You know the military's policy on a mandatory mental wellness treatment that must take place shortly after any personal trauma or high-casualty situation."

Jonathon couldn't help but chuckle at her amusing impersonation. Bringing a smile to Jonathon's face had become second nature for Kate, even when she was feeling low in spirits herself. Her compassion for others was one of the many attributes Jonathon found so attractive.

Having relaxed her face, Kate cleared her throat and resumed speaking in her normal voice. "Go take your happy pills, Jon. I know Dr. Whyte can be a little on the annoying side, but she's right. Everyone could use a little help dealing with what happened today, especially you, so please take care of yourself. I'll see you in a little while."

As Kate's face faded from the monitor, Jensen's image popped in, looking rather smug with the temporary increase of his responsibility. "Captain, I just wanted to let you know that most of the ship's repairs have been completed. They were all fairly minor issues, aside from five starboard laser turrets that had to be replaced. Our technicians are mainly repairing light fixtures and computer consoles at this point and they should be finished within a few hours. The *Pathfinder's* engineers have also departed and with my thanks. Everything's perfectly under control, so take as much personal leave as you need. Jensen out."

The message ended and Jonathon pushed himself up from the bed, feeling a little more at ease with the knowledge that the ship was almost fully functional. He began unfastening his jacket as Dr. Whyte's face appeared on the monitor again, looking more irritated than before.

"Computer, terminate message."

Dr. Whyte's image disappeared before she could deliver her predictable speech.

"That's one persistent lady," Jonathon uttered while making his way to the closet, numbly going through his nightly routine. He removed his jacket and draped it across the wire-frame chair that was pushed in against the corner desk. But in so doing, he inadvertently caught a glimpse of his father's picture out of the corner of his eyes and looked quickly away. He couldn't help but feel as if he had disappointed his childhood hero, even though deep down he knew his father wouldn't think so. The details of the failed experiment were still vivid in Jonathon's mind, as were the consequences. He had collapsed on his bed before he had a chance to properly deal with the full impact of the lunar catastrophe. But he was alert now and feeling miserable.

Jonathon closed his eyes, hoping to shut out the unforgiving reality that was bearing down on him, but instead the indelible images of the lunar destruction flashed through his mind. He saw the moon burning, the colony vanishing, and he imagined the faces of so many people screaming. Their cries of pain and horror were mingled with desperate pleas for help and at least a few blameful curses spoken against Jonathon's name. It was a powerful manifestation of his emotions, so powerful, in fact, that he couldn't contain them. As his eyes burst wide open, Jonathon clenched his right hand and cried out while slamming his fist into the mirror. A resounding thud and a sharp crack sprang from the mirror as it split from top to bottom, leaving behind a web-like pattern of shards that masked Jonathon's troubled reflection. He didn't even feel the pain in his hand, having become consumed with his thoughts. And at that moment, he began to weep. He tried to fight it at first, but he soon relented and dropped to his knees, permitting the outburst to ease his conscience, even cleanse his soul.

For several minutes Jonathon wept, shedding tear after bitter tear for all of the innocent lives that were lost. And he could feel the new scar on his heart, throbbing beside the emotional wounds that still lingered from the war with Mars. He had seen more death and destruction in his relatively young life than he had ever thought possible and it weighed heavily on him. But Jonathon was strong and he wasn't about to let despair consume him. He knew better.

With a few deep, soothing breaths and a reliance on the basic principles of his mental conditioning, he worked to bring his emotions under control. Wiping away the remaining tears, he exhaled one final cleansing breath and rose to his feet, standing before the shattered reflection of his former self. There he lingered for a quiet minute or two until he felt reasonably satisfied that he had permitted himself to grieve. His thoughts eventually shifted back to the present, to his pending rendezvous with Kate. It would still take time for things to normalize, but he had no intention of sitting idly by. He knew how destructive it could be to dwell on the past and those things that were now out of his control.

Shedding the remainder of his military attire, he felt quite relieved to get out of his uniform, as if the military outfit itself was the source of all his burdens. Jonathon dressed in his usual off-duty duds—casual and comfortable, yet still professional enough for a captain. The change enabled him to feel more at ease, even look forward to spending his last night onboard the ship with Kate. He had a lot on his mind that he wanted to talk to her about, other than Black Thursday. But as he approached the portal leading out of his quarters, he tensed and stopped. Doubts had started to creep in—doubts about venturing out of his safe, isolated environment, and more specifically, doubts about whether he deserved to venture out.

Kate was definitely planning on getting together. But now I'm not so sure I'm up for this. The last thing I want to do is talk about the day's events with everyone I bump into. He stared at the door while continuing to weigh his options. *I certainly don't want to leave Kate waiting, though. She'd kill me. Besides, I always feel better after I've been around her. I suppose a peaceful evening with Kate is exactly the kind of medicine I could use right now. And I do need to talk to her.*

Satisfied with his decision, Jonathon departed. He continued out into the hallway as his quarters darkened, the door sealing shut behind him. And as he strolled toward the elevator, he noticed that the hall lights had stabilized, which confirmed Jensen's earlier report. Though he knew the day's tragedy would inevitably leave behind emotional scars for many of his crew, he was glad to see that the ship, at least, was beginning to heal.

Stepping inside the elevator, he opened his mouth to issue his destination request, but Dr. Whyte's face flashed through his mind. *I'd better stop by sickbay first,* he thought while exhaling a slight groan.

"Please state your destination," the computer beckoned, drawing a glare from Jonathon.

Clearing his throat, he reluctantly stated his request. "Sickbay."

The elevator closed its doors and ascended toward the ship's state-of-the-art medical center, where few expenses, if any, had been spared. Staffed with highly skilled doctors and surgical specialists, sickbay was equipped for virtually any operation or medical procedure that was required. They also attended to the emergency medical conditions of other military personnel and any space-faring civilians in need of assistance beyond the capabilities of their own ship's physicians.

Upon reaching his destination, Jonathon stepped beyond the retracting elevator doors and out into a small, enclosed reception area. He immediately took notice of the ten people who were sitting patiently on the metal benches that decorated the perimeter of the sterile room. Not wishing to enter into any casual conversations, he marched straight ahead, toward the young female medical assistant who was sitting behind a small, glossy-black desk near the main entrance to sickbay. She was dressed in a hospital-white military uniform with green trim, signifying her medical affiliation and low rank. Staring uninterrupted at the erect flat-panel monitor in front of her, she seemed unaware of Jonathon's presence. Her fingers were busily tapping the angled pressure-sensitive surface of the desk, accessing the data-entry commands that were illuminated within. And the magnetic soles of the polished white dress shoes that clothed her feet clicked rhythmically against the metal floor as she tapped to the tune a nearby crewman was humming.

"Excuse me, Ensign," Jonathon interrupted politely.

Brushing her wavy amber hair aside with one hand, the assistant glanced up. "Oh, hello, Captain," she greeted. "What can I do for you?"

"Dr. Whyte had requested I pay her a visit."

"Oh, right. She had just asked about you a few minutes ago. Why don't you go on in to exam room six and I'll let her know you're here."

"All right."

Jonathon stepped around the desk and walked toward the sealed doors, which retracted hastily as he approached. Continuing through the entrance, he strolled down the passageway, courteously returning the greetings from a few of the doctors that ambled in and out of the adjacent rooms. Each exam room was numbered. With a quick tap of the access button, the door to number six slid open and he peeked inside the small, vacant room before stepping with a hint of caution beyond the threshold, acting as if he was facing imminent danger. That was absurd of course, but Jonathon had never looked forward to a trip to the doctor's office. He didn't know why exactly, perhaps it was something from his childhood or just basic human instinct. All he knew for sure was that the ripe smell of sickness and medicine made him a little edgy.

Once the door closed behind him, Jonathon moseyed over to the half-sized metal bench that angled along one of the corners and sat down, intentionally bypassing the reclined examination chair that patients were expected to use. With his legs crossed, his arms folded, and his pulse elevated, Jonathon waited as patiently as he could. His eyes eventually wandered, though there wasn't much in the room worth looking at aside from metal cabinets and powered-down display screens. Along one armrest of the chair, however, he discovered a misplaced datapad and opted to borrow the device. He then spent the next fifteen minutes glancing at the latest sports news from Earth, suspecting that Dr. Whyte was intentionally keeping him waiting as a means of getting even.

Upon hearing footsteps outside the door, Jonathon tossed the datapad back into the chair and sat up straight. With a swishing sound, the door opened and Dr. Whyte entered the exam room, dressed in her red-trimmed medical uniform.

"Good evening, Captain," she stated while glancing at the medical datapad that was grasped between her hands. Taking another step forward, she permitted the door to close behind her.

"Hello, Doctor," Jonathon replied as he crossed his legs and wrapped his interlocked hands around his elevated knee, looking more comfortable than he actually was.

Dr. Whyte slid her datapad into one of the side pockets of her jacket and glared down at Jonathon. "It's been a very busy day, so let's get this over with," she suggested, almost ordered. "The medication you're about to take will remain in your system for a full twenty-four hours before dissipating. If you begin to feel emotionally distressed after that period you may come back for one additional treatment. In most cases, however, one dose is more than sufficient. Now, do you require some water in order to take your medication?"

"No, and I don't require any happy pills either," Jonathon replied, sounding rather defiant. "You know the kind of mental conditioning I've been through, Doctor," he continued, unaffected by the scowl on Dr. Whyte's face. "This is all a big waste of both your time and mine. I'll be fine. I've been trained to handle far worse situations than what we experienced today."

"First of all, they're called Tetra-Prozomamine, not happy pills. And secondly, I don't care what kind of training you've been through. You're not exempt from your obligation to take this medication. The policy on this matter is clear."

"The policy is flawed," argued Jonathon, returning a scowl of his own. "Those pills won't help me. All they'll do is numb my emotions. And they certainly won't reverse the tragedy that occurred. They'll just make it seem less tragic, as if the people who died had suddenly become expendable—a prospect that I find rather offensive."

Dr. Whyte's expression intensified, as did her tone of voice. "Don't be absurd. Tetra-Prozomamine is a proven, effective treatment that has helped countless individuals."

"That's your opinion."

Jonathon stood up from his chair and prepared to leave. In all honesty, he hadn't intended to engage Dr. Whyte in a verbal confrontation, but for some reason she had always managed to rub him the wrong way. And with High Command having stripped him of virtually all authority, the last thing he needed was for her to dictate orders.

"You're not going anywhere until you've taken this medication, Captain," Dr. Whyte insisted as she reached into one of her jacket pockets and retrieved a small plastic container. "Failure to comply with medical regulations will lead to an immediate suspension of your command."

Jonathon all but laughed at her statement. "That's not much of a threat at this point. High Command's already beat you to the punch."

Dr. Whyte stood quiet for a moment, rethinking her habitual tendency to butt heads with anyone who disagreed with her opinions.

"Look," she said calmly. "I'm only trying to help you. Why don't you simply take one of the pills with you and we'll leave it at that. I won't require you to ingest it while under my supervision, but at least I will have done my part in prescribing the treatment. Does that sound like a fair compromise?"

Jonathon nodded and held out his right hand.

Dr. Whyte opened the small container and placed one of the thumbnail-sized beige pills into Jonathon's extended hand. "Try to have a quiet evening, Captain. And best of luck with everything."

Jonathon started to leave, but stopped, turned back and said, "Thanks. And for what it's worth, I do appreciate your efforts. Take care."

He continued out through the retracting doors and back down the hallway toward the exit. After stepping through the main doors to the reception area, he promptly tossed the pill into the small trash receptacle beside the medical assistant's desk.

"Have a good night, Captain," the young assistant called out, her eyes still focused on her work.

"Thanks," Jonathon replied politely as he tapped the elevator's access button. The doors opened and he stepped inside. "Recreation deck," he ordered to the computer.

The elevator sealed itself and descended, passing through the two decks that housed the living quarters before coming to a complete stop. Jonathon stepped out into the hallway and strolled through the intersecting corridors, making his way toward the port side of the ship. He soon approached the entrance to Murphy's, the most popular recreational area onboard. It was clearly marked by a red neon sign that hung above the door's frame, producing a faint hum as it beckoned people to come inside. Such displays were against regulations, but Jonathon had considered it too trivial of a matter to deal with, despite objections from Jensen.

Entering the spacious room through the off-center doorway, he took notice of a recently posted sign that was fastened to a waist-high pole off to his left. The hand-written message was short and to the point:

Take care of my antiques! The last person that damaged one of them was promptly jettisoned out the nearest airlock. Now seat yourself and have a good time.

Don Murphy
(a.k.a. The Management)

A thin smile crept across Jonathon's face as he finished reading the sign. Raising his eyes a bit, he started surveying the atypically quiet surroundings. The room was like every other location on the ship: framed in metal. But the decor and patrons made it quaint, unique. It was almost like you could step through the door and right back into any dimly lit pub on Earth. Sprawling out from the antiquated jukebox that idled in the near corner was a wooden dance floor with more scuffs than the crew had battle scars. Jonathon slipped firmly into the grip of fond recall as he eyed the dance floor. He remembered how much Kate loved to dance and how often she had dragged him out there, despite his pleas to let him retain his dignity.

Both edges of the dance floor faded out into the dining area and its assembly of rounded white tables with their companion chairs. At the peak hours close to one hundred people would eagerly flood the room, squeezing into their seats and familiar social circles. The stresses and repetitious boredom of isolation onboard a warship would be checked at the doorway, leaving only the buzz of friendly conversation as everyone feasted on what was arguably the best food on the ship.

At the present time, however, the room was mostly empty. Under normal circumstances Jonathon would have found the sparse signs of nightlife to be disconcerting, a sign of problems among his crew. But tonight was far from normal. Life had changed for everyone, some more drastically than others, and it would be a little while before customary notions of entertainment or simple enjoyment could find their place on the ship again, before Murphy's lived up to its reputation again. For now, at least, Jonathon welcomed the tranquil atmosphere, feeling that anything livelier would border on disrespect.

An unexpected burst of laughter shot out from the far corner, catching Jonathon's attention. His eyebrows popped up, then sunk upon recognizing the source of the irreverent outburst. Six casually dressed Black Lance fighter pilots were huddled in the corner, talking loudly amongst themselves while chugging drinks. A couple of them were engaged in a game of eight ball, hovering around one of the archaic pool tables like male predators marking their territory. They glanced back, taking notice of their captain's presence, yet their eyes smugly washed across him and through him as if he wasn't even there. They were, after all, the best of the best—elite space jockeys within the most highly renowned squadron in the system—and that, apparently, gave them the right to be choosy about whom they would acknowledge and socialize with, regardless of rank. Jonathon tried to ignore them back, but their attention had already gone full circle, so he strolled toward the bar.

The smooth mahogany countertop stretched along the starboard wall, leaving scarcely enough space behind it for Retired Sergeant Donald Murphy to maneuver. He stood next to the centralized kitchen access door, dressed in a wrinkled red T-shirt and blue jeans, with a lightly soiled apron that straddled his oversized midsection. Despite his obvious retired status, the sergeant was only in his early forties, still young enough for combat duty. But that was no longer up to him. His brutal tour during the Martian war had left him with more than his share of physical injuries, including an irreparably damaged spine that had forced him out of the military and plunged him into a world of binge eating, isolation, even good-old-fashioned depression. Jonathon had tried to keep in touch, although Murphy's deliberate withdrawal from life had left the friendship somewhat one-sided. But at Jonathon's request Murphy had eventually obtained a worker's permit and set up shop on the *Intimidator*, getting as close to the military as his civilian contract would allow.

Holding a towel in one hand, Murphy dried a couple of freshly washed glasses as Jonathon strolled up. "Evening, Jon," he called out in his usual low, scratchy voice.

Jonathon gave a friendly nod in response and sat down on one of the soft, brown bar stools. "How's it going, Don?" he asked while liberating a few pretzels out of one of the inset snack baskets that were even-spaced along the countertop.

"I've got no complaints," Murphy replied, scratching the scraggly brown beard that clung desperately to his portly face. "Haven't seen you around here in little a while. High Command must've been keeping you on a tight leash."

"Yeah, you know how it goes."

"Something on your mind, Jon?"

Murphy began filling a small glass with what appeared to be Jonathon's favorite cherry-flavored synthetic alcohol. All intoxicating drinks had been banned by the ICP in the early twenty-third century, due to the numerous socioeconomic problems that were caused by an increasingly drunken society. The synthetic alternative still enabled people to relax and feel good, but without compromising their ability to function. In other words, you could not become "drunk" by consuming synthetic-alcohol-based drinks, regardless of the quantity you ingested.

Jonathon looked up as his old war buddy placed the drink in front of him. "Thanks," he said with a discernable sigh. "There's a great deal on my mind, I'm just not sure I want to talk about it."

"Come on, Jon, you can talk to me. We've been through our share of hard times together and we've always managed to pull each other through. Now lay it on me."

Jonathon raised his glass and swallowed a gulp of his drink, figuring it would help him relax. His eyes suddenly bulged and he almost dropped the glass. "Whoa," he uttered in a strained, scratchy voice and between coughs. "What is this?"

"Whiskey," Murphy replied with a big grin. "I keep a bottle on hand for emergencies. Just don't ask me where I got it. Given everything that happened today, I figured you could use something with a little more kick. You look like hell, man."

"I feel like it too," Jonathon replied before downing the remainder of the strong contraband.

"Care for another?"

"Tempting, but no thanks."

"Kate meeting you here for dinner?"

"Actually, I'm supposed to head up to her quarters in a few minutes, which reminds me: could I get two steak dinners to go?"

"Sure thing."

Dragging a smudged datapad from his apron pocket, Murphy said, "Let's see, that'd be one medium-rare steak for Kate and one prime cut that's charred beyond all recognition and flavor for you, right?"

Jonathon simpered. "Yeah, that's right. And give me a bottle of that lime shooter Kate likes to drink."

"All right. It'll be ready in a few."

Murphy punched in the order on his datapad before squeezing it back into his apron. He then retrieved a narrow red bottle from under the counter and poured its synthetic cherry-flavored contents into Jonathon's empty glass.

"Now, you gonna share what's on your mind?"

"I don't even know where to begin," Jonathon explained as he rubbed a finger across the rim of his glass. "Everything happened so fast. I had expected a few problems. You know, the usual kind of crap that tends to bog these operations down, but nothing major, nothing to suggest that all life on the moon was about to come to an end." He took a sip of his drink before continuing. "And the thing that really kills me about this is that I knew something wasn't right. All the signs were right there in front of me, but I didn't react. This whole thing was so political that I hesitated and it all came crashing down around me, around all of us." Jonathon downed the last of his drink. His forehead wrinkled as he glanced back up at Murphy. "I also had the strangest feeling come over me when I saw that alien ship. I know this'll sound crazy, but I felt like the thing was actually watching me. I don't know…maybe I just needed more sleep. All I can tell you for sure is that it's been one hell of a day."

"Don't stress about it too much, man. It's easy to see what could've been done in hindsight. Nobody knew what was coming. Even those big-brained scientists had no clue. If they were as smart as they thought they were, God rest their souls, then none of this would've happened. If anyone's to blame, Jon, it's them. You didn't really have anything to do with the experiment itself, anyway. Oh, I'm sure you did your assigned duties as you always have. And don't get me wrong, the accident that occurred today was certainly tragic. I mourn for the dead as much as the next guy, but I don't blame you for what happened just because you were sitting in the captain's seat at the time. That ain't right and I think everyone else will see it the same way."

"I suppose so," Jonathon replied, sounding a little more at ease. "But you know High Command's going to want a scapegoat for this mess, and I think they've got their sights set on me."

"Yeah well, you already know what I think of the brass. They try to crucify you for this and I'll be the first one on the comm telling them what they can go do with those fancy medals they like to brag about."

Jonathon chuckled a little and raised his glass in a toast to Murphy before downing the rest of his drink. "Thanks, Don. You're the man."

Murphy returned a friendly smile and a nod before resuming his dish-drying duties.

"Are you the only one running the place tonight?"

"Yeah. I would've closed up shop all together, but I figured there'd be a few stragglers that'd wander in to escape reality for a while. And besides, I've got nothing better to do."

Sounds of laughter rang out from the gaming area again, albeit from the opposite corner and in a more subdued tone. Jonathon glanced over at the five oval-shaped virtual-reality combat simulators that occupied the remaining space within the gaming area. He recognized Chang near the corner, standing beside the only sim that was in use. Dead Eye was sitting inside the authentic cockpit replica, leaving only his head in view. Both men were still in uniform despite being off duty.

"Did you get some new VR games?" Jonathon inquired, pointing in the direction of Dead Eye.

"Yeah. Young Dead Eye over there had been bugging me for several weeks to update those things. If you can imagine it, he actually asked *me* to toss out something old. Fortunately for him I wasn't very attached to 'em. They're too high tech for my taste. So I finally caved in and got a couple of new ones on the last supply shipment. He's been over there since he got off his shift, blowing off a little steam and trying to achieve the only fame and glory he'll probably ever get in life."

Jonathon chuckled and stood up from the barstool. "I'll swing back around in a few minutes."

Murphy replied with a relaxed, half-completed salute before disappearing into the kitchen. Jonathon walked on by, brushing his right hand across the edge of the countertop along the way.

"Would you stop stuffing your face while you're playing," Chang insisted as he peered down at Dead Eye and the speckles of rye bread that dotted his friend's lap. "You're getting crumbs all over the place."

"Man, what's with you and your obsession with cleanliness?" Dead Eye replied before shoving the remaining quarter of his sandwich into his mouth, deliberately trying to appear disgusting. And to top it off he immediately resumed talking, though he was barely understandable with his mouth full. "You're starting to sound like my mother."

"Hey, at least I don't have a highly-evolved civilization of mold growing in my quarters."

"Actually, they're gone now. The cleaning guys made me commit genocide against the whole lot of 'em. And I think the poor little spores were on the verge of establishing contact with me, too. Ah well. There's always next month."

"Evening, boys," Jonathon interrupted as he strolled up beside Chang.

"Evening, Captain," Chang replied.

"You wanna play a game, Cap'n?" Dead Eye asked in his usual jovial manner. "They always help me relax after a bad day."

"Nah, I've got other plans tonight. Besides, I wouldn't want to embarrass you," Jonathon responded lightheartedly, trying to maintain an upbeat attitude in front of his fellow officers and friends.

Chang burst into laughter.

"Yeah, real funny guys," Dead Eye mumbled.

"So how is the new sim anyway?" inquired Jonathon, admiring its reflective black surface.

"It's pretty cool. The main combat scenarios are a little predictable and look a lot like what we use for training, but the side game of Alien Onslaught more than makes up for any shortcomings. Oh, and they've also enhanced the rumble packs in the seat and back rest, so you can really feel it when your ship gets hit."

"Well your butt must be pretty sore then, Chuck, because you were pummeled in that last mission," Chang retorted with a big grin.

"Hey, it takes me a minute to warm up. And besides, the controls are flaky. I'm telling ya, Captain, they just don't make 'em like they used to."

"Don't start that again," urged Chang, rolling his eyes. "The controls worked fine for the last guy that played. You just plain stink."

Tilting his head back, Dead Eye stared up at his friend and said, "You wanna put your money where your mouth is?"

The two of them continued their raillery as Jonathon listened in amusement. He noticed, however, that the third member of their close-knit group was missing. "Where's Lieutenant Parker?"

"Oh, he went to talk to one of the ship's counselors about what happened today, with the operation and all," Dead Eye replied. "I guess the meds didn't do enough for 'im."

"Don't worry about Darin," interjected Chang. "He'll be fine. He went to the counselor for a little proactive treatment is all."

"He always has been on the cautious side, hasn't he?" remarked Jonathon.

"Big time," Chang responded.

"Well, I'll see you guys later. Try to stay out of trouble."

"No promises there," Dead Eye wisecracked. He then resumed fiddling with the flight stick, still insisting the controls were hampering his ability to achieve the high score.

Jonathon turned around to head back toward the bar, but was startled by Kate's unexpected presence. She was standing right in front of him wearing high heels and a sleek strapless black dress with a slit that ran part way up her right leg. Her soft flowing hair was draped down her back. She looked incredibly sexy, despite standing at full attention with her arm raised in a salute.

"Lieutenant Hayes reporting for duty," she announced with a semi-serious expression. Even though she wasn't entirely in the mood to dress up, she had always felt that going through her normal activities when calamity struck would facilitate her return to a normal life. And most of the time it worked.

"At ease, Lieutenant," Jonathon replied with a receptive smile.

"With pleasure."

Kate's face lit up as she leaned into Jonathon, wrapped her arms around his neck, and kissed him on his lips.

Jonathon placed his arms around her slim waist and countered with a kiss of his own.

"Care to brief me on the mission, Lieutenant? I thought we were going to rendezvous in your quarters."

"Change of plans, Captain. Tonight we're dining out. And then later we can return to my quarters and debrief each other," Kate suggested with a frisky smile and a wink.

"Oh, come on," Dead Eye objected, having witnessed the flirtatious encounter. "Do you two have to do that in front of us?"

"Jealous, Chuckles?" Kate teased, tilting her head to one side and glancing over at Dead Eye.

"Yes. Now go away unless you brought a couple of cute friends for me and Li to play with."

Chang grinned and bounced his eyebrows in approval.

"Sorry, boys, maybe next time."

"Well, I guess I might as well score on a few aliens then," Dead Eye sighed. He pressed a button that caused the canopy on his sim to lower and seal the cockpit shut. The inside of the simulator came alive with photo-realistic visuals of outer space and holographic star fighters that approached in the distance.

Chang folded his arms and watched the simulcast projection boot up along the rear exterior of the canopy, permitting him to observe the action as well.

Taking hold of Jonathon by the hand, Kate led him toward one of the empty tables by the portside wall, away from the few patrons that dined quietly nearby.

"You look incredible, Kate," declared Jonathon, courteously sliding out her chair.

"Thanks," she replied as she sat down and made herself comfortable. "And might I say that you look like hell."

"So I've been told," Jonathon said with a wry chuckle. He scooted over and sat down in the adjacent chair, sliding in a little.

"Did you go see Dr. Whyte?" Kate asked with her arms folded and resting on the edge of the table.

"Yeah."

"And did she give you a happy pill?"

"Yeah."

"And did you take it?"

"Yeah, but just briefly."

"Jon," Kate exclaimed in a disapproving tone. "What did you do with the pill?"

"I tossed it. You know I don't care for those things."

"Oh, that's right. You're a big tough guy that can handle anything."

"Yup," Jonathon agreed with an askew smile. "Are you mad at me?"

"Yes."

"Well you don't look mad."

Kate shook her head and smiled back. "You can be really frustrating sometimes, you know that?"

Murphy strolled up to their table, carrying a green bottle in one hand and a pair of ice-filled glasses in the other hand. "Evening, Kate."

"Hey, Don. What's the special for tonight?"

Murphy shook his head and smiled. "Why do you keep asking me that? You know I don't do specials."

"Yeah, but you're so fun to tease, Donny," replied Kate, batting her eyes in his direction.

"Uh huh. Well, did you two decide to dine in tonight?"

"Yes," Kate confirmed enthusiastically, preempting Jonathon's reply.

"All right then, here's your drinks."

Murphy placed the bottle and glasses on the table prior to embarking on his return trip to the kitchen.

"It's all right with you if we stay here, isn't it?" Kate asked, gazing into Jonathon's eyes. "I just didn't feel like staying cooped up in my quarters all night. I hope you don't mind."

"It's fine, Kate. This place is practically deserted anyway."

Taking hold of one of Jonathon's hands, Kate gave it a little squeeze. "How are you feeling?"

"Better, now that you're here."

"Glad to hear it. You know I worry about you, Jon. And please don't hesitate to come find me whenever you feel the need to talk. It's not good to keep your emotions bottled up."

"Oh, they're not bottled up any more," Jonathon replied while inconspicuously rubbing the bruised knuckles on his right hand. "And I appreciate your concern, but don't worry. I'll be fine."

"So what did our beloved leaders have to say about everything that happened today?"

"Well," Jonathon began, his face tensing a bit, "as you can probably imagine they were all pretty furious, though Admiral Breckard stole the show. If General O'Connor hadn't stepped in and kept things civil I think the admiral might've had a heart attack in mid sentence."

"Oh, I don't think that man will ever die. Death's too chicken to take him on."

Jonathon let a small laugh escape before continuing. "Aside from the obvious tension of the meeting, everything else was pretty straightforward. They're mostly in fact-finding mode at this point, but as usual there'll be a hearing before the Coalition's cabinet members." Pausing briefly, his countenance dimmed a little. "In fact," he continued, "I have to leave on a shuttle tomorrow morning."

"What?" Kate objected with a concerned, almost outraged expression on her face. "Why?"

Jonathon looked out the window, taking a brief moment to organize his thoughts. He gazed at the distant view of Earth, which seemed so peaceful as to nearly contradict the day's events.

"I have to testify during the hearing."

"During the hearing or during your trial?" Kate asked, demonstrating that she understood the political forces that were in play.

"Probably both. Even though they didn't officially state it, I will most likely face a trial after the general hearing is complete. They'll either strip me of my rank or discharge me from the military altogether. Commander Jensen will finally get his long awaited promotion."

"That's not right, Jon," Kate huffed, although her frustrations weren't directed toward her companion. "They can't do that! They can't punish you for what happened. It wasn't your fault."

Jonathon didn't respond. He simply reached over, grabbed the chilled bottle, and removed the glass top while Kate continued to fume over his announcement. The sparkling green liquid was poured into each of the glasses, causing it to hiss as it cascaded down the ice. After setting the bottle down, they both lifted their glasses and took a sip.

"Well, I'm coming with you," Kate insisted. "Maybe I can testify on your behalf."

"They won't allow you to testify. And besides, the verdict will be decided long before I arrive. I've seen this kind of thing before. The trial will be swift and conducted behind closed doors. It's merely a formality."

"Then don't go. Let's hijack the ship instead and head over to Mars. We could get immunity there. I'm sure there are plenty of people on Mars that would love to stick it to High Command."

Jonathon grinned at her suggestion. "As tempting as that sounds, I don't want to be responsible for starting another war between Mars and Earth."

"Well, then I'll resign my commission and go to Earth with you. Once High Command has finished with their little song and dance we can settle down...get married...have a couple of kids. You could even pretend to be their captain. I'm sure I could teach them to salute whenever you walk into the room."

"That sounds like a great plan to me." Jonathon leaned in and kissed her before continuing. "I'll make the arrangements."

Kate stared at him for a moment, looking suspicious at first, then pleased. She opened her mouth to continue the discussion, but Murphy had returned, so she bit back her words for the moment.

"Here's your dinner," he interrupted, placing their freshly prepared meals in front of them. "Everything's on me tonight, so just relax and enjoy yourselves."

"Thanks, Don," they both stated in unison before Murphy headed back to the bar.

"Were you serious about wanting to settle down and get married?" Kate inquired with guarded optimism.

Jonathon took hold of her hands, looked into her eyes, and said, "You know how I feel about you, Kate. And while we've never formally discussed marriage before, it is something that's been on my mind. Once things settle down with all this, I'd be honored if you'd walk down the aisle with me."

Kate's smile returned, though she remained speechless, which was rather unusual for her.

"I still have the deed to my father's house and property in Montana. It's a modest place, but it's also far enough out of the way that we'd be able to start a new life together. I know it's probably not what you had in mind, but—"

"It sounds nice. I don't need a big house or a flashy lifestyle to be happy."

"My bank account thanks you."

Kate chuckled. "Let's eat. I'm starving."

They both unfolded the thick, white napkins that contained their utensils and prepared to dig in. Their food was steaming hot with a rich aroma, making Jonathon's mouth water. Kate had already cut into her meal, but Jonathon was still examining the exquisitely prepared steak, savoring the moment. The past several days had been so busy that the only food he'd had time to consume was from the ready-made meal packets. And while they were certainly nutritious, the company that manufactured them didn't seem to feel that flavor was a priority.

"Are you going to eat it or try to establish a telepathic link with it?" Kate asked in jest.

"I'm enjoying the aroma. I don't like to rush good food."

"Been eating a lot of those meal packets again, huh?"

"Is it that obvious?"

"Let me put it this way: I'm starting to feel a little jealous about how much attention your steak is getting."

Jonathon laughed. His countenance was noticeably more cheerful than when he had first set foot inside Murphy's a short while ago. He seemed to have almost forgotten about the day's events, or, at least, they had been buried deeper in the back of his mind.

Kate kept the tone of the conversation as upbeat as she could. She was trying her best to ensure that Jonathon's last night onboard the *Intimidator* would be memorable, and it would be, but not for the reasons she had envisioned. The darkness among the stars was in motion and it was approaching.

"I'm really going to miss this ship," Jonathon admitted after taking a moment to enjoy his first few bites of steak. "She's the finest vessel in the fleet."

"I know what you mean. I've always felt safe onboard, almost invincible. From the moment I first arrived on the *Intimidator* I felt completely secure. And that was a big deal to me, considering that awful encounter I had with those mercs a few years back. Anyway, for the first few months I thought it was the ship's size and firepower that kept me at ease. I mean, who in their right mind would assault a Juggernaut-class warship? But you know, as time went on I came to realize that it wasn't the impressive technology that was reassuring. Technology always fails, eventually. It was you, Jon. Having you in command of the ship is what has made me feel so safe. Without the right person in command, the *Intimidator* just doesn't live up to its name."

"Thanks, Kate. That really means a lot to me, especially now. I—"

Jonathon shuddered as a chilling sensation coursed through his body, as if someone had just stepped over his grave. The unexplainable feeling was similar to what he had experienced during Operation Giant Leap, when the alien starship had first come into view. He began looking around the room suspiciously, which made Kate a little nervous.

"What's wrong?" she inquired.

Turning back around, Jonathon jerked and almost screamed as he stared horrifically at the rotting corpse that was sitting in Kate's chair. His eyes darted around the room but were met with the same macabre imagery everywhere he looked. There didn't seem to be a single living creature within the vicinity aside from himself. A clammy hand latched onto Jonathon's arm and as he snapped his head back toward Kate, the ghastly images were gone. They had been nothing more than a figment of his imagination, but they still troubled him deeply.

"Jon, are you all right?" Kate probed as she squeezed his arm and tried to pull him back into reality.

"I...I don't know. I've got a really bad feeling that—"

The lights within the room began to flicker before fading completely, leaving the window-framed starlight as the only source of illumination. The *Intimidator's* reactor had mysteriously shut down.

"Hey, what gives?" shouted Dead Eye from across the room, trying to pry open the simulator's canopy.

Jonathon spun his head partway around as he heard strange whispers scatter through the darkness. He couldn't understand the words but their harsh tone left him feeling like he was surrounded by a threatening presence. At that precise moment, he caught a glimpse of a bluish shadow out of the corner of his eye. He looked out the window in time to see the star-fighter-sized object streaking away from the *Intimidator*, heading toward Earth. It was eerily familiar and as it faded into the blackness of space, so to did the ghostly whispers.

"What was that?" Kate inquired, having caught a brief glimpse of the unidentified object.

Jonathon didn't respond. He was tapping his wrist-comm, trying to activate it so he could contact the bridge. But the communicator didn't utter so much as a single beep, having lost power as well.

"I need to get up to the bridge," he exclaimed, rising in such a hasty fashion that he sent his chair tumbling over behind him.

"Wait for me," Kate hollered, stumbling through the darkness.

The lights flickered again and eventually stabilized as both Jonathon and Kate raced out of the room.

"The captain sure left in a hurry," Dead Eye relayed to Chang, "which means something big must be goin' down. Come on. I don't wanna miss anything."

Chapter 5
A Bullet Through the Heart

The lights on the bridge had a slight red tint to them, indicating the ship's elevated alert status and the command staff's heightened tension. Aside from Jensen and Parker, everyone else on the bridge was part of the night shift and they were all busily engaged with an assessment of the confusing situation. Parker would have preferred to be off duty, but Jensen had ordered him to return and finish the engine diagnostic he had started before leaving his shift early to speak with the ship's counselor. Jensen tended to push the crew a lot harder than Jonathon did. He also had a habit of working a double shift whenever Jonathon had given him temporary command of the bridge, savoring every last minute of the power and attention.

"What's the status of the sensor sweep?" Jensen called out while peering through the portside windows, making his own visual scan of the area.

"Still nothing, sir," the auxiliary weapons officer reported.

Turning around, Jensen headed back along the rear balcony, rubbing his forehead with one hand as he pondered his options. "Lieutenant Parker, how many ships are within lunar space?"

"I'm showing six destroyers in orbit, sir. Five of those are in a very low orbit, near the disaster site."

"Lieutenant," continued Jensen, turning to face the communications officer, "contact the ship that's in high orbit and find out if they experienced the same problem we did. And ask them if they saw or detected anything out of the ordinary. If our power outage wasn't an internal system failure, then it must have been external in origin. We may have fallen prey to a mercenary weapons test. And if there are mercs out there, I want them found and dealt with."

"Yes, sir," the communications officer replied.

Jensen turned around and began pacing. He wasn't supposed to, though, according to the command officer's code of conduct. To pace demonstrated anxiety, fear, and lack of confidence, all of which were never to be openly displayed to an officer's subordinates. Emotions had a way of trickling down the chain of command, and though he hadn't intended to, Jensen was making the command staff nervous. But he couldn't help it because he was nervous, frustrated. He hated being in the dark, not knowing how or why a situation had happened. Conspiracy theories began to churn and wander through his mind. Suspicion had already started to seep into his bloodstream and there was little he could do to stop it.

"Weapons systems are online," the senior weapons officer announced, glancing over at her commanding officer.

"Power up the defensive grid."

"Yes, sir."

"Commander," said the communications officer, "the *ICS Challenger* has reported a similar blackout experience. But here's the weird thing: they've also reported seeing some sort of odd-looking starship racing through lunar space. It didn't seem to match any known configuration or profile."

The elevator doors suddenly opened and both Jonathon and Kate stepped out, breathing a little heavy from their hasty trip up from Murphy's. They were still dressed in their casual attire, but that didn't stop them from immediately getting down to business.

"Status report," Jonathon ordered, marching toward his chair. Kate relieved her counterpart at the communications station and sat down, eager to hear an explanation for the blackouts and Jonathon's peculiar behavior.

"The ship appears to be fully operational," Jensen reported, walking back to his station, reluctantly yielding command. "We've completed several sensor sweeps, but nothing out of the ordinary has shown up. It's all quiet out there, as far as we can tell. However, the *Challenger*, which is in a similar orbit to our own, has reported a short power outage, comparable to what we experienced. They also reported seeing some sort of vessel move through lunar space at high speed. It's possible it was an experimental prototype of some kind."

"Don't we have any other details?"

"No, Captain. In fact, nobody can confirm much of anything about the situation because of the blackouts. We were fortunate enough to record a few sensor readings before the *Intimidator* powered down, but the data's inconclusive."

"Let me see the sensor report."

"As you wish."

With a few taps of his command interface, Jensen transferred the data.

Pushing the console-activation button on the right arm of his chair, Jonathon caused the small display screen to slide up and activate. He then examined the brief sensor readout that had been recorded by the *Intimidator's* powerful sensors.

Meanwhile, the elevator doors opened again and both Chang and Dead Eye stepped out and moved to their command stations, relieving the junior officers who currently occupied them.

"There's no way that energy signature is coming from the ship's engine," Jonathon mumbled while studying the data. "It's too erratic for propulsion. It must be carrying some sort of cargo…or weapon."

"Captain, I insist that you tell me what's going on," Jensen demanded, feeling certain that Jonathon was deliberately withholding information from him and thus relegating his command position to one of lesser importance—a delusion he often suffered from.

"Do you remember what the alien ship in the Polaris System looked like?" inquired Jonathon, turning to face Jensen.

"If my memory serves me right, it had sort of a dark-blue shimmer to it, but what does that have to do with…don't tell me you're implying it was an alien vessel that came through here?"

"I'm not implying it, I'm stating it. I believe that it was the source of the power outages. And based on the direction it was moving, it appears to be on a direct intercept course with Earth. I'm afraid all hell's about to break loose, Commander."

Anxious chatter filled the bridge on the heels of Jonathon's bold announcement.

"Lieutenant Parker, bring us about and move in on an intercept course at maximum burn."

"Belay that order, Lieutenant," snapped Jensen, his eyes bearing down on Jonathon. "Need I remind you, Captain, that we're not authorized to leave lunar orbit? High Command gave us strict orders—"

"I understand that, Commander, but we have bigger issues to worry about. The Earth itself could be in serious danger."

Jonathon cocked his head back toward Parker and said, "Execute your orders, Lieutenant."

"Yes, sir," Parker replied, fidgeting in his chair. He felt more than a little uncomfortable about being in the middle of the power struggle that was mounting between the two senior officers.

"Lieutenant Hayes, start broadcasting an automated hail using conventional radio frequencies. Set the communication to rotate through the usual spectrum and let's see if we can get that ship's attention."

"Will do."

"You have absolutely no proof of any hostile intentions, *Captain,*" snarled Jensen in a tone that suggested the argument was heating up. "You don't even know for sure that it was an alien vessel. And you can't go running off on a personal crusade simply because you have a *bad feeling* about what might happen. It's an absurd abuse of power—"

"We don't exactly have time to research the situation, Commander. We've already wasted enough time as it is. That unauthorized vessel needs to be intercepted, regardless of what it may or may not be. And if I'm right, if it is in fact from the Polaris System, then the stakes are far too high for us to sit back and do nothing."

Jonathon hated fighting with Jensen, but he couldn't ignore his gut instincts, not again. He had to do what he knew was right or risk soaking his hands in more innocent blood.

"Lieutenant Hayes, contact High Command…no wait." Jonathon took a few seconds to ponder his dwindling options. "Contact General O'Connor."

"Shouldn't you be speaking with High Command directly?" Jensen objected.

"I don't have time to deal with their bureaucracy. I need someone who can act quickly."

"Don't you mean someone who thinks exactly like you?" Jensen said pointedly.

"That's enough, Commander," Jonathon shot back, asserting his authority.

"Captain," Kate interrupted, and not a moment too soon. "I've located the general. He's on the *Endeavor*, which is holding position roughly one thousand klicks outside of Earth Dock."

"Perfect. Establish an ultra-priority comm link and put the video feed through to the main screen."

Turning his attention back to Jensen, Jonathon hoped that by giving him something to do he could distract him from pursuing the argument further, even stave off his annoying tendency to play devil's advocate. "Commander, contact all ships in this sector and ask them to scan for anything out of the ordinary. We need to know what that unauthorized vessel is up to and whether it's alone or part of a bigger force that we've yet to discover."

"As you wish, Captain," Jensen assented reluctantly, taking an additional second or two to glare at Jonathon in protest.

"General O'Connor's transmission is coming through now, sir," Kate reported.

The main display screen flickered and O'Connor's image popped into view.

"Captain Quinn, this is a surprise," admitted O'Connor. "I didn't expect to hear from you until tomorrow. What's the emergency?"

"I'm sorry to be the constant bearer of bad news, General, but we have a situation developing."

"I'm listening."

"We're tracking an alien ship that's headed on a direct intercept course with Earth. It's emitting—"

"I'm sorry, did you say *alien* ship?" O'Connor interrupted, looking more than a little confused about Jonathon's unusual statement.

"Yes, General, I did. The ship appears to have some of the same characteristics as the one we observed in the Polaris System. It's also emitting a strong and erratic energy signature, which I believe could be some manner of weapon."

"Are you certain about that, Captain? Do you have any proof?"

"I'm positive about this, General, but I don't have any hard evidence to offer you. The only thing we know for certain is the alien vessel has a very disruptive effect on all electronic systems within several klicks of its location, and the effect seems to linger for a minute or two after the ship departs. Whatever dampening field it's emitting has made it extremely difficult to gather any kind of useful information about the vessel, almost like it doesn't want to be scanned.

"Physical evidence aside, General, everything adds up. During Operation Giant Leap we destroyed the Polaris System. Now you and I both know it was an accident that resulted from a failed scientific experiment. But from the point of view of the aliens—"

"It would be viewed as an act of war," O'Connor finished. He was growing increasingly concerned about Jonathon's theory. The dilemma was unprecedented, but if Jonathon was right, if mankind was on the brink of war with an alien civilization, all reasonable steps had to be taken to diffuse the situation. And if that wasn't possible, O'Connor knew he had to at least ensure that the war started on humanity's terms. It was a grim prospect either way.

"How could they possibly have known how to find us?"

"I don't know, General, but they appear to be more advanced than we are. Perhaps they were able to identify our star system based on the wormhole we created. The fact that they got here so fast suggests they have wormhole technology of their own, or something similar."

"You're probably right. I'll speak with the other members of High Command immediately, but it's not going to be easy to get all of them to agree with your assessment. Admiral Hughes in particular will resist any sort of action until we have proof of the aliens' intentions. Has any contact been attempted with the vessel in question?"

"We're broadcasting a standard hail, but so far there's been no response. And there probably won't be one either. It seems to me that if the aliens were interested in making contact they could have done so already. That ship has raced right by several of our own, including the *Intimidator*, without sending any kind of transmission or even pausing to analyze us. The fact that it's traveling on an unwavering course toward Earth demonstrates a preconceived mission objective, and that makes me more than a little nervous."

"Good point. I'll try to persuade High Command to evacuate Earth Dock, but that's easier said than done, especially given the short time frame. Most of the Coalition's cabinet members have already arrived for tomorrow's hearing. There's going to be a lot of resistance to the idea of abandoning the space station. I trust your judgment, Jon. I always have, but you know how red tape tends to get in the way. However, I'll do my best to press the issue with Admiral Hughes and the others."

"Thank you, General. I also wanted to inform you that the *Intimidator's* currently en route to Earth. I know that's a violation of our orders, but it seemed the appropriate thing to do, in case we could be of assistance."

"I support your decision, Captain, but based on your observations it sounds as if the alien ship will be here before you arrive. Fortunately, we've got three other destroyers in the area that we can use to form a defensive perimeter, in the event our uninvited guest proves to be a Trojan horse. In the meantime, continue on your current course. I'll send out a priority alert to the rest of the fleet to keep an eye out for more of these unexpected visitors. We can hope this one's only the advance scout."

"Understood, General. Be sure to warn the fleet about maintaining a reasonable distance. Otherwise, they'll risk losing power and become easy targets."

"Acknowledged, Captain. O'Connor out."

Jonathon began running through possible scenarios in his mind, half of which played out to disastrous results. He eventually glanced down at the time on his communicator. "How long before we reach Earth orbit?" he inquired.

"Approximately twenty-five minutes, sir," Parker replied. "The *Intimidator's* moving as fast as it'll go, but the alien vessel got a big head start on us. It'll probably reach Earth within the next ten to fifteen minutes."

General O'Connor was sitting in the captain's chair on the compact bridge of the *ICS Endeavor*. Space within the

Destroyer-class warship was at a premium, with a cramped internal layout and design that made the *Intimidator* look like a luxury cruiser. But O'Connor didn't seem to mind. He had the whole of space beneath his feet, which to him was very liberating. The *Endeavor* served as O'Connor's personal vessel whenever he needed to conduct specific assignments away from Earth, or even when the desire struck him to escape the stresses of his job. For a marine who had spent a good portion of his life planetside, he was quite fond of the stars. The constellations and their mythological tales were of particular interest to him. He didn't believe the ancient yarns of course, but he enjoyed their mysterious symbolism and dramatic flare.

The *Endeavor's* command staff was comprised of five relatively inexperienced young officers, all sitting at their command stations along the perimeter of the circular room. O'Connor had been serving as a mentor of sorts for the young crew, helping to mold them into the MPF's finest, as he had done with Jonathon and others.

"Put me through to High Command," O'Connor ordered, glancing over at his communications officer.

"Yes, sir," the lieutenant replied, looking more than a little uptight about the prospect of engaging an extraterrestrial vessel. He was remembering all of the science-fiction holograms he had watched in which a powerful alien species decimated the unsuspecting humans. And the more he let his imagination run rampant, the more convinced he was they were about to face certain death.

"The video link's coming through now, General."

Straightening up, O'Connor faced the display screen that angled down from the ceiling a short distance in front of him. Admiral Hughes and five other members of High Command came into view around their conference table. The other three officers were out and about the station, busily overseeing preparations for the upcoming hearing.

"General O'Connor, how can we be of assistance to you?" Admiral Hughes inquired politely.

"We have an extremely serious situation developing, Admiral. I've received information indicating that an extraterrestrial presence has entered our system. Its last known position has placed it on a direct intercept course with Earth."

"Extraordinary! We'll prepare to make contact with it when it arrives. This—"

"It's not here on diplomatic business, Admiral. We believe it's from the same civilization that occupied the Polaris System. We also believe it to be hostile."

"Based on what grounds?" Breckard inquired, sounding intrigued rather than argumentative.

"For starters, the alien vessel has an incredibly disruptive affect on our technology. It's emitting some sort of dampening field that temporarily disables any ship within several klicks of its location. It's also been heading on a specific course toward Earth, without making any efforts to contact the ships in this sector. And given the destruction our scientists caused in the Polaris System, it seems only logical the aliens view us as an aggressive species. The approaching ship may be their initial response to our apparent declaration of war."

An energetic verbal debate promptly broke out among the prestigious group. The overall atmosphere within their conference room had become exceptionally tense.

"I'm sorry to interrupt," O'Connor continued, "but we need to make some decisions and we need to make them now."

"What do you propose, General?" asked Breckard.

"Earth Dock should be placed on full alert and all nonessential personnel and dignitaries should be evacuated immediately. I also suggest placing Earth at DEFCON 3."

"I agree," Breckard replied.

"Well, I do not," Admiral Hughes objected. "You've provided very little evidence suggesting that we're about to be attacked. This situation could very well be a turning point for humanity. Therefore it is imperative that when we contact the alien ship, we do so under normal operating conditions. We don't want to send the wrong message—"

"With all due respect, Admiral, we've already sent them the wrong message," O'Connor countered, disappointed with her conflicting point of view.

"I stand firm on my views, General."

"I agree with Admiral Hughes," Vice Admiral Kreider added. "We need to approach this fully as a diplomatic situation."

The other three officers in the room nodded their heads in agreement. Only Breckard, being the hardened man of war that he was, understood O'Connor's perspective on the situation.

"We've got to at least evacuate the station, as General O'Connor suggested," Breckard argued, sounding quite annoyed with his fellow officers.

"I think that action's premature," Admiral Hughes retorted. "We will instruct all civilian and corporate vessels to immediately vacate the area, but the occupants of this station will remain. We're only talking about one alien ship, not an invasion force. We should be perfectly safe here. However, if the circumstances change and evacuation is warranted, then we will proceed accordingly. In the meantime, we will maintain a diplomatic posture. Do *not* engage that ship in any way, General."

"I will, of course, respect your decision. The *Endeavor* will form up with the local destroyer group and maintain a defensive perimeter around the station. We will engage only if fired upon. O'Connor out."

As the communication terminated, the display screen switched to an exterior view of Earth Dock.

"Commander," stated O'Connor, "instruct the other destroyers in the area to close formation and take up defensive positions around the station, maintaining a distance of ten klicks. And give them strict orders that no one is to fire without my approval."

"Yes, sir."

"What have we brought upon ourselves?" O'Connor mumbled to himself, feeling dysphoric about mankind's current predicament. He gazed thoughtfully at the image of the glistening white space station on the main display screen. Earth Dock looked more like a fortress than a docking hub, with its enormous defensive barriers rotating slowly around the perimeter and weapons of every kind bristling from the upper and lower platforms. While it seemed unlikely to him that such a daunting structure could be destroyed, he was still concerned.

Information was power and with little known about the aliens he felt almost powerless.

The alien ship made its final approach toward Earth, slowing to a crawl, then lingering in orbit, as if surveying the area. It was a pause that lasted but for a moment. Coming about, the elusive vessel accelerated directly toward Earth Dock. The *ICS Lionheart* came about as well, positioning itself on a pursuit vector and matching speed. Square panels on the undersides of the twin extensions that jutted down from the destroyer's main body slid open, enabling a pair of missile launchers to pop into view while a third launching rack rose out of the midsection of the ship, surrounded by defensive lasers. Several more hidden compartments slid open as well, revealing an assortment of quad-barreled plasma turrets, or stinger cannons as they were more commonly known, the largest of which was located above the bridge, at the front of the heavily armored warship. Though its captain had been ordered to maintain a defensive posture, the *Lionheart* continued advancing with its gun ports hot, poised to strike at the slightest sign of provocation.

"General," the commander called out, "we've sighted the unauthorized vessel. It's approaching the space station."

"Put it on screen and zoom to full magnification."

O'Connor stood up from his chair and stared in amazement at the unusual image that filled the display screen. He had never seen anything like it before.

"Is that a ship or a life form?" one of the officers mumbled as they all looked on in awe.

The bizarre-looking otherworldly visitor was both a dazzling and a frightening sight, leaving many individuals wondering if the alien craft was real or merely a figment of their own dark imaginations. The main body of the vessel was comprised of rounded overlapping strips, like muscular tissue that had meshed together in a spherical wad. Its midnight-blue surface shimmered in the untamed sunlight, drawing considerable attention to the black patterns that slithered along its hull. The effect was similar to watching the undulating shadows that form on an underwater surface as light refracts through the depths.

Four talon-like extensions protruded out from around the forward surface of the main body, curving in toward each other in a threatening manner. From the rear extended eight tentacles, almost enclosing the main body as they arched beyond the front of the ship where they restrained a reflective black sphere. The malignant jewel was approximately one third the size of the vessel's main body and occasionally pulsated with faint white energy waves that beat in rhythm like a heartbeat.

Such peculiar attributes did indeed give the vessel the appearance of a life form rather than an interstellar starship. From a distance it resembled a spider that had trapped its prey—imagery that made it difficult to think of the alien presence as anything but hostile.

"General, the space station is losing power," the commander reported.

"Maintain our current position, but go to full alert and instruct the other ships to do the same. Let's also try hailing the alien vessel. I want to see if we can get its attention."

"Yes, sir," the communications officer replied, looking obedient at first, then confused. "But, uh, what do I say to it?"

"Just send a standard hail, Lieutenant. They most likely won't understand a word of what you're saying, but we've got to try something, anything that might trigger a non-lethal response. We don't exactly have set protocols for dealing with first-contact situations."

"Understood. I'll get right on it, sir."

O'Connor looked on with bated breath as the alien ship crept to within one hundred meters of Earth Dock—a menacingly close stance and certainly not one that any reasonable diplomat would use.

"What is it doing?" he whispered to himself, his concerns mounting. The extraterrestrial vessel was idle, ignoring all transmissions from the *Endeavor* and making no attempts of its own to establish contact. It seemed to O'Connor and others of his command staff that whoever was onboard that ship was either unwilling or unable to communicate. Most hunters don't talk to their game before pulling the trigger.

Within the protected inner zone of the space station, all was ominously quiet. The countless windows that dotted the exteriors of the glistening white mesh of towers had become dark. And the sweeping barriers that rotated around the station had slowed, giving the impression that life itself was being drained from the heart of the proud human empire.

Meanwhile, the *Lionheart* was still advancing on the unwelcome visitor, which was well within its targeting sights. But before the *Lionheart's* captain realized it, his aggressive nature and lack of caution had brought the *Lionheart* within range of the dampening field. The warship's power faded, though its momentum continued to carry it forward, drawing it toward an uncertain fate.

"Any response?" O'Connor inquired.

"No sir. It's all quiet across the board except for an odd energy reading coming from whatever that thing is that it's transporting. Hold on…we've got a problem. The *Lionheart* has broken formation and is advancing on the alien's position."

"Who's in command of that vessel?"

"Captain Russell Erickson, sir."

"I should've known," O'Connor groaned, returning to his chair. Though he was usually pleasant natured, he had little tolerance for anyone who willingly disobeyed orders, especially when lives were at stake. "Get that man on the comm ASAP."

"Too late, sir. The *Lionheart's* lost all power."

"Curse that man!" O'Connor growled. "He'd better have a good reason for his obvious lack of judgment or I'll have him busted down to ensign and working in the mess hall before he knows what hit him."

"Uh, I think we have a bigger problem here, sir," the weapons officer reported, glancing over at his superior. "I'm detecting a massive energy spike. Your orders?"

O'Connor didn't respond, mainly because he wasn't sure what to do. He was torn between protecting the station and being careful to not misinterpret the aliens' actions, thus preventing an interstellar incident that would only deepen the potential conflict.

"Sir? Your orders?"

"Just wait, Lieutenant," O'Connor replied, his eyes fixed on the target.

The tentacle-like extensions on the alien vessel separated from the black orb and retracted toward the main body of the ship, which drifted backwards several dozen meters before holding position. And there it lingered while the energy surges along the orb intensified.

"Energy readings are off the scale," the commander reported. "I'm also detecting strong gravitational fluctuations coming from the alien device. And both Earth Dock and the *Lionheart* are still dead in space."

"Unfortunately, Commander, I think your choice of wording is more accurate than you realize," said O'Connor. "I feel like I'm watching a spider paralyzing its prey in preparation to consume it." Pausing for a moment, he decided on the appropriate course of action to take. "I want that ship destroyed, Commander. Order all warships to lock onto the alien vessel and fire at will."

"Gladly, sir. I hate spiders."

A constant stream of plasma bursts was unleashed from the three active destroyers. The luminous green fire struck the hull of the alien vessel, causing its energy shield to ignite in a coruscating display of multi-chromatic lightning. Reacting to the assault, the vessel spun around and tried to flee, but one plasma stream after the other pounded its shields and eventually ruptured its surprisingly resilient hull. A tremendous explosion ensued, sending debris scattering into space before slowing and drifting back toward the mysterious orb. Each of the small fragments accelerated into orbit, spinning around the pulsating device like planets circling a star.

"That object appears to be some sort of localized gravity well," the commander cautioned, sounding uneasy about his assessment. "Destroying the alien ship has had no effect on the device. It's still intensifying in power. The dampening field is also still in effect, so it must be emanating from that thing as well."

"Target the alien device and fire!" O'Connor ordered.

Several rounds of plasma stingers shot out of the *Endeavor's* forward cannons and streaked toward the orb. Initially the energetic bursts appeared as if they would strike their target, but at the last second they curved down and away, having veered along the warped space that enveloped the alien mechanism.

"What the—" the weapons officer stuttered.

"I saw it, Lieutenant. Increase power to the weapons and keep firing. Order all ships to fire at will."

As more plasma ordnance deflected along the intense curvature that surrounded the orb, it shone with a searing white light for several seconds, prior to undergoing an instantaneous collapse, releasing a compression wave that rattled the neighboring ships and personnel. There, rotating like a whirlpool in blackened water, was a four-meter-wide rift in space.

"Cease fire and back us up to a safe distance," O'Connor ordered, gripping the sides of his chair tightly as the *Endeavor* trembled from the violent forces that tugged at it.

"Yes, sir," the navigation officer responded, speaking with a light Hebrew accent. A glimmer of fear could be seen in her eyes as she stared in disbelief at the disturbing images on the overhead display.

Parts of Earth Dock were beginning to buckle and break away as the entire facility drifted toward the shadowy rift like a helpless victim dragged to its death, shedding its outermost layers in a vain attempt to escape. The *Lionheart* appeared to be gaining speed as well, despite its lack of propulsion. It too was caught in the unforgiving gravitational pull.

The crews of the destroyer group watched in horror as the symbol of mankind's triumph, that indomitable fortress in space, yielded its structural integrity. One chunk of metal after another was ripped free and pulverized as it approached the rift. Even the largest of fragments crumpled, as if they had been constructed out of nothing more substantial than paper.

Power to the station came back online, which caused several commanding explosions to erupt from the sides of the weakening pearl spires. A chain reaction ensued, producing several smaller explosions all around the station, blasting debris into space. It wasn't long before the entire facility depressurized and collapsed, resulting in more explosions that expelled the twisting, churning shards into the mouth of the spatial anomaly. Earth Dock had been reduced to a swirling sea of metal that writhed defiantly before vanishing into the rift, leaving not so much as a single atom behind.

Having regained power, the *Lionheart* engaged its reverse engines at full burn, spewing dazzling yellow exhaust as the powerful warship tried desperately to veer away from its pending doom. But the intense gravitational forces refused to release their hold. Drawing inexorably closer, the forward section of the destroyer eventually buckled and imploded, generating a tremendous blast that blew the *Lionheart* apart. The mangled wreckage was crushed beyond recognition as the detritus spiraled into the deadly rift.

With the remaining debris consumed, ripples in the fabric of space itself soon radiated from the perimeter of the distortion as it destabilized. Its dark, ferocious mouth closed slowly, swallowing all traces of its prey.

O'Connor's shocked expression transitioned quickly to one of outrage. "The *Lionheart*...Earth Dock...nearly four thousand dead. And there was nothing we could do to stop it," he uttered, gritting his teeth. His hands gripped the arms of his chair even tighter as anger swelled within him.

Disheartened, the command staff stared at the monitor in silence. The communications link was beeping, yet nobody seemed to notice or even care.

Far off in the distance, the *Intimidator* was approaching, but the pride of the MPF didn't seem so intimidating any more.

"Captain," Kate called out, breaking the thick silence that had overtaken the bridge, "General O'Connor's finally acknowledged our communication request."

"Put him through."

Despite the apparent lack of emotion in Jonathon's voice, he was torn up inside about what had taken place. The empty void that had replaced Earth Dock's once-grand profile was too horrifying to contemplate.

"General, I'm sorry we didn't arrive in time to—"

"Don't apologize, Captain. There was nothing you could have done even if you had been here."

"What happened?"

"The alien ship was transporting a weapon that created some sort of gravity well. It crushed and swallowed the space station while we sat here and watched like helpless children. We were able to destroy the hostile vessel, but the damage was already done."

Jonathon remained speechless until he noticed that only three destroyers were in the area. "General, I thought you claimed there'd be four ships guarding the station. I notice one's missing and I'm a little hesitant to ask where it is."

O'Connor sighed and shook his head. "The *Lionheart* drifted within range of the dampening field and was destroyed in the same brutal fashion as Earth Dock," he reported grimly.

Jonathon's countenance dimmed as he mourned his fallen comrades. He felt at least partially responsible, surmising that the attack never would have happened had Operation Giant Leap turned out differently. And perhaps he was correct. If he had listened to his instincts and aborted the operation at the right moment, then conceivably death and destruction would not have become his bedfellows. Or perhaps the darkness would have been set in motion anyway. Only time would tell.

"How many casualties did we suffer?"

"Nearly four thousand. But it's even worse than the numbers indicate. We lost the other nine members of High Command, as well as other high-ranking officers. We also lost nearly all of the Coalition's cabinet members. The aliens hit us a lot harder than I think they realize. And it's going to take a long time for us to recover from this, time that we most likely don't have."

"I suspect this initial attack was primarily a test of our technology and defenses," Jonathon opined.

"I agree. They're probably waiting to see how we'll respond. And given that we have no way to take the fight to them, it shouldn't be long before they realize that and send a full invasion force. We've got a lot of serious work to do so that we're not caught off guard like this again."

"How can I be of assistance, General?"

"As the sole officer within High Command, I'm afforded emergency powers under these grave circumstances. These additional powers give me the authority to do whatever is necessary to ensure the security of the Solar System. But in order to do that I'm going to need some help. I need someone to organize the fleet, someone that has the experience, leadership, and courage to defend mankind at all costs. You're the first person who comes to mind, Jon."

"General, I—"

"I'm promoting you to the rank of admiral and giving you a seat within High Command. You now have autonomous control over the entire fleet. A joint announcement concerning this matter will go system-wide in the next few minutes. Do you have any questions, Admiral?"

"No, General. I'll begin the war preparations immediately."

A look of determination had swept across Jonathon's face. He already seemed more distinguished, more powerful. Though he took no pleasure in being promoted under such tragic circumstances, he was prepared to fill the full measure of his position. He had been well trained for war.

"Good. Now, as the highest ranking officer in charge of our ground forces, I need to head down to Earth and organize our soldiers and planetary defenses in the unfortunate event that aliens set foot on human soil. I'll also arrange to have all available marines near Martian space transferred down to the colony, to bolster the few thousand peacekeeping troops that are currently stationed there. And I believe you already know the standard wartime protocols, so as soon as you're ready we'll begin the broadcast."

"Understood, General."

The command staff was quiet, withdrawn, and unsure whether they should congratulate Jonathon on his promotion. By tacit agreement, it seemed appropriate to remain silent and dwell on those who had fallen and those who would no doubt fall in the coming weeks and months.

The day's medication treatments were still in effect, aiding the disheartened officers as they came to terms with the severity of their situation. Even so, the mood on the bridge was somber. And Jonathon, fed up with the death toll that continued to mount from the consequences of the failed experiment, sat stone-faced in his chair. His thoughts were focused on the imminent broadcast and his new role in upcoming events. But having already heard countless moving, motivational speeches from the likes of O'Connor and others within the military, the words flew to him effortlessly.

After clearing his throat, Jonathon perfected his posture and smoothed the last few wrinkles from his shirt in an attempt to look as proper and authoritative as he could, despite his casual attire. Yet Jensen looked on with disapproval. The thought of an admiral appearing out of uniform before the entire fleet made him cringe. And so, in what mistakenly appeared to be a rare display of camaraderie, he walked up to the captain's platform, removed his military jacket, and held it out to Jonathon.

"Thank you, Commander," said Jonathon as he graciously accepted the jacket and quickly put it on.

"Lieutenant Hayes, synchronize our video link with General O'Connor's and prepare to initiate a system-wide ultra priority broadcast to all military personnel."

Straightening his borrowed jacket, Jonathon listened as O'Connor spoke.

"This is General O'Connor of High Command. It is with deep regret that I inform you that the Intrastellar Coalition of Planets is now at war. We were attacked moments ago by a hostile extraterrestrial presence. We've suffered a devastating blow with the loss of Earth Dock, the *ICS Lionheart*, and approximately four thousand brave men and women who gave their lives in the line of duty. In addition, our political and military infrastructure has been substantially weakened, capped by the loss of the other nine members of High Command. Therefore, I am hereby promoting Captain Jonathon Quinn to the rank of admiral and elevating him to the position of supreme commander of our fleet and I urge you to give strict heed to his orders. Admiral."

The video feed transitioned to a close-up image of Jonathon. "Thank you, General. Our first priority is to tighten security throughout the system. We have an obligation to see that the savage attack that occurred today does *not* happen again. All warships are hereby ordered to abort their current missions and return to the nearest planetary docking ports to await further orders. Maintain full alert status and report any unusual sensor activity. A full account of the events that transpired today will be forthcoming, as will particular assignments to each ship and crew.

"Stand firm and remain vigilant. Today has become a day of infamy, but our enemies will soon realize that our courage and determination are unmatched in the universe. Victory will be ours to claim. Quinn out.

"Lieutenant, prepare to initiate a system-wide emergency broadcast."

All across the Solar System, on transports and cargo ships, in restaurants and shopping centers, even within peoples' homes, video terminals abruptly displayed the ICP logo.

Kate's voice came through. "This is an emergency broadcast of the Intrastellar Coalition of Planets. Please stand by for an important announcement. I repeat: this is an emergency broadcast of the Intrastellar Coalition of Planets."

Silence swept through the system as people flocked anxiously to their video terminals. The ICP logo was replaced with split-screen close ups of Jonathon and O'Connor, as if sitting side-by-side.

"This is General O'Connor of the Military Protection Force. It is with a heavy heart that I inform you that mankind is now at war with an unknown extraterrestrial civilization. Our enemies have already struck at the very heart of our society and today we mourn the loss of those who have fallen in defense of our freedoms. But rest assured, their brave sacrifice will not be in vain. We are stronger than our enemies realize and we will bring them to justice."

"In an effort to ensure security throughout the system," added Jonathon, "we are declaring martial law. All corporate and civilian transports are hereby ordered to return immediately to their appropriate planetary docking ports. All space-based mining platforms must be evacuated within the next twelve hours. And all travel within the Solar System is strictly forbidden without appropriate military authorization. If you need assistance in complying with these orders, please contact the nearest military authority.

"There's no need to panic. Please remain calm. With your cooperation we will get through this difficult time. If you require further information or feel the need to evacuate to other locations, please contact your local authorities. They will assist you in any way they can."

The ICP logo once again appeared on the screen. Despite Jonathon's plea, panic was already spreading throughout the system.

Chapter 6
Portents

"The first evacuation transport has cleared Jovian space, sir," the young assistant reported to Commander Bruso. "And the last bunch of workers has boarded the second transport now awaiting departure."

"Good, now get out of here! Grab the reactor-shutdown crew and get onboard the transport. I'll be there in a few minutes."

"Yessir," the young assistant replied, looking relieved that he'd finally been given permission to bail. Bruso had run the poor lad ragged for the last few hours, using him as a beast of burden to ensure that corporate protocol had been followed with respect to station shutdown—a duty that Bruso and his administration team should have tended to personally. Despite being exhausted, however, the assistant had more than enough energy remaining to dart out of the *Jupiter III's* control room and down to the awaiting transport.

Taking advantage of the empty room and his complete privacy, Bruso lumbered over to one of the consoles. A small, translucent-blue data card was inserted into the adjacent slot, activating the console. He spent the next few minutes interacting with the touch-screen interface, deleting the various streams of data that popped into view while keeping an eye on the doorway.

After a few minutes had passed, Bruso's morally suspect chief of security came bursting into the room, looking frustrated, as usual. "Why are you still up here?" Warren complained. "It's been almost ten hours since the evacuation order was given. We need to get our butts outta here!"

"Not yet. I need to delete the financial records first. I'm not leaving any traces of our activities. It's too risky."

"Risky?" Warren squawked as a puzzled, almost flabbergasted expression washed across his face. "Man, your priorities are way outta whack. Risky is stayin' here on this floating death trap. Don't you remember what happened yesterday? That alien thing that took out the space station came through that weird opening that popped out next to us. And I don't wanna wait around for any more of 'em to show up."

"Relax, I'm almost done. Besides, what are the odds they'd appear in the same place twice? We'll be just fine." Bruso brushed aside Warren's concerns and continued destroying the evidence of their crimes. He seemed to fear prison more than death—a point not lost on his uptight cohort.

Before Warren could continue the argument, however, the sensor panel started beeping, bringing unpleasant feelings of déjà vu.

"Oh, that's real friggin' great. They're here, aren't they?" Warren grumbled, nervously running both hands through his hair. "Man, we're gonna die. I knew I should've left on the first transport instead of waiting around for you. You've screwed us all this time!"

"Shut up and let's get out of here," Bruso yelled, lumbering like an elephant and leading their hurried retreat from the control room.

Within the relative calm of space near the mining platform, along the rim of Jupiter's rings, a new wormhole had formed. The unnatural distortion was significantly larger than the one that had appeared a day earlier, hinting at the greater threat that lay in wait. Ghostly bursts of blue energy spiraled away from the perimeter of the ominous opening while faint ripples glided from one side to the other, slowing in frequency as the wormhole stabilized. The imagery quickly transitioned from breathtaking to terrifying, however, as a distant fleet of alien warships came into view. And while their exact location was a mystery, their intentions were clear: they were advancing on the humans' home territory.

"Power up the engines and get us out of here," Bruso demanded in between deep gasps as he stepped inside the cramped cockpit of the final evacuation transport.

"Yes, sir," the pilot replied calmly, having grown accustomed to the constant ranting of his boss. He picked up his half-eaten ham sandwich and took a generous bite before continuing.

"We'll be able to disembark in five minutes," he mumbled while spit-soaked crumbs sprayed from his mouth.

"We don't have five minutes, you idiot!" Warren shouted. "We need to leave right now."

"We can't," the pilot snapped in a knee-jerk reaction, unaware of the looming danger that was fueling Warren's furor. "The launching procedure is an automated process. It takes *five minutes*, no more, no less. There's nothing I can do to change that. I didn't design the freaking system. Now go sit down and buckle up."

The obtrusive exhaust ports on the back of the transport eventually ignited, burning with a subtle rusty glow as the engines came online. But the vessel was still fastened to the starboard side of the mining platform, unable to depart until its aging technology was primed and ready.

Brilliant flashes of light arced across the dark opening of the wormhole as the tip of one of the alien warships crept out, rippling the space around it. Small gravitational currents pulsed toward the transport and caused it to vibrate against the docking clamps, making the ship appear as if it was trembling before the approaching predator.

Onboard the transport, the sensor panel in the cockpit was abuzz with activity.

"What's going on?" the pilot demanded, glaring back at Bruso.

"We're about to become space dust unless you get this friggin' piece of junk moving," Warren growled, preempting what would have been a similar remark by Bruso.

Reaching over with one hand, the pilot powered up the overhead display screen and adjusted the external cameras to monitor the sensor disturbance, bringing an image of the wormhole into view. But that wasn't the worst of it. He also caught a glimpse of the first alien warship. With his eyes wide and his jaw slack, the stunned pilot was almost speechless. "Holy—"

"Now you can see why we're so anxious to blow out of here," Bruso bellowed. "I've got no interest in becoming the next casualty in this frigging war."

The pilot's eyes shot down at his instrument panel. "Another sixty seconds and we'll launch. Maybe they haven't noticed us yet." He sounded optimistic, but the frightened expression on his face betrayed his words.

The alien warship was in full view, with an overall size comparable to the *Intimidator*, but an appearance that was far more intimidating. Dark shadows slithered across the fleshy segments that meshed together along its midnight-blue hull, creating an appearance that was every bit as disturbing as the smaller alien vessel that had violated Earth's space a day earlier. The dusky variegated patterns gave the illusion that the vessel was fading in and out of view against the blackened backdrop of space. Engine exhaust ports, weapons, and other components that usually bristled from the exterior of a warship were noticeably absent, adding to its mysterious aura.

Its main body was roughly triangular, with a rift dividing the forward-most section, creating spear-like projections that continued out into the darkness. From the aft corners protruded four black talons, each more massive than a Destroyer-class warship. The upper pair curved forward, mirroring the pair that extended beneath the ship. And as if that wasn't threatening enough, the rest of the hull was covered with blackened spikes that appeared as if they had torn through the outer layer. Such a design seemed to have its roots in terror more than any defensive or functional purpose.

Centered a short distance above the vessel was another structure roughly the same shape as the main body, but much thinner and only half as big. It was secured by two dozen bulky tentacles that extended down from both sides.

Simply put, the alien vessel looked like something straight out of a nightmare, or at least that's what Bruso and his two companions were thinking. And all they could do was tremble in its shadow until the launch sequence had finished counting down—a seemingly drawn out experience that left them feeling more afraid than they had ever been in their lives.

As the alien warship halted its advance, the docking clamps that were attached to the port side of the *Jupiter III's* remaining evacuation transport finally released their stubborn grip. And with its lateral thrusters engaged, the transport drifted sideways until it had sufficiently cleared the mining platform. Exhaust from its engines spewed out with a fiery glow soon after, as the technologically inferior starship began moving through the Jovian rings that had served as a home to the mining operation for so long. The evacuation was underway, but the escape was far from complete.

Glimmers of blue light appeared along a small portion of the alien warship's starboard hull. And as the individual sparkles intensified, they glided along the surface, collecting in a central location. The energy pool that had formed suddenly burst away from the hull, creating a powerful beam that lashed out at the fleeing transport. It pierced the aft hull of the unshielded vessel with ease and quickly channeled through the forward section, gutting every compartment and passenger in between. Untamed explosions shattered what remained of the transport, spraying a maelstrom of mangled shards that ricocheted off the *Jupiter III's* dented exterior and in some cases punctured its hull.

Satisfied with the kill, the alien warship glided forward, enabling a companion vessel to begin its incursion into Jovian space. The invasion had begun.

Cruising in his star fighter, Jonathon peered out through the canopy and scanned the space near Jupiter. Though the surrounding area seemed peaceful enough, he couldn't shake the unsettling feeling in the pit of his stomach. Something bad was about to happen. He just knew it.

"Intimidator, this is Admiral Quinn. Everything's all clear in Jovian space. I'm going to make one more pass through the area, though, just to be sure."

The comm system remained unusually silent.

"Intimidator, come in. Is everything all right back there?"

Faint clicks of static crackled through the comm link as the air within the star fighter turned unexpectedly frigid. Shivering, Jonathon opened his mouth and inhaled the brisk air, but he was unable to release it from his lungs. Panic swept across his face as he struggled to breathe. He began pounding frantically on the command console, trying to get the environmental controls to respond, but the ship was drifting without power or purpose. Feeling weak, Jonathon slumped back into his chair and stared at his fading, frightened reflection in the canopy. The tinted enclosure began to bear a striking resemblance to the lid of a coffin, albeit transparent. He could sense death drawing near and he felt the urge to give in, but he fought it. His lungs finally relaxed and with a strong exhale his foggy breath streamed out into the cockpit, as if it had been ripped from his chest.

While his breathing normalized, a low-rumbling voice came over the comm link, uttering a strange phrase that was barely perceptible: "Ish dracorum ven Drak'Rasha ex udrokem, pur'qui ish vurloi preta hem."

Jonathon's eyes were immediately drawn to the foggy residue that still lingered. The cloudy formation began pulsating in sync with the rhythmic beat of his heart, which pounded stridently against his chest. The thumping grew louder and louder, then stopped abruptly. It was at that moment, when an eerie silence had filled the cockpit, that the misty collection coalesced into the shape of a dragon. With its wings spread, the vaporous creature lashed out at Jonathon, slashing his right cheek. He winced in pain and raised his arms as a shield, at which the hellish apparition snarled before soaring out through the top of the canopy, streaking toward the center of Jupiter.

"I must be hallucinating," Jonathon mumbled to himself, bewildered by the bizarre events that were transpiring.

Crackles drifted across the comm link once again. And with them came a return of the low-rumbling voice, repeating its previous message but with a soft, hissing echo that spoke in words that Jonathon could understand. "The shadow of the Dark God has come, cleansing the way before him."

As apprehension swelled within his mind, Jonathon peered out through the icy canopy, having noticed a dark, spherical shadow that had formed near Jupiter's equator. The murky discoloration began to grow, devouring the vibrant clouds that swirled around the gas giant. Before long, the entire planet was plunged into darkness, yet the shadow spread, plucking the stars from the heavens.

Jonathon remained still, captivated by fear as he watched the darkness swallow his ship whole.

Awakening from the nightmare, Jonathon screamed and practically leapt out of his bed. Beads of sweat trickled down his forehead as his heart pounded to the point of discomfort. The lights within his quarters brightened at a slow, steady pace, reassuring him that he was safely onboard the *Intimidator*. Breathing a sigh of relief, he collapsed back onto his bed, pondering the disturbing and harrowingly realistic dream.

"Admiral Quinn, you have an emergency communication waiting," the computer announced in its usual calm tone, contradicting the pressing nature of the matter.

Jonathon groaned, slowly pushing himself back up. Though his mind was fully alert, his body remained stubbornly sluggish, his strength sapped by the potency of his dream and the long night of war preparations that had preceded it.

"Admiral Quinn, you have—"

"Computer," Jonathon interrupted, massaging the crick in his neck, "receive communication, audio only."

Speaking with great urgency, Lieutenant Commander Stephen Vance addressed Jonathon. "Admiral, I'm sorry we weren't able to give you more time to rest, but we need you on the bridge immediately."

"Very well. Wake my command staff and have them report in. You and the rest of the graveyard shift are relieved of duty. Thank you for your efforts, Lieutenant Commander."

"Acknowledged, sir."

The communication terminated and Jonathon rose from his bed, still wearing his boots and the gold-trimmed military uniform he had changed into the night before. He snatched a meal packet off the dresser and dashed out the door. The luxury of a soothing shower and a decent breakfast would have to wait.

Chapter 7
Regressing Borders

Seven alien warships had advanced into Jovian space beyond the mouth of the wormhole. There they closed into a relatively tight formation while thirty star-fighter-sized ships darted through the collapsing spatial distortion and danced energetically around their larger companions, like a pack of hounds eager to begin the hunt.

As with the warships, the alien star fighters demonstrated an unusual design. The main body of each ship was a mesh of fleshy material, woven into a sphere that was straddled, almost enclosed by four triangular wings that projected forward, crowned with menacing spikes. And the eerily shifting darkness that masked their dark-blue hulls not only helped maintain the consistent, threatening appearance of the invasion force, but it gave the star fighters the advantage of stealth, making them every bit as dangerous as they looked.

All things considered, the alien fleet was a daunting presence, despite a ship count that was significantly fewer than their human counterparts. It was unclear whether their limited presence was a result of caution or arrogance. But either way, their ships would no doubt instill fear in all those who were unfortunate enough to cross their path.

Two energy pools began forming along the surface of one of the warships, nearest the *Jupiter III*. Seconds later, twin energy beams burst out and ravaged the abandoned mining platform. It was a swift and decisive action that not only awarded the aliens full control over Jovian space, but would serve to send a clear message: humanity's borders and sphere of influence among the stars had started to collapse.

With their initial strike complete, the alien warships accelerated, collectively vanishing into the darkness with tremendous speed. The star fighters proceeded to head out as well, but on seemingly random exit vectors. They departed in packs until only one ship remained. The lone star fighter swung around and accelerated past the wreckage of the *Jupiter III*, having already honed in on a closer target.

The initial evacuation transport from the mining platform was moving at full speed on its long trek to Mars. Having been alerted to the plight of the second transport moments before its unfortunate demise, the grim-faced passengers huddled nervously in the overcrowded compartments, praying that war would pass them by. Though they knew the odds were against them, the Solar System was a big place after all, and perhaps they'd be able to slip away unnoticed, or, at least, that was their hope.

Their lives rested in the hands of the baby-faced pilot who was sitting alone in the confined cockpit, altering the ship's course every few minutes out of paranoia. Dressed in ragged jeans and a dusty black T-shirt, the young indentured miner looked out of place behind the controls of the sizeable vessel. He had never been formally trained to pilot corporate-grade transports, yet he was the only person onboard who knew anything about flying a starship—a reckless oversight by Bruso and his habitual disregard for ICP regulations.

As the fidgety pilot stared out into the endless night of space, the sensor panel started beeping, warning of a nearby disturbance. Glancing over at the sensor readout, he noticed a peculiar energy signature, which barely registered on the transport's dated equipment. He turned and peered out the portside window, but all he saw was his own nervous reflection. Breathing a sigh of relief, his attention returned to the sensor display.

"This useless piece of junk's probably detecting an energy pocket in its own exhaust," he fussed while smacking the console with his fist. Under normal circumstances he would have chuckled at how jittery he had become, but there was nothing funny about his current predicament. He was spooked and cursing every little creak and rattle.

The pilot eventually cocked his head toward the starboard wall and gazed at a crooked photograph of his beautiful wife and their infant son. The cherished picture had been taped to the wall in an effort to help preserve his sanity during the long, nerve-wracking journey. It worked—to a certain degree—bringing a thin smile to his face as his thoughts flew to his family and their humble Martian abode. But try as he might, the more paranoid side of his conscience simply wouldn't allow him to slip completely into a peaceful trance, filling him instead with a nagging suspicion that he and his passengers were being hunted, or at least watched.

An unfinished beep hiccupped from the sensor panel, momentarily interrupting the quiet atmosphere that had settled in the cockpit. The pilot heard it, but tried to ignore it, disregarding it as one more annoying glitch in the computer system. But as he stared more intently at the photograph, his brow scrunched up with puzzlement upon noticing that the picture and everything around it was beginning to brighten. Turning his head back toward the forward window, he was startled by the presence of an alien star fighter that had positioned itself directly in front of the transport, matching its speed and course while traveling backwards. The front of the hostile ship's rounded body was glowing menacingly and before the young pilot could react to the situation, continuous bursts of energy slammed into the cockpit. A rapid chain of explosions propagated from the front of the transport back toward the engines, shattering the vessel and every life onboard.

The elevator doors on the bridge of the *Intimidator* opened, through which Jonathon stepped out onto the rear balcony and back into the madness of war. He approached the captain's chair and dropped back into his seat while his sagging, red-rimmed eyes immediately zeroed in on Lieutenant Commander Vance. The thirty-seven-year-old officer was dressed neatly in his red-trimmed uniform, with dark, slicked-back hair and a commanding presence that reminded Jonathon of Breckard, whom the lieutenant had respected a great deal. He was standing tensely on the forward balcony, examining his datapad.

"What do you have to report, Lieutenant Commander?"

Snapping his head to attention, Vance said, "As you've no doubt already surmised, Admiral, we have confirmation of an alien fleet within the Solar System. They first appeared near—"

"Jupiter," Jonathon interrupted, remembering the images from his dream. As absurd as it seemed, he was beginning to realize that someone or something had made contact with him while he slept—a realization he found to be most troubling.

"That's right, sir, near Jupiter," Vance replied, staring quizzically at Jonathon. "But how did you—"

"Continue with your report."

"Yes, sir. The aliens appeared near the mining platform that is…was operating there. The Hadlock Interplanetary Mining Corporation, which owned the station, had received an emergency broadcast that was transmitted across their channels. We just barely got hold of the recorded message, although it has a timestamp indicating it was originally broadcast approximately twenty minutes ago."

"What's the reason for the delay?" Jonathon inquired with an edge of irritation in his voice.

"Unknown. I had requested an explanation, but none was provided. I suspect they were busy assessing the financial ramifications of the attack."

"That figures. Play the message on the main screen."

"Yes, sir."

The central display screen flickered and the recorded transmission came into view.

"This is David Bruso, Chief Labor Commander of the *Jupiter III*. We need a military escort out here immediately! Those frigging alien ships have—" Bruso's distraught face was abruptly replaced with static before the message ended.

"That's all there is, sir. According to the report we received from their corporate headquarters, the identification beacons for both the transport and the mining station went offline shortly after the transmission ended. We're presuming no survivors. The aliens seem to…one moment, Admiral." Vance examined his beeping datapad before sharing his latest update. "An addendum to the report has come through. It appears there was a second transport that had evacuated the mining station about twenty minutes prior to the initial attack. According to this update, its identification beacon has gone offline as well." Lowering the datapad, Vance reestablished eye contact with Jonathon before continuing. "If you ask me, Admiral, I'd say the aliens were out for blood."

Frustrated over the news of civilian casualties, Jonathon seemed alive for the first time that morning. Most of the fatigue had worn off as his adrenaline spiked from the troubling news. The intensity of his stare, which rivaled even the classic outraged expressions of Admiral Breckard, made Vance feel a little uncomfortable, despite knowing full well that Jonathon's anger wasn't directed at him.

"Do we have any knowledge of the alien fleet's size or current whereabouts?" Jonathon inquired.

"Part of the report contained a brief sensor log from the mining station prior to its destruction. As you know, corporate-grade sensors aren't nearly as sensitive as what we employ, but they did manage to record an unusual jumble of readings. At first it appeared to be one large energy surge, which was most likely the result of the enemy's method of entry into our Solar System. However, I ran the sensor report through our computers and they were able to enhance and separate out seven faint but distinct signatures. Unfortunately, I can't say with any degree of certainty whether that's a full count of their forces. And those readings tell us nothing about the ships themselves, or their current whereabouts. In fact, nobody's been able to detect them on their sensors at all and I don't know if that's because they haven't advanced any further or if their ships have engaged some sort of stealth capability."

"The way things have been going, Lieutenant Commander, I think it's safe to assume the worst. And according to our initial intelligence estimates, we expect the enemy will have total supremacy of movement throughout our system. Whatever technology they used to get here could permit them to hot drop right on top of us without much, if any, warning. We have to keep a sharp eye out."

"Understood, sir."

Jonathon pondered the status and last known positions of his own fleet, ensuring that every piece of his plan was in place. "Is the *Chameleon* still within the asteroid belt?"

"Affirmative. They were assisting in the evacuation of one of the mining platforms and should be en route to Mars as we speak."

Jonathon nodded before drifting into deep thought, oblivious to the change in personnel going on around him. The command staff for the morning shift had arrived on the bridge, with Jensen leading the way.

"Lieutenant Hayes," Jonathon called out, having finally noticed the fresh group of officers.

"Yes, Admiral?" she called back while getting situated at her post.

"Contact General O'Connor and put the link through to the main screen."

"I'll have him patched through momentarily."

Jonathon activated the small console on the armrest of his chair and viewed the latest statistical information regarding the fleet while he waited to speak with O'Connor.

"The transmission's coming through now, Admiral."

O'Connor's image faded in on the main display screen. "Good morning, Admiral. Do you have any news to report?"

"Unfortunately, yes. The enemy's on the move, General. Hostile contact first occurred approximately twenty minutes ago, within Jovian space. They destroyed a mining platform and attacked its transports without provocation, murdering the civilian personnel that were onboard."

"It sounds as if the aliens are so determined to get revenge they're not distinguishing between civilian and military targets. I'll double my efforts here on Earth to ensure that our forces are ready, in case they manage to break through the fleet's defenses. I'm concerned about Mars, though. Their planetary defense grid has yet to be rebuilt since the war."

"I know, and unfortunately, evacuating the colony isn't an option. We don't have the resources or time to undertake that big of a task. We'll just have to hold the enemy as best we can."

"Well, if the aliens do try to occupy Mars, they'll be forced to deal with the third and fourth infantry regiments, comprised of six thousand marines and a full battery of anti-personnel drones. They'll put up a good fight, though I'd prefer the battles stay in orbit. Is the fleet ready?"

"Fortunately, our fleet's in a good position. As luck would have it, most of our warships were in close proximity to either Mars or Earth, allowing us to quickly organize into defensive formations near both planets. Seven warships are already in orbit above the Martian colony, with another five destroyers that should take up position shortly. And ten ships, including the *Intimidator*, are in position around Earth. There are another six warships on the way, which leaves only the *Chameleon* and two security frigates still out in the field. They were assisting with the evacuation of the asteroid belt's mining cluster and will provide escort for that convoy. Overall, General, I feel good about our defenses, but I'd feel a lot better if I knew exactly what we were going up against."

"I know what you mean. It's difficult to engage an enemy you know nothing about. Do we even have any idea as to the size of their fleet?"

"We think seven warships may have been involved in the initial blitz, but we've yet to confirm that data. We're still working on gathering intelligence at this point. So far we haven't seen so much as a flicker on our sensors. All eyes are still looking, though, so it's only a matter of time before we see them."

"Very well, Admiral. Keep me informed of any new developments. O'Connor out."

Jonathon stared out the forward windows, watching as the MPF's mighty warships gathered into a perfect defensive formation. It was a sight he hadn't seen since the conflict with Mars, only this time it wasn't quite so reassuring. Despite all of the firepower at his disposal, he felt uneasy about going into a fight blind. It was a known fact that in war, intelligence was every bit as valuable as high-tech weaponry. But it took time to gather intelligence, time that he most likely didn't have. Frustrated and anxious, he had no choice but to wait.

Vance marched toward the elevator, leaving Jensen behind to monitor the fleet's activities. Real-time holographic recreations of the two groups of MPF warships were projected above the left and right tactical displays. The central unit was currently offline.

Tapping a few of the command functions on his console, Jonathon brought a holographic projection of the asteroid-belt's mining cluster into view above the central tactical display station. He studied the three-dimensional images for a moment and became puzzled.

"Commander, why isn't the *Chameleon* showing up on the tactical display?" he inquired. "What's her status?"

Jensen glanced down at his datapad before looking back at Jonathon. "Her identification beacon isn't registering. We don't have any data on her current situation, Admiral."

"Who's the captain?"

Jensen studied his datapad once more before responding. "Captain Hiroshi Masuko, sir."

"Lieutenant Hayes, raise Captain Masuko on the comm link."

The *ICS Chameleon* was by far the most unusual Destroyer-class warship in the entire fleet. It had been specifically designed to deal with the increasing threat of corporate raiders and mercenaries that had plagued the asteroid belt's mining cluster for the past thirty years. And up until the *Chameleon's* arrival nearly five years ago, black-market mineral trading had been an exceptionally lucrative business.

Surprise and deception were the trademarks of the *Chameleon*. As suggested by its name, the prototype destroyer made use of experimental yet highly effective cloaking technology. The ship's hull was coated with an unusual liquid-crystal material that possessed light-altering effects. Through the use of sophisticated computers and camera systems, the *Chameleon* was able to project the images of its surrounding environment onto its hull, which essentially rendered the ship invisible. The liquid-crystal mask also provided the added benefit of radar absorption, permitting the surreptitious security vessel to police the asteroid belt virtually undetected, catching many criminals by surprise. It didn't take long for the *Chameleon's* name to become a curse and its existence to become the bane of every space-faring thug throughout the entire system. It truly was a remarkable vessel, but despite all of its success, the *Chameleon* had yet to be tested to its limits.

With the evacuation of all mining personnel complete, the asteroid belt had returned to its naturally dark and barren state. Each of the mining platforms within the main cluster had been shutdown indefinitely and left as nothing more than scrap embedded among the space rock. The jointly owned trading hub had also been abandoned, leaving the restrained blue glow of the *Chameleon's* thrusting engines as the only sign of activity.

The archetype destroyer was cruising at a comfortable pace along the inner edge of the dense asteroid ring, en route to rejoin the mining convoy and their two-week trek to Mars. But that progression was soon halted. Its reverse engines had engaged, bringing the ship to a complete stop beside a prominent asteroid. And as its engines powered down, the camouflage system activated, washing its deceptive cloak across the blackened hull until the ship had faded from sight, vanishing like a wily animal taking shelter from a hunter.

Captain Masuko was alert and sitting in his chair on the bridge of the *Chameleon*. His handsome face was drawn with age and unreadable for the moment as he stared at the overhead display screen, scanning footage of the surrounding asteroids.

"Captain," the communications officer called out in a whisper, sounding nervous that someone would overhear her conversation.

Masuko smiled and turned his chair to face the young officer. "What is it, Lieutenant? And speak up. I'm pretty sure the aliens can't hear you."

"Sorry, sir, I'm just a little jittery," she answered, sporting a sheepish grin between the locks of blond hair that framed her face. "The *Intimidator's* hailing us. Should I respond?"

"Of course, but audio only."

"Captain Masuko, this is Admiral Quinn speaking. I'm quite curious as to what you're doing out there."

"Sorry about disappearing like that, Admiral, but we seem to have unwelcome guests."

The alien fleet had decelerated outside of the mining cluster and was advancing slowly, apparently undecided about which of the many targets to strike first. An attack was imminent, though, as indicated by the energy pools that formed along their shady surfaces while each of the warships fanned out along the extensive stretch of asteroids. A torrent of powerful beams was unleashed, resulting in continuous explosions that rocked the mining cluster, littering the region with debris. The aliens proved unrelenting in their systematic annihilation of every last bit of human technology within reach.

With its crew anxiously watching the shocking parade of destruction, the *Chameleon* remained hidden, shielding itself from the targeting sights of the approaching enemy, or at least that's what Masuko hoped. He knew full well that his ship and crew couldn't stand alone against such impressive firepower. Five years of laying traps for criminals had taught him the importance of patience. He was content to wait for the hostile ships to depart. And in the meantime, he and his command staff would gather what intelligence they could, knowing that it would prove useful to the rest of the fleet.

"You've sighted the enemy?" asked Jonathon with twinges of surprise and concern. "First contact occurred within Jovian space a short time ago and involved at least seven warships, so either their forces are moving with the kind of speed and efficiency that we've feared or we're facing a multi-pronged assault. It's a rotten scenario either way. I need useful intelligence on them, Captain, and I need it now."

"Well," Masuko began, still awe stricken by the carnage that occupied the overhead display screen, "the good news, Admiral, is that there appear to be only seven warships here, which correlates with the initial sighting. But the bad news is they're each comparable in size to the *Intimidator*. And their design is totally unconventional. In fact, I get the creeps just looking at them. Their hulls look more like flesh than metal, and they seem to be missing the usual pieces of hardware that you'd expect to see flaunted along the exterior of a warship, including weaponry. They're armed to the teeth, though. There's certainly no doubt about that. Their primary weapon appears to be an energy beam that seems to burst right out of their hull, enabling them to fire in virtually any direction. And their firepower is destructively thorough. They're tearing through the mining structures like ancient samurai lopping off heads. In my thirty-five years of military service I've never seen anything like this."

"Please tell me the mining platforms have been safely evacuated," Jonathon requested, hoping the casualty report wasn't going to climb any higher.

"Oh, yes, sir. The convoy and its escorts left nearly an hour ago. We're carrying thirty of the miners ourselves, due to overcrowding on the last couple of transports. And we would have been well on our way by now too if we hadn't experienced a few electrical problems that temporarily set us back. We're all right for the moment, though. I don't think they've detected us."

"Good. Have you been able to gather any sensor readings from the alien vessels? We need any information that might help identify a potential weakness."

"I wish I could help with that, Admiral, I really do. Unfortunately, aside from some very faint energy signatures, we can't detect a darn thing. They don't even show up on radar, which is going to make engaging them in battle a real bugger."

"Captain," one of the officers called out, "we're detecting three more energy signatures heading this way. The signals are barely within the detectable range. I think we might have incoming fighters, sir."

"Did you hear that, Admiral?"

"Yes, Captain. Can you—"

Thunderous tremors unexpectedly rumbled through the *Chameleon* as a sizeable piece of debris from a nearby mining platform slammed into the rear section of the elusive ship. Its shields lit up in a brilliant flash of amber light, illuminating the surrounding asteroids and drawing unwanted attention.

"Get the engines online now!" Masuko demanded. He was shaken, but uninjured.

"The cloaking field's offline, sir," the commander announced, his face reflecting the tension within the room. "Our cover's blown."

"Gunner, bring the weapons online and fire at will. You'll have to aim the plasma cannons with your own eyes, son."

"The alien ship's plenty big, sir," the weapons officer replied. "Hitting it shouldn't be a problem."

"Move the ship within the lower edge of the asteroid belt and maneuver through it as fast as you can handle, Lieutenant. The added cover should work to our advantage."

"I'll do my best, sir," the navigation officer responded.

"Admiral Quinn, are you still with us?"

There was no response.

"Our comm system's down," the communications officer reported.

She glanced over at her captain, projecting the fear in her eyes. Masuko knew what she wanted. He could see it in the eyes of the other officers as well. They were all waiting for him to share his plan, his clever vision that would lead them to victory, or at least to safety. He had done it before on so many other occasions. In fact, he had never failed them, and for that reason alone he couldn't bear to look into their eyes any longer. He simply stared quietly at the overhead display screen, keeping his thoughts to himself. There was no plan, no vision. There was only darkness.

The *Chameleon* accelerated, weaving through the asteroid belt as quickly and gracefully as the laws of physics would permit. One of the alien warships gave chase, promptly matching the *Chameleon's* speed but traveling in a parallel path above the asteroids, wisely avoiding potential collisions.

Several green plasma bursts shot out of the *Chameleon's* rear guns, illuminating the narrow space that separated a collection of asteroids. Sprays of blue light flickered across the underside of the alien vessel as the weapons fire struck the heavily shielded warship. Every hit was precisely on target, yet the superheated munitions might as well have missed for all the damage they were doing.

Multiple energy beams lashed out at the *Chameleon*, but the aliens' first attempt failed as well. Several asteroids exploded into dozens of smaller fragments, having interfered with the enemy ship's targeting abilities. Masuko's strategy was working, but at the same time he knew his luck couldn't last forever.

A square panel atop the destroyer's midsection slid open, permitting a rotating missile rack to rise into view. The launcher tilted upward, acquired a targeting lock with its image-recognition system, and fired a full spread of Hellfire-II guided missiles. One of the missiles accidentally collided with a stray space rock. The other nine warheads, however, accurately approached their target, leaving yellow trails of ionized exhaust as they streaked between the asteroids.

Thin violet laser beams burst out from the hull of the alien ship, destroying eight of the advancing missiles. The final warhead managed to slip through and detonate against its target, producing a rather large and satisfying explosion. But despite the direct impact, there weren't any visible signs of damage, leaving the alien warship to continue the hunt undaunted.

The *Chameleon's* gunner followed with a continuous round of plasma bursts, letting up only when an asteroid blocked his view. And once again the underside of the enemy warship flickered repeatedly as the energy projectiles struck their intended target, but without the intended results. Despite their best efforts, Masuko and his officers were unable to overcome the technological superiority of their foe.

Both tips of the alien warship began to glow, warning of an imminent assault. Masuko took notice and pushed his navigator to boost speed, but the extra momentum didn't come soon enough. A pair of energy beams targeted the asteroid-filled region in front of the *Chameleon* where a rather prominent asteroid was utterly blown apart. Fragments of various sizes scattered randomly, with much of the debris storm striking the port side of the *Chameleon*. The rocky bombardment caused the ship to lose navigational control and its back end to slide forward and slam into the jagged surface of another asteroid. A fierce explosion tore through those portions of the destroyer that weren't crushed during the impact.

Having removed all traces of the human presence within the asteroid belt, the alien warships returned to formation and accelerated into the darkness once more.

"Any word from the *Chameleon*?" inquired Jonathon, staring at the empty space above the central tactical display station. The mining cluster's array of security sensors had been destroyed, severing the link that had sustained the holographic projection of the region. This loss, combined with the abrupt termination of the previous communication link with Masuko, had left Jonathon feeling especially uneasy.

"Sorry, Admiral, but they're still not responding," Kate replied.

"Sir," Jensen interrupted, "we've lost the *Chameleon's* identification beacon again."

Jonathon exhaled with a bitter sigh and said, "I think it's safe to assume the enemy is now on its way to Mars. Is Beta fleet in formation within Martian space?"

"Affirmative. They're all at full-alert status and maintaining a defensive holding pattern above the colony."

"Transmit what little data we have on the aliens to each of our ships, in the off chance it'll prove useful to them. And instruct Beta fleet to keep a watchful eye on their sensors. Order them to engage in coordinated attacks of four or more warships per target, avoiding single ship-to-ship encounters all together. It's imperative they concentrate their firepower."

"Understood, sir."

Concerned with their lack of progress in the war thus far, Jonathon leaned back in his chair and began analyzing battle strategies in his mind. Yet as he thought about the alien warships, he couldn't help dwelling on Masuko's comments regarding their appearance. *He claimed their hulls looked more like flesh than metal. And General O'Connor's report on the destruction of Earth Dock made similar claims about the alien ship that was encountered there.* "I wonder…" Jonathon muttered to himself as a glimmer of inspiration began to twinkle in his eyes.

"Commander, you have the bridge," he stated, rising from his chair.

"Sir?"

"I need to look into another matter, but contact me if there are any further developments."

"Yes, sir."

Jensen resumed his duties, as ordered, but he suspected Jonathon was up to something, once again leaving him out of the loop.

Jonathon stepped down onto the rear balcony and walked toward the elevator, pausing long enough to say, "Lieutenant Hayes, I need you to contact Specialist Tippits and have him meet me in the main weapons lab, ASAP."

"Certainly, Admiral."

Upon entering the elevator, Jonathon issued his destination request. "MORAD Unit, first floor."

With its doors closed, the elevator descended, passing through the two-deck Mobile Research and Development (MORAD) section at the rear of the ship. The secured area functioned like a civilian facility that had been embedded within the *Intimidator*. It had a military purpose to be sure, focusing on all kinds of research in the realms of weaponry and defense, but its personnel were civilian, leaving them somewhat segregated from the crew.

Having reached the designated floor, Jonathon stepped through the parting doors, walking at a hurried pace toward the secured weapons lab at the end of the hallway. As he reached the sealed entryway, he placed the back of his right hand against the adjacent security pad, permitting it to scan his embedded identification chip. The hefty doors clicked and separated, exposing a sophisticated laboratory into which Jonathon marched, his eyes darting around. It had been a while since he had paid a visit to R&D, but he had always enjoyed the experience, finding the research to be fascinating.

The walls, floor, and ceiling were all coated with a white, static-free film, emphasizing the need to maintain an immaculate environment. All kinds of research equipment, holographic computer projections, and experimental weapons components were spread across the tops of workbenches, behind which a host of contracted civilian scientists were working. The room was bustling with activity yet completely quiet except for the sounds of Jonathon's footsteps.

"Good to see you again, Admiral," Dr. Lynn Vandegrift hollered from across the room. The bald, aging chief weapons scientist stood up from his desk and strode forward, straightening his full-length, white laboratory coat along the way. The surprise visit had his curiosity piqued.

Though he wasn't in a cheerful mood, Jonathon forced a receptive smile and shook Dr. Vandegrift's hand. "Hello again, Doctor. How goes the research?"

"Slow, as usual, but interesting nonetheless. How can I be of assistance?"

"Have you seen any of the data on the alien ships we've encountered?"

"I've seen a little information, only what's in the ship's data banks. Why?"

"There's speculation that the aliens are using organic-based technology in their ships. The recurring statement from those people who have witnessed them up close is that their hulls appear to be more like flesh than metal. I know this may sound crazy, but is it even possible for organic material to be used in the hull of a starship?"

"Actually, Admiral, mankind has been pursuing organic technology since the early twenty-first century. Unfortunately, it's proven to be an incredibly difficult medium to work in. Success with organics has been extremely limited, focusing primarily on medical and bio-engineering applications. But I suppose it's feasible to use it in the manner you suggested. Organics are excellent conductors."

"But wouldn't metal be better for absorbing the impact from weapons?"

"Not necessarily. Organic matter can be amazingly resilient. There are also other issues to consider besides resistance to brute force. For instance, an organic hull could theoretically be designed to automatically repair any damage it sustained, similar to how the human body works."

"Interesting, but what about weaknesses? Would chemical and biological weapons be useful against organic technology?"

Jonathon's comments gave Dr. Vandegrift pause. "You do realize that chemical and biological weapons have been outlawed? The Macmillan Act officially declared them to be illegal and *unethical* to use in war."

Although he understood the sensitive nature of the topic, Jonathon was still somewhat offended by what Dr. Vandegrift was implying. He chose, however, to keep the conversation civil. "They've been outlawed for use against humans, not aliens. Besides, I don't have any desire to unleash them on an alien civilization. I simply want to know if they could be used to weaken or even destroy an organic warship."

Relieved by Jonathon's reply, Dr. Vandegrift's face relaxed. "Well, I suppose they could be effective. It's hard to say what the exact results would be, though, without knowing more about the organic material itself."

A buzzing sound that emanated from the laboratory's locked doors momentarily interrupted the conversation. Someone without proper security clearance was requesting entrance.

"That should be Specialist Tippits," said Jonathon, glancing back at the doors. "I asked him to meet me here."

"Susan," Dr. Vandegrift called out to the engineer that was located near the front of the room. "Please open the doors and let in our guest."

She politely nodded and stepped toward the door, pressing the lock release switch. With a distinctive click, the doors unlocked and slid open. Tippits stepped through, dressed in a standard, albeit dirty, blue engineering jumpsuit. He brushed back his dusty-red hair and looked around before noticing Jonathon, who was motioning for him to approach. He promptly marched forward, as requested.

"Hello, Admiral, Doctor. What's going on?" Tippits inquired, sounding curious about the impromptu meeting.

"We've been discussing the alien warships and the possibility of using chemical and biological weapons against them," explained Jonathon.

Tippits looked stumped by such a seemingly odd suggestion. "I don't follow you, sir."

"It's been theorized that the alien species that has attacked us has constructed their ships out of organic matter," Dr. Vandegrift expounded.

"Right," Jonathon added. "And if they're organic, it's possible they're susceptible to chemical and biological weaponry."

"Makes sense," said Tippits, nodding in agreement. "Let me guess: you want me to help you modify some of our weapons, right?"

Jonathon smiled. "That's exactly why I called you here. I need you to work some of your magic and help Dr. Vandegrift construct what I need. Unfortunately, we have three big problems to overcome.

"First of all, I don't know if this will even work. We're at a severe disadvantage when it comes to intelligence regarding the aliens' technologies. We need to find some way to maximize the effectiveness of the warhead without any knowledge of the genetic makeup of their warships, assuming they are in fact organic.

"Secondly, we're under a time crunch. The aliens are advancing through our system at an alarming rate. We need to construct as many warheads as possible in the limited time we have.

"And finally, we need to come up with a method of bypassing any shielding they might possess. I'll gladly take whatever you can devise, even if we can only punch through their defenses temporarily."

Tippits thought about Jonathon's request for a moment. "Well, if you want to do some punching, sir, nothing works better than the *Intimidator's* slam cannons. I believe an EMP mine could be modified to serve as a projectile for the cannons. You deliver three or four of those bad boys to the same location and I guarantee you'll wreak havoc with the aliens' shields, even if the effect only lasts for a second or two. They'd be a lot more effective than our sapper guns. I could have some of my techs get started on the modifications pronto."

"That works for me," Jonathon confirmed. "Could chemical and biological agents be delivered in the same fashion?"

"I believe so, Admiral," Dr. Vandegrift interjected. "With Specialist Tippits help we should be able to construct a delivery package that could be fired from the mass-driver cannons and dispersed across the surface of the alien warships."

Tippits nodded in agreement. "We can also adjust the firing sequence of the cannons to ensure both kinds of ordnance hit at the right time, just in case their shields recover quickly from the EMP burst."

"That all sounds good, but what about the final piece to this puzzle? I know we have a generous quantity of chemical and biological agents stored in the secured cargo hold. The containers were supposed to be jettisoned into the sun early next week, in accordance with their mandated destruction. I also know we have a small amount of Ketogen-13."

"Ketogen?" exclaimed Dr. Vandegrift with a look of shock. "I thought the last vials of that ungodly concoction were destroyed decades ago."

"The original batch was destroyed, yes. What we're carrying was seized from a Martian suicide transport during the final days of the war. I have no idea why it took High Command so long to authorize the chemical's destruction, but their delay may work to our advantage."

"What's Ketogen-13?" inquired Tippits, his eyes glancing first at Jonathon, then at Dr. Vandegrift.

"You probably know it as the Angel of Death," Dr. Vandegrift explained. "That was its nickname, and a most appropriate one at that. It scrambles DNA. There's no treatment, no cure. If you're infected with it, you die within minutes."

"Oh."

"Perhaps we could include several different kinds of agents in the payload," Dr. Vandegrift continued. "Without being able to test a sample of their tissue, we can only make our best guess as to what will work."

"Smart thinking," Jonathon replied. "Delivering multiple agents would certainly increase our odds of success. Check the ship's classified manifest for a full listing of the toxins that are now at your disposal and do what you can with them. I'll check on your progress in a little while, but if you run into any major snags, be sure to contact me immediately."

"I'll have Dr. Shepherd select the appropriate specimens. She's quite knowledgeable about them."

"That's fine. Oh, and one last thing: I'd prefer that information about this project stay classified. I don't have the time or desire to enter into any legal debates, should the Coalition's army of lawyers catch wind of what we're planning. I'll—"

"Admiral Quinn, please report to the bridge immediately," Jensen's voice rang out through Jonathon's wrist-comm. "We've received a distress call from the mining convoy. The *Protector* requests assistance."

"I'm on my way, Commander."

An exploding transport illuminated the interior of the *Protector's* cramped bridge, spotlighting the outraged expression on Captain Mary Perkins's rigid face.

"We've lost another transport, Captain," the commander reported in a frustrated tone.

"I can see that, Commander," growled Perkins, speaking with a discernable British accent.

"Sir," the communications officer interrupted, his young voice ringing with optimism, "Admiral Quinn is responding to our distress call."

"Put him through, audio only," Perkins ordered, sounding relieved at the prospect of reinforcements.

"What's your situation, Captain?"

"Three alien star fighters are assaulting the convoy. They're bloody fast and using the transports for cover, making it difficult to target them. We'd appreciate any assistance that can be spared, Admiral."

"I'm sorry, Captain, but it would take almost two weeks for the nearest warships to reach your current position—"

"What about the *Chameleon*?" Perkins protested.

"It was destroyed in battle near the asteroid belt. You and the *Defender* are going to have to handle this on your own, Captain. And I'd suggest you start by drawing those star fighters away from the convoy. A little harassing fire should get their attention, but be sure to coordinate your efforts with the *Defender*. And above all else, do not underestimate their capabilities. Quinn out."

Perkins gritted her teeth at the disappointing news, cursing under her breath. Despite her frustration with the situation, however, she was determined to do her duty. Thousands of lives were at stake. The odds also seemed to be in her favor. There were only three enemy star fighters, after all—a tactical mismatch against a pair of security frigates. That was what she kept telling herself, anyway. It had also been her first instinctive thought when the attack had originally begun, yet she had still made a request for reinforcements. She didn't doubt that there was a mismatch, but she did have serious doubts about whether the advantage was really hers. There was only one way to find out.

"We need to destroy those fighters quickly, gentlemen. Lock onto the closest target and fire."

Though it measured only half the size of a destroyer and looked more like a transport than a warship, the *Protector* was still a force to be reckoned with. Its arsenal was on full display and its gunner eagerly waiting for a clear target. His wish was soon granted. One of the enemy star fighters completed a strafing run and darted up above the convoy, leaving an explosion in its wake. Acting without delay, the *Protector's* gunner acquired an image lock and fired a full spread of Sunfire-IV guided missiles from the frigate's upper launching rack.

The alien vessel countered with a sequence of erratic maneuvers, swooping through the zero-gravity environment as if it was arrogantly disregarding the laws of physics that restricted the movements of the manmade vessels. Trailing behind were the six speedy warheads, each creating fantails of yellow ionized vapor as they streaked through the blackness, making wide turns for each sharp zigzag of the enemy. The missiles weren't gaining even an inch on their target, but their pursuit was so unrelenting as to persuade the alien to employ a surprising tactic. It charged straight toward a transport, as if to ram it, but at the last second dived down and away, causing two of the powerful missiles to fail to make the abrupt turn. They detonated against the edge of the unshielded transport, triggering several explosions that tore through its hull. Those passengers who weren't burned alive were sucked out into the vacuum of space. It was a gruesome sight that weighed heavily on the conscience of the lieutenant who had pulled the trigger.

Continuing defiantly on its way, the alien star fighter was soon caught off guard. One of the more modern transports within the group, and the only one equipped with defensive weaponry, had opened fire, striking the enemy with a single red laser beam. No damage was inflicted, but the alien instinctively jerked away and inadvertently into the path of the remaining missiles. They detonated in swift succession, consuming the vexatious star fighter in a triumphant flash of light.

"We're going to have to control the collateral damage, Lieutenant," groaned Perkins to her weapons officer, who was reluctant to make eye contact. "We'd better refrain from using missiles this close to the convoy."

"Captain," the commander interrupted. "We appear to have gotten the aliens' attention. They're approaching on an attack vector."

"Contact the *Defender* and tell them to close on our position."

"Yes, sir."

The two remaining star fighters had veered toward the *Protector* with their hulls glowing, primed to fire. Several energy bursts were unleashed and slammed into the starboard side of the security frigate, causing its shields to flare before weakening.

"Shields are down to thirty percent," the commander announced. "We can't take another hit like that."

"Then reinforce the blasted shields with power from the engines," Perkins bellowed. "We won't be going anywhere for a while."

"The enemy fighters are moving too fast," the weapons officer complained. "I'm not having any luck targeting them, sir."

"Then stop relying on luck and start utilizing your training, Lieutenant. Pick a bloody target and fire!"

The *ICS Defender* began dropping back from the convoy, toward the slowing *Protector* in an attempt to combine efforts. Both warships fired their plasma guns in rapid succession, hurling countless high-energy projectiles toward the swiftly approaching star fighters, which scattered in response.

Having avoided the initial counterattack, the alien star fighters circled back toward the *Protector* and unleashed another wave of energy bursts. The shields around the *Protector* flashed brightly before burning out.

"Shields are offline," the commander shouted, his face tense with panic. "You've got to do something. If those ships hit us again, we're finished. I don't want to die!"

"Then start praying, Commander," urged Perkins, scowling at the enemy ships that had stolen her victory. All she could do was curse them with every last fiber of her being.

As the star fighters accelerated past the two frigates, one of the alien ships spun around and unleashed another volley, piercing the *Protector's* aft engines. Several explosions engulfed the defeated warship, leaving the *Defender* to face the enemy alone.

"Target the nearest hostile and blast it with an EMP burst," Captain David Reynolds yelled to his weapons officer, infuriated by the destruction of the *Protector*.

"Sapper guns firing now, Captain."

Streaks of elongated blue light shot toward the advancing star fighter, with several of the electromagnetic pulses hitting their mark. The resulting electrical arcs circulated around the alien vessel's fading shields, and within seconds the protective energy barrier had dissipated, though the star fighter itself was still functional, still deadly.

"Direct hit," the weapons officer announced enthusiastically, looking as if vengeance would soon be his.

"Fire at will, Lieutenant. Blast that piece of alien filth back to whatever hell it came from."

"Stinger cannons charged. Firing now."

Swift spurts of plasma were fired toward the vulnerable alien ship, which was attempting to flee. A few of the bursts struck the star fighter and blew apart two of the tentacles, severing one of its wings. The ship tumbled a little way before regaining control and swinging back around on an attack vector. Flickers of blue light popped all around the vessel as its shields recharged. The second alien ship came into view as well and joined the assault.

The *Defender* was ready. It opened fire with everything it had. Plasma stingers raced toward the damaged star fighter while the second alien ship quickly altered course at the sight of the approaching volley of missiles. The mangled star fighter didn't stand a chance. It was pummeled in the attack, spraying gooey remains that splattered along the starboard side of the frigate and sizzled against its shields.

Six missiles were tracking the last enemy vessel, which soon spun around and raced back toward the *Defender*, its energy pool charging. The lone fighter accelerated toward the underside of the frigate, firing continuous rounds before pulling up hard, skimming the starboard hull of the warship and soaring right past the bridge. A pair of defensive laser beams fired at the star fighter, but it was no longer the main threat. Five of the trailing missiles collided with the *Defender* and produced a series of devastating explosions that plowed through its weakened shields, shredding the hull. The remaining missile managed to strike the alien star fighter and sent it spiraling out of control.

The bridge of the *Defender* was dark, save a few small pockets of light that emanated from the fires that had broken out, and the occasional smattering of electrical sparks that crackled as they bounced along the floor. Captain Reynolds pushed himself up to one knee, winced in pain, and slipped back down beside the fallen beam that had stopped short of crushing him. A cough or two escaped his lips as his lungs began to take in the smoke that had surrounded him.

"Damage report," he called out, streams of blood trickling down his battered face.

There was no response. The bridge was deathly quiet, except for the hiss of a small hull breach that taunted menacingly from the back of the room.

The lone alien fighter had regained control and closed on the crippled frigate. It hovered for a moment, as if gloating over the damage, then delivered the fatal blow. One energy thrust after another raced toward the frigate, pierced its aft engine section, and triggered a sweeping explosion. The *Defender* had fallen.

"Admiral," Jensen called out, sounding shocked, "we've lost both security frigates. I don't know how they did it, but the enemy star fighters must have outgunned them."

Outraged, Jonathon slammed his fist against the armrest of his chair. It was an instinctive reaction, his body's way of channeling at least a bantam portion of his anger and frustration in a harmless manner. "That means the mining convoy is completely unprotected and there's nothing we can do to stop the slaughter," he huffed, fuming over the fact that he had no other choice but to sit idly by while the aliens rampaged across the Solar System, unhampered by the limits of technology.

After a little while had passed, Jonathon calmed, turned, and faced Kate. "Lieutenant, contact all mining corporations that had charters within the asteroid belt. Order them to recall and ground any supply ships that were going to rendezvous with the convoy. Inform them of the situation and send our deepest regrets."

"Of course," Kate replied in a soft voice. Though the situation still seemed surreal to her, she shared in the grievous mood that abounded. And her heart went out to the remaining survivors that were about to face certain death.

Like his fellow captains, Jonathon was eager to face the enemy in battle, yet he couldn't help but feel at least a little nervous about the fleet's chances. The aliens' phenomenal technology made him especially uneasy. *Losing two frigates to a few fighters shouldn't have happened.* Jonathon worried that their destruction was a portent of the conflict to come. But there, among the grim prospects, was a sliver of hope. *If the biological weapons prove successful, it'll negate their technological advantage and place us on an even playing field, or possibly better. It just might be the trump card we need to force an end to this war and stave off any future aggression.*

Jonathon turned toward Kate and caught her attention. "Get ahold of Dr. Vandegrift in the weapons lab and ask him to contact me. Just transfer the video link to my console."

"Certainly."

Jensen growled in disgust as he viewed the information that channeled through his datapad.

"What is it, Commander?"

"We've received reports of other civilian vessels that have come under attack by enemy star fighters. The aliens seem to be sweeping through the Solar System and destroying every starship they come in contact with. Everything's a legitimate target to them."

"Are any of the endangered ships close enough for us to be of assistance?"

"No. They're all several days away and as good as dead. All this blasted technology at our disposal and we still can't get where we need to in an efficient manner."

Jonathon remained surprisingly calm, though it took a great deal of effort on his part. His emotions were still simmering from the loss of the mining convoy. But with the rapid advancement of the enemy fleet, he knew he had to keep a cool head. His own forces were depending on him to lead them to victory—a task that would be near to impossible if he allowed himself to be blinded by rage.

"The communication you requested has come through, Admiral," said Kate.

Jonathon's attention turned immediately to the small console on the right armrest of his chair. The image of Dr. Vandegrift came into focus.

"Things are progressing exceptionally well, Admiral," reported Dr. Vandegrift. "Barring any unforeseen problems, I'd estimate that we should be finished with the first batch in the next thirty to forty minutes."

"That's excellent, Doctor, and exactly the kind of good news I needed to hear. Continue with your work and I'll check back with you later. Quinn out."

Jonathon resumed his previous state of meditation, gazing thoughtfully at the tactical display stations. *The aliens seem to be methodically destroying everything they come in contact with. Their bloodlust won't allow them to spare any man or woman...or facility. Perhaps their blind aggression is their weakness.*

"Tell me, Commander, what remains between us and Mars, in terms of facilities?"

"One moment, Admiral," responded Jensen, punching in a few commands on his datapad before continuing. "The only structures of importance are the lunar shipyard and the antimatter reactor. They're both abandoned, but still valuable."

Well, the reactor's underground and not likely to be noticed. But the shipyard's certainly big enough to catch their eye. It'd make a perfect site for an ambush. After a few minutes had passed and a plan had been formulated, Jonathon spoke up again. "Who's the captain of the *Hades*?"

"That'd be Captain William Concevich, sir."

"Perfect," Jonathon uttered. "Lieutenant Hayes, contact the *Hades* and put the link through to the main screen."

"Yes, sir."

"What are you up to, Admiral?" Jensen pried, eyeing his superior officer suspiciously.

Jonathon responded with a sly smile and said, "I'm going to lay a trap for those alien savages, assuming we don't destroy them near Mars first."

The main display screen flickered as the rugged face of Captain Concevich came into view, his left eye twitching atop the thin scar that stretched most of the way down his face. He was as battle-hardened as a captain could get, and one of the most feared men in the entire fleet, due primarily to his ruthless, sometimes questionable battle tactics. "What do you need, Admiral?" he asked in his usual gruff voice.

"Correct me if I'm wrong, Captain, but doesn't the *Hades* have Omega-class nuclear warheads?"

Stroking his black, short-trimmed beard that curled around his mouth and chin, Concevich chuckled at the question. "That's right, Admiral. You gonna let me play with 'em?"

"In due time, Captain. For now, I want you to head to the lunar shipyard at maximum burn. Report in once you've arrived and I'll give you further details."

The unorthodox captain smiled roguishly and saluted before terminating the transmission.

"Admiral," Jensen called out, "Beta fleet has detected the alien energy signatures. They appear to be approaching Mars. We should have visual confirmation at any moment."

"Reroute the video relays from a few of the colony's security satellites to the overhead screens. I want to be able to clearly see what's going on out there. And order Beta fleet to engage the enemy as soon as they're within range. It'd be nice if we could take the first shot for a change."

"Yes, sir."

Jonathon carefully studied the left tactical display, waiting for the alien warships' unusual profiles to be recorded by Beta fleet and loaded into the MPF's system-wide data network. Three-dimensional replicas of the alien vessels soon popped into view, donning red auras that accented their unmistakably hostile nature. And as they drew ever closer to the twelve MPF warships that anxiously awaited their approach, a hushed anticipation settled over the bridge.

Chapter 8
Martian Twilight

Captain Nikolai Petrov was sitting proudly in his chair on the bridge of the recently commissioned *ICS Peacemaker*. It was the newest addition to the fleet and the first of three Cruiser-class warships that had been planned for construction. Though its architecture was similar in nature to a Destroyer-class vessel, it was twice that size and its firepower was comparable to that of the *Intimidator*. But despite its offensive prowess, the *Peacemaker* still yielded the title of most powerful ship in the fleet to the *Intimidator*—a point that seemed lost on its vainglorious captain.

"Bring us to the front of the formation," Petrov ordered, speaking with a thick Russian accent. His dark eyes peered out from beneath his heavy brow, glaring at the images of the enemy fleet on the overhead monitor. "I want to draw first blood and make them pay for the lives of our fallen comrades."

"Gladly, sir," the navigation officer responded, echoing the common desire for revenge.

"The enemy will be within firing range in ten seconds," the veteran commander cautioned while studying the holographic battlefield that lit up one of the tactical display stations at the front of the room, beside the windows.

"Do we have permission to fire, sir?" the senior weapons officer inquired.

"Bring death to their soldiers, Lieutenant."

As the alien warships approached Beta fleet, the *Peacemaker* unloaded a full spread of Hellfire-III guided missiles from several turrets along its heavily armored exterior. The other ships in the group joined the fray as well, sending a deadly wave of warheads and plasma bursts surging toward the enemy. It was an awesome display of firepower, until the alien fleet responded.

Multiple rounds of defensive energy beams were fired from the enemy warships, drastically weakening the strength of the initial attack. Yet there were several missiles that managed to slip through along with the plasma projectiles, slamming into the forward sections of their targets. The attack left the shields around the enemy vessels glowing brightly, but showing no signs of weakening. It was an ineffective first strike that did little more than provoke the aliens. Energy pools had begun forming along their hulls.

The twin tips of the lead alien starship were also showing signs of activity, albeit in a more bizarre fashion. They had begun to bend inward, as if the space directly in front of the vessel was on the verge of collapsing. This continued until a dark and most peculiar beam discharged from the ship, warping the starry region that it passed through before striking the *Peacemaker*. The cruiser's shields ignited and appeared to be holding firm, but the section of its hull directly beneath the focal point of the weapon started to buckle and implode, as if the shielding were nothing more than an illusion. Gravity had once again heeded the call of its master, crushing the *Peacemaker's* metal framework without mercy. And as the beam progressed from bow to stern, mankind's latest technological triumph was reduced to a mere fraction of its former size. The crumpled wreckage became a catalyst for spreading fear throughout the human fleet.

Shocked by the ease at which their most prominent warship had been destroyed, the remainder of Beta fleet was thrown into disarray, scattering and firing their weapons while frantically trying to avoid being targeted themselves. But there was little chance of that. The aliens unleashed their fully charged arsenal with deadly precision, adding to the chaos that had engulfed the region.

The *ICS Reliant* was the next ship to fall. It was severed in half by one of the energy beams, sending each of its ravaged sections tumbling into low orbit.

"We've lost the *Herakles* and the *Vigilance* as well," Jensen reported, watching each warship vanish from the tactical display.

"Our weapons aren't having any discernable effect on the enemy's shields."

Jonathon stared in disbelief as the fleet was being dismantled right before his eyes. The battle was swiftly heading toward a disastrous conclusion. He had to do something. "Commander, order the remaining ships to concentrate all firepower on the starboard hull of the lead enemy vessel. I want it hit hard and fast."

"Yes, sir."

Sparks were flying within the bridge of the *ICS Centaurus*. The aging frigate had become the latest victim of the aggressive alien war machine.

"Full power to the shields!" Captain Gerard Moreau demanded as the overhead display screen exploded, sending hardened plastic and electrical discharges cascading down onto the floor.

"Shields are off—" the commander started to announce before being shaken violently to the floor, his head striking the edge of his station.

The ceiling of the bridge turned fiery orange, then yielded to the energy beam that burst through at an angle, consuming the room on its way down through the floor.

The forward section of the *Centaurus* exploded, causing a chain reaction that shattered the frigate and bounced debris among its companions.

Having received their new orders and a new sense of focus, all remaining warships came about and targeted the starboard hull of the lead alien vessel. A torrent of plasma stingers and missiles surged toward the enemy warship, overwhelming its defensive weaponry and pounding its stubborn shielding incessantly until, at long last, the weapons fire broke through. A cluster of magnificent explosions followed, leaving behind visible signs of damage along the ship's hull. It was precisely what Jonathon needed to buoy morale.

With confidence returning, the remaining destroyers closed formation and continued firing at the exposed section of the damaged vessel. The enemy countered the attack by rotating until it was upside down, deflecting the approaching munitions to its shielded underside in the process. Then came a companion vessel, closing with great haste toward the starboard hull of the besieged ship until it had achieved a tight, parallel alignment. Once in formation, the pair initiated what appeared to be some sort of docking procedure. The portside tentacles that had secured the upper section of the supporting ship to its main body detached swiftly and stretched across the damaged vessel, pulling the elevated section into a central position above the narrow gap that separated the two warships. Then the tentacles reattached themselves along the far side of the other vessel, securing the link. The elevated structure that was located on the damaged ship moved as well, centering itself beneath both vessels before attaching to the far side of the supporting warship, completing the symmetrical union.

The crews of the remaining destroyers were stunned by what they had witnessed—the merging of two enemy vessels into a single, monstrous warship. And in a further blow to morale, the tattered hull of their initial target had begun to automatically repair itself, sealing the gashes that had formed.

With a heightened sense of self-preservation among their crew, the remainder of Beta fleet intensified their assault, firing nonstop at the resilient vessel, yet they were unable to penetrate its reinforced shielding. The tide of war simply refused to turn.

Dazzling streams of energy began arcing between the narrow gap that separated the adjoined alien warships. The chaotic discharge propagated along the dividing rift, growing more intense as it surged forward. Upon creating an energy bridge between the inner tips of the merged pair, the powerful weapon was unleashed on the *ICS Perseus*, striking its forward shields. A tangent arc of energy immediately leapt toward the *ICS Gemini*, which had taken up position alongside the *Perseus*. The fierce, rapid strikes of the searing bolts swiftly overwhelmed the defensive capabilities of both destroyers, clearing a path to their destruction. Random patterns of explosions erupted all around their shredded hulls and culminated in a violent death scene. The shock wave that radiated from the exploding remnants of the *Perseus* accelerated the demise of its companion vessel, sending the crew of the *Gemini* to join their fallen comrades.

The bridge of the *ICS Inquisitor* trembled from the forces unleashed by the *Gemini's* destruction, intensifying the panic that had risen up against Captain Estefan Moreno. The Venezuelan-born veteran was at a loss for a solution to their desperate situation.

"Captain, our weapons aren't having any effect," the petrified weapons officer griped. "And another stinger cannon has overheated."

Before Moreno had a chance to respond, an excruciatingly intense blue light pierced the forward windows of the destroyer as an alien energy beam struck the shielding around the bridge.

"We're losing shields!" the commander shouted.

"Take evasive maneuvers and lower the blast plating."

The intrusive light started to fade as thick metal barriers slid down over the windows.

Glancing back at Moreno, the commander started to convey his urgent status report. "Shields are—" His statement ended abruptly as his body was thrown forward, ahead of the explosion that had burst through the front of the bridge.

The *Inquisitor* swelled from the tremendous fireball that consumed the interior of the warship. Tongues of fire leapt out from fractures in the hull moments before the entire ship exploded.

Outnumbered and hopelessly outgunned, the four remaining MPF warships continued to engage the enemy fleet as best they could. Surrender was not an option.

"Bring us right up next to the underside of one of those alien ships," Captain Lukas Richter ordered from the bridge of the *ICS Redeemer*. "I want to see what kind of damage we can do at point-blank range."

"Are you nuts?" the navigation officer balked.

"Do as you're told, Lieutenant," the commander reprimanded, glaring back at the navigation officer.

"This is suicide," the young lieutenant grumbled while reluctantly obeying his orders.

"They've spotted us, sir," the weapons officer announced, glancing over at her superior. "The enemy is preparing to fire."

"Route all available power to the shields," Richter instructed, tightening his grip on the armrests of his chair.

The bridge trembled as an energy beam struck the bow of the *Redeemer*.

"Shields are weakening," the commander called out. "We're not going to last much longer."

"If I'm going down, I'm taking one of those abominations with me," vowed Richter, his face consumed with anger and determination. "Continue straight ahead at ramming speed."

"Yes, sir."

The bridge became unusually quiet as the officers recognized and accepted their fate.

"Computer, initiate core overload. Authorization: omega, gamma, four."

"Authorization code recognized. Requesting confirmation—"

"Confirmed," the commander shouted. "Authorization: beta, sigma, five."

"Core overload in progress."

"Fire all weapons, Lieutenant," Richter demanded.

"Yessir."

Glaring at the enemy ship, Richter uttered one last statement, "Die, you son of a—"

Explosions radiated out from the forward section of the *Redeemer* as the alien beam penetrated the destroyer's hull. But it was all in vain. The barrage of weapons fire from the *Redeemer* impacted against the shielded underbelly of the alien warship seconds before the two vessels collided, generating a sequence of intense explosions that penetrated the enemy's shields. And as the *Redeemer's* overcharged reactor core ruptured, the ensuing chaos shredded a large section of the targeted vessel, gutting its innards in the process. The pyrotechnic display culminated in a blinding flash of light that consumed the alien warship, scattering a cloud of detritus in all directions.

Although the crew had lost their lives in the process, the *Redeemer* had been successful in its task. The alien fleet had finally suffered significant casualties of its own.

The *ICS Magellan* was annihilated by a retaliatory strike from the remaining enemy warships. In desperation, the *ICS Aries* and the *ICS Agamemnon* tried to employ the same kamikaze tactics that had worked for the *Redeemer*, but the aliens weren't about to fall for the same trick twice. A spread of energy beams pierced the hulls of the two remaining destroyers, bringing about their fiery destruction before they had a chance to ram their targets. Beta fleet had been eliminated, leaving Mars vulnerable to an invasion.

"Get me the Prime Minister of Mars," Jonathon demanded.

"I'm already working on it," said Kate. "The link's now active."

The image of the respectable, pasty complected politician appeared on the main display screen. His face was sagging with age and newfound despair. Having been in office for only two Martian months, the once ambitious politician had never counted on alien invasions becoming part of his political agenda or even his survival.

"We all saw the disastrous battle, Admiral. The local news service broadcast footage of the conflict against my wishes, and in the process fueled the panicked mobs that have begun to overrun the colony."

"It's imperative that you calm your people, Prime Minister. Have the governors of each dome gather their citizens into shelters as quickly as possible. Our ground forces should be moving into defensive positions as we speak. Use them to help establish order if you must, but do it quickly. We're running out of time!"

"I'll do my best, Admiral."

The communication link terminated.

The lush cultivated grounds and intersecting walkways within the Martian colony were flooded with terrified civilians, many of whom felt hopelessly trapped within the enclosed metal domes. Memories of the war with Earth were still fresh, including imagery of the conquering army marching into the city-sized domes like combatants entering an arena. The fighting had been brutal and many innocent civilians had been caught in the crossfire. It was a nightmare, the return of which appeared inevitable. But this time the local population didn't fear stray weapons fire. They feared that they were the primary targets and that left them shackled with panic. Rioting had quickly become the norm.

Colonel Mathew Clark stood confidently atop the ivory steps of the towering Martian headquarters, which overlooked the entirety of the central dome. The highly decorated veteran was attired in a black, armor-plated battle suit, accentuating his striking physique. Scenes of rioting Martians were all too familiar to Clark, bringing back the bitter recall of his tour of duty. Staring spitefully at the mob that was encroaching on his position, he activated his helmet-embedded communication system.

"All right, boys, let's get this crowd under control before the real fight begins. And I don't want to be held accountable for civilian casualties, so be gentle with them, but not too gentle."

Hundreds of marines marched out from their defensive positions dressed in the same protective battle suits. They swept through the alleyways and open spaces between the glistening white buildings of every shape and size, joining forces with police officers clad in riot gear. Canisters of tear gas and sonic stun charges were fired into the sea of people, forcing many of them to run for cover. But several localized clashes erupted nonetheless, as some of the more frustrated, more violent citizens lashed out at the security forces that were trying to help them.

Coolly detaching a sonic stun charge from around his waist, Clark thumbed the red button that rested atop the small, spherical device, then tossed it forward, watching the non-lethal weapon bounce down the long stairway. Upon reaching the ground it rolled toward the advancing masses and detonated, releasing a punchy sonic shock wave that knocked the unruly crowd off their feet.

"Worthless Martian trash," Clark muttered to himself, looking on with perverse amusement as the stunned civilians scampered out of sight. But more people soon strayed into his view. Adjusting the power level on his pulse rifle to its highest non-lethal setting, he took aim at each and every civilian who was unfortunate enough to cross his targeting sights. With each squeeze of the trigger, he sent a painful jolt through the legs of the frenzied Martians, prodding them back into the residential districts like cattle.

Warning sirens began drowning out the chorus of screams that permeated the recycled air, encouraging people to seek shelter. Moments later, the Prime Minister's voice echoed from an array of loudspeakers that had been networked throughout the colony.

"This is Prime Minister Keller speaking. I'm pleading with all of the citizens of Mars to *please remain calm*. I encourage you to either stay in your homes or proceed to the nearest secured shelter. Marines and security personnel are taking up defensive positions in an effort to ensure your safety. The best way you can assist them is by staying off the streets and out of their way. We need your full cooperation in this matter so that the capable men and women of our armed forces can do their jobs. There's no need to panic. The situation is under control."

After a short pause, the Prime Minister repeated his message.

"Admiral," Jensen called out, "the colony's sensors are detecting some markedly odd power readings coming from one of the alien warships."

"Adjust the main display to zoom in on that ship," Jonathon ordered as he stood up from his chair, anxiously watching the overhead display. "I've got a really bad feeling about this," he uttered to himself.

A small opening had formed along the underside of the ship in question, as if an incision had been made in its belly. Several dozen small black spheres emerged from the hole and plummeted toward the Martian colony. The objects were similar in appearance to the larger orb that had ravaged Earth Dock and the *ICS Lionheart* during the initial alien incursion into human space.

"No!" screamed Jonathon, his eyes wide with horror. The terrible realization of the aliens' savage intentions had stung him to his core.

The dark objects rained down on the manmade structures, generating incandescent flashes as they impacted on and around the interconnected domes. Tremendous gravitational fields followed, producing widening cracks along the thick metal exteriors of each dome. And through those fissures hissed the artificial atmosphere that had been so carefully contained.

As the air rushed up around him, Clark glared at the dome's ceiling, watching as small fragments broke free and started to fall. "Come down here, you cowards!" he yelled, cursing the aliens with every embittered thread of his being. He even raised his pulse rifle into the air, eyed one of the larger fissures, and squeezed the trigger, lashing out at the enemy even though he knew his weapons fire would be unable to reach their warships, let alone inflict any damage. He wanted a fight, fair or otherwise, but all he got was an irreversible death sentence. Everywhere above him the ceiling was losing structural integrity, sending hefty shards of metal slamming onto the buildings and inhabitants below. One of the resulting tremors knocked Clark off his feet, sending him tumbling down the steps and into the path of a falling slab. He was crushed instantly.

Several deafening explosions ripped through the area as the fusion power plant that had sustained the electrical needs of the colony was leveled. Falling debris smothered countless scores of civilians and marines alike. And those few who managed to survive the deadly cave-in suffered death by asphyxiation as the dome's oxygen supply made a hasty exodus. It was a gruesome scene that played out over and over again in each of the domes that surrounded the ruined capital, until the entire colony had been reduced to nothing more than a series of grotesque burial mounds scattered across the unforgiving Martian landscape.

"I don't believe it," yelled Jonathon, tensing with anger. "They just murdered over four million people." Outraged, he grabbed the datapad that rested on the left armrest of his chair and hurled it toward the holographic projections of the alien fleet, lashing out at the enemy in the only way he could. Jensen took a precautionary sidestep as the datapad raced by and shattered against the forward window, but he otherwise paid no attention to the outburst since he would have done the same thing, perhaps worse.

Jonathon stood rigid, glowering at the taunting holograms. "They'll pay for their atrocities," he promised himself, his crew.

The bridge was silent as each of the stunned officers stared in disbelief at the horrifying images on the overhead display screens. Dead Eye had his arm around Parker, trying to offer what little comfort he could to his sobbing friend. The Martian native's family had been killed during the attack.

Turning toward his grieving navigator, Jonathon said, "Lieutenant, you're welcome to excuse yourself if—"

"No sir," Parker interrupted, his eyes swelling with a lust for vengeance. "I want a front row seat for the payback we're going to dish out. We can't let them get away with this. They deserve...they deserve to die for what they did, every last one of them."

The lieutenant's remarks gave Jonathon pause, forcing him to reflect on his own unhealthy thirst for revenge. Even though emotions were running high, he realized that civility had to be maintained. The function of the MPF was to protect lives and freedoms. Killing out of hatred or revenge wasn't an option and he knew it. Vengeance would only cloud his judgment and undermine his leadership, resulting in further misery.

"Admiral," Kate called out, wiping the tears from her eyes, "General O'Connor is hailing us."

"Put him through."

Jonathon turned to face the image of his old friend and mentor, wishing he could report a victory rather than the appalling events that had transpired.

"I saw what happened on Mars, Jon. Earth can't withstand that kind of an assault. Our defenses are designed to protect us from occupation, not extinction."

"We may have lost the first round, General, but we're not out of the fight yet. If those savages think they're going to march in here and destroy the Earth without any resistance, they're gravely mistaken. I've still got a few surprises waiting for them."

"That's exactly what I wanted to hear, Admiral. I've brought the solar defense grid online and I'm transferring control to the *Intimidator* so you can add it to your arsenal. The planetary guns are also at your disposal. Use them at your own discretion. In the meantime, I've got to do a little shifting of our ground forces. But don't worry, I can promise you that my troops will be ready, though it wouldn't disappoint me in the least if you should decide to keep all of the glory for yourself. The privilege and the burden of protecting the Earth is yours to bear, Admiral. Godspeed."

"And to you, General. The next time we speak, it'll be to celebrate our victory. Quinn out."

Despite all of his brave talk, Jonathon was still unsure about the fleet's chances. Victory wouldn't come easily and would most certainly require further loss of human life. But he'd be ready.

Chapter 9
The Tides of War

"Admiral," Kate called out. "The *Hades* has reached the lunar shipyard. Captain Concevich is requesting further orders."

"Put him through," Jonathon acknowledged, focusing all attention toward the main display screen.

Looking as stone-faced as ever, Concevich popped into view. "We've arrived at the shipyard, Admiral," he reported. "Now please tell me you're gonna let me nuke those friggin' aliens."

"That's exactly what you're going to do, Captain. Since the alien fleet is destroying everything in their path, it stands to reason they'll swing past the moon and take out the shipyard. It's a very tempting target that I don't think they'll be able to resist. They're addicted to destruction and it's your job to make sure they get an overdose."

"You want me to mine the area?" Concevich asked, sporting a mischievous grin.

"In a manner of speaking. I want you to plant several bombs inside the shipyard's main facility. Its reinforced walls should keep the nukes sufficiently shielded from sensor sweeps. You'd better get moving, though. I estimate that you'll only have between twenty to twenty-five minutes to complete your task once the enemy fleet leaves Martian space."

Concevich nodded and pledged, "I'll give 'em a welcoming party they won't soon forget."

The communication link terminated.

"Are you sure it was wise to send *him* to booby trap the shipyard?" Jensen inquired. Concevich had always managed to give him the creeps, especially considering the man's unhealthy fascination with weapons of mass destruction.

"The guy's got his quirks, but he's also good at what he does. He'll get the job done."

The lunar shipyard resembled a gargantuan steel ribcage, primarily due to the long cranes that curved down from the outer edges of the main structure. It was once a bustling hub of engineering activity, but all signs of life had since vanished, fled as soon as the alien fleet had made its presence and intentions known. All that remained was the charcoal-gray framework of an unfinished Cruiser-class vessel fastened between each row of cranes. Loose scrap and a variety of tools drifted through the bowels of the ship, emphasizing the degree of haste with which the area had been evacuated.

"We've safely docked, Captain," the navigation officer announced, glancing over at his captain.

"Good, but keep the engines warm," said Concevich, rising from his chair. "Commander, you have the bridge. If I'm not back before the enemy closes within sensor range, you're to return to Earth without me. The safety of the crew is your top priority. Is that clear?"

"Yes, sir, and good luck," the commander replied, rising to attention and initiating a proper and heartfelt salute as his captain set foot inside the waiting elevator.

The remainder of the command staff rose as well, following the commander's lead and leaving the room exceptionally quiet. Concevich turned around and acknowledged their collective salute while peering briefly into each officer's eyes, all of which were fixed on him, as if to preserve the captain perfectly in their memories. But not being fond of outward displays of sentiment, Concevich quickly spoke to the computer, saying, "Cargo and munitions deck," bidding the elevator to descend into the depths of the *Hades*.

Upon reaching its destination, the elevator doors swished open and Concevich stepped out into the narrow corridor. His footsteps echoed through the passageway as he double-timed his march toward the secured cargo hold. Two armed guards stood at ease near the entrance, dressed in black military fatigues with twin-handled pulse rifles held loosely and angled toward the floor. As their captain approached, they broke from their casual conversation and sprang to attention, pressing their weapons against their chest and becoming as immovable as bronze statues.

Concevich smiled a little from having caught them off guard and said, "Relax, boys, and step aside."

"Yes, sir," the guards replied in unison, parting from the door. Their stance slackened, but barely enough to comply with the request. Their captain's mere presence made it impossible for them to be fully at ease.

Concevich smacked the back of his right hand against the security panel, eliciting a faint beep as the computer recognized his embedded identification chip and granted him access to a numbered keypad. After the authorization code was punched in, two sets of armored doors made a loud clanging noise as they retracted at a moderate pace, exposing a vault-like room.

"Follow me," Concevich instructed, leading the two guards into the secured cargo hold and toward the first of four metallic spheres, all of which were a full head taller than he was and commanded at least as much respect. For there, staring back at the three men, was the image of a dark-red skull, decorating the exterior of the first warhead and hinting at its destructive purpose.

"Beautiful, aren't they?" said Concevich, running his hand along the smooth surface of one of the spheres. "Omega-class fusion bombs are the most lethal weapons in the fleet. They bring a smile to my face just looking at 'em. Each of these technological terrors contains the fires of hell itself and we're gonna unleash 'em on our new enemies." Looking back at the two guards, he sported a roguish grin.

They both glanced sideways at each other, unsure of how to respond to their captain's remarks. So they chose to play it safe and remain quiet.

Concevich chuckled at the nervous expressions on the faces of his young companions before continuing. "Come on, boys, we've got a lot of work to do."

The lights within the main cargo facility of the shipyard activated ahead of Concevich's arrival. He entered the room from the rear, followed closely by the two guards. They were accompanied by remote-controlled flatbed transports, which emitted a muffled whirring sound as their engines struggled to ferry three of the fusion bombs into position.

"Bring 'em over here," Concevich called out, his voice echoing through the spacious room. "Give the transports a little push if you have to, but hurry it up. We don't have much time."

Guiding their cargo to the middle of the room, the guards halted the transports once they were in position, then started the unloading process.

"What do you think you're doing?" Concevich barked, glaring at the startled soldiers.

"Um, we're unloading the bombs so we can take the transports back with us," one of the guards replied, sounding more like he was seeking confirmation than offering an explanation.

"Why? You gonna do something with 'em later?"

The guard was feeling rather uncomfortable, which was the standard reaction whenever a conversation with Concevich began. "Well no, sir, but—"

"We don't have time to unload. Just leave 'em on the friggin' transports and prep for arming. It won't kill the military to give us a couple of new ones, assuming we even survive this."

"Yes, sir."

Both guards crouched down and started interacting with each of the small security terminals that were located near the base of the bombs. Meanwhile, Concevich made his way toward one of the consoles along the starboard wall and entered in a sequence of commands on the touch screen interface, bringing the shipyard's sensor grid online. The video feed from one of the external cameras was also transferred to the primary display screen at the front of the room, providing a clear view of the region of space outside.

"That should keep those buggers from sneakin' up on us," Concevich mumbled to himself before heading back to the warheads. "Hurry it up, you two, unless you want a front row seat for the alien barbecue."

"They're prepped, sir," said one of the guards. "All that's left to do is for you to enter your authorization code."

Concevich dropped to one knee and keyed his eight-digit code into the first bomb's security terminal. "Access denied?" he exclaimed in an irritated tone. "What do you mean access denied? It's a valid code!" He began cursing at the warhead as his repeated attempts to arm its payload failed. Scooting to the next bomb, he initiated the same procedure but yielded the same results, so the cursing resumed.

One of the guards piped up with a suggestion. "Maybe if you pause for a moment and try to remember—"

"I haven't forgotten the blasted code," Concevich growled. "The geniuses in High Command—God rest their souls—must've given me the wrong code…again. We don't exactly use these babies a lot, so the code-delivery system's got a few kinks in it."

The guards didn't buy his explanation, but they weren't about to argue with him. They were, however, anxious to depart. "Can't we just leave them as they are?" one of the men asked.

"They won't detonate properly if the atomic trigger isn't armed. There'll be an explosion all right, but not nearly as grand as what we're going for."

"So now what?"

Exhaling with a deep breath of disappointment, Concevich pushed himself up and turned to face his companions. "The two of you are going to return to the *Hades* and tell the commander to hightail it back to Earth."

"But—"

"That's an order, soldier. There's a way to override the security code, but it's gonna take some time and that's one thing that we've about run out of. Now get out of here!"

Though they hated the idea of leaving a man behind, even one as odd as their captain, the guards reluctantly made their way out of the room and back to the airlock.

Concevich continued to curse at the bombs while using a small pocketknife to disassemble each of the security terminals. He worked as fast as he could, determined to arm the warheads before the aliens arrived. But the task was complicated at best and fraught with the possibility of error. After a few minutes had passed and little progress had been made, his wrist-comm started beeping. Ignoring the communication request, Concevich continued fiddling with the exposed color-coded wires of the first bomb's security terminal, trying to remember the correct rewiring sequence. "I hope I don't accidentally detonate this thing," he mumbled to himself. "That'd sure ruin everyone's day."

Though consistent in its tone, the incessant beeping from the communicator had caused Concevich's facial expression to grow increasingly twisted with irritation. Finally pausing from his work, he activated the comm link and said, "I'm unavailable right now. Leave a message at the sound of the boom."

"Not funny, Captain," the commander responded. "Now please return to the *Hades*. We still have time to get out of here. Forget about the bombs. We'll—"

"I can't do that, Commander, and you know it. Besides, I've had a good run and I plan on going out with a bang, if you know what I mean. Now get outta here, Marty, before this whole place goes to hell."

The commander sighed before conveying his final message. "It's been a privilege serving with you, Bill. Your heroism won't go unnoticed. I'll make sure of that."

The transmission terminated, leaving Concevich feeling alone, yet more determined than ever. His work resumed.

"Well, that does it for this one," he mumbled after completing the arming process on the first warhead. Scooting over to the next bomb, he began implementing the same hot-wiring trick as before, though at a more efficient pace.

The shipyard's sensor panel started beeping, raising Concevich's level of anxiety. "It's just my rotten luck that we had to go to war with punctual aliens," he grumbled, trying to speed his work along. Darting to the final warhead, he frantically tried to arm it, glancing up at the video display periodically to check the progress of the advancing fleet. And sure enough, the enemy warships slowed to a crawl alongside the shipyard. But just when Concevich thought he had them right where he wanted them, all except one of the warships picked up speed again, racing away from the shipyard and its frustrated occupant.

"Oh, you've got to be kidding me," he shouted at the display screen. "Now's not the time to get picky with your targets."

Scowling at the screen, he seemed quite dissatisfied with the lone warship that had stayed behind and which was currently approaching on an attack vector. But Concevich finished his work nevertheless and stood up, brushing his hands across his knees while maintaining eye contact with the overhead display.

"Come and get your present, you little bug-eyed freaks."

The starboard tip of the alien warship brightened until a single energy beam lashed out at the shipyard, slicing through each of the large cranes as it swept across the underside of the main facility. And as the first beam dissipated, more energy pools formed along the vessel's hull, resulting in a series of attacks that ravaged the shipyard's critical structures.

Concevich fell to the ground from the thunderous tremors that stampeded through the doomed facility. And as the ceiling began to collapse, he reached up and prepared to hit the detonation switch on one of the bombs, unwilling to leave anything to chance. "See you in Hell!"

The shipyard vanished amidst the apocalyptic explosion that soared into space, consuming the surrounding darkness and all traces of the lone alien presence. At that instant the Solar System had two suns.

Sensor readouts on the bridge of the *Intimidator* were beeping wildly, coinciding with the brilliant flash of light that had appeared near the moon and illuminated Jonathon's attentive face. Even though he didn't know the full extent of the damage to the alien fleet, he was certain they had suffered casualties. Cracking a smile of satisfaction, he glanced at Jensen and said, "Looks like the *Hades* put on a good show."

"It certainly appears that way, sir, although we won't know exactly how successful they were for a few more minutes."

"Admiral," hollered Kate, "the *Hades* is sending out a distress call."

Jonathon's smile vanished. "Put them through."

The image of the *Hades*' commander flickered into view, his face beaming with anger and a hint of desperation. "Admiral, the remainder of the alien fleet is closing on our position."

"What happened? Where's Captain Concevich?"

"He's dead. There was a problem with the warheads, so he stayed behind and gave his life to make sure they detonated. And he would have sent every one of those ships straight to hell if they had all taken the bait. But the aliens cheated him and only sent in one of their warships to do their dirty work. The rest are itching for a fight and I aim to give them one."

Jonathon nodded, looking rather glum, and said, "Do what you have to, Commander, and Godspeed."

With a farewell nod, the commander terminated the communication.

"Which ships do you want to send to assist the *Hades*?" inquired Jensen.

"None of them."

"What? But—"

"I don't like the situation any more than you do, Commander, but there's nothing we can do. They'll be dead long before any of our ships could reach them. Now instruct the fleet to prepare for battle. We make our final stand here."

"You can't just sentence them to death. We should move out and assist the *Hades* instead of waiting here like..." Jensen hesitated, biting back the remainder of his statement.

"Like what, Commander?" snarled Jonathon. "Like cowards?"

Jensen remained quiet, staring icily at his superior officer.

"Courage alone doesn't win a war," Jonathon lectured. "Caution and strategy are equally as important. By remaining here we can fight on our own terms and with Earth's defensive weaponry at our disposal. We need every advantage we can get. And it pains me to no end to lose more good men and women to this war, but I can't in good conscience gamble the lives of billions of people for the sake of the crew of only one ship. Can you?"

"No, sir!" Jensen snapped. Realizing that the command staff was staring at him, he turned away and resumed monitoring the fleet, pretending the verbal exchange hadn't taken place. He certainly wished he had kept his mouth shut, knowing that Jonathon was right, which annoyed him. But worse than that, he had been rebuffed in front of his peers and that angered him. He cared little for the friendship of his subordinates, but their respect of his command meant everything to him. And intentional or not, Jonathon had shaved away a small sliver of that respect, placing himself directly in front of the emotional targeting sights of Jensen, whose trigger finger was already twitching.

Jonathon could feel his pulse quicken as the alien fleet encroached on his home territory. The chaos of war was about to consume the remainder of his fleet and he had to make sure they were ready. "Lieutenant Hayes, open a fleet-wide priority link."

"Done."

After clearing his throat, his speech began. "This is Admiral Quinn speaking. The enemy will be here within minutes and we are all that stands between them and the Earth, between survival and utter defeat. We simply *cannot* and *will not* fail in our task. And rest assured that while our enemy is every bit as impressive as they are ruthless, they are *not* invincible. In fact, they've already suffered casualties of their own and we will continue inflicting damage until their savage hearts no longer beat within human space. Our fallen comrades have shown the enemy that there are no limits to our bravery and determination. We will never surrender. We will not taste defeat. We will be victorious.

"All ships are hereby ordered to target and engage the first alien vessel that moves within firing range. We need to hit them hard and fast in order to minimize our own losses. Remember, our unity is our strength, and by concentrating our firepower we can effectively repel their assault.

"Enemy star fighters will no doubt join in the battle. Several clusters have been spotted throughout the system and are converging on our position. I want them taken out before they have a chance to inflict any damage on our warships. Get our star fighters out there and give them a welcoming party they won't soon forget. This is the moment you've all been training for, now make the Earth proud. Quinn out."

The bridge became quiet for a moment, before a disturbing update beamed across Jensen's datapad. "We've lost the *Hades*," he announced indignantly.

Jonathon simply nodded in acknowledgement, choosing to ignore Jensen's tone. The crew of the *Hades* had been added to the mounting casualty list and there was nothing that could change that, nor was there time to mourn. Jonathon had already shifted focus, thinking only of his current responsibilities and what would soon become the most important battle of his career.

"I want the Black Lance prepped for launch immediately, Commander," ordered Jonathon. "Contact Lieutenant Hunter and tell him to scramble his squad."

"Yes, sir."

Jensen temporarily buried his ill feelings toward Jonathon so he could focus on his own duties, though with some selfish motivation. He was thinking of the honor and recognition he would earn for doing his part to ensure the fleet's victory.

"Gunners, bring all of our weapons online and man the defensive lasers," Jonathon instructed. "Target all enemy fighters that move within range and respond with deadly force."

"Sure thing," said Dead Eye, "but can't we just turn on the Rapid-Track-and-Attack system?"

"Unfortunately, no. It primarily relies on radar tracking and the alien ships have proven to be too stealthy to show up on our radar. You'll have to gun them down yourselves."

"We won't let anything slip through," Chang vowed.

"Lieutenant Hayes, I need you to contact Dr. Vandegrift in the weapons lab. Tell him it's urgent and transfer the link to my console."

"Yes, sir."

Peering out the forward windows, Jonathon watched as the *Intimidator* flexed its military muscle. Dozens of missile racks, lasers, and quad-barreled plasma guns rose out of the secured compartments that had been strategically placed around the Juggernaut's elongated hull. There was an unprecedented arsenal at Jonathon's disposal, yet it did little to calm his nerves. He knew that timing was going to be everything in this battle, with no room for mistakes.

"Dr. Vandegrift's communication is coming through now, Admiral," Kate reported.

Jonathon turned his attention toward the small console on the right armrest of his chair and activated the comm link. "The alien fleet will be here within minutes, Doctor. What's your status?"

"Tippits' men have successfully finished their modifications to the EMP mines and we've nearly completed the second biological projectile. I wish we could have created more of them, but we had to use excessive precautions in order to avoid exposure."

"Then we'll just have to make the best use of what we've got. Be sure to pass along my gratitude to everyone that assisted in this effort. These weapons could very well turn the tides of war in our favor. Now, let me speak with Specialist Tippits."

"Of course, Admiral."

"What do you need, sir?" Tippits asked, stepping into view.

"I need you to get the slam cannons loaded with the modified projectiles as quickly as possible. Notify me when you're done, then stay put, just in case something goes wrong."

"Understood, sir. I'm on my way."

The communication link terminated.

"Admiral," Jensen called out, "we've detected the enemy fleet on our sensors. I'm reading three energy signatures, two of which are larger than the third, possibly due to vessel mergers." Additional tactical data streamed across his datapad, catching his attention. "Sir, we've got incoming fighters…twenty-eight of them. They're advancing ahead of the warships."

"Get our fighters out there!" demanded Jonathon.

The lights within the spacious forward hangar bay were flashing red as the emergency launch siren wailed. Fifty Black Lance fighter pilots were dressed in shady flight gear and scrambling out onto the flight deck, preparing to justify their reputation. Their reflective helmets were proudly decorated with varying quantities of tiny red skulls, identifying the number of enemy kills that had been achieved over the course of each pilot's career. Lieutenant Dale Hunter's helmet was almost completely covered.

"Let's move it, hot shots," he prodded while rushing toward one of the elevator tubes along the starboard wall. "We don't want to be late for the party."

The squad split in half and scattered throughout the room, which was divided into three different docking zones, each denoted by a thin colored stripe that ranged along the perimeter. From green zone they ascended the ladders and elevators. Half of them stopped at blue zone and sprinted along the railed catwalk that led to twenty-six Phoenix SG-11 stealth fighters—

thirteen along each side, facing the walls. The rest of the squad ascended to red zone and the remaining twenty-four stealth fighters, which were staggered in a docking pattern above the ships in blue zone.

A chorus of loud metallic clanging sounds echoed through the hangar bay as the reinforced launch doors in front of each stealth fighter retracted, exposing the darkness of space that lay beyond the invisible containment field.

"Come on, girl," coaxed Hunter, hopping inside the cockpit of his jet-black stealth fighter. "Don't let me down."

The tinted canopy closed around him with a faint hum and sealed itself shut as he powered up his vessel, the whole of which was a clever mixture of firepower, stealth, and maneuverability, with a fair amount of sexy design features thrown in for good measure. For starters, it had three curvilinear wings—two jutting out and back at a slight downward slant, with a shorter third wing centered underneath. And each wing was accented by rapid-fire stinger cannons, which, when combined with the fixed missile launcher that was positioned directly behind the cockpit, made the Phoenix a force to be reckoned with.

The faint sapphire glow of Hunter's engine exhaust brightened as he disengaged his docking clamp and accelerated out into space. The rest of his squad launched as well, departing the *Intimidator* several fighters at a time.

"Form up," broadcast Hunter as his translucent-red targeting reticle faded in on the inner surface of his canopy. "We've got twenty-eight bogies incoming. Take them out fast before they can harass the fleet, and be sure to check your friendly fire. The pilots who score the most kills get a free round of drinks. Now light 'em up."

Eighty Tsunami star fighters, comprising two separate squadrons, took up position as well, having launched from the two Carrier-class warships: the *ICS Pegasus* and the *ICS Titan*. The design of the Tsunami fighters was similar to that of the Phoenix except they only had two wings and their hull was composed of a light-gray alloy which was void of any stealthy attributes. The Tsunami fighters weren't as lethal or maneuverable as the Phoenix either, but they had still proved their value over the years.

Accelerating into view, the alien fighter squadron scattered, opening fire on everything within range. A cluster of six Tsunami fighters was pummeled by the initial onslaught, exploding before their pilots knew what hit them.

"Whoa!" one of the fighter pilots shouted. "How are we supposed to track those things? They don't show up on radar and they're moving faster than anything I've—"

"Pipe down and get moving," his flight officer interrupted before darting away and into the thick of battle.

Meanwhile, Hunter was closing in on one of the alien ships, keeping pace with its erratic movements. And as soon as he had a clear shot, he took it, unleashing a rapid pulse of plasma bursts that hammered the rear shields of his target. Reacting to the attack, the enemy began zigzagging at high speed, trying to shake the determined lieutenant off its tail. It didn't work. Hunter continued firing, predicting the alien's every move.

"Come on," he shouted at his target. "Blow up already!" His weapons fire eventually wore down the shields of the alien vessel and tore through its hull, triggering a decisive explosion that caused his star fighter to shudder. As usual, the honor of the first kill was all his.

"I can't shake him," one of the Tsunami pilots called out across the comm system, feverishly arcing his ship in an attempt to avoid destruction. "Somebody get this thing off my—" The pilot's message terminated as a few well aimed energy bursts shattered his star fighter. The alien ship that had been pursuing him tore through the exploding wreckage and continued on toward the perimeter of the destroyer group.

Two Black Lance pilots immediately took notice and gave chase, trying to intercept the enemy fighter before it could inflict any damage. As the alien ship approached, the *ICS Challenger* fired its defensive lasers. Most of the intense red beams missed their mark, but a few of them managed to connect, igniting the target's shields and placing it on the defensive. Swerving sporadically, the enemy vessel darted out of the destroyer's targeting sights and inadvertently into the cross-hairs of the two advancing Phoenix star fighters.

"Let's burn 'em up, Maniac," the first pilot said to his wingman.

"Roger that, Hawkeye. My finger's already on the trigger."

Both veterans unleashed a rapid succession of plasma stingers that streaked toward their target, striking its port wing. The alien responded by swinging around and returning fire, easily overwhelming the inferior shielding around one of its attackers.

"Eject, Hawkeye, eject!"

Before Hawkeye could react, his fuel line ignited in a measured explosion that ripped through his engines, crippling his fighter. Had the shot struck the main reserves, his life would have been snuffed out in a fraction of a second. Such an outcome would have been preferable to what he experienced next. Fuel had begun to leak into the cockpit, and as the clear liquid contacted a live wire, the air surrounding Hawkeye erupted in flames, burning him alive.

Maniac stared in horror as Hawkeye smacked his charred hands against the canopy several times, his blood-curdling screams shrieking through the comm link, then dying down once he finally succumbed. The battered wreckage drifted past Maniac's ship before exploding, interrupting his ability to return fire on what had become a personal crusade of revenge.

"You're going to pay for that," Maniac yelled, veering his star fighter back toward the alien that had slain his friend. He thumbed his missile-firing button three times and unleashed his rage. The corresponding volley of Starfire-III guided missiles quickly acquired an image lock and streaked away, as did the enemy. But try as it might, the alien fighter was unable to escape the vengeance that had been wreaked on it. Three commanding explosions sealed its fate.

"That's for Hawkeye," proclaimed Maniac, banking his ship toward new targets.

The sounds of fast-paced, adrenaline pumping music blared through the comm system as another of the Black Lance pilots called out for assistance. "Big Dog, this is Loose Cannon," he said, speaking scarcely louder than the music. "I've got one of those alien fraggers on my tail and I can't seem to shake him. If you're not too busy—"

"I see him," Hunter responded. "Just hold on."

Maneuvering his ship onto an intercept vector with the alien star fighter, Hunter prepared to engage the target. "Delta-five, on my mark," he advised.

"Roger that, but make it snappy."

Hunter guided his cross-hairs slightly off-center from his squad mate's location, then fired his stinger cannons along a curved path. "Engage."

Loose Cannon complied, banking his star fighter hard starboard. The alien ship followed suit, moving right into the spread of plasma bursts that Hunter had laid down. As its shields lit up, Loose Cannon spun his fighter around and fired his trio of linked weapons while soaring backwards. The combined assault broke through the shielding on the enemy ship and seared through its hull, resulting in a satisfactory explosion.

"I owe you one, buddy. Drinks are—"

The premature celebration was terminated by enemy weapons fire that rained down on Loose Cannon's position, blowing his ship apart. Hunter peered furiously out through his canopy, unable to locate the alien ship that had dealt the fatal blow to his friend. But someone had to pay for such an outrage. It didn't matter who, so long as they were alien. Zeroing in on the nearest enemy star fighter, he punched his afterburners and raced ahead with his gun ports hot.

"We're losing a lot of fighters out here," one of the younger Black Lance pilots complained. "Our forces easily outnumber them four to one, but the aliens are too fast and their shielding is freaking unbelievable."

"Then double up," Hunter snapped, frustrated with his squad's lack of progress in the battle. "The enemy ships might be impressive, but like the admiral said, they're not invincible. Now get out there and kick some alien butt."

"Roger that," the young pilot replied before joining up with a pair of Tsunami fighters that brushed by his ship en route to a fresh target. Their collective arsenal was sufficient for the kill, or would have been, had the alien not been so effective at out-maneuvering its pursuers. The starlight dance continued until the enemy had grown sufficiently tired of being on the defensive. At that moment, the wings of its fighter angled out into a perpendicular alignment with the main body. Then, as the ship spun clockwise, the tops of each wing started to glow. A barrage of energy blasts shot out of the rotating vessel and thrashed its three pursuers, leaving their corresponding explosions to illuminate the alien's next victim.

"Did you see that?" someone yelled over the comm system, watching as the alien fighter closed its wings and darted away. "What in the—"

"Stay focused, pilot," her flight leader encouraged. "Why don't you try impressing the enemy with some moves of your own?"

Amid a frenetic display of defensive laser fire, a sweeping explosion emanated from within the destroyer group. Six alien star fighters emerged from the scene.

"Admiral," Jensen called out, "we've lost the *Challenger*. An enemy fighter group took her out."

Jonathon scowled at the news. "Instruct the flight leaders to provide better protection. We're taking a beating out there and we can't afford to lose any more destroyers. We've yet to engage their capital ships. Tell Lieutenant Hunter I want to start hearing about enemy losses for a change."

"Yes, sir."

Staring at the right tactical display station, Jonathon watched as the holographic projections of the alien warships popped into view. They were drawing closer to the raging battle that had already lit up the three-dimensional display.

"Gunners," said Jonathon, "Target the nearest warship with all of our weapons except the slam cannons. *Do not* fire those cannons until I give the order."

"Aye, aye, Admiral," replied Dead Eye.

"Commander, how long until the warships are within range?"

"Thirty seconds, sir."

"Bring the solar-laser grid online and target the forward section of the nearest warship. Prepare to fire on my mark and let's see if we can split one of those merged abominations apart."

Sixty spherical laser devices had been placed into high orbit around the Earth, evenly spaced from one another in a sequential array. The glistening, diamond-like exterior of each device was composed of a special crystalline material that served as a powerful solar-energy collector and magnification lens, storing the sun's lethal radiation into energy cells residing within their shielded cores. Once a sufficient energy pool had been acquired, a deadly chain reaction could be unleashed in a precision strike that would pulverize its target. During the war with Mars, the solar laser had served as more than sufficient deterrent to ward off a direct assault against Earth. It was a weapon greatly to be feared and the aliens would soon understand why.

As each of the devices activated, they began to sparkle, emitting a fiery yellow glow.

"The alien warships are within optimum range of the solar laser," Jensen announced, his finger twitching above the firing switch.

"Fire!" Jonathon ordered, almost yelled.

A thin saffron energy stream was discharged from the first solar weapon, striking the next device in the sequence. The potent beam merged with the power stored inside the second device and burst out through the weapon's pulsating exterior, magnifying in strength as it continued rapidly along the chain. Upon reaching the final device, the death-dealing ray was redirected toward the designated target, burning with an intensity that rivaled the sun. The shields around the merged alien warships ignited in a magnificent explosion of blue light as the solar laser struck the forward section of the starboard vessel.

"Direct hit," proclaimed Jensen, his eyes shifting between the scenery outside the windows and his sensor readout.

"Fire at will, Lieutenants," said Jonathon.

"One massive pummeling coming up," Dead Eye responded as he and Chang engaged the *Intimidator's* weapons array.

A cluttered swarm of plasma stingers and missiles streamed toward the weakening shields of the adjoined alien vessels. And like a guiding flare being fired in the night, the attack signaled the remainder of the fleet to follow the lead of their flagship, sending a wave of weapons fire into the fray.

Having finally succumbed to the power of the solar laser, the shielding around the front of the targeted warship faded, triggering a chain of massive explosions as the solar laser burned clear through the interior of the invading warship.

With its energy supply drained, the solar laser grid powered down, leaving secondary explosions to rock the bow of the damaged vessel, which was remarkably still functional. In an effort to curb any further damage, the merged warships fired dozens of defensive energy beams, destroying a significant number of the approaching warheads. But the remaining ordnance slipped through and detonated against the front and upper portion of their target, producing explosions that propagated throughout the vessel. A frantic separation got underway, with the portside vessel abandoning its ravaged companion. The discarded wreckage exploded in a blinding flash, releasing a considerable shock wave that hammered a nearby alien star fighter and destroyed the two Tsunami strike craft that had given chase.

It was a small victory for Jonathon, but the aliens were quick to put a damper on any celebration plans. Three converging energy beams assaulted the *ICS Pathfinder*, ripping the destroyer apart.

"They're not paying us by the hour, people, so don't let up," Hunter announced while engaging another enemy star fighter.

"I'm only counting eleven bogies left," one of the Black Lance pilots called out. "And at least two of those are mine."

"Man, you're either blind or stupid," another pilot commented, "'cause there's twelve of those fraggers left. And don't be hoggin' the targets."

"You make another remark like that and you'll be my next target," the first pilot snapped back.

"Less talking, more killing," a third pilot interjected.

"My thoughts exactly," Hunter added, prior to finishing off his latest kill. "And for the record, gentlemen, I just bagged my third."

"Looks like the Big Dog's gonna come out on top…again," one of the pilots replied. "Nice shooting, LT."

With the MPF's fighter groups having finally taken charge of the dogfights, their alien counterparts turned their full attention on the destroyers, harassing them. And as one of the enemy star fighters emerged from a strafing run against a cluster of warships, it drew within range of the *Intimidator* and Dead Eye's targeting sights. He greeted it with a spread of eight defensive laser beams, hitting his mark dead on and overwhelming its shields. The alien fighter spiraled out into the darkness and disappeared in a spray of colorful explosions.

As the battle intensified, several more coruscating explosions lit up the surrounding region, originating from within the destroyer group. The remaining pair of adjoined alien warships had unleashed an arc of energy that was tearing through the hulls of two destroyers that were in a tight formation.

A pair of Tsunamis happened to be racing through the area, pursuing a rather truculent alien star fighter. They launched a couple of Starfire-II missiles at their target, expecting a sure kill. But the alien promptly veered toward the besieged destroyers, and, like a lightning rod in a storm, attracted a bolt of energy from the capital ship's weapon. The chaotic stream channeled through the hull of the star fighter and belched out through its aft surface, prematurely detonating the missiles that were giving chase. From there, the energy bolts popped out in strings until they struck the advancing Tsunami fighters, incinerating both ships before their pilots had time to react.

"We've lost the *Taurus* and the *Scorpius*," Jensen announced ruefully. He hated reporting ship losses and it seemed to him as if that was all he had done since the dreadful day began. Traces of Tetra-Prozomamine were still flowing stubbornly through his veins, but the waning medication was now fighting a losing battle. The war was pounding through the commander's emotional defenses and taking a heavy toll.

"Admiral," Kate called out, "Specialist Tippits is reporting in, stating that we can fire when ready. He suggests a two-one-two firing sequence, timed at your discretion."

"Lieutenant Adams," said Jonathon, turning to face the expert marksman. "Target the merged warships with the slam cannons. Fire the outer four cannons first, followed by the inner cannon two seconds after. Your aim and timing have to be dead on."

"They don't call me Dead Eye for nothing, sir."

"What's going on?" Jensen inquired, curious about the unusual firing request.

"Keep an eye on those ships and you'll see soon enough. Our weapons specialists have developed a little surprise for the enemy."

Five hefty, destructive mass-driver cannons had been mounted in plain view atop the *Intimidator's* forward section. These slam cannons, as they were more commonly known, were unique to the *Intimidator*, as it was the only ship in the fleet large enough to house mass-driver weaponry. And it was high time to put it to good use. Once the cannons acquired a trajectory lock, four high-velocity projectiles burst out of the long barrels, followed by the fifth projectile soon after. The shields of the merged warships ignited as the modified EMP mines impacted, triggering a wave of electrical discharges that produced a small but adequate hole. The remaining projectile soared through the opening and slammed into the hull of the portside vessel before its fluctuating shields recovered and sealed the breach. It was a direct hit, yet the warship seemed unscathed.

"Nothing happened," Jensen reported snidely.

Jonathon waited for several seconds before responding, studying the alien ship and hoping the ace up his sleeve hadn't turned into a joker. But he finally yielded to Jensen's assessment. "Well, it was a long shot anyway," he admitted, sounding disappointed. "Prepare to—"

"Hold on," Chang interrupted. "I'm showing a decrease in the power readings from that ship. Its signal is fading."

The hull of the portside alien warship acquired a dark-green discoloration as the dreaded Angel of Death and other chemical agents were absorbed into the fleshy surface. Abruptly halting their advance, the merged vessels began to separate. The departure was in vain, however, as the discoloration had already expanded onto the tentacles that bound the ships together, contaminating both warships at a surprising rate. And as they drifted apart, cracks began to form along their tainted hulls. The attack had worked and far better than Jonathon had dreamed.

"Target both ships and fire at will," Jonathon ordered. He could almost taste the awaiting victory.

"With pleasure," acknowledged Dead Eye, sporting a big grin.

Intertwining gold vapor trails extended from the *Intimidator* as sixty Hellfire-III guided missiles raced toward the crippled ships. The deadly warheads burst through the brittle hull of each vessel unchallenged and detonated within the bellies of the subdued beasts. Their exoskeletons swelled from the burning carnage before shattering violently, unleashing a blizzard of charred remains.

Snapping his head toward Jonathon, Jensen beamed with astonishment and said, "How in the world did you do that?"

"The aliens are using organic technology, so we countered with an appropriate weapon. We spread several chemical and biological toxins across their hull."

"Brilliant thinking, sir. Possibly illegal, but brilliant."

Jonathon chuckled. "It's a gray area, but I'm sure it'll be deemed justified once all this is over."

"Admiral," Dead Eye interrupted, "the remainder of the enemy fleet's on the run. You must've really freaked 'em out."

Relieved by news of the almost certain victory, Jonathon's muscles finally relaxed and he exhaled a triumphant breath. "Commander, tell the fleet to target the nearest vessel. I don't want those warships escaping."

"Yes, sir."

"Lieutenant Adams, we've got one more round left in the slam cannons. Target the far ship and put the fear of God into its crew."

"You got it, Admiral," Dead Eye replied, looking exceptionally pleased with his orders.

With its shields lit up from an onslaught of weapons fire, the besieged enemy vessel tried to speed away from its attackers, but its efforts were proving futile. Another round of high-speed projectiles raced past the assaulted vessel and impacted against the protective force field of its retreating companion, creating a small opening through which the last of the toxins soared, embedding themselves under the ship's skin.

Despite their continued retreat, explosions from the first alien vessel soon illuminated the green discoloration along the exterior of the infected warship. Its hull was becoming terribly brittle from the effects of the toxins that were spreading across its surface like a rampant disease. Crippled and vulnerable, the contaminated warship drifted at a lifeless pace.

The weapons fire from the destroyer group had ceased. Their target had been pulverized and its tattered frame was replaced with a bright flash of light, followed by an intense shock wave that radiated outward, shattering the debilitated vessel. The alien fleet had been defeated.

"Commander," said Jonathon, leaning back into his chair, "instruct Lieutenant Hunter to mop up the remaining enemy star fighters and return home for a well deserved rest."

"Yes, sir," Jensen replied, looking relieved almost to the point of smiling.

"Let's get this over with," Hunter urged his squadron while pursuing one of the last hostiles. "I've got a dinner date that I don't want to miss." He confidently thumbed his missile-firing trigger three times, unleashing the remainder of his payload. The warheads streaked toward their target and detonated against its hull.

"Chalk up another kill for the Big Dog."

Multiple defensive laser beams fired from two of the surviving destroyers as one of the alien ships tried to scurry past them. The lasers intersected along the fighter's shields and burned for a time before slicing into its main body, severing all four of its wings. What little was left exploded.

The remaining three hostile star fighters were quickly overwhelmed by the superior numbers of Tsunami strike craft that vengefully pursued them. Their destruction signaled an end to the alien presence.

"Woohoo!" one of the fighter pilots shouted through the comm system, celebrating the win.

"My sentiments exactly," his flight leader replied. "Let's head back to the *Titan*."

"Well done, gentlemen," proclaimed Hunter. "The enemy was no match for the Black Lance. Let's head home."

Resting comfortably in his chair, Jonathon felt relieved, though not anywhere near as much as he had expected. He was undoubtedly satisfied with the hard-fought victory. The men and women under his command had been successful in sparing the Earth and its inhabitants from certain destruction. That alone should have been enough reason to celebrate, but it wasn't. Something was bothering him and he couldn't quite put his finger on it. The tremendous loss of human life that had occurred was weighing heavily on his conscience, to be sure, but it wasn't the source of his mounting trepidation. For some reason he was beginning to feel as if their victory was nothing more than the lull that came while standing within the eye of a storm. It was as if he could sense the enemy all around him, waiting for an opportune moment to retaliate.

"Should I give the order to stand down, Admiral?" asked Jensen against a backdrop of cheering officers who were patting each other on the back.

"Not yet," Jonathon cautioned, probing the darkness around the fleet with great suspicion. "Have all ships fall in and remain at full alert as a precaution."

"Admiral," Kate called out, "General O'Connor wishes to speak with you."

"Put him through—"

The sensor readout interrupted with a series of distressing beeps.

"We're detecting multiple energy signatures...big ones," Jensen reported. His victor's countenance was immediately cast down as the grave realization of an alien reprisal sunk in.

"Tell the general to stand by," ordered Jonathon, rising from his chair. "Commander, get any of the fighters that have docked back out there. This isn't over."

"Already underway, sir."

Jonathon pressed one hand against his stomach as it wretched wildly in discomfort. "Will this nightmare ever end?" he muttered to himself, staring out the forward windows. The storm of war was about to swallow the fleet whole.

Over a dozen massive wormholes had formed all around the fleet, permitting scores of alien star fighters and warships to flood the surrounding region. Fear and despair quickly spread through the human ranks like a plague.

"Commander, what's the status of the solar laser?" inquired Jonathon, expecting to utilize the same effective tactics as before.

"It's only at seventy percent of capacity. We can't fire for another five minutes."

Jonathon gritted his teeth in frustration and leaned forward against the railing, gripping it tightly with both hands. "Bring the planetary guns online," he ordered, determined to employ every last bit of firepower at his disposal. "Set them to automatically target all enemy vessels that move within range."

"Yes, sir."

"All officers on the lower command level are to abort their current duties and assist in the defense of the fleet. Bring the manual weapons controls online and help man the guns. Target everything that moves and fire at will!"

The region erupted into chaos once more as the remnants of the human fleet fought for their survival, discharging munitions of every kind. But the alien armada had encircled their quarry and unleashed a torrent of weapons fire of their own. The *ICS Victory* was the first to fall, followed immediately by the *ICS Avenger*.

"There's too many of them," one of the fighter pilots screamed. "We can't—" His ship exploded before he could finish his statement. The Black Lance was facing elimination for the first time in its proud history.

"Protect the *Intimidator* at all costs," Hunter demanded, squeezing his firing trigger repeatedly as alien star fighters streaked all around him, more numerous than the stars themselves. His blasts struck several of the enemy ships and though he was unable to inflict any damage, he did manage to draw attention to his efforts. A barrage of energy thrusts converged on his location and shattered his starboard wing. As his star fighter trembled, he glanced up in time to see a flash of enemy weapons fire fill his view. Part of his canopy fractured and his command console showered him with sparks while his ship was sent hurling through space.

With the air hissing out through the cracks in his canopy, Hunter wrapped both hands around the trembling flight yoke and tried to pull his Phoenix out of its inertial tumble. His eyes widened when he saw the *Intimidator's* bow rushing into view. He was on a collision course.

"Come on, open," he shouted, staring at the sealed hangar bay doors.

Fortunately for Hunter, the *Intimidator's* deck officer had detected his approach and initiated emergency docking procedures. The large doors at the front of the hangar bay began to separate at a modest pace. Hunter did his best to level off and decelerate, but his Phoenix was fighting him all the way. His portside wing clipped the retracting doors and tore off as his fighter rushed through and slammed hard onto the evacuated floor. A loud screeching noise echoed through the room as the mangled stealth fighter scraped along the floor and broke through one safety net after another before colliding with an idle shuttle. Medical personnel rushed to the scene and liberated Hunter's unresponsive body from the wreckage. He was alive, but just barely.

A portion of the enemy armada broke away from the battle and accelerated toward the solar laser chain, attempting to prevent its future use. Four of the devices were promptly destroyed by the first wave, but in so doing, the enemy ships had drawn within range of Earth's automated defensive grid.

Emerald fireworks dotted the surface of the Earth as the MPF's hefty planetary guns fired, sending broad strokes of plasma plunging into space and slamming against their targets. One of the alien vessels was struck multiple times, causing its shields to fail.

Reeling from the defensive volley, the strike group initiated a strategic withdrawal as a second round soared into orbit. Significant damage was inflicted on several of the warships, one of which exploded. But it was little consolation, as a fresh group of reinforcements had moved in, replacing their retreating companions. The undersides of the advancing vessels were glowing in preparation for a retaliatory strike. Searing balls of energy shot out like torpedoes and rained down on the inimical gun array. Earth was becoming more vulnerable by the second.

The familiar ionized vapor trails of the *Intimidator's* Hellfire-III guided missiles painted the region once more as a full salvo of the powerful warheads raced toward one of the alien warships. But before they reached their final destination, the entire surface of the targeted vessel glimmered briefly, followed by a bright pulse of energy that encircled the ship. The resulting energy field expanded and incinerated every last one of the incoming missiles before fading away, repelling the *Intimidator's* best efforts.

The bridge of the *ICS Incursion* trembled as it traveled alongside the exploding wreckage of the *ICS Orion*.

"What's our status, Commander?" inquired Captain Hugo Dugas in a dejected French accent. His ship appeared to be falling apart all around him.

"We've sustained heavy damage, sir. Just about everything's offline."

"Captain," one of the officers called out, "the *Titan's* come under fire."

"Move the *Incursion* between that enemy vessel and the *Titan*," Dugas ordered. He then leaned back in his chair and closed his eyes, calmly awaiting his fate.

"Y-yes, sir," the navigation officer stuttered solemnly. His face had become pale with the realization that his captain was sending them to their death.

The *Titan* veered toward the *Intimidator*, seeking to come under its protection, but it wasn't going to make it. Promptly moving into position, the *Incursion* absorbed the brunt of the energy beam before exploding in a heroic last light show. The *Titan* had been spared, but only for seconds before two more enemy warships closed on its position and mercilessly crushed the tattered carrier with a pair of focused gravity beams.

"This is hopeless!" one of the few remaining Tsunami fighter pilots yelled, sounding absolutely terrified. "I'm getting out of here."

"Get back here and fight," his superior demanded. "I'm giving you a direct—" The flight leader's ship exploded, adding to the fleeing pilot's determination.

Weaving around the few remaining destroyers, the petrified pilot tried desperately to cheat death. He glanced nervously out through the portside section of the canopy, attempting to discover if he was being pursued. Upon returning his attention to his flight path, he screamed and crossed both arms in front of his face as his ship compressed and exploded against the starboard shields of an alien warship that was descending on the *ICS Pegasus*.

Several more explosions swept away the remainder of the MPF's star fighters, leaving their alien counterparts to focus their attention on the countless satellites that orbited the Earth. Multiple strike groups spread out around the planet and began a systematic elimination of the web of expensive technology, crippling most communication among the inhabitants below.

"We've lost both carriers, sir, and their full complement of fighters," Jensen reported as he stared dully at the mass of enemy holograms that overwhelmed the tactical display. "We've also lost the Black Lance. Lieutenant Hunter managed to survive, but he's been rushed to sickbay with serious injuries."

Jonathon stared quietly out the windows, almost numb to the casualty reports that had been coming in far too frequently. Though he was ready to accept his own death, he was baffled by the fact that he was even still alive. *Why is the Intimidator still functioning? If I was commanding the alien fleet, the Intimidator would have been my first target.*

"Lieutenant Chang, give me a damage report."

"We haven't sustained any damage, sir," Chang replied, looking surprised by his own words. "They haven't even fired a single shot in our direction."

"Interesting," Jonathon mumbled to himself before resuming his watch over the waning battle. He knew that sooner or later the aliens would focus their attention on the *Intimidator*, but only time would tell how cruel its onslaught would be.

"The *Endeavor* has been destroyed, along with…" Jensen sighed and powered down the tactical display. Having grown weary of reporting the fleet's losses, he walked back toward his command station. Jonathon sympathized and let him go, unchallenged.

Sweeping explosions rocked the area as the remaining destroyers met their doom. The *ICS Liberty*, *ICS Independence*, and *ICS Freedom* had been destroyed. The chaos soon subsided as the alien fleet temporarily ceased its genocidal activities, filling the region with an eerie calm. The *Intimidator* had stopped firing as well. Jonathon was waiting to see what the enemy had in store and which of their warships would become his final target. Though he knew little regarding the aliens, Jonathon was well educated in war and its universally constant tactics.

"Why aren't they attacking?" inquired Dead Eye.

"Because," Jonathon began, returning to his seat, "you don't attack a target that you intend to capture intact."

"Oh, I definitely don't like the sound of that."

"The admiral's right," Jensen added. "The *Intimidator's* a prime target and for the enemy to leave us alone like this can only mean they want prisoners…or worse."

"So what do we do now?" asked Chang.

"The same thing that we've been doing," Jonathon instructed. "We fight."

"Good," said Dead Eye. "Now, can someone please give me a target? We've got a lot of ammo to burn."

"Lieutenant Hayes," beckoned Jonathon, turning to face her, "send a priority communication to General O'Connor. Tell him…tell him we've fought with honor and done all that we can, but the burden of defending the Earth is now his to bear." Realizing how quiet the room had become, how much of the command staff's attention had been diverted his way, Jonathon spoke one last statement that was intended as much for them as it was for O'Connor. "And let him know that our final act of service will be to make that burden a little lighter."

"Understood," Kate replied softly, her eyes lingering on Jonathon's face. She could sense the personal surrender taking place behind his resilient soldier's mask, and she sympathized. I've always felt safe onboard the *Intimidator*, almost invincible, she remembered confessing to him during their last meal together. But with the prospects of one final, glorious battle bearing down on her, she felt little more than vulnerable.

"We've got a hostile warship approaching on an attack vector," Chang announced. "Looks like we've found our target."

Jonathon zeroed in on the merged alien monstrosity that was encroaching on the *Intimidator's* position and said, "Gunners, bring all weapons to bear on the approaching vessel and fire at will. Don't hold anything back."

Lashing out with all its might, the *Intimidator* hammered the shields of its surprisingly restrained target. The alien vessel took the beating for a short time before discharging a thin blue energy beam that struck the forward shields of the spirited flagship. As the beam intensified, a concentrated ring of energy straddled it, increasing in size before slamming into its target. The protective force field enveloping the *Intimidator* flickered dramatically, then burned out.

"Shields are offline," Jensen reported. "They must have hit us with an electromagnetic pulse."

"The enemy vessel has sustained only minor damage," Chang announced, glancing over at Jonathon. He was searching for guidance, for that one elusive strategy that would somehow give the *Intimidator* an edge. But the look Jonathon lobbed back confirmed what Chang had been reluctant to accept. The *Intimidator's* fate was almost entirely in the hands of the enemy.

"I'm detecting a massive energy surge from the alien vessel," Jensen interrupted, his muscles tensing, his eyes glued to his sensor readout.

"Do something!" implored one of the junior officers on the lower deck, but it was too late.

A second energy ring collided with the *Intimidator's* hull, sending electrical arcs all around the defiant warship. The mighty beast of war had been declawed.

"The reactor's offline," Jensen grumbled from the darkness. "We're defenseless."

Jonathon scowled at the alien warship as it soared over the bridge and out of view. The aliens had defeated him in battle and denied him escape through an honorable death. And he was certain they were coming for him and his crew. He could feel their hatred and it made him shudder.

"Lieutenant Chang, gather your security officers and prepare for an enemy boarding party. I *do not* want any member of this crew becoming a prisoner of war."

"Yes, sir."

"Gather the ship's personnel into tight, defensible areas and arm them with every weapon that can be spared. You can use your communicators to maintain contact between groups. Once your forces are in place, return to the bridge with a complement of pulse rifles. We'll make our stand here."

"Understood, Admiral," said Chang, grabbing a portable light from one of the junior officers who had begun handing them out. "I'm heading to the armory now."

As the wieldy lights brushed aside the darkness, Chang made his way toward the emergency escape hatch near the elevator tube. The small door was tugged away, exposing the ladder. Grabbing hold of both sides, he jumped down into the pool of shadows and proceeded to carry out his assigned tasks.

Tremors soon rumbled through the ship as it slowed unnaturally.

"They must've latched onto us," Parker commented nervously, his eyes bouncing from one window to the next. "What are they—?"

The *Intimidator* jerked unexpectedly hard and rotated until a view of the Earth consumed the forward windows. Then the vibrations stopped, leaving the disabled warship completely still and its crew sufficiently spooked.

"Anyone else feel like we've just been given front row seats to a public execution?" Dead Eye blurted out while staring at the Earth. Nobody responded, though everyone agreed with him.

Dragging his feet as he walked, Jonathon headed over to the forward balcony and peered out, looking more dejected than ever. He quietly cursed the aliens for sparing him. Having to bear witness to whatever cruel acts they were planning for his crew and the rest of humanity was, in Jonathon's opinion, a fate far worse than death.

Kate walked up beside Jonathon and laid her head on his shoulder. Gently wrapping one arm around her, he tried to provide what little comfort he could as she began to cry.

Chapter 10
Ashes to Ashes

Standing atop a majestic mountain, Jonathon admired the breathtaking view. Down beyond the rolling plains and forests he could see a sprawling city, with its remarkable skyscrapers dotting the landscape. The tranquil scene helped ease the grueling effects of the unusually hot noonday sun. Reaching up with one hand, he wiped away the beads of sweat from his forehead and glanced up at the clear sky. Just then, the sun started moving, arcing swiftly toward the horizon. And as it set near the bustling metropolis, its descent slowed, painting the sky in vivid, fiery colors.

The fading daylight brought an unseasonably chilling breeze that roamed across the mountaintop, sending shivers through Jonathon's body. He folded his arms snugly against his midsection in an effort to keep warm while watching the sun vanish behind the jagged skyline. Suddenly, the fiery sunset transitioned into a wave of blood that washed across the entire firmament. A new nightmare was beginning to take form.

As the gentle wind became colder still, an ominously low voice thundered through the air, speaking in an unfamiliar tongue. "Ish Drak'Rasha edrox'ta, jorshu'qui mortalum un killraxun ra tox orlaban. Retamba preta hes gorgon."

The soft breeze strengthened into a commanding wind, perturbing the bloodied sky while blackened clouds formed directly overhead, swirling and rumbling as they stampeded across the heavens. Though vulnerable, Jonathon held his ground, focusing his attention on the funnel cloud that descended a fair distance in front of him. The bottom of the voracious twister curved toward him and morphed into the head of a snarling dragon. Expanding its ferocious mouth, the vaporous creature exhaled a powerful growl that shook Jonathon to his core. The resulting gust of wind tore away the medals and ribbons that adorned his military jacket, removing every last symbol, every testament of his courage. The three gold bars along his collar were ripped free as well, stripping him of all visible power and authority until he resembled nothing more than a common mortal. Growling incessantly, the head of the turbulent beast ascended until the tempest became its wings. It soared across the sky, leaving darkness in its wake—violent, loathsome darkness.

Realizing that he had slipped into another induced dream, Jonathon seized the opportunity to try to communicate with the alien presence that was contacting him. With his head raised, he shouted into the wind. "The destruction of your star system was a terrible accident, a mistake for which I am willing to atone. Stop this madness now and spare this world. Further bloodshed is not the answer. We can find a peaceful solution—"

The thunderous voice drifted across the wind once more, repeating its previous message, but with a soft, hissing echo that spoke in words that Jonathon could understand. "The Dark God approaches, bringing death and destruction to this world. Tremble before his power."

Plenipotent bolts of lightning pierced the veiling shadows, drawing Jonathon's attention toward the distant city. With his heart pounding and his eyes undistracted, he bore witness to the streaks of blue fire that rained down on the Earth, scorching everything in their path. The searing flames roared across the landscape, which itself began to tremble and fragment, reducing the city to nothing more than rubble and ashes. Even its population had diminished, leaving behind a shrill chorus of ghostly screams that lingered in the air and grew fainter over time. The Earth was becoming desolate.

Outraged that his plea had been ignored, Jonathon shouted toward the heavens once again. "If you destroy this world I'll find a way to strike back. I'll—"

The mountain shook with tremendous force, rebuffing Jonathon's bold words and sending him stumbling hard onto the ground. A cylindrical tower erupted out of the rocks in front of him, climbing high above the mountaintop until it nearly touched the clouds. Its dark, mirror-like exterior reflected the ravaged landscape that continued to burn around it.

Though shaken and bruised, Jonathon rose defiantly to his feet and studied the alien edifice for a moment, staring at his shadowy, faceless reflection along its eerie surface. Creeping forward at a cautious pace, he drew closer to the tower until he heard the commanding voice and its companion echo drift across the wind once more. "Ish ledgegon ven mani pax jel onlo matray: The knowledge of man shall be no more."

At that precise moment, Jonathon's reflection changed into the ghostly image of a pale-skinned old man. Reaching his bony hands out of the tower, the elderly figure latched onto Jonathon's arms. His cold, clammy grip was like a steel trap, immovable and crushing, preventing Jonathon from escaping, though he did struggle. The old man's eyes had rolled back into his head, as if he was unconscious, yet he remained focused on Jonathon's terrified expression.

"Don't let them take me," the old man pleaded in a frail, wispy voice. "I don't want to forget. I don't want to be forgotten." Without uttering another word, the elderly figure released his grip and faded back into the shadows that danced around the surface of the tower.

A familiar, soothing voice suddenly called Jonathon's name. Feeling a warm presence draw near, he spun around, but saw only the molested landscape. He was alone, hopelessly encircled in flames, yet death had stayed its hand. Puzzled, he took a step toward the fires that threatened to reduce him to ashes, but the hungry flames withdrew from his presence as if afraid of his touch.

The soft voice called Jonathon's name again.

"Jon," Kate whispered, kneeling down beside him. "Wake up."

Jonathon's eyes popped wide open and he sat up straight against the wall, flush with panic.

Realizing that she had inadvertently startled him, Kate grabbed hold of his arms to try to calm him. "Whoa. Relax, Jon. It's just me."

"Kate, what's going on? What happened?"

"You dozed off a little while ago. Are you all right?"

"I had a bad dream is all," Jonathon replied in a tired voice, feeling as if he hadn't gotten any rest at all. "I didn't mean to fall asleep, but I just couldn't seem to keep my eyes open."

"Don't worry, you didn't miss anything."

Pushing himself up from the floor, Jonathon rose quicker than expected. His weightless body tilted forward and right into Kate's arms. "Gravity's still out, huh?"

"Yup," she replied, helping him regain his balance.

"Any word on when the reactor will be back online?"

"We can talk about that later. You'd better look out the window."

With the magnetic soles of his boots keeping him grounded to the catwalk, Jonathon turned around and stood in front of the main window, still holding onto Kate for support, both physical and emotional.

"The fleet started moving again before I woke you," said Kate, pointing out at the source of her concern. "We haven't the slightest idea what they're up to. Their ships had just been drifting around us without any sort of activity at all, despite having gone out of their way to leave us intact. I guess I should be relieved, but in all honesty it's got me spooked."

"This doesn't make any sense," Jonathon responded, squinting suspiciously at the nearest alien vessel. "Why would they rampage across the system and then just stop?" The answer came to him as he remembered the gist of his disturbing dream. "They must be waiting for *him,*" he mumbled.

"Waiting for who?" Kate asked. "What are you talking about?"

Placing one hand on the glass to stabilize himself, Jonathon sidestepped to his left, away from the other officers that had been drawn to the scenery outside the windows. Pulling Kate closer, he whispered into her ear. "Do you remember when I told you about the nightmares I used to have as a child?"

"Yeah, why?"

"They weren't just dreams. At first they seemed like the usual kind of nightmares your average kid would have after overhearing adults talk about the latest murder in the news. But there was one night in particular that changed everything. On the eve of my eighth birthday, I had a dream in which I saw a man sneaking into Greg McGuire's house. He was my best friend at the time. Well, the guy accidentally knocked a glass picture frame onto the floor, waking Greg's parents. His father came into the family room and startled the burglar, who turned and shot him. I woke up screaming and my dad came into my bedroom to try to calm me down. He kept telling me that it was only a dream, but I wouldn't listen. I just couldn't accept that. And once I heard the police cruisers rush over our house, I had the most awful feeling come over me. I begged my dad to take me to Greg's place and he did, figuring it'd help calm me down. Well, by the time we arrived, police officers had already secured the area and were taking a man into custody on charges of murder. I'll never forget that man's face. He was the same guy from my dream.

"I was never able to understand how or why the nightmares occurred and I think they might have been the reason my biological parents abandoned me when I was little. Fortunately, after a few years had passed, the dreams just stopped, enabling me finally to lead a normal life."

"I take it the dreams have come back?"

"Yes, but it's different this time. Our encounter with the aliens has awakened something inside me, Kate. I see strange visions not only of the present, but also the future and they seem to be growing stronger. And while I don't fully understand what's going on, one thing is clear: the aliens have no intention of backing down. They're preparing to strike the Earth in force, but they're waiting for—"

"Check it out," Dead Eye shouted, pointing off to the right, toward a cluster of ships that were located less than two kilometers from the *Intimidator*. "They're scattering like something scared 'em off."

"What's going on, Jon?" Kate said with an edge of fear.

"I'm not sure," Jonathon mumbled, inching toward the starboard window and staring out into the empty space that had been left behind by the alien fleet. The stars within that region started to fade away, leaving a blackened void. Overcome by a steadily escalating sense of foreboding, Jonathon seemed unaware of the vibrations that had begun to rumble through the *Intimidator* as the space outside was perturbed.

Clasping Jonathon's arm, Kate felt his muscles tense, triggering a raise in her level of anxiety as well. "What is it,

Jon?" she pleaded, almost demanded, though not so loudly as to draw too much attention.

But Jonathon remained silent, hearing only the heavy thumping of his own heartbeat. A cold shiver shot through his body, ahead of the low-rumbling voice that had returned from his haunting dreams. It echoed a familiar, disturbing message, though Jonathon was the only one who heard it. *"Retamba preta Drak'Rasha'sa gorgon:* Tremble before the Dark God's power."

The statement was followed by the image of a ferocious black dragon that flashed through Jonathon's mind, startling him to such a degree that he jerked his muscles out of reflex.

"Jon? What is it?" Kate pleaded in a progressively panicked tone. "What's out there?"

Turning his head, Jonathon looked into her eyes and said, "You don't want to know."

A vast tenebrous void had formed in the vacated region of space beyond the *Intimidator*, repelling even the sun's warming rays from its blackened boundaries. Unnatural flashes of crimson light emanated from within the abyss, like bolts of lightning in a raging storm. With each luminous burst, the fleshy exterior of a colossal warship flashed into view, displaying an eerily shifting pattern of shadows that slithered across the hull.

The main body of the ominous vessel was approximately twenty kilometers in length, though its exact shape was difficult to discern against the blackness and even seemed to shift subtly. But it was its appearance more than its size that inspired so much terror. Its dark and gnarled hull was bristling with curved spikes of various sizes, some larger than even the *Intimidator*, and all appeared as if they had torn through the dense organic casing. Further examination revealed small clusters of tentacles that were tangled among the sharpened protrusions, probing the darkness around the vessel with great vigor.

"What in creation is that?" Jensen uttered while peering though a pair of digital binoculars. He scanned the surface of the gigantic warship and upon making an unexpectedly gruesome discovery, he jerked his head back. His eyes had witnessed something he wished they hadn't, yet his morbid curiosity persuaded him to look again.

"You'd better take a closer look at that ship, Admiral," he advised before flinging the binoculars toward Jonathon.

Reaching over with one hand, Jonathon snatched the hovering device out of the air and quickly complied. With each flash of lightning inside the void, he was able to clearly see the ghastly images. The hull of the dreadful warship was comprised of an innumerable host of bodies, most of which appeared humanoid in form while others had rather exotic shapes. The blackened carcasses were meshed together in a chaotic pattern. And though they all appeared to be dead, Jonathon wasn't so sure that was the case. He heard a host of screams stampede through his mind, as if the tormented souls of those imprisoned individuals were crying out for help.

"Do you see them?" Jensen inquired, verifying that he wasn't going mad.

"How could I not?" Jonathon confirmed with an edge of disgust. Lowering the binoculars, he glanced over at Jensen and said, "It looks like there are no limits to the atrocities our enemy's willing to commit."

"You think that…thing is part of their fleet? They seem to be frightened of it, judging by the distance they're maintaining."

"I don't blame them. It gives me the creeps as well."

"What are you guys talking about?" Dead Eye interrupted. The unusual topic of conversation had his curiosity piqued.

"See for yourself," said Jonathon, tossing the binoculars to Dead Eye.

After raising them to his eyes, his jaw dropped. "Whoa. That ain't right. That ship looks like it's made out of dead bodies."

"What?" Chang exclaimed. "Give me those." Reaching in with one hand, he yanked the binoculars from his friend's clutches, pulling Dead Eye off balance, and used them to verify the claim with his own two eyes. "That's barbaric. Darin, you've got to see this."

Parker quietly shook his head and toddled back to his command station. He had seen enough already.

"Look," Kate interrupted, pointing out the starboard window. "Those two merged vessels are approaching that...whatever it is."

The adjoined warships crept toward the abyss at a cautious, almost hesitant pace, stopping outside its oscillating boundaries. There they lingered like a pair of timid servants that stood fearfully before their cruel master, bracing for the worst. It came. A red energy pool formed near the midsection of the colossal warship, prompting the starboard vessel of the merged pair to make a hasty exodus. So swift and desperate was its attempt to flee that it tore several of the adjoined tentacles in the process. The vessel managed to veer away as a searing energy beam struck its idle companion, triggering a dramatic explosion that consumed the entire warship. The resulting shock wave slammed into the retreating vessel and shredded its aft section. Damaged and burning, the ravaged warship drifted a little further before exploding in a brilliant burst of light, even releasing a shock wave of its own that caused the *Intimidator* to tremble.

"What just happened?" Dead Eye inquired, gripping the railing until the shock wave had passed.

"Hard to say," answered Jonathon, "but I wouldn't be surprised if it was some form of punishment. After all, we did manage to destroy several of their warships and repel their initial invasion. That had to have angered someone. But at any rate, it appears their brutality extends to their own people as well."

"Oh, that's just great!" said Dead Eye. "We would have to get into a fight with the species from hell."

"Looks like the fleet's moving again," Jensen announced, getting everyone's attention.

The alien warships systematically encircled the Earth, gathering in large clusters above each of the densely populated continents. And there they waited, poised to strike. But the first shot wasn't theirs to take. It came in the form of a strange, turbulent black sphere that had been launched from the menacing capital ship within the abyss. The peculiar warhead streaked toward the Earth's tranquil atmosphere and, upon penetrating the soft white clouds, exploded in a sharp flash of lightning. Dark thunderheads formed soon after, twisting and rumbling as they spread across the Earth like a plague.

General O'Connor was stationed atop a prominent hill within a wooded area outside of New York City, laying in wait with his handpicked squad of four marines collectively designated Alpha One. They were all armored in light-grade, camouflaged battle suits and helmets, affording them a decent amount of protection while still providing a great deal of mobility—a theme accentuated by the compact jetpacks that were fastened to the backs of each soldier's form-fitting armor. With the aid of their jetpacks, the squad would be able to move quickly from one area to the next while avoiding any dependence on vehicles. It was an advantage that would no doubt prove useful, should the aliens decide to test their mettle in a ground war.

The general blended in fairly well with the terrain and his squad. He had always preferred to be on the battlefield rather than simply directing the action from the safety of a secured military installation. He truly thrived in a combat environment, but that was only one of the factors in his decision to deploy with his troops. O'Connor was well versed in the history of war, from the ancient Greeks on up and he greatly admired those military leaders who had stood shoulder to shoulder with their compatriots in battle. It was partially about honor, but more than that, he would gain invaluable insights into the nature of the enemy and the ebbs and flows that fed the tides of war—the kind of information that was difficult to absorb from digitized battle reports.

During the engagement between the alien armada and Jonathon's fleet, O'Connor had ordered all of Earth's ground forces to divide into small groups and spread out around the globe, increasing their chances of survival during the anticipated bombardment. They moved as much weaponry as possible, hiding armored vehicles near major cities and scattered throughout the surrounding terrain. It was a defensive move, but O'Connor and his top advisors weren't satisfied to remain in a defensive mindset for long. They would go on the offensive as soon as the time was right, or at least, that was their hope.

O'Connor was passing the time by polishing the third-generation Bowhouzer sniper rifle that lay across his lap. Its combination of a high-powered ultraviolet laser and precision targeting scope enabled skilled marksmen to snipe targets from an incredible distance without drawing unwanted attention to themselves. And although O'Connor was a little out of practice, he was still more than capable of giving even Dead Eye a run for his money.

His thoughts also strayed from time to time, wondering what fate had befallen Jonathon and his crew. Though communication with the *Intimidator* had been lost, certain forces within the military had been making use of special telescopes designed to monitor the alien fleet's activities and they had spotted the idle Juggernaut's predicament. News of its survival brought both comfort and concern—concern that the enemy was planning on extending the suffering of those individuals they didn't target directly.

The air was quiet and breezy, doing little to interrupt the somber mood that dominated each marine's thoughts. But a bone-jarring clap of thunder soon stole their attention. The violent storm front was swiftly approaching New York, darkening the blood-red sky that had been stained by the setting sun.

"What in the world..." one of the soldiers uttered, staring up at the rolling thunderheads. Flashes of lightning reflected off his dark, bewildered eyes as the storm's shadow fell upon him. Feeling vulnerable, the middle-aged major grabbed his helmet off a nearby rock and slid it over his head, all the while keeping his eyes fixed on the unearthly tempest.

The sergeant sitting next to him was every bit as jittery. "Where'd that storm come from?" he shouted, ducking a little while trying to talk over the noise of the commanding wind that had started to blow through. "I don't like this. I grew up in Tornado Alley and saw more storms than I cared to. But this...this couldn't possibly be a natural occurrence. There's just no way."

"I think you're right, Sergeant," O'Connor shouted back. "Though I'm at a loss as to how they're doing it, I think this storm was induced by the enemy. They must be using it as cover for their assault. Get the word out to all squadrons to keep their eyes open and brace for the worst. I don't want anyone caught unprepared."

"Yes, sir."

The sergeant retrieved the datapad from the right hip of his battle suit and broadcast O'Connor's message across the MPF's land-based Command and Control Network (CCN), which was integrated into the Hub.

"General," hollered the major, "we've got forest fires erupting all over from those lightning strikes. If Mother Nature doesn't let up, we may need to relocate."

"Negative. We have to hold our ground as long as we can, Major. We can't risk moving until we know what the enemy's up to."

The major nodded in response before dropping to one knee and initiating a scan of the surrounding area. He was keeping an eye out for anything out of the ordinary, anything alien.

"Sergeant," O'Connor called out. "Contact the fire department of the town that's a few klicks to the west and have them dispatch any dousing drones they can spare to our position. We need to get these fires under control."

"You got it, sir."

Staring up at the rumbling tempest, O'Connor felt uneasy about their worsening situation. The superiority of the aliens' technology was a nightmare in and of itself, but with Mother Nature having turned traitor and allied herself with the enemy, O'Connor found himself debating whether he and his forces would survive the night, let alone mount any meaningful resistance.

"God help us all."

The command staff onboard the *Intimidator* stood in stunned silence, staring out the windows at their unrecognizable home world. Earth was completely shrouded in darkness and surrounded by hostile warships. It was a sight to dishearten even the bravest soldier.

"I can't even imagine what it must be like down there," said Dead Eye.

"The worst is yet to come," Jonathon interjected, despondent over the realization that his prophetic dream was coming true. He didn't have to imagine the nightmare the inhabitants of Earth were about to experience. He had already seen it and the images were forever burned into his mind.

"Admiral," Jensen shouted, peering through the binoculars, "something's descending out of the warships." After a brief moment, he lowered the binoculars and discarded them in Jonathon's direction. Then, while bowing his head against the cold window, he uttered one last statement. "The bombing's started."

Jonathon snatched the binoculars and peered furiously at the alien fleet, watching them rain thousands of their death-filled spheres down on the Earth. The cold-blooded rejection of his dream-spoken plea to end the war was now cemented in reality. Angered and disgusted, he turned and threw the binoculars at the rear wall, shattering them along with the remaining sliver of delusional hope that he had clung to—the hope of preventing the weight of more innocent lives from being added to the albatross of responsibility that already hung around his neck. Back to the captain's chair he trudged, powerless to do anything about the unfolding apocalypse.

Feeling alone and dejected, Kate folded herself and slumped below the window, down onto the unsympathetic catwalk. She pressed back against the wall, keeping her body from bobbing, and placed her hands over her dolesome face, trying to defend herself from the cruel reality that was bearing down on her. It did little good. Her thoughts turned to her parents, and realizing that she would most likely never see them again, she wept.

The rest of the command staff broke down emotionally as well, flooding the room with their angry, grievous outbursts. Many of the officers turned away from the windows, unable to watch any further destruction without losing all control of their emotions. And one of them did lose control. A junior officer on the lower deck tottered toward the center of the room and vomited, having become sick to his stomach. His liquefied projection of despair drifted through the air, unhindered by gravity, and splattered against the starboard wall while he clung to the base of his command station, coughing and sputtering before bursting into tears.

Fierce winds raced through the darkened streets of New York City, pushing against the panicked mobs that were desperately trying to flee certain destruction. Even though orders had been given to evacuate the populous capital, a significant number of people had chosen to remain, congesting the residential districts with their stubborn and foolish defiance. Martial law no longer governed the region. It had deteriorated into the law of the jungle, with the terrified inhabitants heeding only their individual sense of self-preservation, pummeling and shoving their way into the streets in an effort to steal safe passage aboard any personal or public hover-transports within reach. They trampled those who weren't fortunate enough to keep pace with the frenzied masses. And many others were killed simply because they occupied one of the coveted seats onboard the inadequate supply of transportation. Not a single bomb had impacted, yet the work of death had already commenced.

Rectangular transports of every size and color engaged their antigravity engines and lifted off, floating a stunted distance above the heads of the infuriated masses left behind. They raced through the streets and shed those individuals who had clung to the roofs and sides of the low-flying vehicles, discarding them like garbage onto the unruly crowds.

Pernicious bolts of lightning began discharging throughout the city, setting the skyline ablaze. One building after another was ignited, burning in the night sky like fuses on a massive powder keg. A resounding explosion soon thundered from the western edge of the city as an aging nuclear power plant was struck by the fury of the storm, setting off a chain reaction within the system of transformers that had maintained a steady flow of electricity to the power-hungry metropolis. The capital was plunged further into darkness, drawing what little light it could from the eerie glow of the towering infernos that burned unchallenged and the unpredictable light show that flashed high above.

Amidst the madness, standing alone atop the concrete steps of City Hall, was a lively old man, dressed in dirty, ragged clothing and clutching a worn-out black book against his chest. A long, bushy beard hung from his bony face and the fury of God seemed to burn within his eyes, strengthening the words he bore energetically from his soul. "You cannot hide from his wrath! God has seen your sins and sent the destroying angel to punish you. Judgment Day has come to the wicked. Repent of your immoral acts or burn in the fires of hell." The wind and lightning strikes grew fiercer, magnifying the power of the elderly man's words as he continued his tirade. "The devil has abandoned his followers. Turn away from his dark path before the Almighty Lord strikes you down."

The self-proclaimed mouthpiece of God continued to condemn everyone within shouting distance, especially the cluster of transports that had begun racing past him, trying to cheat death. He cursed them vehemently and smiled sadistically when, as if in answer to his prayers, a bolt of lightning struck the engine of one of the vehicles, triggering an explosion that sent the burning transport crashing down into the congested streets. Many innocent people were killed in the impact.

Viewing the smoldering wreckage as the handiwork of God, the old man continued shouting his prophetic message. "The end of the world is at hand and only the righteous shall be saved. You cannot escape your judgment. Now listen and bear witness to the thunderous voice of your God—"

A streaking ball of fire impacted near the crash site, jolting dozens of people to the ground and interrupting the old man's train of thought. Curious about the strange object that had rained down from the heavens, he hobbled down the steps, drawing closer to the smoldering crater.

"What strange gift is this, Lord?" he mumbled, staring inquisitively at the black orb. A blinding flash of light suddenly burst out from the alien sphere, followed by a compression wave that forced a wide area of the street to sink. The old man fell hard on the cement walkway, groaning in pain from the intense gravitational forces that were crushing his fragile body. Hundreds of neighboring citizens fell upon the earth as well, unable to escape the extreme forces that overwhelmed them.

Their bones shattered, their internal organs burst, and their lives vanished as their bodies were dragged toward the impact site. The disfigured carcasses collided with the alien sphere, collapsing into a swirling vortex of organic matter that was joined by debris from the transport wreckage. Even the grandiose stone pillars that decorated the face of City Hall cracked and crumbled down into the street. Nothing seemed capable of escaping the alien weapon's appetite for destruction.

Another of the deadly warheads plummeted through the top of an enormous skyscraper near the heart of the city and descended several stories until it lodged between a set of floor braces. As its extreme gravitational field was activated, creaks and moans resonated through the building's framework before a substantial section imploded. The upper floors of the towering edifice leaned forward and crashed to the ground, burying two smaller buildings in the process. Then, with gravity as its slave, the alien weapon descended through the destabilizing structure, forcing each floor that it passed through to collapse inward and crumble, adding to the devastation that already blanketed the surrounding area.

The fate of the rest of the city was no different. One building after another collapsed as if an earthquake of unbelievable magnitude had struck. Scores of the city's inhabitants were obliterated in the concrete hailstorm, leaving dense walls of smoke and dust that quieted all but a smattering of the screams that continued to pierce the surrounding darkness.

O'Connor and his squad looked on in disbelief as the once-proud metropolis, which had miraculously survived the Third World War, was leveled within a matter of minutes. And with the squad's attention so completely focused on the smoldering horizon, they soon found themselves startled by a stray warhead that impacted only a few hundred meters from their position, forming a considerable depression in the earth. The surrounding trees bent and fell toward the center of the unnatural disturbance, creating a new clearing in the process. And even though Alpha One was encamped at the limits of the weapon's range, each marine felt as if their skin was crawling, due to the artificially induced forces that tugged at their bodies. Back down the hill they crept, away from the bombardment but in direct view of the wind-fueled fires that continued to advance on their position.

"General, we've got to fall back to a safer location," his second in command pleaded.

"And go where, Major? There's nowhere to hide from this kind of assault. No, we make our stand here."

Nodding reluctantly, the major turned his attention skyward, searching for any stray bombs that might threaten him and his squad. He knew O'Connor was right, but that did little to change how vulnerable he felt, how afraid he was.

The last of the warheads streaked through the blackened heavens and impacted against the side of the Statue of Liberty, one of mankind's greatest and longest-enduring symbols of freedom. The midsection of the statue buckled in several places before shattering inward, along its right side, leaving the top half of the towering figure to tip forward and fold awkwardly, almost apologetically, onto the island below. Lady Liberty had fallen.

Though the storm raged on, the bombardment of New York City ceased almost as quickly as it had begun. Its lofty buildings were gone, its economic might reduced to a cipher, and its population brutalized and decimated. The city had, in effect, been reduced to nothing more than a memory.

O'Connor crawled back up the hill and surveyed the damage. "We need to get emergency personnel in there to search for survivors," he yelled back to his stunned communications liaison. "Sergeant, I gave you an order!"

"Huh?" the sergeant mumbled, snapping out of his trance. "Sorry, sir. I'll send in a request for medical aid right away."

Like his companions, O'Connor had known the bombardment would happen, yet the outcome was still difficult to bear. The images of the devastation on Mars were still fresh in his mind, but even they paled in comparison to what he had just witnessed. Such utter destruction was overwhelming, almost debilitating. Even so, O'Connor knew he had to press on. His troops were depending on him for their survival, as was the rest of humanity.

After a moment of silence, O'Connor turned to face the others and said, "I doubt this is the end of the enemy's assault. If they're determined to extinguish our civilization, they'll have to send down ground forces to hunt for survivors. And when they do, we'll be ready for them. Stay vigilant. I don't want any enemy units slipping through that cloud cover unnoticed."

"Understood, Boss," said one of the lieutenants, while her compatriots simply nodded and looked skyward. Pressing a tiny button on the side of her helmet, she caused a thin transparent visor to slide down and mask her entire face. Then another button was tapped, tinting her visor a dark shade of green as its night vision mode was activated. She started scanning the hostile sky as ordered, but her thoughts were scattered, wondering how many other cities had suffered the same fate as New York.

All across the Earth the alien assault had ravaged the helpless population, plunging the entire planet into chaos. The combination of the supernatural storm and deadly munitions created a cataclysmic situation from which few could escape.

Along the western seaboard of North America, many of the enemy's bombs fell near sensitive coastal fault lines, triggering unforgiving earthquakes that magnified the severity of the bombardment. Entire oceanfront cities crumbled, with the lowest portions submerging beneath an onslaught of tidal waves, drowning those people who had managed to survive the initial blitz. Earthquakes also thundered throughout Asia and the Middle East, leveling the smaller cities and towns that had been spared from a direct assault.

Volcanic eruptions dotted the Central and South American landscape as the intense gravitational fields from the alien bombs perturbed the magma within the bellies of the sleeping giants, spreading an explosive sea of fire that transformed the landscape.

The relentless global storm also induced sprawling hurricanes that dominated the oceans, as well as voracious tornadoes that rampaged across the embattled landscape.

Within half an hour the enemy bombardment, combined with the wrath of Mother Nature, had molested the entire planet, leaving mankind facing the threat of extinction for the first time in recorded history.

Chapter 11
Dissension in the Ranks

Jonathon sat quietly in his chair with his right foot pressed against the railing in front of him, keeping his weightless body in check. He was content, for the time being, to remain in self-imposed isolation. His eyes simply stared up at the dull ceiling, intentionally avoiding the alien-polluted scenery that filled every window. Many officers in his command stuff were following suit, though they had the luxury of closing their eyes to shut out reality. Jonathon couldn't do such a thing, or rather, he didn't dare. The last time he closed his eyes he got a lot more than he had bargained for.

Glimmers of blue light suddenly danced across the ceiling, directly in Jonathon's field of view. Shifting his eyes toward the brightening starboard windows, he witnessed the spawning of a new wormhole. "They must've run out of bombs," he muttered to himself, his anger simmering.

"Admiral," Jensen called out from the right-most portion of the forward balcony. "There's something unusual coming through the wormhole. It's some manner of starship, but different from those we've already encountered."

Jensen's observations had caught Jonathon's attention, persuading him to drift upright from his chair and slog over to the few officers who were still peering out the windows at the extraterrestrial newcomer.

The alien vessel seemed to stretch on forever as it progressed steadily out of the wormhole. It was roughly of a rectangular form and about as wide as the warships, but significantly longer. It was also fashioned from the same organic material, complete with dozens of large talons that curved out above and below the vessel in mirrored rows along each side. A blackened, serrated strip rose from the center of the vessel, stretching from bow to stern. But it was the underside of the ship that proved most intriguing. There, dangling from its belly by a web of tentacles, were about one hundred hefty, cylindrical objects that appeared to be based on organic technology as well—objects that vaguely resembled the tower from Jonathon's dream.

As the alien vessel cleared the wormhole, an identical companion ship followed in its wake. The second phase of the alien invasion was clearly underway.

"What are those?" inquired Jensen, even though he knew full well that nobody had the answer.

"Looks like some sort of transport convoy," Dead Eye commented.

"That much is obvious," Jensen replied snidely, "but what are they transporting?"

"Infantry, for their ground invasion," Jonathon opined. "They're probably going to hunt down and exterminate the remaining survivors."

Most of the other officers quieted down, realizing that Jonathon was probably correct. Jensen, however, disagreed with Jonathon's assessment and made a point of being vocal about it. "You don't know that," he countered, staring at Jonathon. "They could be preparing to strip-mine the planet or—"

"They've only demonstrated one purpose since they arrived in our system, Commander, and that's to eradicate our species. We destroyed the Polaris System, so they've come here to return the favor. Isn't that how war works?"

"What makes *you* such an expert on their behavior?" Jensen snarled, sounding intent on starting a fight even though the topic of discussion didn't warrant a heated debate.

Kate snapped out of her depressed state of mind and stood up beside Jonathon, wobbling a bit until she grabbed the railing for support. She listened to the verbal exchange, or, more specifically, listened for an opportunity to interject, even diffuse the argument.

"I didn't claim to be an expert," Jonathon replied. "I just think their intentions are obvious." Turning his head, he gazed out the window again as a means of indicating that he no longer cared to continue the debate, especially not with Jensen. But that decision wasn't entirely up to him.

"You know, none of this would have happened if you had supervised Operation Giant Leap properly," Jensen continued.

"What did you say?" Jonathon growled, swinging his head around and glaring at the commander. Though he had already contemplated the issue himself, the fact that Jensen had vocalized it really struck a nerve and Jensen knew it.

"You heard me. You should have ordered Dr. Nazarov to close the wormhole the instant it displayed signs of instability. Your poor judgment and lack of action has cost us—"

"Not even the scientists knew what was going to happen," Kate interrupted. "We were assigned to the job primarily for security reasons, not to provide guidance on a complicated experiment that only a handful of brainiacs understood. It was a scientific experiment. You can't blame—"

"That's the typical answer I'd expect from you," said Jensen with an edge of disgust. "Tell me, Lieutenant, who gives the orders when you climb into his bed?"

Kate was speechless, having been caught off guard by Jensen's personal attack. He had never outwardly expressed such contempt for her before, leaving her stunned. Then again, it wasn't really necessary for her to say anything since Jonathon was preparing a response of his own. Cocking his fist, he threw a punch that landed squarely against Jensen's nose. The commander fell back with such force that his boots were plucked free from their stabilizing bond with the floor, sending his body flying headfirst into the portside windows. Even Jonathon stumbled a bit, having thrown himself off balance with his own momentum.

Stepping out of the way, Kate permitted the other officers to ease between the two men and bring an end to the fisticuff, though a part of her felt that Jensen got exactly what he deserved.

"Come on, guys," Dead Eye pleaded. "The situation's bad enough as it is without us goin' at each other's throats."

Wiping away the sporadic droplets of blood that floated out through his nose, Jensen disregarded Dead Eye's plea for civility. He pushed off from the windows and lunged through the air, directly toward Jonathon. Everyone else had become irrelevant except for Chang, who wasn't about to be ignored.

Stepping in the way, the security chief gripped the railing with one hand while snatching a fistful of the commander's jacket with his other hand. In one well-timed maneuver, Chang had turned himself into an anchor, jerking Jensen to a stop and facedown onto the floor with a groan. He then stepped over the commander with one of his legs and used the resistance of his boots to maintain his leverage atop Jensen's back, restraining him like a common criminal under arrest.

"Get off me!" Jensen demanded, squirming between Chang and the floor.

"Not until you calm down," Chang insisted, tightening his hold.

Jensen wrestled one arm free and swung his elbow back into Chang's chest, knocking the lieutenant's nearest foot loose and sending his body pivoting awkwardly into one of the computer stations on the forward balcony. As Chang struggled to regain his balance, Jensen was free and clear and ready to seize the moment. But after pushing himself upright and cocking his clenched fist, he hesitated. Several officers were huddled beside Jonathon, protecting their leader more than they were restraining him.

"This isn't over," Jensen huffed, glaring spitefully at his superior. Turning partway around, he climbed atop a tactical display station, narrowly dodging Chang's outstretched tackle, and pushed off, soaring toward the emergency exit. The sealed hatch was hastily unlocked and yanked away, forcing one officer to duck as the metal disc hurled up into the air, bounced off the ceiling, and down into another officer's arms, knocking him back half a step into his command station. But Jensen didn't even notice. He simply snagged a portable light and pulled himself down into the darkness, mumbling an inaudible curse.

With Jensen gone, Jonathon calmed himself and looked into the weary yet trusting faces of the officers that remained faithfully beside him. "Do you all feel the same way?" he asked as the crowd dispersed a little, granting him his space.

"No, sir," Dead Eye replied without hesitation. "Kate's right. That mishap was way out of your control. And I'd bet you good money that if the commander had been in charge things wouldn't have ended up any different."

"I agree," Chang added, drifting upright and balancing against one of the computer stations. "You're a good man, Admiral, and we've always been behind you."

The other officers nodded in agreement.

"Thanks," said Jonathon. Though he appreciated their comments, he wasn't so sure he deserved their confidence.

"Don't pay any attention to Paul's outburst," Kate spoke, drawing closer to Jonathon. "He was just frustrated and felt the need to lash out at someone. He's always been a little cold to you."

"I know," Jonathon sighed. "Believe me, Kate, I understand perfectly well how he's feeling. I only wish I could do something to change all this."

Kate quickly searched her thoughts for anything that could help raise Jonathon's spirits, knowing that as an added bonus she'd most likely help herself feel better as well. "Did I ever tell you about my father's experience as a POW during the war?"

"I thought he finished out his career as a deck officer onboard the *Titan*?" Jonathon replied in a quizzical tone.

"He did, but during the battle of Gentry IX, one of the *Titan's* fighters was disabled near the trading hub. The fighting around the mining cluster had been pretty heavy that day."

"I remember reading the battle reports. We suffered our worst casualties during that engagement."

"Right. And according to my father, the *Titan* had suffered more than its fair share of losses. The crew was shorthanded and so he decided to take a shuttle out and go rescue the stranded pilot by himself. Well, they were both captured in the process and taken to Mars where my father spent four of the longest weeks of his life. And he had plenty of company while he was there. Most of the prisoners spent their free time fighting with the guards and taking a beating because of it. Or, as my father put it, they suffered an exceptional amount of unnecessary pain.

"He spent his time carefully studying his surroundings and the guards' daily routines and habits. Then, when the time was right, he organized a breakout. Though nobody onboard the *Titan* ever expected to see him again, he made it back in one piece and even brought back the pilot he had originally set out to rescue.

"My point, Jon, is that you may yet have your opportunity to get us out of this. Just be sure to keep the unnecessary pain to a minimum."

Jonathon smiled and although he didn't usually display affection on the bridge, he wrapped his arm around Kate's shoulder and gave her a soft kiss on the cheek.

Chapter 12
Slipping Away

Dead Eye looked on as the bow of yet another alien transport crept out from the mouth of the wormhole. The all-too-familiar sight had left him wondering if he'd ever see an end to the mounting alien presence. He longed to be at the controls of his weapons station again, feeling the warm touch of the command console as the ship's power hummed faithfully through its circuits and placed control of the *Intimidator's* awesome firepower at his fingertips. But as long as the ship was without power, so too, he felt, was he.

With a strong exhalation of his warm breath, Dead Eye fogged a small portion of the chilled window, partially obscuring the elongated alien vessel that loomed beyond. He then reached up with one hand and used his index finger to draw a targeting reticle across the hazy glass. "Bang, you're dead," he whispered as he watched the enemy transport move through his targeting sights unscathed.

Kate started to shiver, catching Jonathon's attention as her body vibrated against his. "It's getting cold in here," he commented, taking notice of the drop in temperature himself. "How long before the reactor's back online?"

"At least another couple of days, possibly a week," Kate replied. She crisscrossed her arms over her chest and cupped her elbows in her palms, as if bracing for the next shiver. "I guess the EMP burst really fried the reactor's circuits. Fortunately, the manual pumps for the oxygen converters are still working, so as long as we've got able-bodied crewmen to run them, we should have a sufficient oxygen supply."

"Where's Lieutenant Parker?" Jonathon asked, speaking more to the unseen lieutenant than to Kate.

"Back here, sir," he called out in his usual quiet voice. He was curled up in a fetal ball in his chair, pressing his feet against the front edge of his command station. Though such a position was commonly associated with that of frightened children, the lieutenant had curled up more for warmth and stability than anything else.

"Head down to the lower command level and retrieve some blankets and portable space heaters from the emergency supply kit. We're going to need them if the temperature keeps dropping."

"Yes, sir," Parker acknowledged while spinning a quarter turn in his chair and dropping his feet, waiting for his magnetic soles to hug the floor before rising. He then moseyed over to the stairs and down the steps to the lower command level where two junior officers stood waiting to assist him, having overheard the orders.

"Are you going to be okay?" Jonathon whispered to Kate, though he knew there was little he could do about it if her answer was "no."

"I'll survive," she whispered back. "Is there anything I can do to help out? I'd like to get my brain thinking about something else, anything besides what's going on out there."

"Actually, yeah. Go ahead and send out a general broadcast to all officers, asking them to ensure the rest of the crew is warm and has enough food for the night. And when you're done with that, see if Lieutenant Parker needs any help with the space heaters."

"That'll work."

Kate returned to her defunct command station, looking eager to resume her duties, though she really wasn't. She simply needed a diversion, something to distract her for a little while. It wasn't much, but she took it.

"And tell them to make use of flight suits as well, if there aren't enough blankets to go around," Jonathon added.

Kate nodded, but without looking back at Jonathon. Her eyes were fixed on her communicator, which was floating a fair distance above her head. She had left the item sitting atop her console prior to the artificial gravity going offline, and something had knocked it into high orbit around her command station. But it was a curiosity more than a problem. Stretching up until she was practically tiptoe, she snatched the communicator, slapped it around her wrist, and went about her business.

"I guess that's the last of their transports," Dead Eye reported as the lingering wormhole closed.

"It also looks as if their warships are being recalled," Jonathon observed while staring out at the scattering vessels, each departing the system through one of the many new wormholes that had spawned round about. "That must mean their bombing campaign is over."

Though the sight of the departing warships was welcomed, it did little to change the heavy mood that persisted. The Earth and its inhabitants had been forever changed, plunged into a dark age of historic proportions and nothing short of a miracle could spare them from further ignominy. Or at least, that was the growing consensus.

The convoy of twenty alien transports moved into a low orbit around the Earth, joining the five warships that had remained as watchdogs over the major geographic regions. Once in position, multiple incision-like slits appeared along the tops and sides of the transports, retracting into wide circular openings that permitted a steady stream of objects of varying size and shape to accelerate out, heading planetside in clusters.

"Are they launching fighters?" inquired Dead Eye, squinting at the distant entities.

Jonathon looked around for the binoculars before remembering that he had thrown them against the back wall in a fit of anger. There was little reason to regret that action though, since another pair was stored safely in the raised cabinets at the rear of the bridge. And so with a strong jump he sailed toward the back wall where he retrieved the spare binoculars before pushing off and embarking on the return trip. Dead Eye waited for him to approach, caught hold, and pulled him back down onto the forward balcony.

"Thanks," said Jonathon, securing his footing.

"No problem."

Raising the binoculars to his eyes, Jonathon studied the alien vessels for a moment prior to sharing his findings. "It looks like they might be launching shuttles, possibly troop transports. But there's something else out there—something really strange."

He took another few seconds to study the mysterious dark-blue objects before lowering the binoculars. "With the limited amount of intelligence we have on the aliens," he explained, glancing over at his companions, "it's impossible to tell what they're deploying,"

"Well," Chang pondered aloud, "if they are deploying ground forces, then I suppose the remaining warships are sticking around to serve as a support mechanism."

"I agree. And unfortunately, they've got total space superiority, so they'll be able to pick off any of our forces that move out into the open. General O'Connor and his troops are going to have a brutal fight on their hands."

"Yeah, but fighting on the ground should help equalize the battle somewhat," Dead Eye interjected. "The aliens' technology's pretty wicked, but they're deploying their soldiers on our home turf. We also have one other thing going for us."

"And what would that be?" Jonathon inquired, looking rather baffled.

"My cousin's stationed down there. I know you've never met him, sir, but I can promise you that he'll do some serious alien butt-kicking."

"Oh yeah," Chang agreed. "The brute's an army all by himself."

Jonathon cracked a barely perceptible smile, taking a modest degree of comfort in Dead Eye's remarks. The idea that one man could tip the odds in favor of Earth was absurd, of course, but it did drive home an important point: the military was full of similar individuals, equally brave and capable. Divided they would be little more than pestering insects to be swatted away, but united, and especially under O'Connor's command, they could mount stiff resistance and do a little swatting of their own.

"If your cousin's anything like you, Lieutenant, I'm sure he'll put up a good fight."

"I just wish I was down there with him," Dead Eye sighed, then became frustrated. "I really hate having to sit here on the sidelines."

"Amen to that," Chang agreed, peering out at the last of the enemy's deploying ground forces before they dove into the storm.

The sounds of Jonathon's beeping communicator interrupted the conversation. "Admiral, we've got a problem," said Tippits with a degree of urgency in his voice. The officers beside Jonathon immediately quieted down in order to listen in on the details.

"Go ahead," Jonathon replied, raising his wrist-comm a little.

"Someone just did a manual detach of one of our escape pods. But—"

"The escape pods are still working?" Dead Eye blurted out, sounding surprised. His voice was just loud enough for Tippits to overhear through the comm link, prompting a response.

"Well, see, that's the thing. The emergency systems on the pods are as fried as everything else onboard. I know because I was down there trying to salvage a few circuit boards to use with the reactor."

"How was it able to launch, then?" asked Jonathon.

"The launching mechanisms are spring mounted, not electrical. It's only a matter of releasing the clamps. The initial kick gets the pod away from the *Intimidator's* hull before the thrusters are supposed to fire. But without power, he's going to continue to drift until he either runs out of oxygen or—"

"He's spotted by the enemy," said Jonathon, finishing the statement that Tippits was reluctant to say. He took a few seconds to peer out the windows, keeping one eye on the enemy while trying to locate the wayward capsule. "Which side did he launch from?"

"Port side, sir, less than a quarter of the way across. Odds are the pod's momentum has already pushed him into view from your vantage point."

Lumbering over to the portside catwalk, Jonathon and his trailing entourage worked to spot the escape pod, which soon came into view as a small charcoal speck drifting steadily away from the ship.

"I think I see it," Dead Eye reported, pointing out at the cylindrical vagrant.

Shooting his eyes toward the alien vessels nearest the *Intimidator*, Jonathon verified that they were still holding position before resuming his communication with Tippits. "We need to get that AWOL crewman back," he ordered.

"I'm way ahead of you, Admiral. I've already contacted our search and rescue grunts and they should be suiting up for a spacewalk as we speak. It'll no doubt be a hazardous retrieval, but they didn't even flinch at the idea."

"Good. And it doesn't look like the enemy's detected the escape pod yet, so there's a chance they might be able to pull this off."

"Who's onboard that thing, anyway?" Chang inquired, using the digital binoculars to zoom in on the pod, which unfortunately, was oriented in such a way as to keep its small porthole window and its occupant's panicked face out of Chang's line of sight.

"I'm not sure who jettisoned the pod, sir," said Tippits. "I managed to catch a glimpse of his face before he sealed the hatch, but I didn't recognize him. He might have been one of the new crew transfers. He was definitely young, barely old enough to be onboard."

"Thanks for the heads up. Your quick action just might save his life."

"It was luck more than anything, sir. I simply happened to be in the right place at the right time. And I'll be sure to reseal the access door before heading back to the reactor, unless you want me to stay put for a while and guard—"

"No. I'll send down security to seal off the area. You've done enough already."

"Understood, sir. Tippits out."

As the communication link terminated, Jonathon turned toward his security chief and was about to issue an order when Chang preempted him, saying, "I'll get some of my men down there to secure the remaining pods, ASAP."

Jonathon nodded his acknowledgement and turned his attention back to the drama outside the windows.

"What's going on?" Kate inquired as she approached the group from the right, having placed the last of the small, rectangular space heaters atop the central tactical display station, being careful to secure its magnetic base so it wouldn't float away and accidentally burn anyone.

"One of the new guys freaked out and jumped ship in a defunct escape pod," Dead Eye replied rather bluntly while scooting past Kate so he could better soak up some of the warmth radiating from the space heater.

"Really?" said Kate, stepping into the vacant spot to the left of Jonathon and peeking out the windows, but she couldn't locate the capsule in question.

"In a nutshell, yeah," Jonathon replied, looking mildly annoyed with Dead Eye's less-than-sensitive summary of the situation. Using his index finger, he guided Kate's attention toward the escape pod. "Search and rescue should be—"

The sounds of his beeping communicator once again interrupted the conversation.

"This is Rescue Leader, reporting in," came a confident and masculine voice over Jonathon's wrist-comm. "Are we cleared to deploy, Admiral?"

"You're all clear, Rescue Leader," confirmed Jonathon, giving the region of space surrounding the capsule another visual once-over. "Get out there and bring that AWOL crewman back. We'll watch your back and keep an eye out for hostiles."

"Roger that, Admiral. Tag and grab underway."

The communication link terminated.

"You don't think the enemy's spotted him yet, do you?" Kate asked, her eyes still fixed on the tiny drifter. Like her companions beside her, even the junior officers on the lower deck who had begun to congregate near the portside windows, she had become immersed in the tension, the emotion of the moment. And she couldn't help but let her heart go out to whoever was onboard the pod, worrying that his rash decision to try to escape his virtual imprisonment onboard the *Intimidator* would end up costing him his life. The situation was, ironically enough, the very thing he had been trying to avoid.

"Not that we can tell," Jonathon responded. "They still seem preoccupied with their ground invasion, but it's only a matter of time before he shows up on their sensors."

Using one hand, he motioned for Chang to pass along the binoculars. And with them he performed a thorough scan of the nearest alien starships, all of which seemed deceptively still. Shifting the binoculars further to the right, he finally spotted some movement among the enemy. "Looks like they've started deploying the rest of their cargo," he reported, focusing everyone's attention in the direction he was looking.

Four of the cylindrical towers had dropped free from one of the transports and were descending planetside. Then two more disengaged from one of the furthest transports in view, followed by half a dozen that dropped from its neighboring companion, scattering to predetermined coordinates beneath the Earth's turbulent atmosphere. After a curious pause, more vessels deployed their towers, but only a few at a time, leaving the majority dangling in wait.

"What's up with that?" said Dead Eye, having returned to his position beside Chang. "Why'd they bring so many of those things if they're only droppin' off a few of 'em?"

"There goes some more," Chang observed. "It looks like they're only being called down as needed, maybe as extra support or…who knows."

"There's the rescue team," Parker chimed, inadvertently startling Kate a little. He hadn't been standing beside her for long, but his approach had been so quiet that she hadn't noticed him until he spoke up.

Turning his attention back the other way, Jonathon spotted the two-person rescue team. Both individuals were dressed in cautionary-yellow space suits and thrusting repeated bursts of blue exhaust out through their jetpacks. Slowly but surely they were gaining on the pod.

The command staff looked on in silence, watching what appeared to be a routine retrieval operation. As Jonathon had suggested, the enemy seemed preoccupied with their invasion efforts, leaving the rescue team to operate with a lesser degree of danger. Yet as Jonathon's eyes lingered on the capsule, he couldn't help but feel afraid. At first he thought simple concern for the isolated crewman had triggered an empathetic reaction, but the fear quickly escalated, became irrational. He even began to feel claustrophobic, as if he was the one trapped onboard the escape pod. And as his respiration began to quicken, he felt his heart pounding away until it resembled the sounds of someone banging their fists in desperation. Then came the hysterical cries. They were merely a whisper at first, almost like stray thoughts or memories. But as they grew louder, they drowned out all other sounds and took on a distinctively young male voice—the voice of the ensign that had jumped ship.

Feeling as if he was about to break down and lose control, Jonathon inched back from the windows and turned away, staring down at his trembling hands, which he clasped around the railing in an effort to forcefully calm them. But as his eyes rose slowly back up, he found himself staring out the far windows, past his own alarmed reflection and into the depths of the abyss. At that moment, his vision went black and he froze in place.

The darkness soon faded away, but the familiar scenery of the bridge was no longer before him. He could see a distant view of the Intimidator's starboard profile, as if he had been whisked away in a bizarre out-of-body experience. The idle Juggernaut was hazy, almost dream-like in appearance, and it was getting closer. The progression was steady at first, but a sudden spike in Jonathon's uncontrollable fear caused the pace of the approach to quicken. The powerful emotion served as a catalyst, a beacon to whatever was really approaching the ship.

Jonathon's body jolted a little as his mind snapped out of the disorienting, trance-like experience, and he inhaled a short gasp of air, just loud enough to catch Kate's attention.

"Are you all right?" she asked, not thinking too much of his withdrawal from the group, at least not yet.

"I'm...I'm fine," he replied, pressing against the railing and massaging the side of his head with one hand while his breathing and pulse normalized. The screams had also faded away. He was becoming himself again, but his eyes remained fixed on the abyss and the alien capital ship that lurked within. It had launched something. He was certain of it. As bewildering as it seemed, he had witnessed the approach of something alien in origin, from the point of view of the incoming hostile.

Activating his communicator, he promptly established a link with the rescue team and said, "The enemy's spotted you! Get that crewman out of there and get back to the ship, now."

"Roger that, Admiral," was the only reply that came through, and in a tone that was surprisingly calm and confident under the circumstances.

"We've got incoming?" Dead Eye inquired, turning around to look at Jonathon, following his line of sight out beyond the starboard windows. But he couldn't see anything out there and neither could Jonathon. Even with the aid of the binoculars, there was nothing detectable in view and that worried him.

"Something was deployed from that capital ship," Jonathon revealed, making his way to the right-most portion of the forward balcony. Kate joined him, as did Dead Eye, leaving the others to keep watch over the rescue team.

"Are you sure?" Kate questioned, squinting out into the starry darkness near the *Intimidator* and beyond. "I don't see anything."

"Trust me," Jonathon replied, "it's out there."

Kate glanced over at him for a moment, looking concerned, almost spooked. She managed to catch a brief glimpse of his troubled eyes before he looked away. From the moment he had told her about his dreams, she had begun to worry about him. She didn't understand why he had been singled out by the aliens, why they were communicating with him, privately tormenting him. Perhaps it had to do with his position of leadership over the fleet, or at least, that was the rationale she used for comfort. But it was the possibility that the enemy had a more diabolical agenda in store that troubled her so deeply.

"Man, I'm not seeing anything," Dead Eye complained, his face all but touching the starboard window.

"They've almost caught up with the pod," Chang announced, glancing back at Jonathon. "Maybe they'll make it in time."

"Maybe," Jonathon uttered, feeling less confident than Chang. His repeated scans of the space between the *Intimidator* and the abyss kept coming up empty, which should have been comforting, even cast doubt on what he had witnessed. But as much as he wanted to believe it was only a hallucination, it had felt far too real to simply shrug it off, especially with three lives at risk.

"Stand by to attach, Rescue Two," instructed the veteran search and rescue leader to his companion, speaking to her privately over their comm link. "Let's keep this short and simple."

"Right, uh, grappling tow ready to fire," she replied, trying to stay as collected as she could. The gold-tinted visor on her helmet kept her edgy expression hidden, but her tone of voice was plenty revealing. She couldn't help it. Her thoughts were scattered, dwelling partly on the mission at hand but mostly on Jonathon's last transmission, which served to magnify the inevitable feelings of helplessness that usually accompanied a space walk.

"Stay focused, Lieutenant," Rescue Leader snapped, catching her attention.

"Sorry, sir," she replied while tightening her grip around the base of the grappling gun she had palmed in her right hand. A thin, retractable chain stretched from the back of the gun to a secured hook on the rear of her utility belt, making her the anchor for their efforts to slow and reverse the capsule's movements. "Tagging the pod now," she announced while thumbing the firing switch.

The front half of the grappling gun discharged from its base and soared straight toward the door of the escape pod, uncoiling a towing line in the process. Once the grapple struck the pod, a flash of red light burst away from its perimeter as the device fused with the metal door, creating an unbreakable seal. The Lieutenant then locked the towing line and let go of the base, letting it retract back toward the hook in her utility belt while she used the thrusters in her jetpack to rotate until she faced the *Intimidator* and the airlock they had deployed from.

"Perfect shot, Rescue Two," said Rescue Leader while using his thrusters to slow his approach. "Now, reel it in, but don't worry about saving the pod. There's no time for that."

"Copy that, Rescue Leader," she replied, waiting until she felt a tug in the fully extended towing line before engaging her jetpack at medium burn. The capsule was slowed to a complete stop, then gradually picked up speed en route to the *Intimidator*.

Rescue Leader continued toward the pod and raised his feet so that the magnetic soles of his boots touched down on the shell's metal casing. His body compressed a little, bending at the knees, but he managed to maintain his balance long enough to grab onto the circular handle to the door.

"I'm attached," he confirmed to his companion. "Stand by to scrap and run. We'll only get one shot at this."

"How's their progress?" Jonathon called back to Chang.

The lieutenant kept his eyes fixed on the rescue team and cocked his head slightly to the side while relaying what he observed. But Jonathon was only able to hear part of the report before Chang's words faded into unnerving silence. Uncomfortable, almost painful feelings of fear were once again coursing through Jonathon's veins. And as he whipped his head back toward the abyss, the imagery before him changed in an instant.

He could see the starboard profile of the Intimidator again, and it was close, very close. Then his vision became erratic, shifting slightly in one direction and another, until it zeroed in on the bridge. Jonathon could see himself staring back through the glass. His petrified expression rushed into view as if a collision was imminent.

A loud thud resonated from the glass directly in front of Jonathon, snapping him out of his induced trance and nearly giving Dead Eye a heart attack. Kate jerked as well and let out a scream while backtracking, almost stumbling against the railing, though she couldn't see whatever it was that had impacted. What followed was a series of scrapes and muffled thumps that scurried across the windows, toward the port side of the bridge, then disappearing. The experience sufficiently rattled the entire command staff, prompting everyone to back away from the windows. Some even retreated to their command stations and ducked down, fearing they were under attack.

"What the freak was that?" Dead Eye uttered once the sounds had stopped.

"I didn't see what it was that hit us," Chang replied, peering from one window to the next. "Did anyone else?"

"No, but it certainly wasn't space junk," Kate added, shuddering a bit from the close encounter. She turned toward Jonathon to ask him if he had witnessed anything, but he brushed past her, heading toward the portside catwalk.

He had regained control of his emotions again, though he was still afraid, not for himself, but for the rescue team. The hostile entity that had grazed the bridge was practically right on top of them. Activating his wrist-comm, he yelled into it, saying, "Get out of there!"

"Just a little closer," Rescue Leader muttered, eyeing the waning gap that remained between the pod and the *Intimidator*.

"Hurry," Rescue Two pleaded, her panic escalating. Procedure required them to minimize the distances involved in the retrieval, reducing potential harm for the soon-to-be ejected ensign. At the moment, however, she didn't care. Her eyes were darting from one location to the other, visually probing her vicinity and the perimeter of the *Intimidator's* obtrusive profile, which concealed a great deal from her view. The enemy was out there, but she couldn't see any signs of its presence, which only served to freak her out further.

"I'm blowing the door, now," Rescue Leader advised, standing up and stepping away from the door as two micro-charges shattered the metal hinges, followed by a third explosion that fractured the lock. Oxygen began streaming out through the cracks.

Re-engaging her jetpack, Rescue Two yanked the door free at a slight upward angle before detaching the towing line. The maneuver caused a quick but not explosive depressurization of the escape pod's interior, sending its horrified occupant hurtling out into the vacuum of space and right into the clutches of his awaiting rescuer. A self-sealing emergency breathing apparatus was hurriedly attached over the ensign's exposed face, pumping a thick, oxygenated fluorocarbon liquid into his airway, temporarily stabilizing his lungs at the expense of making him initially feel as if he was drowning. Despite the benefits of the breathable liquid, the relative discomfort and sheer surprise of its

introduction into his system were enough to send the ensign's
hysteria into overdrive. Rescue Leader had to wrestle with the
young man while engaging his own jetpack and heading toward
the airlock, securing the ensign under one arm like a lifeguard
aiding a distressed swimmer. "The target's secure," he said,
sounding composed. But that soon changed.

As he glanced back at the escape pod to ensure that its
trajectory and that of his own were no longer the same, he saw
the pod stop abruptly, mysteriously, and begin to tremble. It
caved in along several points around its frame, as if an invisible
fist had snared the pod in its grasp and crushed it to a mere
fraction of its original size. Staring in shock, the veteran was
only able to come up with one viable explanation: the elusive
hostile that Jonathon had warned them about had found them,
using some manner of stealth ability to its advantage.

"Get in the airlock," he shouted to his companion through
the comm link while accelerating to a critical threshold. He had
only done a rapid dock once before, and that was a long time
ago. But he had no other choice. It was either barrel into the
airlock full speed, knowing that the jarring impact would likely
result in injuries, or approach slowly and by the book, in which
case he'd be as good as dead.

"What's wrong—" Rescue Two started to say before
catching a heart-pounding glimpse of what remained of the pod.
She instinctively jammed the ignition button for her jetpack's
main thruster and worked to bring her legs in front of her as she
surged into the cramped airlock. At the last second, she fired her
reverse thrusters, but her rate of approach was so fast that the
thrusters did little good. She smacked hard against the inner wall,
stressing her knees and back as her body compressed rapidly and
before she could get her hands up to serve as a brace. Her
momentum sent her upper body tumbling forward until her head
ricocheted off the wall, soliciting a groaned exhale and leaving
her dazed.

Rescue Leader's approach was even more treacherous.
Though he tried to initiate the same maneuver as his companion,
his rescued charge had witnessed the destruction of the escape
pod first hand and it left him drenched in terror. His kicking and
struggling was frustrating the veteran rescuer's ability to pivot

into a landing posture. All Rescue Leader could do was spin around and use himself as a cushion to soften the ensign's landing. He cringed as he soared backwards into the airlock, narrowly missing the lieutenant, and collided with the wall in a bone-crunching impact that fractured his right shoulder blade and knocked him unconscious.

Having shaken off some of the effects of her rough landing, Rescue Two immediately noticed that the door was still open, leaving the group exposed and vulnerable. A tense couple of seconds followed as she stared wide-eyed into the darkness, almost too frightened to move. But once her survival instincts kicked in, she lunged for the door, sliding between it and the wall, which she used for leverage. Pushing with all of her strength, she sent the door swinging outward. Her starry view narrowed at a steady pace, until the door was on the verge of closing, the group's safety nearly secure. But with scarcely a three-inch gap remaining, the door refused to budge any further and she felt a series of unsettling vibrations resonate through the metal framework. Something was on the opposite side of the door, pushing back.

Struggling to maintain her footing, the lieutenant braced her body sideways against the door, trying to keep it from reopening. But her efforts were proving futile and the rescued ensign wasn't in any position to help. Between his fear-induced paralysis and the mounting pain in his vacuum-exposed and swelling body, he could do nothing more than cower in one corner until he blacked out.

The situation worsened when something sliced across the lieutenant's visor, tearing a gash in the impact-resistant plastic. Screams of horror were ripped from her lungs as her space suit depressurized, leaving her gasping, fighting to suck down the streams of oxygen that rushed up past her face. But upon feeling a sharp pain in her chest, she quickly yielded the remaining air from her lungs in order to prevent them from rupturing, leaving her with precious little time to act. Then something slashed across her right arm, sending globules of blood spurting away from the deep wound at an alarming rate. The attack produced excruciating pain and she wanted to cry out, even opened her mouth wide, but all that came out was a silent whimper. And at the moment when she was about to lose all hope, some instinct prompted her to utilize her jetpack as extra leverage.

Securing her shoulder-braced hold on the door, she freed one hand long enough to fire her thrusters. Her jetpack generated enough thrust to stop the door's inward progression and slam it shut. Little time was spared in securing the lock. She could still feel vibrations resonating through the metal, growing more intense as the alien presence outside pounded at the door in vain. It had been denied its prey. She was safe, along with the others, and anxious to breathe again. But as she reached for the manual re-pressurization lever, she was startled by three severed appendages that seemed to have appeared out of nowhere, floating amongst scattered drops of dark blood near the doorframe. The lifeless appendages were slimy black and almost finger-like in appearance, though each was as large as her forearm. And at the tips were razor-sharp talons, one of which was coated with her blood. It was a haunting realization of exactly how close she had come to a gruesome death.

"Come on," Jonathon uttered to himself, staring out the window for any signs of the rescue team or the alien presence. He had tried contacting the team leader over the comm link, but there was no response, leaving him worrying there had been casualties.

The officers beside him all had their eyes glued to the window, watching and waiting with bated breath for the silence to be broken. And after a nerve-wracking minute had passed, Jonathon's communicator finally produced the awaited beeps.

"This is Rescue Two," the lieutenant reported, sounding short of breath. "Mission accomplished."

Jonathon exhaled a sigh of relief against a backdrop of cheers that filled the bridge. The command staff was behaving as if a major military victory had been achieved, despite the fact that the rescue mission meant little to nothing in the grand scheme of things. They were simply elated to finally hear some good news.

"Good work, Lieutenant," said Jonathon. "Is everyone all right?"

"As good as can be expected, sir," she replied between coughs and against a backdrop of vomiting sounds that were emanating from the freshly resuscitated ensign. "The doc's got someone coming down to check us out. We've got a few minor injuries and the ensign will need to be treated for exposure, but at least we're alive."

"Did you encounter the enemy?"

"Yeah, I definitely wanna hear about this," Dead Eye interrupted, stepping between Chang and Jonathon. "Something freaky rattled the windows up here and took off in your direction, but we couldn't see what it was."

"We did encounter some form of hostile presence, but we couldn't visually detect it either. It was cloaked, I guess, and I think it's gone."

"Good riddance," Dead Eye mumbled, though he knew there was no way to confirm her claim. He simply preferred to believe the hostile had departed, rather than entertaining the notion that it might still be prowling around outside the *Intimidator*.

"You seem pretty confident it's gone," Jonathon pried. "Is there something you're not telling me?"

A hushed sigh crept over the comm link, followed by the lieutenant's reply. "It's really nothing, sir," she responded hesitantly, not wanting to talk about or mentally relive the specifics of the frightening ordeal. "It's just that I managed to wound it when I sealed the airlock."

"Come again?" Dead Eye chimed, his forehead wrinkling.

"You mean that thing was a life form?" said Kate, sounding rather shocked.

"It sure seemed like it," Rescue Two responded. "The blasted thing was vicious, too. It almost took one of my arms off, but I got three of its limbs in trade, or at least part of them, anyway. But don't bother wasting your time coming down here to have a look. They decomposed pretty fast and left behind quite a toxic cloud. I don't think we'll be using that airlock anytime soon."

"Well," said Jonathon, "at least you're safe. Get patched up and go get some rest. You've both earned it."

"Roger that, Admiral," came a grateful reply before the communication terminated.

"Man, that's just creepy," Dead Eye commented.

"Maybe it was actually one of the aliens," said Parker, which sparked a nod of agreement from both Dead Eye and Chang. Even Kate was warming up to the idea. Jonathon, however, disagreed.

"I'm not so sure about that," he countered. "Granted, we don't know anything about their physical appearance, but they do seem to be just as dependent on starships as we are, regardless of their technological differences. And who knows how far their use of organics extends. That thing might've just been another weapon in their arsenal."

"Well, I guess it doesn't really matter," said Chang, but Dead Eye begged to differ. He drew Chang into a friendly debate, discussing what the predator might have been. Even Parker interjected from time to time, offering more outlandish theories that leaned toward genetic mutations, but Jonathon had grown disinterested in the topic and let them be. He chose instead to ponder his own thoughts quietly beside Kate.

The ambient chatter on the bridge brought a certain warmth to the air, even a sliver of normality. But as much as Jonathon wanted to savor it, he just couldn't. Something didn't feel quite right. Shifting his eyes toward the darkened Earth, he wondered how many more lives needed rescuing, how many survivors were struggling to endure, to escape, to fight back. He wanted to believe that O'Connor and his troops would be able to mount a campaign of resistance against the enemy, most likely using guerilla warfare to their advantage. But the more he stared at his gloomy home world, the more his countenance fell. Then came the grim observation from Dead Eye.

"Uh, guys," he called out in a nervous tone, staring back toward the starboard windows. "That monster alien ship's headin' right for us."

The colossal alien warship had indeed come about and was creeping toward the *Intimidator*. The abyss moved as well, as if it was one with the ship. Drawing ever closer, the darkness was poised to consume the immobile remnant of the human fleet.

As Jonathon turned to face the enemy, his strength began to fade, as did the sounds from his ears. With his surroundings becoming unnaturally quiet, his vision soon blacked out.

A murky mosaic of smoke and ash jolted through his mind, bringing with it the heavy thumping of footsteps, produced by something that was no doubt impressive in size. The smoke churned and twisted toward him. He was moving, and as the gritty veil began to thin, he saw the demolished remnants of buildings straddling a debris-laden street, which itself was a fair distance below him, placing his field of vision almost eighteen meters above ground.

Amidst the hazy ruins he could sense no emotions, no fear, no hope, only the emptiness of death and destruction. Then he saw the bodies—a sea of human corpses that were strung atop the rubble that littered the street. At that instant, Jonathon was aghast with the realization that he was witnessing the unfolding destruction on Earth first hand and once again from the point of view of an alien presence. But this time he was utterly helpless to change the outcome. He was simply an unwilling bystander, forced to watch for the perverse pleasure of the alien being that had touched his mind.

A strong sense of desperation shot through his body as his vision shifted down toward a narrow alley where he saw a lone and battered marine trying to sprint away to safety. And for a brief moment Jonathon thought the soldier would make it. But as his vision shifted back up, toward the opposite end of the alleyway, only one outcome seemed likely.

Approaching from across the razed building near the alley's exit was an eighteen-meter-tall alien assault unit, which was every bit as extraordinary as the orbiting warships that had decimated Jonathon's fleet. Its shape vaguely resembled that of a man, albeit much larger and much more frightening. Its thick, black frame was almost completely covered with overlapping segments of bulky, organic armor, which were connected to each other and the frame through a complex system of interweaving tentacles. As with the other instruments of destruction that had been employed by the aliens, its dark-blue surface was masked by undulating patterns of shadows, slithering around the assortment of sharpened black spikes that had torn through its armor.

The lower arms of the giant resembled the barrels of wide cannons, with twin-pronged bayonet extensions along the rim. And around the base of its legs were rings of razor-sharp claws, digging into the asphalt with each crushing step. Its head was also enclosed in organic armor, with four fang-like protrusions curving in along the top and bottom of its otherwise featureless face. From the rear, the head draped down and split into a pair of tentacles, each of which straddled the giant's black serrated spine prior to connecting with the lower sides of the torso.

It fired a glistening ball of blue energy from one of its arms directly into the path of the fleeing marine, triggering a lethal explosion that shook the pavement and incinerated his body, along with the remnants of a partially crumbled corner wall. As the ungodly warrior continued on its patrol, its head turned and looked straight toward Jonathon, matching his eye level and leaving him with the impression he was staring back from the vantage point of a similar enemy unit.

"Jon," Kate called out, grabbing one of his arms and snapping him out of his waking dream. "Are you all right?"

He turned to look at her and offer what response he could, but he wasn't even able to see her face. Her soft visage was ripped from his view and replaced with another vision.

He was once again seeing things from the viewpoint of an alien assault unit, but this time he was immersed in a heavily wooded area, much of which had been set ablaze by the torrid bolts of lightning that crackled down from the tempest. Lying scattered at the base of a partially felled tree were the smoldering remains of the upper half of a marine, no doubt sliced apart while confronting the walking weapon. Jonathon could also sense other soldiers taking cover slightly beyond his field of view. He could feel their measured degrees of fear, sometimes dread. And though he was sure there was at least a shred of bravery amongst the lot, he couldn't feel anything but their negative emotions, conveying a potentially misleading sense of complete dominance by the alien ground forces. It tormented him, driving every last bit of hope from his mind.

Seeing the assault unit raise its arms slightly, he felt a surge of panic, followed by a volley of energy bursts that shattered the trees in front of him in an effort to flush out the targeted squad. But in the process, a small explosion rumbled from behind him, causing his vision to rotate until he found himself staring down at a second squad, the leader of which seemed strikingly familiar. Concentrating to peer beyond the visor of the lead marine, Jonathon saw O'Connor's face, illuminated by the alien's charging weapon.

"Run!" he tried to holler, but the images vanished.

He found himself staring at Kate. She was visibly upset, staring into his eyes, which were glossed over. His strength was still fleeting and he could barely hear her voice, which had become muffled in his ears.

"What's wrong?" she pleaded. Before Jonathon could struggle out a response, Chang hollered from across the way, catching his attention. He turned his head to see what the problem was, but he once again fell into a trance.

A strung-out pile of human bodies littered a portion of the downtrodden grassy plain that rolled out into the profile of a smoke-engulfed city. His vantage point was that of an average sized man, looming over the horrified civilians who were alive yet unable to move, save involuntary twitching in their muscles. Their trembling eyes stared blankly up at the writhing thunderheads, some even seemed to be looking right at Jonathon, as if begging for mercy. But it wasn't his to grant. From behind him came a soft pulsing blue light that washed across the region at regular intervals, bringing an eerie glow to their pale, agonized faces.

The emotions that radiated from the civilians were overwhelming. Such raw terror and pain, like nothing Jonathon had ever experienced. It was both exhausting and maddening, yet there was nothing he could do to stop it.

"Grasha con ki ish lash'menta tore," came a snarling, low-rumbling order spoken in the alien tongue. Jonathon wasn't able

to understand the words because the order wasn't spoken to him, but rather to the alien soldier through whose eyes he was watching.

His field of vision rotated to his left until it fell upon a commanding presence that stood beside one of the organic towers that had deployed and taken up roots in the earth like a noxious weed. A ring of blue light shot up the tower, casting its radiance down on the alien figure that was staring back, looking surprisingly humanoid in form. Jonathon had expected the aliens' appearance to be unusual, almost monster-like, since only a monster would engage in the kind of savage acts the aliens had perpetrated since the start of the war. Even so, the true appearance of the aliens remained a mystery. The soldier he was eyeing was completely enclosed in battle armor, with a shiny-black faceplate that reflected the terrified expressions of its victims.

The black underlayer of its ornate combat attire was composed of a sturdy yet flexible thin metal mesh. Smooth armor plating with the luster of a black pearl attached to the mesh and molded perfectly around the majority of its body. The meticulous design and near-majestic sheen also magnified the haughty posture with which the alien held itself. But through Jonathon's eyes the alien looked more of malice than majesty. The plating atop its shoulders was dark red, as if they had been dipped in blood. Even the flowing cape that draped its back was oozing red. This imagery was compounded by a limited assortment of small but menacing spikes that protruded from various armor segments around its body. And between the breastplates was an embedded jeweled insignia of a black dragon, rimmed in fire and flanked by a pair of small, blood-red ideograms that added a degree of evil distinction.

A slug-like weapon stretched along the backside of its right forearm, clinging to its host via thin interwoven tentacles. The bizarre organic armament looked more like a symbiotic life form than an instrument of destruction, but its power was not to be questioned, nor was its host.

With his vision shifting back the other way, Jonathon watched as a pair of armored hands stretched down toward the nearest civilian man, grabbing him by the legs and dragging him back toward the tower as the alien commander looked on and laughed.

Having seen enough, Jonathon screamed at the top of his lungs, "Get out of my mind!" The demand was made with such boldness that even the most boisterous clap of thunder was unable to drown him out. And with his words echoing through his own thoughts, he felt his surroundings grow quiet and dim, as if his senses were simply shutting down. Even his strength was nearly spent, his heart weakening. He could feel himself slipping away to the darkest corners of his mind.

Jonathon's eyes rolled back into his head and his body fell limp, prompting Kate to take hold and pull him closer, yet he remained unresponsive to her concerned cries. The pervasive sense of darkness that flooded his mind took firm hold over him as the abyss swallowed the *Intimidator* whole. At that moment, he felt a presence, a terrible presence. It was cold yet radiated hatred like unquenchable fire. And its voice was like thunder. It spoke into Jonathon's mind, causing a chilling sensation of overwhelming despair to course through his veins.

"Vail pax nalak traden folushan ki rotkillrusha'qui nox'la peshtoy angelatra, chosh ven ablyotum: I shall take great pleasure in tormenting your wretched soul, child of oblivion."

With a deep, baleful laugh, the voice of the being that called itself Drak'Rasha faded, leaving Jonathon in isolated darkness and unable to awaken from his new nightmare.

Chapter 13
Prey

"Somebody get Dr. Whyte up here!" Kate demanded against the panicked murmurs that had overrun the bridge, which itself had grown darker within the shadows of the abyss. A few tears floated away from her cheeks as she clung to Jonathon's flaccid body and descended gently to the floor of the catwalk, pulling him down into her lap.

Chang broke away from the horrific scenery outside the windows and promptly activated his wrist-comm, saying, "We have an emergency medical situation on the bridge. Admiral Quinn is in need of immediate assistance. Please respond."

"I'll be right there, Lieutenant," Dr. Whyte's voice called back.

After terminating the communication, Chang crouched down beside Kate. "What happened?" he asked while studying Jonathon's condition.

"I don't know," she replied in a shaky voice. "He just passed out."

"Well, Dr. Whyte's on her way. Keep an eye on him. I'm sure he'll be all right."

Kate responded only with a subtle nod before casting her eyes back down at her unresponsive companion. Tenderly caressing the side of his face, she shivered. Jonathon's flesh had become icy cold, as if his life force was being drained away. Reaching over with her other hand, she took hold of one of the blankets that had been stacked nearby and pulled it around him as snugly as she could.

"Don't leave me," she whispered into one of his ears. "You're all I've got left, so don't you dare give up on me. Please, Jon…we need you…I need you."

"I've got a really bad feeling about this," professed Dead Eye, standing against a backdrop of sporadic flashes of crimson lightning. "Something's definitely going down and the Admiral's creepy illness is just the start of it."

"I'm with Chuck on this one," Parker interjected, breaking his self-imposed silence.

"Now don't freak out on me, guys," Chang appealed. He was doing his best to assume the role of acting officer in charge. It was a job that he took upon himself reluctantly, yet necessarily since Jensen was still AWOL.

"What do you mean don't freak out?" Dead Eye objected. "Have you glanced out the windows? We're surrounded in darkness with Satan's floating ship of horrors right above us. I'd say it's a pretty good time to freak out."

Parker nodded in agreement.

"Look, I get what you're saying," whispered Chang, "but if you get all worked up about it, you're going to spook everyone else, which will only make matters worse. So if you're going to freak out, can you please do it quietly?"

"I suppose so, but it won't be nearly as satisfying."

Activating his communicator, Chang initiated a ship-wide broadcast. "This is Lieutenant Chang. The enemy capital ship has moved into a position directly above us and may be planning hostile actions against the crew. Those of you who still have weapons at your disposal should arm yourselves and prepare to engage an enemy boarding party, just like we've already planned. Stay alert and watch each other's backs. Chang out."

"I could use some assistance over here," Dr. Whyte requested. She had emerged partway from the emergency shaft near the elevator.

"I'll be right there," Chang hollered back. He climbed atop the railing and jumped toward the rear balcony. His weightless body soared gracefully to the elevator doors and upon reaching them, he pushed his way down to the floor. It was then a simple matter of sidestepping to the left before he was standing beside the emergency entryway.

"Thank you, Lieutenant," said Dr. Whyte as she handed him her oversized medical bag. After taking one look at its bulging white exterior, he felt relieved that gravity was still offline.

"Where's the admiral?" she inquired, stepping wobbly onto the rear balcony.

Chang pointed the way and said, "He's right over there and completely unresponsive. He mysteriously collapsed a few minutes ago and we don't have a clue what caused it."

"Well, that's why I'm here, Lieutenant. Now step out of the way and follow me."

Having been temporarily demoted from acting senior officer to junior medical assistant, Chang rolled his eyes and followed behind the overbearing medical chief.

"Can you help him?" Kate pleaded.

"Relax, Lieutenant," Dr. Whyte advised, kneeling down beside her. "I'm sure I can, but I need to diagnose the problem first. Now, tell me exactly what happened and don't leave out a single detail, regardless of how insignificant you think it might be."

"There really isn't much to tell. He was a little tense while we were watching the rescue team bring that crewman back, but then his behavior changed. He was distracted and seemed really bothered by something. I tried talking to him, to see what was wrong, but he...he passed out on me and he's been unconscious ever since."

"I see," Dr. Whyte replied while retrieving a black ophthalmoscope from her medical bag, which hovered beside her. "Well, perhaps I can shed some light on this mystery." Holding the T-shaped instrument in one hand, she reached over with her other hand and used her index finger and thumb to pry Jonathon's eyelids open, eliciting a startled reaction from each of the officers who were standing nearby. The entirety of Jonathon's eyes had unnaturally become black as night.

To Parker it appeared as if Jonathon's very soul had been drained from his body. He had read about such occurrences in the disreputable paranormal investigation journals that he fancied. Out of sympathy for Kate, however, he decided that it'd be best to keep his diagnosis of Jonathon's condition to himself.

"Whoa!" Dead Eye blurted out. "That ain't normal."

Chang gave him a little jab in the ribs and a sideways glance that suggested he should keep the rest of his comments to himself, so as to avoid upsetting Kate further.

"What's wrong with him?" Kate cried. "What's wrong—"

"Calm yourself, Lieutenant," Dr. Whyte ordered while grabbing hold of Kate's arm and snapping her out of her emotional outburst. Kate covered her face with both hands, and feeling helpless, she burst into tears.

"I'd like to hear an explanation for this myself, Doc," said Dead Eye.

"I wish I had one to give you, Lieutenant, but I've yet to form any opinions regarding his condition."

Dr. Whyte rummaged through her medical bag and retrieved a small rectangular brain scanner. She tapped a few of the pressure-sensitive areas along its worn, black surface and placed it atop Jonathon's forehead where it began monitoring his brain activity.

"Interesting," she mumbled, watching the thin green lines on the scanner's display bounce dramatically from top to bottom. "He has an extraordinary amount of cortical activity, more so than your average person that's fully coherent."

Kate's head immediately popped up above her cupped hands. "That means he's going to be okay, right?"

"It is a good sign, yes, but his situation is still serious, Lieutenant. It's as if his body wants to give up, but his mind is too busy to take notice. And his eyes—"

"They don't seem human," Dead Eye blurted out again, expressing what his comrades felt but were too inhibited to say. He blocked another elbow from Chang before continuing. "The aliens have done somethin' to him. I don't know how, but they got to him, and when I get my hands on 'em, I'll make sure they regret it."

"That's absurd," Dr. Whyte argued. "They've yet to set foot on our ship. And unless he's had a physical encounter with them that I'm not aware of, his illness couldn't possibly be extraterrestrial in origin."

Kate opened her mouth in preparation to reveal the information that Jonathon had shared with her about his dreams, but she hesitated and bit back her words instead. He had confided in her and she was reluctant to break that trust. And besides, as peculiar as she found his dreams to be, she wasn't entirely sure they were relevant to his health dilemma, nor did she want Dr. Whyte scoffing at her for what would most likely be perceived as superstitious nonsense.

Several overly bright flashes of crimson suddenly illuminated the bridge, drawing Dead Eye's attention back to the outer darkness. He leaned against the portside window and peered up at the uncomfortably close alien capital ship that was holding position overhead. A black, star-fighter-sized spherical object was descending from the belly of the beast and advancing toward the *Intimidator*. Its gnarled surface shone clearly with each explosion of lightning that streaked through the abyss.

"Something's been launched at us!" he announced, his heavy breath fogging the window and his eyes bulging with anticipated doom.

The bizarre organic wad moved steadily into a central position above the main deck of the *Intimidator*, where it remained motionless for a time. It was of a hostile nature to be sure, but its exact intentions remained a mystery, increasing the sense of foreboding that permeated the hearts and minds of the human spectators. For several minutes it seemed to sadistically taunt the *Intimidator's* command staff. And when the level of anxiety had reached its peak, it unleashed a swarm of thin tentacles that wrapped securely around the *Intimidator's* hull. Like a spider spinning its web, the strange entity had ensnared the defeated flagship.

With its victims secured, the alien capital ship began to vanish. The stormy flashes within the void subsided and through the diminishing abyss shone the starry backdrop that had been blotted out by the darkness. The *Intimidator* was free from the void, but no longer under its own sovereign control.

"Not that I'm complaining or anything, but where'd it go?" Dead Eye inquired, scanning the calm, star-filled region around the *Intimidator*.

"I don't know, but good riddance," said Chang, plodding up beside his friend.

"What did it do to our ship?" Parker asked, staring nervously out the forward windows at the strange mass of organic spaghetti that had attached itself to the *Intimidator's* hull.

Subtle vibrations began rumbling through the bridge, confirming Chang's suspicions. "I think we're—"

"We're moving," Dead Eye interrupted in an energetic tone. As he drifted back from the force of the sudden propulsion, he flung one arm over the handrail and latched on, pulling himself into a secured position before his body could tumble the rest of the way over the railing.

Parker fell back against the railing as well and remained there with his eyes still fixed on the alien entity. He felt as if he had been forced onto some perverse amusement park ride, more terrifying than thrilling. And he was concerned about where the ride would stop.

Chang also secured himself, keeping his body in sync with the ship's acceleration. He wrapped his right arm under the top railing and quickly activated his wrist-comm, saying, "Link to all personnel."

The communicator replied with a pair of beeps.

"This is Lieutenant Chang. The *Intimidator* has been captured by an enemy vessel and is in the process of being towed. I suggest you brace yourselves against anything secure in order to avoid injuries until this ride's over. Chang out."

Still clinging to the handrail, he stepped past Kate and sat down beside her sliding body. Using himself as a brace, he pushed his feet against the corner post, assisting Dr. Whyte in keeping Kate and Jonathon safely contained.

As the *Intimidator* moved out of Earth's orbit, an expansive wormhole spawned directly in its path, spewing burning stellar gas. The flaming yellow vapor steamed along the Juggernaut's hull before dissipating.

"Whoa," exclaimed Dead Eye, his widened eyes reflecting the disturbing imagery that lay beyond the mouth of the cosmic gateway.

"I see it," confirmed Chang, his head cocked toward the forward windows. The tugging effects on his body subsided once the *Intimidator* reached a steady pace. He was then able to move about unhindered, though he did so with greater caution.

"What's going on?" Kate inquired, wiping away the remnant tears from the corners of her eyes. The bridge was aglow with a luminous panoply of fiery colors, aggravating her already stressed emotional state.

"A new wormhole's opened," Chang answered.

"Yeah, opened right into hell," added Dead Eye, gripping the railing even tighter. Terrible vibrations had begun to stampede through the ship as it approached the wide-open distortion.

The *Intimidator* was towed through the wormhole and into the heart of a nebula, far beyond the prying technology of mankind's most advanced telescopes. The once mighty flagship was forced to sail upon a turbulent sea of volatile plasma and through a churning fog of superheated gas, through which little else could be seen. Lively blue sparks flickered all around the vessel as the nebula's unrelenting explosions and electrical discharges assaulted the energy shield that was superimposed on the Juggernaut's hull. Oddly enough, the controlling alien vessel was shielding its victims from certain death within the cosmic storm. Even still, the journey was far from uneventful. Strong stellar winds and gravitational currents from an unseen pulsar shook the *Intimidator* and its occupants, rattling the crew's nerves with each unpredictable jolt.

For what seemed like an eternity, but lasted no more than a few minutes, the alien subjugator dragged its ensnared prey toward a city-sized shadow that loomed within the masking vapors. There, hidden safely inside the stellar cloud, was an enormous mass of rock—the only discernable remnant of a destroyed planet. Its fractured and mountainous surface was mirrored by a jagged base that disappeared down into the roiling gases. In all, the planetary fragment seemed plain and barren until glimmers of light came into focus, revealing a complex hive of artificial structures.

"That asteroid, or whatever it is, looks like it's inhabited," said Dead Eye with a bewildered expression that lingered behind the forward window. "What kind of sadistic person would place an outpost in a place like this? I mean, how could anything survive out here?"

"Maybe that's their point," Parker opined. "That we're *not* supposed to survive out here."

"Whatever that thing is, it looks like we'll be docking with it soon," Chang warned. "Grab your pulse rifles and secure the bridge."

"You got it, Chief," replied Dead Eye with a half-executed salute. "They're not getting me without a fight."

While his two cohorts made their way back around the catwalk, Chang raised his wrist-comm and prepared to deliver his regretful message to the crew.

"This is Lieutenant Chang with an update on our situation. The *Intimidator's* approaching an enemy installation and will most likely dock within the next few minutes. Remain in your battle-ready positions and prepare for enemy contact. I want to know the minute anything hostile boards this ship. Chang out."

"Heads up, Li," Dead Eye shouted while tossing a weapon from across the room.

Chang waited for the pulse rifle to drift closer, then snatched it out of the air. "Thanks," he shouted back before marching up to Dr. Whyte.

"Well, I've done all I can for him," she uttered with an edge of frustration, packing the last of her ineffective medical devices into her bag.

"What do you mean you're done?" Chang protested. "He's still unconscious."

"I'm well aware of that, Lieutenant. I've tried every procedure at my disposal, but his stubborn body simply won't respond. For the time being, we'll simply have to wait for him to come out of the coma on his own."

"In case you haven't noticed, Doctor, we're running out of time. As soon as we reach that outpost we'll most likely be boarded by enemy soldiers and I don't want to leave the admiral in such a vulnerable condition."

"I understand that, Lieutenant, but as I said, there's nothing I can do. Based on my observations I can tell you that his condition isn't worsening and there doesn't seem to be an immediate threat to his life. In fact, he's surprisingly stable. We can transport him to sickbay if you wish, but it won't change anything."

"No, let's keep him here. I'll feel better guarding him myself."

"It's your call," said Dr. Whyte, rising cautiously to her feet. "Now if you'll excuse me, I need to return to sickbay and check on Lieutenant Hunter's condition."

"Yeah, I heard about his crash landing. He was the only one of the Black Lance that made it back alive, wasn't he?"

"Yes, and he's doing fairly well, although he's going to have a long recovery."

"Well, you'd better hurry back before we dock. And you'd better follow the orders of the security officers that have been assigned to protect you and—"

"Don't worry about me, Lieutenant, I'll be perfectly fine," she insisted while clumping back toward the emergency exit. "Contact me if the admiral's situation changes."

"You can count on that."

After assisting in her departure, Chang slid the metal hatch back over the exposed shaft and fastened the lock. He then turned and glanced over at Dead Eye and Parker, who were both standing quietly nearby. "You two keep a close watch on this hatch. If anything starts to come through, shoot it."

"Aye, aye, Chief," Dead Eye replied with a nod.

Chang traipsed over to the railing that overlooked the lower deck and checked on the officers below, most of whom were still staring out into the nebula. "Get away from the windows and arm yourselves," he ordered. "I want three of you to take up defensive positions on the forward balcony, three near the commander's station, and the rest of you to hold position down below."

Each of the officers carried out their orders without hesitation, moving to their designated posts. Some of them had never been on the front lines before, but when it came to defending themselves and the lives of their peers there was little doubt they'd put up a brave fight.

"That looks like some sort of cave up ahead," said Dead Eye, pointing at the murky shadows that lurked beyond the *Intimidator's* bow.

"Yeah, I see it," Chang acknowledged. "Just stay down and don't get killed."

"Hey," Dead Eye replied, "it's me we're talkin' about."

After a brief chuckle, Chang returned to a position beside Kate and Jonathon. "Let's get you two down below. You'll be safer there." Strapping his pulse rifle around his back, he leaned down and scooped Jonathon's limp body into his arms, then carefully stood up and sauntered back toward the stairs.

Kate pushed herself upright and trudged behind Chang, feeling as if she had to exert all of her strength to keep up. The sight of her comatose companion being carried away like a soldier who had fallen in battle was almost more than she could bear.

Down the stairs they plodded, heading toward the dark, rounded corner near the back of the lower deck. Chang paraded past the officers that stood guard near the base of the stairs, triggering a hush of respect. He waited for Kate to crumple her blanket into a makeshift pillow before lowering Jonathon's body onto the floor. She slid the wadded blanket under Jonathon's head and sat down beside him, with her back pressed against the stair supports.

"I'll get him strapped down," Chang offered while opening one of the overhead cabinets. "Odds are it's not going to be a smooth landing."

He retrieved a pair of magnetic securing harnesses out of the cabinet and kneeled beside Jonathon. One harness was used to fasten Jonathon's legs to the floor while the other harness draped across his chest.

"That should keep him snug for the rest of the ride."

"Thanks," Kate replied quietly.

"Here, take my pulse rifle. If any aliens manage to make it down here—"

"It'll be the last thing they do," Kate interrupted as she took and armed the weapon.

"Amen," Chang echoed with a smile.

Moving back out from under the balcony, he turned, looked upward, and jumped. His body floated up beyond the edge of the rear balcony, at which point he took hold of the top railing and spun into a backwards flip, planting his magnetic soles squarely on the balcony's floor and aborting his forward momentum by bracing one hand against a command station. His acrobatic maneuver elicited a smattering of applause from Dead Eye and Parker.

"Now come on, hot shot, get over here," said Dead Eye.

Chang grabbed a spare pulse rifle from one of the junior officers before taking up a defensive position between his two friends. He was ready and willing to fight by their side, and, if necessary, die by their side.

The *Intimidator* continued moving toward the sizeable cave that was inset within one end of the floating mountain. Jagged rocks near the opening made the cavern look like the mouth of a voracious monster primed to devour its latest meal. And as the Juggernaut was swallowed whole, it passed through an artificial energy barrier, leaving behind the nebula's hostile gasses and gravitational tremors that had persistently harassed the ship.

For several tense seconds the *Intimidator* drifted further into the cave, then stopped with a bone-jarring thud. The air that was trapped in the cave was soon filled with a chorus of whipping sounds as the alien entity recalled each of its strangulating tentacles in swift succession. Having completed its task, it disappeared back into the nebula.

"Is everyone all right?" Chang called out while massaging the minor bump along his right temple. The *Intimidator's* abrupt stop had caught him uncharacteristically off guard, bruising his ego more than anything. His fellow officers responded with varying degrees of groans, acknowledging their relatively unharmed conditions.

"That landing sure brings back memories of basic pilot's training," Dead Eye moaned, pushing himself up from the floor. He stood upright, brushed himself off, and paused, looking almost confused. "I've either gained weight or someone's turned the gravity back on."

"The ship's circuits are still fried," Parker reminded him, "so it must be coming from this outpost."

"Everyone stay sharp," Chang advised. "Things could get ugly at any moment."

"Man, I hate having to sit here and wait," muttered Dead Eye. "That cave's probably crawlin' with enemy—"

"Shh," said Chang, having heard a soft, muffled thud drift down from the ceiling.

"What are you shushing me for?"

"I think I heard something up top..." Chang's statement was sufficient to mute his companions—Parker even held his breath while he listened—just in time to hear the sound again. "There, did you hear it?"

"Yeah, and it's starting to creep me out. Something ain't right here."

Grabbing hold of one of the portable lights that had fallen to the floor, Dead Eye abandoned his post and hurried to the starboard edge of the forward balcony.

"Wait," Chang objected, but his protest had fallen on deaf ears, so he followed behind.

Parker jumped up and joined them. And as they all stared out through the forward windows, Dead Eye focused the beam of light that was emanating from his lantern. With a gentle waving motion of his hand, he probed the outer darkness, guiding the soft light up the jagged walls in search of the doom he felt was certain to befall them.

"So far it just looks like an empty cave," said Chang.

"Well something's obviously out there," Dead Eye replied. "So keep lookin'."

As the spotlight climbed higher still, it grew ever fainter until its long reach was barely able to illuminate the rocky surface that hung overhead.

"Stop," Chang insisted, grabbing hold of Dead Eye's arm. "Keep the light right where it is. I think I saw something up there."

"Saw what?" Parker inquired with twinges of fear in his voice. His face was a little more pale than usual.

"Well, there's nothing there now," said Dead Eye. "Let me move it a little to the—"

"Whoa," Chang interrupted. "The whole ceiling's moving."

"Man, this nightmare just keeps getting' worse by the minute," Dead Eye complained.

"What are those things?" Chang whispered, studying the sporadically shifting patterns that scurried across the cavern ceiling. His bated breath drifted across the glass, forming a thin layer of fog that gradually hazed the middle portion of the window.

Having overheard the conversation, the three junior officers who had been crouching down near the tactical stations popped back up and turned around, staring with mounting jitters at the eerie sight. Feeling vulnerable, they each double-checked their weapons, ensuring they were armed and ready to fire at a moments notice.

With his eyes still drawn to the shifting ceiling, Chang placed one of his palms against the icy window. A bizarre, spider-like creature that wasn't much bigger than his hand suddenly smacked against the outer edge of the glass, opposite his palm, which he promptly withdrew. The creature's pulsating black body suctioned to the window, oozing a clear viscous liquid that dripped freely into the shadows. A chorus of startled outbursts erupted from the five neighboring officers as they each jumped back from the windows. Dead Eye accidentally tossed his portable light and nearly fell backwards over the railing.

"Holy crap!" he shouted after regaining his balance. "What is that freaky thing?"

"Beats me," Chang replied, inching back away from the window. "But at least it's on the outside."

Dead Eye raised his pulse rifle and pointed it threateningly at the unusual life form, as if he was trying to prove to it that he wasn't intimidated.

Several more thumping sounds came from the portside windows as more of the spider-like creatures attached themselves to the ship. They seemed drawn to the human presence, but whether it was out of curiosity or a desire to feed was unclear. Dead Eye assumed the latter and maintained his firing stance, aiming his weapon at each of the new arrivals. "I don't like this," he said. "Those little buggers are lookin' at us like we're they're next meal. Man, what I wouldn't give for a can of bug spray right now."

"Let's back away from the windows and maybe they'll leave," Chang suggested.

"Good idea," Parker agreed as more of the creatures arrived, creating a disturbing mosaic.

The three nearby junior officers fled quickly back along the portside catwalk, trying to ignore the host of thumping sounds that rang out like hailstones beating against the glass. Chang led Parker and Dead Eye in a strategic withdrawal back to the starboard edge of the rear balcony, safely away from the bizarre life forms that proceeded to cover every inch of the windows and most likely other portions of the ship as well.

Suddenly, a hollow banging sound came from the emergency access hatch. Someone or something was attempting to gain entry.

"Cover me," ordered Chang, stepping toward the hatch.

Dead Eye followed, his weapon drawn. "You think they've boarded already?" he uttered.

"Not likely. They couldn't have gotten up here that fast. It's probably one of our own, but be ready, just in case."

Crouching down beside the sealed hatch, Chang shouted, "Identify yourself."

"It's Commander Jensen. Open the hatch."

"Man, what's that jerk want now?" Dead Eye huffed.

"Who knows, but we've got to let him in."

"Says who? Just leave 'im down there."

"I can't. An order's an order, and like it or not, he's still second in command."

"Fine, but if he tries anything funny I'm gonna—"

"I gave you a direct order, Lieutenant!" shouted Jensen, though his voice softened as it penetrated the floor.

Chang unlocked the hatch and carefully removed it. Up popped Jensen, looking smug as ever.

"What are you doin' here?" Dead Eye protested, glaring at Jensen. Chang inched closer to Dead Eye, looking a little stressed as he readied himself to diffuse what was likely to be a heated verbal exchange between the two officers.

"I heard about the admiral's condition, so I'm here to assume command of the ship. And I don't much care for your tone, Lieutenant."

"We've already got everything under control. We don't need you comin' up here and—"

"Don't question my authority, Lieutenant, or I'll..." Jensen became distracted after catching a glimpse of the life forms that smothered the windows. "What in the world..."

"They attached themselves to the ship a few minutes ago," Chang recounted, redirecting the conversation. "But there's no way they can get in."

The distinctive sounds of weapons fire, followed by the scream of an unseen crewman on the deck below, drifted up through the open shaft, casting doubt on Chang's assertion.

"Take your defensive positions," Jensen ordered to the group. "Lieutenant, seal that hatch."

Chang quickly did as ordered, but as he stood up, several thick globs of a clear, rank liquid dropped onto his head. Glancing up at the ceiling, his eyes widened as he stared at one of the spider-like creatures clinging to the inside of the bridge. Before he could reach for his weapon, the creature leapt at his face. A single burst of plasma splattered its frail body less than half a meter above Chang's head, plastering him with malodorous bile and small chunks of gooey flesh.

"That was close...and disgusting," said Chang, scraping organic debris from his scalp. "Nice shot, by the way."

"Thanks," Dead Eye replied with a smirk.

"How did that thing get in here?" asked Parker. His eyes were jumping from one end of the room to the other, frantically searching for more of the creeping invaders.

"The ship's airtight," Jensen explained, "so unless someone let them in it's impossible for—"

"Sir," the strained voice of one of the security personnel called out over Chang's wrist-comm. "We've got big problems down here. There's some sort of infestation...wait...they're attacking. We can't—"

The sound of weapons fire interrupted the communication.

"Ensign Page, come in," Chang hollered into his communicator.

There was no response.

"They're coming through the windows," one of the junior officers shouted, sounding terrified.

All eyes were drawn to the blur of rapidly vibrating creatures that drifted mysteriously through the solid glass that should have kept them at bay. Jensen quickly commandeered a pulse rifle from one of the junior officers near his command station, leaving the lieutenant on his own to locate and obtain the only remaining spare.

"How are they doing that?" wondered Dead Eye, aiming at the nearest creature. "That just ain't right."

"Try telling that to them," said Chang, raising his weapon as well.

"Check your crossfire and fire at will," Jensen commanded, positioning himself near the elevator and safely between defensive groups.

As the ghostly bodies of the creatures emerged from the inner surface of the upper windows, they ceased vibrating, returned to solid form, and plopped down onto the floor. Everyone immediately opened fire, lighting up the forward balcony with a barrage of carefully aimed plasma bursts. As one creature exploded, two more took its place, scurrying along the catwalk and up the walls.

The starboard tactical display station shattered as stray shots pierced its delicate surface. Jensen cringed at the sight of the damaged station, but he wasn't about to order anyone to hold back.

"There's too many of them," Dead Eye complained, repeatedly squeezing the trigger on his pulse rifle. His weapons fire splattered at least a dozen of the threatening creatures, but failed to deter the rest of the advancing horde. "They're coming through faster than we can—" Having caught sight of the creature that was jumping toward his face, he instinctively ducked. The hostile life form soared toward the rear wall and suctioned to it. Dead Eye lunged backward and smashed the butt of his rifle against the nasty intruder before it could make a second pass. He then intentionally crushed two more beneath his feet and opened fire at others scurrying along the starboard wall.

Panicked screams emanated from the portside corner of the rear balcony as the huddled pack of junior officers found themselves overwhelmed by the infestation. The spider-like creatures leapt onto and clung to their faces, wrapping their long, slimy legs tightly around the heads of their squirming prey. And as they arched their rounded bodies, they exhaled a powdery green mist into their victims' airways. Within seconds the officers ceased moving and their bodies collapsed on the floor, leaving the detaching little monsters poised to strike again.

"What the freak did they do to 'em?" Dead Eye worried aloud while sniping the creatures that surrounded the limp bodies in the corner.

"I don't know," said Chang, "and I don't want to..." His eyes were immediately drawn to the wave of space spiders that had begun descending on the lower deck, even coming through the bottom windows. "Protect the admiral," he shouted, rushing toward the railing.

"Hold your ground, Lieutenant," barked Jensen, but his orders were ignored. Chang jumped and tucked into a summersault flip before landing on the lower level, between bursts from Kate's pulse rifle. He immediately withdrew to a defensive position beside Kate and Jonathon, shooting any creatures that drew near.

Dead Eye and Parker tried to follow suit but had become surrounded. A few of the spiders jumped toward Parker, prompting Dead Eye to react. He dropped his weapon and snatched two of the aggressive life forms out of the air, crushing one of them in his hand. The other creature wrapped itself around the lieutenant's forearm, expanded its mouthful of razor-sharp teeth, and bit down, removing a small yet bloodied chunk of flesh from his arm. Screaming in pain, Dead Eye slammed his forearm against a nearby command station and splattered the small assailant. But as he turned around, he realized that his efforts had been in vain. Parker collapsed to the floor with a hollow thud. Reaching down, Dead Eye tried to detach the life form from off his friend's face, but he soon found himself covered from head to toe by creatures that had pounced on him from every direction. One of them scurried up his chest and latched around his mouth. But as it huffed its noxious fumes, he clamped his mouth shut, trying not to breathe in the overpowering vapor. The feisty attacker sensed the resistance and placed its mouth directly under the lieutenant's nose. With a shrill hiss it disgorged a moister puff of gas into his airways. Coughing and sputtering, Dead Eye became dizzy and tumbled over backwards, crushing several of the creatures as his body fell limp beside Parker.

Jensen was next. Feeling one of the nasty things leap atop his right shoulder, he instinctively grabbed it and flung it across the room, but dozens more had already converged on his location. And as they jumped, he tried to flee down the stairs, but slipped on the organic remains that littered his path. Falling hard to the ground, he tumbled down the steps, banging and bruising his body along the way. He wound up face down on the lower level, lying still and drifting in and out of consciousness.

Chang watched with mounting fear as his allies dwindled in number. The four junior officers near the center of the lower deck were the next to fall, leaving himself, Kate, and Jonathon as the only remaining survivors.

"I won't let it end like this," he insisted while laying down nonstop suppressing fire ahead of the creeping floor. The majority of the lower balcony was awash with the creatures' splattered, mushy entrails, yet there seemed to be no end to their numbers.

"Look out!" warned Kate as several of the creatures jumped onto Chang and overwhelmed him. He collapsed onto his side and, having failed to protect Kate, he gazed briefly at her with an apologetic expression before losing consciousness.

Kate continued firing until her weapon jammed. Then she used it as a blunt object to swat away several more creatures until one of them managed to bite her hand and disarm her. Moving closer to Jonathon, she leaned over him and used her body as a shield, though she knew her actions would most likely do little good. As her eyes closed, she cringed and waited for an end that seemed like it would never come. A quiet minute passed, then two. Easing her head back up, Kate opened her eyes to a frightening scene. Every inch of the room was covered with the spider-like creatures except for a tiny perimeter around her and Jonathon. Kate held her breath, fearing that the slightest movement might provoke an attack. And yet the creatures seemed hesitant to finish their task. Feeling Jonathon's cold body twitch, she glanced down at him. His eyes popped open, startling her. They were still black as pitch and inhuman. Cocking his head toward the sea of creatures, he uttered an unusual directive in a language not his own. "*Derashka!*"

A chorus of sharp hisses filled the air as the grotesque entities withdrew. Back along the floor and up the walls they scurried, heading to other parts of the ship in search of fresh victims.

"Jon, are you all right?" Kate asked, sensing that perhaps the danger had passed. "Jon?"

Turning his head back toward his companion, Jonathon stared up at her and smiled in a way that made her feel strangely uncomfortable. Kate opened her mouth as if to speak, but she felt something moving atop her head. A lone creature crept down her forehead and huffed its powdery gas across her face. She coughed and became faint. With her head bobbing, she glanced one last time at Jonathon, who was sporting an uncharacteristically callous expression.

"Who are you?" she stuttered in a failing voice, recognizing that he was not himself. But before any response was given, she passed out.

Fighting to remain conscious, Jensen looked on in disbelief, wondering how it was possible that the creatures obeyed Jonathon's command, sparing only him and no one else. The scene troubled him deeply, but before he could nourish the dark seeds of conspiracy that had been planted in his mind, he passed out and remained that way.

Chapter 14
Traitors in the Midst

Surrounded by darkness and despair, Jonathon remained in a timeless limbo, oblivious to the events that were unfolding around him. His thoughts dwelt on Kate, his trusted officers and crew, even the work of death that continued uninterrupted on Earth. He felt more isolated and helpless than he had ever been in his life, yet he wasn't alone.

Whispers from a stranger fell upon his ears. Jonathon listened intently to each of the words, cursing the alien tongue in which they were spoken. But this time he wasn't able to comprehend them. He waited to hear the hissing echo that had always conveyed their meaning before, but it never came. Even though the stranger's voice had been projected toward Jonathon, he soon realized it was speaking to someone else—a dark and commanding presence.

"Zar ish peshkal'ta malray?" a threatening voice growled. Jonathon shivered upon recognizing the rumbling utterance of Drak'Rasha, the malevolent alien being that had ensnared his mind. And though he didn't understand what had been said, he couldn't shake the impression that something terrible was about to happen to his crew.

"Baylo, valoi lay'rasha," the stranger humbly whispered in acknowledgement.

"Grego. Uluq ish mortalum'quay," Drak'Rasha snapped in a tone that conveyed a perverse sense of satisfaction.

"Baylo, Drak'Rasha," the stranger acknowledged reverently before departing. The soft shuffle of footsteps faded into the distance.

After a brief moment, the enveloping shadows began to shift, altering the scenery around Jonathon until his eyes beheld a gloomy stone hallway. The dull, mud-toned walls and floor had been haphazardly chipped away, leaving a crude tunnel that was sufficient to move through, yet felt more like a tomb than a transitional corridor.

Gazing up, Jonathon watched the ceiling ripple like water, then wash away. In its place he saw a star-filled region of space, which did little to improve his dismal surroundings. He observed one of the stars brighten, then fade away forever. Then he saw another, and another. It was as if the light and life force of entire worlds were being extinguished from the universe. The scene gave him pause, left him wondering when the Earth's light would go out.

Feeling compelled to move, he walked forward, still glancing up from time to time. His journey eventually brought him to a jagged wall at the end of the hallway where he stopped and waited.

"Oknala," demanded Drak'Rasha, causing the ground to tremble at his command. Dust fell from the obstructing wall as the rocks separated, fragmenting like a jigsaw puzzle. The individual segments retracted back into the adjacent walls and revealed an opening, through which Jonathon stepped.

Though he tried to resist going forward, he felt more like a shadow than a man, unable to control his own movements. The room that he had entered was less claustrophobic than the tunnel, yet still narrow with stone framing that stretched as far as the eye could see. And his ears were soon troubled by the pained outcries of many unseen individuals, calling out like specters in the night.

Twin flames suddenly erupted along both sides of the room, rising high and burning untamed. The fire spread like a roaring tsunami, masking the walls as it surged into the distance. Jonathon took another step and the flames subsided, extinguishing themselves far enough to reveal the unfortunate individuals contained behind the fiery barrier. He cried out upon seeing the downtrodden faces of his crew.

His outburst spurred a sadistic laugh from Drak'Rasha. And as the laugh faded into a hiss, the cruel overlord spoke in a rumbling voice. "Pa nox'la haisen'ta wist vail ledgekor'et nox'la orlaban. Un jelai nox'la grabor pax nox'la peshtoy uthun'ta jel lenkillra'et."

A soft hissing echo conveyed the message in words that Jonathon could understand. "For your crimes have I judged

*your world. And by your hand shall your wretched companions
be scourged."*

*The unnerving laugh once again echoed through Jonathon's
thoughts as he was forced to venture forward, walking within his
waking dream.*

Deep within the bowels of the planetary fragment that
resided within the hellish nebula, the *Intimidator's* crew had
been imprisoned, caged like animals in a long and narrow room.
Fiery-orange beams of energy encircled each of the captives,
illuminating the dull-brown locale and the dark, blood-like stains
that testified to past atrocities. Sparks of electricity arced
between the beams from time to time and on rare occasions
struck the magnetic soles of the crews' boots, crackling and
releasing an acrid odor into the musty air.

Though upright and fully coherent, the prisoners were
exhausted and some were battered and bruised. Occasional
screams echoed throughout the room, hinting at the barbaric
treatment that a few unfortunate individuals had already been
forced to endure.

As Jonathon walked forward, whispers drifted through the
air. The crew watched enviously as their beloved leader moved
freely among them. But there was neither hope nor comfort to be
found in his presence. Jonathon's eyes were consumed in
shadows and his face displayed only the hatred the aliens bore
for their human captives. A mounting sense of betrayal followed
him as he walked.

"Traitor!" Jensen shouted as Jonathon drew near to his cell.
The spiteful commander put all of his energy and passion into
each of the words that he hurled at Jonathon. "You couldn't beat
them so you offered us up as sacrifices to spare your own life.
Coward."

"Shut up," Dead Eye hollered from across the way. "The
admiral wouldn't do that."

"Open your eyes, genius," Jensen growled back. "The
evidence clearly speaks for itself. He walks freely while we're
caged here like animals, waiting to die—"

"You don't know what you're talkin' about. I'm tellin' you,
they did somethin' to him, back on—"

"*Sheloq*," an alien guard demanded in a low-pitched voice. It was dressed in typical albeit dimmed battle armor and carried a long black pike instead of the organic weaponry that had been used by the alien soldiers back on Earth. The guard marched up beside Dead Eye and struck the encircling energy bars with its pike, producing an iridescent flash and a jolt of heat that seared the lieutenant's face. He winced in pain and wisely kept his mouth shut.

"Maybe now you finally get it," Jensen sneered.

Stepping toward Jensen, the alien guard struck his energy bars as well. The move was designed to restore order, but it didn't work. Jensen had become consumed with anger and at that moment he lashed out without thinking of the full consequences of his actions. He spat on the alien and cursed it, provoking his subjugator to such a point that it raised its pike and prepared to deliver a fatal blow.

"*Trentosh!*" Jonathon snapped in a commanding tone. Though the alien directive had been uttered in his own voice, it was Drak'Rasha's thoughts that projected from his mouth.

"*Baylo, lay'rasha,*" the guard said humbly, obliging with the order to stand down. It wiped the saliva from its faceplate and cursed Jensen before turning to face Jonathon. Bowing its head, it oriented the pike in a submissive, horizontal position and held it out with its palms open.

Jonathon snatched the pike out of the guard's hands and glared at Jensen.

"Go ahead," Jensen taunted, glaring back. "Finish it, if you've got the guts."

Jonathon scraped the pike along a few of the energy bars, smiling wickedly with each burst of heat that seared Jensen's flesh. Then he turned and walked away, leaving the commander's curses to fall upon deaf ears. He continued walking until he reached one cell in particular.

"Kate," Jonathon exclaimed as he stared at her demoralized face. But she couldn't hear him. He was still caught between a dream and reality.

Drak'Rasha spoke. "Ish may nox gullushui pax jel mog: The one you prize shall be first."

"No!" screamed Jonathon defiantly. "I will not harm her."

"Abrai ish emlafet reka ehmfet yuke'ta nox'la enballe: Strike the female until she curses your name."

As a spine-chillingly malicious laugh filled the air, Jonathon felt his arms rise, angling the pike into a striking position.

"No," he screamed, trying to resist his uncontrollable movements.

The laugh grew louder.

"Jon," Kate pleaded, eyeing the weapon with mounting concern. She wanted to reach out and touch him, embrace him, but that was out of the question. The restricted spacing of the beams would have led to severe burns, possibly a severed limb. Kate also recognized that Jonathon wasn't himself, which frightened her. And so she crept back an inch or two, which was all the extra room she had.

With a vicious scowl on his face, Jonathon closed the gap and raised the end of the pike until it was mere centimeters away from Kate's face. Then he withdrew the weapon slowly. His arms began to tremble and his face became twisted under the great physical and emotional stress that he bore. "I won't do it," he uttered in a strained voice. The shadows that had consumed his eyes faded for a brief moment as newfound strength mounted within him. Having temporarily regained control of his body, Jonathon emerged from his waking nightmare and looked at Kate, staring at her through his own two eyes. "Forgive me," he whispered.

"Jon?" Kate cried out. "What's happening?"

Feeling the darkness overtake him again, Jonathon crept backwards and groaned, almost fell to his knees. With his arms shaking, he angled the pike toward his own neck and muttered a statement under his breath. "My will is my own. I will not harm her." He then struck himself with the pike, provoking a flash of red as it contacted and singed his flesh. His hands convulsed and lost their grip on the weapon and his veins started to glow as if his bloodstream had been set on fire. With an ear-shattering scream that exhausted all of the air from his lungs, he collapsed to the ground, writhing from the unbearable pain that coursed through his entire body.

A scream of anger thundered through his mind as Drak'Rasha was forced to abandon its control over Jonathon's paralyzed body. *"Illgrata! Nox'la nixkillrusha'qui zil ungali alph'hati'qui."*

The hissing echo repeated the threatening statement to Jonathon, though he was barely conscious enough to hear it. "Fool! Your suffering is just beginning."

The crew looked on with shock and bewilderment, unaware of the events that had led Jonathon to inflict such horrendous pain on himself. But one crewman in particular was about to get a glimpse of the nightmare that had besieged Jonathon's mind. The timid young ensign, who looked more like a child than a man, stood nervously within his containment cell beside Jonathon's twitching body. A cold numbness came over him and he exhaled with a faint whimper as his eyes widened, then plunged into darkness. Like a parasite searching for a new host, the nefarious being that had tormented Jonathon took control of the quivering ensign's mind. His face became tense with anger and he cursed Jonathon in the alien tongue. And as the cursing softened into a hiss, he snapped his head toward the guard and barked out an order. *"Jorshu hem ra ish mortalum'quay."*

"Baylo, Drak'Rasha," the guard acknowledged, smacking a clenched fist against its left breastplate. The alien promptly moved toward Jonathon, whose physical suffering had already started to subside. Reaching down with one hand, the guard grasped Jonathon's throat and yanked him up until his feet dangled above the floor. Jonathon squirmed and gasped for air, but the guard's grip remained firm.

The young ensign groaned and became dizzy as Drak'Rasha severed the telepathic link. Staggering in place, he almost fell into the energy bars and what would have been a great deal of pain or even death.

Several meters away, flashes of blue light and a faint humming sound drew everyone's attention. A barely elevated circular platform was pulsating along its hardened black base, which was encrusted with four long, equal-spaced talons that curved inward at a slight angle. A mirrored platform hung from the ceiling, pulsating in sync with its counterpart. The unusual apparatus extended from one side of the corridor to the other, producing gaps in the spacing of the prisoners. And within seconds of activating, a bright-blue ring of energy shot from the bottom platform to the top, after which the device powered down. There, standing within the center of the platform, was a rather burly guard who seemed to have appeared out of thin air. The newly arrived alien stepped off the platform and walked toward one of the containment cells.

"*Onlo,*" stated the guard that was restraining Jonathon. It turned and pointed directly at Jensen. "*Jorshu tau may,*" it said with great loathing in its voice.

The other guard nodded, marched up to Jensen, and placed its right hand flat against the rectangular device that was mounted to the wall near the commander. With a pop and a crackle, the energy bars deactivated and a jolt of electricity shot through Jensen's body, stunning him long enough for the alien to wrap one hand around the commander's throat and yank him into custody. Back to the platform it walked, dragging Jensen along the way.

With their two prisoners held close, the aliens stepped up onto the platform and stood side by side while it activated. As the ring of energy flashed before Jonathon's eyes, he saw his surroundings change in an instant. He was no longer in the cramped prison corridor, but was now standing on a platform within a dark and dismal arena. The room's size was difficult to discern at first, with nothing more than a faint cascade of light illuminating the center. But as the guards walked, their echoing footsteps were almost swallowed up within the veiling shadows, revealing that the room was more spacious than it seemed.

A multitude of whispers drifted out from all directions, growing louder until they became snarling laughter at the sight of both men being dragged to the center of the cold, seemingly barren room. There they were discarded, sent stumbling down onto the bloodstained ground. The laughs became uproarious for a time, then quieted gradually while the two guards moved back to the platform and vanished from sight.

"*Saetenta ish traden uluqzon'ta,*" Drak'Rasha shouted from on high, speaking in a low but mocking tone. The statement caused a fresh uproar of laughter that echoed through the room, eventually fading into a rhythmic chant. "*Krey*," a chorus of low-rumbling voices shouted in unison while the sounds of metal clanging against stone resonated through the room. Their taunting pattern was repeated over and over again, increasing in volume with each round.

Jensen rose to his feet and immediately began a visual hunt for an exit. He wanted no part in whatever was about to take place.

Pushing himself upright, Jonathon groaned and staggered a little. His diminished strength had yet to fully return. He stood still while his eyes adjusted to the dim lighting, but he soon struggled to maintain his balance as the ground quaked, much to the delight of the unruly crowd. The outer perimeter of the room separated and retracted back into the walls, producing a harsh grinding noise in the process. The arena acquired a yellowish hue and became noticeably brighter as the outer stone flooring disappeared, giving way to a clear view of the violent nebula that raged outside. Flickers of blue light revealed the force field that had replaced the missing floor segments, keeping the cosmic storm at bay.

The stone segment twenty meters in diameter that remained in the center of the room was hovering yet stayed firmly in place. It hung mysteriously in the air over the nebula, leaving a queasy feeling in both Jonathon's and Jensen's stomachs.

Though some shadows still lingered along the walls, Jonathon could now see the host of bloodthirsty spectators that chanted for his death. Hundreds of armor-clad alien soldiers were standing within carved-out walkways that ranged around the entire room. A half-sized stone wall kept each of the aliens safely contained within the narrow corridors, which were evenly spaced all the way up to the jagged ceiling where darkness still reigned supreme.

Jonathon's eyes inched up the walls, scanning his grim surroundings. He searched for signs of the evil being that had tormented him, but he couldn't see through the blackened veil. And yet the cold tingle in his spine told him that Drak'Rasha was near.

Another minor quake shook the ground and a small opening formed in the center, drawing the attention of Jonathon and Jensen. From within the hole came a hovering, thin black device with pulsating red edges. Up it floated beyond the resealing stone until it had achieved a height even with Jonathon's waist. A pair of polished ruby orbs rested on the surface of the device.

Jensen eyed the unusual items and crept toward them, causing the unnerving chanting to grow louder, more intense. He felt an inexplicable urge to reach his hand out and snatch one of the orbs, as if someone was whispering into his thoughts. Without realizing it, he was playing right into Drak'Rasha's hands. Jonathon felt the urges too, but he recognized the source of the temptation and fought it.

"Stay away from them," he cautioned.

"I don't take orders from *you* any more," Jensen snapped, permitting his contempt for Jonathon to cloud his judgment.

"Those things could be dangerous."

Ignoring Jonathon's advice, Jensen reached in to take hold of one of the orbs, but as he drew near it produced a soft glow. He became apprehensive and withdrew his hand, stepping back and watching as the peculiar jewel came to life. With a startling flash of light, it disintegrated, leaving behind a hazy red mist that showed no signs of dissipating. The throbbing discoloration spread out and gravitated toward Jensen, keeping pace with his nervous movements. He backtracked several more steps, checking behind him to ensure he still had sufficient room to maneuver, that he wasn't being cornered. But before he could take another step, the mist shot forward and swarmed around his body until he was completely covered from head to toe. He flailed his arms about, trying in vain to swat it away, but he stopped when he felt his body lift off the ground and levitate almost a meter into the air. The gaseous shroud began shifting, twisting, and reshaping itself until it resembled a mighty battle suit that was similar in design to the assault units that had been unleashed on Earth. Its size was much smaller, though, and it didn't appear to be entirely solid either, leaving the ghostly red armor seeming more fictitious than ferocious.

Jensen remained thunderstruck for a moment, trying to grasp the reality of what had just happened to him. He was unharmed, yet he felt different, powerful. It was an intoxicating sensation and he liked it.

"You were right about one thing," said Jensen contemptuously. "Those things are dangerous...dangerous for you."

Jensen ran toward Jonathon and lashed out at him with one of his armored fists. Diving out of the way, Jonathon narrowly avoided the assault, but he still felt the vibrations trickle up through his feet as the commander's fist slammed against the ground with a resounding thud, surprising both men with the degree of power contained within the vaporous battle suit.

"What's wrong with you?" shouted Jonathon, keeping his distance. "I know we've had our differences, but this is insane."

"What's the matter? Are you afraid to fight me? Afraid I might be better than you?"

"Back off," Jonathon warned while scooting backwards.

"You're not as tough without your alien friends backing you up."

Jensen lunged at Jonathon once again, but he managed to duck and rolled out of the away before the commander could connect with what would have been a devastating blow.

Discontented murmurs began resonating from the restless spectators as they voiced their objections to the one-sided battle.

"I'm not in league with those savages," Jonathon insisted. "I had nothing to do with any of this."

"Prove it," Jensen shouted before taking another swipe at Jonathon. Part of his fist caught the edge of Jonathon's right shoulder, knocking him over hard as he attempted to flee.

Jonathon groaned and scampered back to his feet. As much as he hated the idea of fighting one of his own, he realized he had no other choice. Darting toward the center of the room, he seized the remaining orb. It disintegrated in his hands and released a red mist that snaked around his body.

The crowd reacted favorably to Jonathon's decision and resumed their chanting, encouraging the two men to engage each other in deadly combat. Jensen obliged. He rushed toward Jonathon, who was now enclosed within his own battle suit. The two combatants collided, producing a crackling sound and a hailstorm of light as their ghostly armor interacted. They wrestled for a minute, then, while struggling to push Jensen away, Jonathon inadvertently released an electrical discharge that sent Jensen flying backwards onto the ground. The commander's failed assault spurred scoffing laughter from the unruly spectators.

Amazed by his newfound power, Jonathon looked down at his hands, wondering how he had managed to unleash the defensive burst and how he could use it again, if necessary.

Infuriated, Jensen rose to his feet and scowled at Jonathon. Jeers from the hostile aliens fueled his rage further. He hated them, but at the moment he hated Jonathon more. And so, with the aliens still urging him on, Jensen took half a step forward before noticing a change in the hollowed tips of the mystical armor surrounding his arms. They were glowing with an intensity that matched his temper perfectly. Raising his arms, he vented his rage. Two bursts of energy shot toward Jonathon and detonated against his midsection. The force of the explosion knocked him a little way into the air and down onto his backside, much to the delight of the crowd. Skidding along the ground, Jonathon approached the edge of the platform and stopped, his head hanging partway over. The attack had left his chest throbbing, even bruised several of his ribs, causing him to grimace in pain on his first attempt to stand up.

"Get up," yelled Jensen. "I'm not through with you yet."

Having caught a glimpse of the nebula out of the corner of his eyes, Jonathon found new motivation for rising to his feet. He rolled over onto his stomach and pushed himself upright.

Jensen took a few steps forward, but stopped abruptly when an obtrusive spike erupted out of the ground directly in front of him. Its appearance solicited an energetic reaction from the crowd.

Annoyed with the aliens' interference, Jensen raised his head and screamed at the top of his lungs. "Stay out of it! This is my fight."

Many soldiers in the crowd shouted back a slew of remarks that had a derogatory tone to them, but Jensen ignored them, focusing only on his desire to resume the battle.

As the spike sunk back into the ground, two more took its place in other locations, with still more appearing after that. And so the madness continued. The dangerous obstructions would appear in overtly random locations and with little warning, bringing new possibilities for pain and death.

Jensen moved toward Jonathon with one cautious step after another, glancing down at the ground frequently. As his anger and frustration mounted, his weapons began charging again.

Still reluctant to take any action that might bring serious injury to his former comrade, Jonathon worried about how he was going to defend himself against the imminent assault. As Jensen raised his arms into a firing position, Jonathon took a deep breath and braced for the attack. While doing so he felt a surge of power course through his armor, causing it to brighten. A quick check of Jensen's battle suit revealed that his armor dimmed slightly as his weapons charged. *Now it makes sense. These things feed off our emotions.*

With a venting outcry, Jensen unleashed two bursts of energy that slammed into Jonathon's midsection, but dissipated without inflicting any noticeable damage. The attack had been repelled. And so Jensen decided to employ a more direct approach. "Block this," he growled, rushing head on toward Jonathon. He lunged forward in an attempt to tackle his opponent, but his effort was thwarted by another defensive discharge. Jensen fell awkwardly backwards as a spike burst out of the ground. Its hardened black tip went straight through his ghostly armor and sliced into his right shoulder, narrowly missing his head. Though it was a mere flesh wound, it still stung nonetheless. And the fresh jeering laughter from the alien soldiers stung even more.

"That's enough," demanded Jonathon. "We need to end this now before one of us dies."

"The only way out of this is through death," said Jensen in a strained voice, pushing upright. He stumbled to his feet and stared callously at Jonathon, calculating his next move. The raw power at his disposal gave him confidence, yet through his anger he was inadvertently rendering the defensive capabilities of his armor virtually nonexistent. Either he didn't realize this or, in his rage, he discounted its importance. His right wrist rotated subconsciously in a subtle counterclockwise motion as he studied Jonathon's armor, probing it for weaknesses. A sparkling mist began spiraling out from the front of his arm as it moved, and upon discovering this, Jensen moved his arm more vigorously, strengthening the vaporous trail into an energy whip that crackled as it impacted the ground.

Jonathon was becoming increasingly annoyed with Jensen's refusal to back down. He was at a loss for the means to get through to his obdurate opponent. So he wisely kept his distance, stepping carefully around the sporadically thrusting spikes while maintaining a defensive posture.

Jensen raised his right arm and with a strong snapping motion he cracked his energy whip near Jonathon's head, but missed. He then moved closer and prepared to initiate a second attempt. As the whip snapped, Jonathon snatched the end of it. Then, holding it tightly in both hands, he screamed at the top of his lungs. "Enough!"

His intense emotional outburst produced an energy surge that disintegrated the whip before slamming into Jensen's armor. The force of the blast sent the commander flying backwards. He scraped across the ground and spun part way around as his legs neared the edge. Feeling his body start to fall, Jensen grabbed a thrusting spike, temporarily sparing himself from a gruesome death within the nebula. But he was far from safe. His boots had crossed through the energy barrier and had begun to melt from the corrosive vapors.

Jonathon rushed forward and as the spike retracted, he dove on the ground and latched onto Jensen's arms. "Hold on," he instructed, struggling to prevent himself from sliding further. A spike popped up in front of him, allowing him to brace his legs against it. Relying on the strength of his battle suit, Jonathon pulled Jensen to safety.

The alien spectators became raucous and shouted their objections to the noble act.

"*Krey con ithca!*" Drak'Rasha bellowed in an angry tone that echoed through the room. Jonathon felt the rage shower down and he sensed that the order had been given for his execution.

The missing floor segments extended out of the walls, returning to their former places beside the centerpiece. And the ghostly armor that had encased Jonathon and Jensen evaporated, leaving both men vulnerable and feeling unusually weak. As they lay beside each other on the ground, the strange platform that had brought them into the arena activated, transporting in an alien soldier armed with an organic weapon. It stepped down of the platform and hissed.

Jensen was astounded by what Jonathon had done. All of his anger and frustration had drained away, leaving only an expression of shame that washed across his face. *What have I done?* Remorsefully, Jensen buried his face in his hands and tried to shut out his guilt, but he couldn't. And the footsteps of the alien soldier were drawing closer, prompting him to make a quick decision. Raising his head back up, he saw the prominent figure aim its weapon at Jonathon, who was struggling to push himself up off the floor. Jensen immediately leapt to his feet and shoved Jonathon out of the way. A single burst of energy slammed into Jensen's stomach and burned clear through his clothing and flesh, spraying blood out from the prominent exit wound in his back.

"No!" Jonathon screamed as Jensen fell back onto the floor. Blood gurgled from the commander's mouth as he turned his head toward Jonathon and tried to vocalize his penitence. But his life faded too quickly.

Outraged by the murderous act, Jonathon stood up and was about to lunge toward the alien when a massive explosion rocked the arena. A sizeable chunk of the jagged ceiling plummeted to the ground near the alien soldier and shattered with a loud thud. The partial cave-in was followed by a wailing siren and a voice projecting an urgent statement through the facility's communication system. *"Embatlei gor'ta. Volun zar oshmot raituk."*

Heeding the call to arms, the alien soldier departed swiftly from Jonathon's presence and returned to its point of entry, then vanished. The surrounding crowd departed as well, filling the arena with the sounds of their hurried footsteps. Jonathon was alone.

Two more explosions shook the arena, but Jonathon ignored them. He knelt beside Jensen's lifeless body and removed the small, star-shaped Medal of Courage pendant that had been pinned proudly above the other ribbons that adorned the commander's jacket. Jonathon fastened the rare medal to his own jacket in the empty region opposite his own testaments of courage. This traditional military ritual was performed as a means of honoring a soldier who had died defending his fellow man.

"I hope you've found your peace," said Jonathon, gently closing Jensen's eyes with one hand.

Another, smaller explosion echoed through the barren arena as Jonathon walked with a heavy heart back to the platform. Standing in the middle of the device, he glanced at his fallen comrade one last time before the platform activated. In the blink of an eye Jonathon was standing within the prison corridor again.

"Admiral," a smattering of familiar, friendly voices called out.

"Jon, you're all right," hailed Kate with a look that properly conveyed how relieved she was to see him. "Where's Paul?"

"Yeah," said Dead Eye. "Where is the little rat?"

"He's dead," Jonathon snapped. "He died saving my life."

"Sorry," Dead Eye mumbled, wishing that he could take back his remark.

"What's going on, sir?" asked Chang, standing in the cell beside Kate. "It sounds like someone's started a war out there."

"I don't know, but it's bought us some time to escape. I just need to find a way to deactivate these bars."

Jonathon examined the small rectangular device that was mounted to the wall near Kate's cell. He recalled watching one of the guards use such a device to free Jensen, but there weren't any discernable buttons or controls. It produced no response when he placed his hand on it.

"What gives?" said Dead Eye. "Why won't they shut down?"

"It must have a security measure that only responds to the aliens," opined Chang.

"Any ideas?" Jonathon inquired.

"Only one," Dead Eye continued. "When in doubt, hit it."

"That's your suggestion?" said Chang.

"You got a better one?"

"Well, no."

And neither did Jonathon. He looked around and immediately zeroed in on the alien pike that was still lying on the floor. But as he retrieved the weapon, he heard a guard shouting at him from behind. Turning around, he saw the familiar presence advancing in the distance. And from the other end of the room came a grinding noise. The obstructing wall at the front of the corridor had begun to fragment and separate. Spinning his head back around, Jonathon tensed as he saw six alien soldiers step through. They raised their weapons and fired. The energy bursts sailed right past Jonathon and detonated against the armored chest of the advancing guard, stopping it dead in its tracks. And as Jonathon watched its body fall to the ground, he noticed that the platform near him had activated. Four more enemy soldiers materialized and brushed past Jonathon, as if he didn't even exist. They opened fire on the other six soldiers near the front of the room, killing one of them.

"What's up with that?" said Dead Eye, watching the unexpected battle unfold. "They're killin' each other."

"Don't complain," Chang replied. "Better them than us."

"Good point."

Jonathon ducked to the side as more weapons fired down the corridor. Another of the soldiers near the front of the room fell dead, yet managed to deliver a fatal shot to its attacker before collapsing. With the skirmish intensifying, the human prisoners were soon caught in the crossfire. Two crewmen were fatally wounded while a third was struck in the leg, soliciting a pained outcry.

The platform near Jonathon had started to hum again. Reacting quickly, he ran toward it and jammed the tip of his pike into the base of the platform. An electrical discharge exploded away and the device aborted in mid operation. The severed lower halves of three alien soldiers materialized and tumbled off the platform, down onto the ground. Jonathon had successfully prevented more enemy reinforcements from pouring in.

The firefight continued until only one alien soldier remained on each side. Having reached the front of the room, the more aggressive alien cursed the other soldier as it grabbed hold of it and shoved it into the energy bars of a nearby prison cell. The bars seared partway through the soldier's armor. It promptly pushed back and moved itself out of harm's way. Grabbing hold of the more belligerent alien's arms, it flipped its body over its own shoulders and down onto the ground, where it placed one foot firmly on top of the downed alien's chest and delivered a lethal shot to the head.

Jonathon crept back into the open and held the pike to his side, looking defensive but not afraid. Holding perfectly still, he waited for the surviving alien to make the next move. The surprising turn of events had left him wondering if he now had a new ally or if he was simply caught in the middle of a more treacherous plot.

As dark pools of blood formed alongside the fallen bodies, eight more alien soldiers entered from the front of the room, but they were noticeably different than the others. The mesh underlayer of their combat attire was white instead of black, matching their reflective faceplates. And their polished armor shone like silver, with a blue-tinted patina devoid of any wreathing spikes. The crest that was embedded between their breastplates was different as well—a ruby fist instead of the black dragon that marked the armor of their more vicious counterparts. Decorating their breastplates were three distinguishing ideograms, though the symbols were of gold, not blood. And their weapons, while organic in nature, were a much softer shade of blue, with patterns of light that danced along their surface. There wasn't a single hint of darkness among the group, which helped put Jonathon's mind at ease, but only a little.

He opened his mouth to try to address them, but he was drowned out by a harsh grinding sound emanating from the ceiling a short distance in front of him. Looking up, he observed that a hole had mysteriously formed within the stone ceiling, exposing an artificial shaft. Slimy residue dripped freely through the opening and splattered on the ground beside Dead Eye's containment cell.

"Not again," Dead Eye moaned, glancing reluctantly up at the shaft. Out crawled a host of the same spider-like creatures that had originally incapacitated the crew. They moved at a frightening pace, scurrying along the ceiling and toward the front of the corridor.

One of the alien soldiers quickly detached a small disc-shaped device from around its waist and flung it toward the ceiling, ahead of the creeping horde. It clung to the rocky surface and activated, releasing a high-pitched tone that was barely within the perceptible range of human hearing. The hostile creatures halted their advance and cried out in a chaotic chorus of shrieks and hisses, as if in pain. Back along the ceiling they fled, withdrawing through their point of entry. Some of them even departed by phase-shifting up through the stone, eager to escape the noise that tormented them. The latest threat had been repelled, bringing an eerie calm that lasted only for a brief moment.

Another explosion shook the room, causing the energy bars on each confinement cell to flicker, then fade away. The crew was free from their imprisonment.

Jonathon discarded his pike as Kate threw her arms around him, expressing her relief and joy at being reunited with him. And while embracing her, he felt a foreign presence reach out to him with its mind. This time, however, he wasn't afraid. He felt strangely peaceful and the room grew quiet until all he heard was a frail, friendly whisper.

"*Follow them. They will bring you and your people to safety.*"

"*How do I know I can trust you?*" thought Jonathon.

"*You do not have any other choice. I will explain everything when you arrive. Now go. We haven't much time.*"

"What is it?" Kate inquired, looking first at Jonathon, then following his gaze toward the alien sentinels at the front of the room. Aside from uneasiness at their presence, she couldn't figure out what could have caught Jonathon's attention so fully.

"We need to go," instructed Jonathon, finally speaking up.

"Go? Go where?"

"With them," he continued, pointing toward the nine soldiers that stood near the corridor's entrance. One of them motioned for him to approach.

"I sure hope you know what you're doing," Kate said with a puzzled expression.

"So do I," Jonathon mumbled back. "Let's move," he shouted while marching toward the aliens. "Everyone follow me and make sure no one gets left behind."

Dead Eye glanced over at Chang and Parker, all sporting looks of bewilderment.

"Don't ask me," said Chang. "I don't have the slightest clue what's going on, but I'll sure be glad to get out of this nightmare."

"I'll second that," added Parker.

Eight of the aliens stayed behind to guard the rear of the group while one of the lighter-colored soldiers moved through the entryway, leading Jonathon and his crew back through the narrow tunnel. It hustled toward a strangely glowing opening, a wormhole that had formed within the corridor. Leaping through the distortion, the alien disappeared briefly before popping back into view on the other side.

Jonathon took a deep breath and jumped through as well. His body became numb as he crossed the boundaries of the cosmic gateway and he felt as if he was falling. Flashes of spiraling dark matter dominated his view during his brief passage through the wormhole's hidden tunnel. His stomach tossed and turned, but quickly mellowed as he stumbled out onto the hardened, bone-white floor beyond the exit. Once he had made the successful transition, he turned around and motioned for Kate to join him, but she hesitated.

"It's all right," he assured her. "It doesn't hurt."

Kate held her breath, closed her eyes, and jumped. Upon clearing the wormhole, Jonathon helped her regain her balance. "That was...different," she said, straightening up and stepping to the side.

"Pick up the pace," Jonathon ordered as the rest of the crew marched two-by-two through the wormhole, some moving more guardedly than others.

Kate glanced around the large windowless room, awestruck by her peculiar locale. Though the floor seemed relatively normal, the ribbed walls and high-arching ceiling were constructed out of organic matter. They gently pulsated with soft light as power coursed through the web of tiny veins that weaved throughout the fleshy tissue. It didn't look like any room that she had ever seen. In fact, it gave her the creeps.

The escorting alien positioned itself directly in front of the arched doorway at the other end of the room. There it stood motionless, but in a non-threatening posture, as if it was simply observing the humans out of curiosity.

A tremor suddenly rumbled through the room, shaking its occupants, though not hard. To Jonathon it distinctly felt like weapons fire impacting against a starship, giving him the impression that he was on one of the alien vessels.

"Hurry it up," he ordered as more of his crew poured into the room. A second wormhole promptly opened parallel to the first and through it Jonathon could see the rear guard of his crew still waiting anxiously to flee the prison complex. He motioned for them to come through, speeding up the exodus as a more violent tremor shook the room in which he stood.

Everyone who passed through the spatial distortions stared in amazement at their new environment while funneling out amongst their peers.

"Whoa...freaky," Dead Eye commented, poking one of the walls with his bare index finger. The organic tissue was warm to the touch and convulsed a little in response to the obtrusive examination.

"*Onlo*," the alien soldier shouted while shaking its head in disapproval.

Dead Eye promptly withdrew his hand. "Sorry," he hollered back.

"What are you doing?" Chang inquired.

"I was just curious. I think the walls are alive."

Dead Eye's remarks caused Parker's eyes to widen and his anxiety to kick in. He continued to stare at the surrounding tissue, letting his imagination run wild.

Once the last of the crew had entered the room, the wormholes began to fluctuate. The alien soldiers that had stayed behind darted through the collapsing openings, narrowly escaping the boisterous chain of explosions that rang out behind them. They had successfully evaded a retaliatory strike by the enemy. A brilliant flash of iridescent lights signaled the end of the sealing wormholes and preceded one last tremor that rumbled through the room, followed by a tranquil calm. The crew of the *Intimidator* had all been safely rescued and for that they were grateful. But many questions still remained.

"Now what?" asked Kate.

"Now," Jonathon began, unsure of the answer himself, "now we wait."

Chapter 15
Revelations

Jonathon had been conversing quietly with Kate when Chang marched up and stood at attention. "Admiral, the medical staff's finished their examination of the crew. All things considered, everyone seems to be in reasonably good condition."

"Good. That's one less issue to worry about."

Chang nodded in agreement and cracked open his mouth as if to speak again, but he hesitated and silently withdrew his lingering question. The troubled expression on his face, however, was sufficient enough to merit Jonathon's attention.

"Something on your mind, Lieutenant?"

"I mean no disrespect by this, Admiral, but…"

"You're wondering what we're doing here? Wondering if we've made a deal with the devil?"

"Well…yes. We don't know anything about who these guys are, or what they are for that matter. They look and talk exactly like the enemy, which makes me more than a little nervous. And it seems to me like all they've done is pull us from one prison and placed us in another. We've been in here for over three hours now without any effort on their part to try to communicate with us. I don't like this and I don't trust them."

"He has a good point," Kate argued. "I seriously doubt they rescued us as a simple act of kindness. They must have an ulterior motive."

"I understand your concerns," said Jonathon. "There are certainly a lot of questions that need answering," he continued in an elevated tone, hoping their mysterious host was listening.

"*Patience, child,*" a frail, yet familiar voice whispered into Jonathon's mind. "*There is far more at stake here than you realize and I must be certain that you are ready.*"

"*Ready for what?*" thought Jonathon as he mentally withdrew from his surroundings and focused only on the peaceful, unseen presence that had touched his mind. "*What do you want from us?*"

"To open your eyes and help you understand."

"Understand?" Jonathon thought in a somewhat irritated manner. *"Understand what? That the inhabitants of my world continue to suffer and die with each passing moment?"*

"He is not ready," a strange new voice whispered into his mind, followed by three others that repeated the same words in agreement.

"No, he is not," the older presence sighed. *"Nevertheless, I will speak with him. Now come."*

"Jon," exclaimed Kate, snapping her fingers in an attempt to pull him out of his trance-like state.

"Are you all right, sir?" Chang inquired.

Before Jonathon could reply, an armor-clad alien soldier walked through the arched entryway at the end of the room and marched forward at a hurried pace, parting the crowd as he approached.

Chang and six of his security personnel instinctively moved into defensive positions in front of Jonathon. Despite having had much of their lives and past realities shattered, they still performed their duties. Some officers acted out of sheer habit while others considered it a matter of honor, even pride. Either way, the aliens would have to go through Chang and his officers if they wanted to get to Jonathon.

"It's all right," counseled Jonathon, placing a hand on Chang's shoulder. "He's not going to harm me. I've been summoned."

"What?" Kate snapped in a concerned tone, speaking against a backdrop of whispers and mumbling that spread throughout the crew. "You can't leave."

"I agree," said Chang, turning partway around to face Jonathon. "This isn't a good idea, sir."

"I'm just going to speak with the individual that's responsible for bringing us here. I'm hoping to get a few answers and possibly even some help with this war. They obviously have no love for the group that captured us, so there might be a chance to form an alliance. And that's an opportunity I can't pass up."

"I still don't like this," Chang objected. "At least let some of us come with you, as an escort."

"No," the alien host whispered into Jonathon's mind. *"What I have to say can only be spoken to you, and you alone."*

"Sorry, Lieutenant, but I need you to stay here and look after the others. I'm placing you in charge of the crew until I return."

"Jon, please," Kate implored, latching onto Jonathon's arm before he could take a single step.

Placing his hand tenderly over her hand, Jonathon looked into Kate's eyes with a reassuring gaze and replied with, "Don't worry."

"That's easier said than done," she countered.

But Jonathon didn't say anything else. He simply walked out, leaving Kate behind to worry. She folded her arms and watched as he followed the escorting soldier out of the room. Oddly enough, the better part of her trusted that he'd be safe and return unharmed. But the more stubborn part of her believed that she'd never see him again and that was the part she listened to.

Jonathon stepped beyond the arched opening and progressed down a long, forked corridor. The light-blue surface of the fleshy tunnel was expanding and contracting subtly, as if the walls themselves were breathing. In fact, the entire passageway resembled the inside of a trachea.

"Follow the guard and do not stray from your path," the frail alien presence whispered.

"No arguments here," Jonathon mumbled under his breath while eyeing his bizarre surroundings.

The alien soldier led the way for a little while longer before stopping in the middle of one of the corridors. It turned and faced Jonathon. A thin incision formed along the surface of the portside wall, producing a soft ripping sound as it stretched from top to bottom, widening into a doorway-sized opening that revealed a small chamber. Inside was a barely elevated circular platform fastened to the floor, with a mirrored disc that clung to the ceiling. The alien stepped to one side and held out its hand toward the chamber.

Jonathon inched closer and examined the hardened white base of the platform. Its simple architecture seemed strangely familiar. "Well, here goes nothing," he mumbled before setting foot inside the chamber. As he stepped up on the platform and turned around, the wall's cleft membrane became whole again, heightening Jonathon's mounting tension. Sporadic glimmers of light and a soft hum soon radiated from the platform, followed by a ring of pure-white energy that shot up around his body. In that instant his location changed.

He was now standing in the middle of a small circular room with a domed ceiling. The walls were ribbed and composed of the same organic material as before, suggesting that he hadn't traveled far. Six guards stood even-spaced around the perimeter, standing with such a regal stature as to lend a majestic feel to the room. Their battle suits were almost identical to those of the other aliens that Jonathon had already encountered, except for a few minor details. Their shoulder armor was plated in gold, securing the finely woven royal-blue capes that draped their backs. And only two golden ideograms decorated their breastplates, one on either side. The symbol on the right was common to them all, whereas the symbol on the left was unique to each individual.

Stepping down from the platform, Jonathon looked around, waiting for further instruction. He held still and kept his distance from the guards, all of whom stood rigidly as if they were nothing more than decorative statues. But despite their unanimated appearance, Jonathon got the impression they were watching him closely and he didn't want to do or say anything that might be misinterpreted.

A soft tearing sound soon broke the silence, drawing Jonathon's eyes to the wall directly in front of him. There he observed that an incision had formed, parting until a narrow opening took shape. Access to the next room had been granted.

"Come forth, Jonathon Quinn," a gentle voice called out from beyond the entryway. Its spoken English was as clear and perfect as any human's, adding to the questions that already crowded Jonathon's thoughts. But it was the alien's foreknowledge of his name that left him feeling especially uneasy.

Moving forward at a cautious pace, Jonathon stepped through the opening and into a multi-chambered room, the whole of which was open, but with distinct dividers that extended partway out from the curved walls on either side. As he took a few more steps, the opening sealed shut behind him, putting an end to any thoughts he had of backing out, even fleeing to the familiarity and safety of his crew.

"Come here, young human," a mysterious figure called out from the other end of the room. It was wearing a royal-blue robe with a hood that kept its face intentionally hidden. The chair in which it sat was smooth, cupped, and suspended a short distance above the ivory floor, dangling by a series of interwoven tentacles that hung from the arched ceiling. And its light-blue organic surface was emitting a soft white glow, producing an aura-like effect around its peculiar occupant.

"Sit down and rest yourself," the elderly figure requested. Just then, a mass of organic tissue tore right out of the ceiling and descended beside Jonathon. As it lowered, it reshaped itself into a chair that was similar to the one that the robed alien sat in, but with a shorter back and void of any lambency.

"I'd prefer to stand, if it's all the same to you," Jonathon replied, feeling apprehensive about the organic make of the chair.

"It is disrespectful for you to remain standing while I am not. Now, please, sit down. We have much to discuss."

Jonathon positioned himself in front of the chair and hesitantly placed both hands along the rounded armrests. They were soft and warm to the touch, bidding him to lower his body in between. Leaning back into the chair, he studied the elderly figure and tried to peer through the shadows that hung from its hood like a thin veil.

"Who are you?" he asked pointedly.

"A friend," the figure replied.

"Maybe, but how do you know my name? Or more to the point, how come you can speak my language?"

"I discerned your name from your thoughts. I know many things about you, some of which you do not even know about yourself. And as far as your languages are concerned, they have been known to my people for countless generations. Though I must admit you are the first *human* that I have had the opportunity to speak with."

"What are you talking about?" said Jonathon, perplexed by the alien's words. "Who are you?"

"No, Jonathon Quinn, the question is: who are you? Do you know your heritage? Your destiny?"

"My destiny? I have no destiny worth speaking of. Now tell me why you've brought me here."

The aging figure sighed. "As I said, I want to help you understand. I want to awaken your mind and bring you out of the shadows."

"You're talking in riddles. I don't understand what you want."

Reaching its trembling hands up, the alien grabbed hold of its hood and pulled it back behind its head, causing Jonathon's eyes to widen in astonishment. There, staring back at him, was the face of a man, wrinkled and worn with age. His long-flowing hair was white as newly fallen snow and his skin was fair, with a subtle blue overtone. The centers of his sagging eyes were glowing like sparkling sapphires, as if his soul was on fire and shining through them.

"You…you look almost human," Jonathon stuttered, staring in awe at the curious figure.

"Actually, it is the other way around. Let me explain.

"Over ten thousand of your Earth years ago, my people walked among the stars like giants, with a vast society that was spread across many star systems. We were known as the Kush'humani, or in the tongue of your people: the Undefeated. We were peaceful and proud, so proud in fact that we were blinded to the darkness that was swelling within the heart of one of our own noble born. His name was Sa'uluq'Voldrok and he was the Dominant Patriarch of House Voldrok, one of the most powerful clans that shared in the governing of our people. His rise to power was swift and cunning, but there was another of our noble born who saw Sa'uluq'Voldrok for what he was. Rael'Kashan, Dominant Patriarch of House Kashan, was a wise and just leader. He was also predestined to ascend to the throne and become Supreme Patriarch over all Kush'humani.

"Sa'uluq'Voldrok used every means at his disposal to usurp the power for himself, for he craved power like no other. It was a drug, a poison that drove him mad.

"On the morning of the twelfth day of the Festival of Light, when Rael'Kashan was to be anointed Supreme Patriarch by the hands of our elder council, unquenchable darkness consumed all of Eden, the heart of our once-beautiful utopia. In his anger, Sa'uluq'Voldrok stormed the sacred temple and massacred all ten of our archelders. To this day there is still not a curse in my own tongue or yours for the unforgivable acts he committed."

The alien quieted for a moment as tears streamed down his cheeks. "Forgive me," he continued, sounding a little frailer than before. "It still pains my soul to speak of such things."

Jonathon remained quiet, unsure of what to make of everything that was being said. And yet there was a small part of him that sensed that the words were true, extraordinary as they were.

After clearing his throat, the alien resumed speaking. "Rael'Kashan managed to escape and flee to Ushun'Kali, the peaceful home world of his brethren. But Sa'uluq'Voldrok followed. He brought his loyal warriors with him, commanding a fleet of dark and daunting warships that had been constructed in secret. Great and terrible was the battle that ensued. The stars hid themselves in shame, becoming less numerous than the host of precious lives that were lost as brother fought against brother. And when it appeared that House Kashan would fall, the fickle tides of war changed. Having caught word of the treacherous acts of Sa'uluq'Voldrok, the other noble Houses joined forces and came to the aid of their one true ruler. The armada of House Voldrok was repelled, but the worst was yet to come.

"In the time that followed, the ruthless minions of Sa'uluq'Voldrok brought death and destruction to every innocent male and female within reach of their blind hatred. Like cowards they lurked in the shadows, striking at the weakest parts of the empire. The noble alliance had to spread their forces so thin they were ill equipped to defend themselves.

"Rael'Kashan was captured and forced to watch his people suffer and his home world burn. Blackened clouds spread across Ushun'Kali, smothering the tranquil planet with the ashes of its dead inhabitants. All save a few hundred of the most prominent Kashanti who had a direct blood relation to Rael'Kashan were executed. The rest were gathered and sentenced to a fate far worse than death. They were exiled to the remote, uninhabited planet of Solunus III, or what is known to you as *Earth*."

Jonathon was stunned by the shocking revelation and his mind was aflutter with one question after another. The history of his world had been thrown into confusion. "You're telling me that the first man to walk on the Earth wasn't even a man at all?" he questioned. "That we share the same blood?"

"Exactly, young Kashanti," the alien replied with a thin smile. "Your eyes are starting to open, but there is much more yet to be revealed."

"Please, continue," said Jonathon, swallowing back the host of questions that had rushed to the forefront of his thoughts.

"In his cruelty, Sa'uluq'Voldrok altered all of the captured Kashanti, including their beloved patriarch. They were genetically modified to be inferior to their fellow Kush'humani. These alterations placed a barrier between their souls and the universe, a barrier that left each of them in bitter isolation. For you see, the mysteries of life that your kind refers to as psychic phenomena are nothing more than an extension of the soul and its connection with all life and the cosmos itself. The Kush'humani life force has always been potent, more so than most other species. And it is the strength of that life force that determines the magnitude to which one soul can commune with or dominate another. This crude matter that we call our bodies does little more than interfere with our true essence. It is but a vessel, a tool of sorts. There are many species out there that are blind to the full potential of their existence simply because their bodies keep their minds and souls trapped, unable to reach out. Sa'uluq'Voldrok knew this and he used that knowledge to turn the bodies of your ancestors into prisons.

"He also purged their minds of all matters concerning technology and the universe itself. They became as young children, knowing little more than how to care for themselves. Rael'Kashan, however, was not made to forget. Instead he was doomed to live out the remainder of his years with a full memory of the world and life he had been forced to leave behind. Though he was with his brethren and family, he walked as a stranger among them, bearing never-ending grief.

"As a final act of insult, Sa'uluq'Voldrok ordered their names to be stricken from the Great Archives on Eden. They were forevermore to be known as Humani, or in the tongue of your people: Defeated. In time you took the name upon yourselves proudly, calling one another *Human* as if it were a noble title.

"And while the history of the Kashanti came to an end, the legacy of the humans was just beginning. Sa'uluq'Voldrok was far from content to leave the newly formed human species alone. He altered their genetic structure further, producing differences in appearance. The eyes, skin, and hair were thrown into a chaotic mix. Even their languages were confounded. The Great Betrayer knew full well that differences breed mistrust, which can lead to hatred and ultimately to bloodshed. That is what he wanted and that is what he got. For many generations to come he kept a watchful eye on your world. He would send his foul servants from time to time, to descend among the humans and tamper with their progress. They walked like gods among your early ancestors, granting power to some while stripping it away from others. They whispered lies into their thoughts and poisoned their minds with war. Sa'uluq'Voldrok was bent on ensuring that the history of your world would be forever written in blood."

"Are you saying that all of the lunatics who started wars on Earth did so because of alien influence?"

"No, not all. Despite humanity's marvelous and enviable achievements, your people have sown many of their own seeds of darkness. But you know this all too well, do you not? I have seen the scars of war on your heart."

Jonathon nodded in agreement as memories of the recent conflict with Mars flashed through his mind. Mankind's last civil war had certainly changed Jonathon's life and left its share of emotional scars. And at the time it had seemed like nothing more than another stain in humanity's long and troubled history. But now it all seemed so pointless, so trivial.

The elderly figure remained quiet for a little while, permitting Jonathon to meditate on the unexpected revelations. And he used the time himself to gently probe Jonathon's thoughts in a non-intrusive manner, discerning his emotional state of being.

Gazing down at his hands, Jonathon studied them reverently as he reflected on his human existence and mortality. The universe had suddenly become much larger, leaving him feeling small and insignificant. He felt as if his entire life had been a lie. And the more he thought about the alien's words, the more questions he had, the more puzzled he became.

"Does my presence trouble you?" the robed figure inquired politely.

Jonathon raised his head and stared at the alien for a moment before responding. "You claimed all Kashanti were either killed or exiled to Earth."

"Yes. All save a small but fortunate group of families who managed to escape during the chaos. Had they not, I would not be here to fulfill my own destiny. For my name is Eolin'Kashan, Dominant Patriarch of the scattered descendants of House Kashan, and my time here is coming to an end. Long have I been searching for another to take my place, one who has the pure blood of Rael'Kashan flowing through his veins, one who can fulfill the ancient prophecy that has driven our meager lives over the ages. I have served my people in righteousness, tending to their needs as best I can, as have all those who have come before me, but none of us are true heirs to His noble legacy. We are Kashanti, yes, but we are not descendants of Rael'Kashan. His bloodline was broken when he and his offspring and kindred were unjustly cast out so long ago. The bloodline must be restored. You, Jonathon Quinn, are the one I have been waiting for."

"Me?" Jonathon replied in a confused and surprised tone. "How could I possibly be of assistance to you or your people? I know nothing about them or their ways of life. I can't help them. I've barely managed to survive myself."

"Ah, but survive you have. As with most humans, you have learned to triumph in the face of great adversity. It is an admirable trait, and one that Sa'uluq'Voldrok has inadvertently empowered you with. Humanity has come far, and you, Jonathon Quinn, have come farther than most. Do you not know that you are different from the other humans? You are an amazing being, whose soul is potent, unwilling to be bound. It is as if you have been touched by the Gods themselves."

Eolin leaned in a little before continuing. "There is a great power burning inside you, Jonathon Quinn, a power that could shake the foundations of the universe and free us all from the darkness that still walks among the stars. You are a gifted leader and warrior, but above all else you *are* a true descendant of the Great One. The noble birthright is yours to claim."

Leaning back in his chair, Eolin finished speaking. "The decision has been laid before you, but you must decide quickly. I am old and tired and I desire to rest, yet I cannot go until my task is complete."

"Isn't there anyone else? One of your own?"

"Yes, there are others that could take my place, but only you can fulfill the full measure of the calling. You have a great destiny before you, Jonathon Quinn, a destiny that should *not* be ignored. You have the power to bring to pass the Great Awakening and rebuild the Houses of old. If you do as I ask, others will follow. We are but a small band of humble wanderers, traveling through the distant parts of the cosmos. But we are not without resources."

"You have your own fleet of warships, don't you?" said Jonathon with a glimmer of hope in his eyes.

"Yes. You are currently aboard one of them."

Eolin's eyes shifted to the starboard wall where a murky discoloration seeped into view along the organic surface, darkening until it resembled a window that peered out into the vastness of space. There, Jonathon could see dozens of alien warships moving parallel to the one he was on. They were similar to the invading vessels that had decimated his fleet and laid siege to Earth, yet these ships didn't inspire fear. They were breathtaking to behold and almost angelic in appearance. Their hulls were light blue in color and completely smooth and organic in design, with undulating patterns of white light that danced along the surface, like sunlight reflecting off clear water. And there wasn't a single threatening spike or talon anywhere to be seen.

"They're amazing," Jonathon uttered.

"They are an abomination," Eolin replied with an edge of sorrow in his voice.

"I don't understand," said Jonathon, his brow wrinkling in confusion.

"In the years following the defeat of the Great Houses, Sa'uluq'Voldrok revealed exactly how black his soul really was. He began experimenting on his own people, dark and forbidden experiments that focused on controlling the forces of life itself.

"Our vessels are not merely a careful arrangement of organic matter. They are living, sentient beings who were once Kush'humani in form. Through foul genetic manipulation and mutilation, Sa'uluq'Voldrok created all kinds of technological terrors to unleash on the unsuspecting universe. Those with the most potent life forces were snatched away from their families and sent to the spawning pits where they underwent a most painful transformation. The souls of those tortured individuals are forever trapped inside these living vessels. They use their telepathic abilities to maintain contact with one another and with us. In fact, every aspect of this vessel is governed by thought. The crew and vessel together form a symbiotic relationship, moving as one through the cosmos."

"But if they were created under such tragic circumstances, then why do you use them for your own purposes?" Jonathon inquired. "I mean no disrespect, but that seems a little hypocritical."

"We do not use them," Eolin said in a slightly impatient tone. "We have freed them from the unending darkness that had kept them bound to the will of the Evil One. We care for them as if they were our kin, for indeed they are. And in return they help us fight our common foe. We do not create such abominations, my young friend. We simply liberate them. They still have minds of their own, and even names. This one is called Ixlyo and it has been my friend for longer than I can remember. It is wise and offers insight of its own, though it also respects my judgments. I serve as overseer of this vessel while others of my brethren have been chosen to oversee the remaining vessels in our fold. It is the vessels themselves who decide which Kush'humani can serve as overseers. Or, to put it more simply using your own terminology: the ship chooses its captain."

"I think I understand," said Jonathon. "Please forgive my ignorance."

Eolin nodded in response. "This must all be quite overwhelming for you."

"It is, and I'm very tired. I haven't slept well since the war started."

"Ah yes, your chance encounter with Sa'uluq'Voldrok and his forces."

"Wait a minute," Jonathon insisted with a perplexed look on his face. "I thought—"

"Sa'uluq'Voldrok has never tasted death. He is immortal, an undying evil that has spread misery since the dawn of humanity. We do not know how he has defeated death, but we suspect that his experimentation on his own people had something to do with it.

"The Great Betrayer is known by many names, though he chooses to refer to himself as Drak'Rasha, which in the tongue of your people means *Dark God.* I sense that he has already revealed himself to you, has he not?"

"Yes," Jonathon sighed, shuddering as he remembered his recent nightmares. "He's haunted my dreams on several occasions."

"That is because he is afraid of you. He fears what you may become. It is for this reason that he crushed your people so mercilessly.

"But I must admit that you surprised us with the bold stand you and your fleet made against his forces. Our spies have informed us that Chief Warlord Uthka'Voldrok, one of House Voldrok's most arrogant and ruthless butchers, was responsible for overseeing the invasion of your star system and the devolution of humanity. He foolishly underestimated you and your people and you wisely took advantage. It was a great embarrassment for his House, forcing Sa'uluq'Voldrok to correct the warlord's mistakes personally. And as I understand it, Uthka'Voldrok received a most deserving punishment. He and his vessel and crew were all executed by Sa'uluq'Voldrok himself, before the warlord had a chance to savor his victory."

"I recall watching them destroy one of their own ships," said Jonathon with somewhat of a spiteful smile. "The scenario seemed rather bizarre at the time, but it makes perfect sense now." As he pondered the recent memory further, his countenance dulled, became more somber. He could see the image of Drak'Rasha's dark and twisted warship clearly in his mind, causing shuddersome feelings to resurface. "The vessel that destroyed the warlord's ship…it was—"

"A most disturbing sight, I know," Eolin interjected with a solemn expression. "It is called the Rashok'Tyre, the exact meaning of which I will not translate into your language. Suffice it to say, its name is a curse against life itself. It is a most abhorrent creation, feared and hated above all of the other dark imaginations of the Evil One. It functions in part as a warship, a vessel of pure destruction that travels without moving, forever remaining in a stationary orbit high above Eden where it casts its long shadow across the heart of the empire. Using dangerous technology that no sane individual would employ, the Rashok'Tyre folds the fabric of space around its dark and twisted body, in effect causing the universe to move around the vessel, rather than the vessel moving through the universe. It is a perverse display of Sa'uluq'Voldrok's arrogance and power. But it is also something far worse. The Rashok'Tyre was forged from the bodies and souls of a vast host of beings, slaves from every sentient species within the galaxy. Collectively they serve as a hive mind, exercising dominion over all of the lesser creations, and thus ensuring that every vessel and all other instruments of destruction remain subjugated to the will of the Dark God. It is through this abomination that Sa'uluq'Voldrok maintains strict order and control over his empire. It is the head of his living war machine."

"So it controls all of the other ships?" Jonathon asked.

"In a manner of speaking. The dark blood of the Rashok'Tyre is infused into the veins of each vessel shortly after they are spawned. It serves as a mind-enslaving poison, forcing subservience to the vessel's overseer and to Sa'uluq'Voldrok in particular. The Rashok'Tyre also probes the minds of each vessel, removing any thoughts that are considered treasonous. And it has also been known to spy on the warlords and other power-craving individuals from time to time, whispering to the Great Betrayer the names of those whom it considers to be a threat to the empire. Many of our courageous brothers who serve in secrecy within House Voldrok risk death every day, knowing that without warning their names may be whispered next.

"The Rashok'Tyre has made it most difficult for us to liberate vessels from Sa'uluq'Voldrok's control. But once the link to the hive mind is severed, and its toxic blood purged, the vessels can be persuaded to rise up in open rebellion, though they will never take Kush'humani form again. If we had the resources at our disposal we would gladly fashion new starships from the hardened elements, as should always be the way. But we must make due with what we have."

"Well," suggested Jonathon, "if we could recover my ship—"

"No," Eolin interrupted with a gentle shaking of his head. "Your warship is nothing but a trophy now, destined to be added to the countless other barren starships that drift in orbit around Eden, forming an artificial ring of shattered hopes and dreams. Your ship has no doubt already left for Eden, departing the Uzun'gal death camp from which we liberated you and your companions. I will tell you now, Jonathon Quinn, to abandon any designs you have of recovering your ship, for it would be folly to attempt to do so.

"You must understand that Sa'uluq'Voldrok's thoughts are now bent on your destruction. He will probe the cosmos looking for you and the others that now walk free. He will not rest until you are dead, even if you should deny your place as head of House Kashan. And should you venture out of our midst, I can say with great certainty that he will find you and strike you down, for he would cleave unto no other purpose. The same holds true for the others.

"Your people are made to suffer because of the blood that flows through their veins, the blood that flows through your veins, Jonathon Quinn. Sa'uluq'Voldrok did not attack your world simply because of your mishap near Ushun'Kali."

"What?" exclaimed Jonathon, shocked. "You mean that inhabited planet we saw in the Polaris System? That was the Kashanti home world?"

"Yes. That great light, that beacon that shone down on your world did not gain its identity from mere myths. Rael'Kashan shared what he could with those who would listen and believe. He tried to teach them of their origins, their way home. But his words were twisted and lost over time."

"I'm...sorry," Jonathon stuttered, feeling a swell of remorse. "We destroyed your home world and—"

"No," replied Eolin sharply. "That crime is not yours to bear. Ushun'Kali had long been desolate before humanity had ever dreamt of visiting the stars. Once a symbol of peace whose name was spoken with great reverence, Ushun'Kali soon became a hiss and a byword. It is from Ushun'Kali that Sa'uluq'Voldrok launched countless raids and genocidal attacks against other worlds, other civilizations, many of which are now extinct or serve as slaves within his empire. The entire galaxy, save for a few isolated star systems, have fallen under his shadow."

Jonathon shook his head, feeling despair return. "And how am I supposed to defeat such a powerful empire? You're asking me to take on an impossible task."

"Do not think that because he commands such great power that he will always control such great power. There are many civilizations that are willing to fight back, but they lack the courage and leadership that is necessary. They have lived with a slave mentality for far too long. Even we have become set in our ways. It is a hard thing to see beyond one's own limitations and the burdens of one's ancestors. But there is hope. I have seen it in your eyes and heart, such courage and strength of will. You could organize them. You could free your own people and the other scattered remnants of the Great Houses, all of whom have suffered the same fate as House Kashan. If you and the rest of humanity are brought out of the shadows it will prove that his stranglehold over the galaxy can be broken. The Great Awakening must commence.

"Though you do not yet realize it, you have already given them a glimmer of hope. Accident or not, the destruction of Ushun'Kali and its companion star sent ripples that were felt in the furthest corners of the galaxy. It was the sign that we had been waiting for. Sa'uluq'Voldrok was there when the great star exploded, there with his most feared warmongers. And although he and a significant number of his minions escaped unharmed, the incident was viewed by many as a deliberate attempt on his life. It was a devastating blow that brought all eyes to bear on your planet. They are watching and waiting for your next move.

"This conversation is now at an end. There is more for you to learn and understand, but the rest can only be shared with my successor. So tell me, Jonathon Quinn, what is your decision?"

Jonathon was speechless and his mind was racing as he struggled with his decision and the short time in which to make it. *By all rights I should be called insane for even thinking about going along with this. A week ago I would have disregarded all of this as nothing more than the rambling of a crazy old man, but with everything that's happened lately I don't have any reason to doubt him. And it's strange how I feel like I've heard all of this before, as if it's a forgotten memory or dream that's suddenly come back. And what about Earth…*

"This is your only chance to save your people," Eolin whispered into Jonathon's mind, carefully directing his train of thought.

"But why is all of this happening now? Why did you wait so long to help us? If you had contacted us earlier we would have been stronger, we could—"

"There was no other choice. Please understand that it has not been easy to watch your people stumble, nor to watch them suffer and die. Your pain is shared among us all. But prior to Sa'uluq'Voldrok's acts of aggression against your people, your world, we could do nothing. Humanity was the crowning jewel atop his thrown of madness. His unrighteous dominion over your people was firm, unbreakable, or at least not without severe risk. To free six billion lives from captivity without his knowledge would have been near to impossible. But now, everything has changed. You are living history, prophecy unfolding. You are the means to the very action you seek."

"But I'm not ready."

"You are more ready than you realize. And I will help you, as will others. You are not alone. You will never be alone."

Jonathon pondered the decision for a little while longer, trying to focus on the opportunity it presented, rather than the unknown future that it would lead him to. But it was a difficult decision and the most important one of his life. While struggling with the weighty issue, he remembered the words that his father had spoken, just before he passed away. He could hear him speaking as clearly as if he was standing right beside him.

"You've made me a proud man, Jon, and brought a great deal of honor to our humble family name. I'm pleased with your decision to join the military and serve the Earth. I don't have any doubts that you'll go far, lad. Just remember that your word is your bond. You must hold to the promises you make and never take your responsibilities lightly. After all else is gone, what we have left is our honor."

The words of his father brought back a recollection of the promises he had made when he had been sworn in as a young officer within the Military Protection Force—promises that required him to do all that was possible to ensure the safety and survival of humanity itself. He now knew what his decision had to be. Raising his head and casting his own fears aside, Jonathon spoke in a quiet, less than confident voice. "I'll do as you ask. I'll do it for my people, for our people."

"As it should be and as I knew you would," Eolin said with a euphoric smile. "I know how hard this decision must have been, but rest assured that it is the correct decision. I have no doubts in your abilities, young Kashanti. Now come, we must begin your transformation."

"My what?" probed Jonathon with a concerned look.

"You do not honestly want to stay human, do you?"

"Uh…"

"Is what I am asking of you really such a difficult thing? Is it your flesh that defines who you are, your essence?"

"I know what you're getting at, but still…the idea of having my genetic code tampered with is a little disconcerting, even if my body is nothing more than a tool, as you put it."

"Do not worry," Eolin chuckled. "The transformation will not hurt. It will simply set your mind and body free. You will still be *you*, yet so much more. Now come."

Chapter 16
Flesh and Spirit Reborn

Jonathon followed Eolin toward the starboard wall where a newly formed incision had appeared. While standing beside Eolin he obtained a closer examination of the small ornate gemstone that clasped together the two ends of Eolin's robe, just below his neck. It was an expertly crafted ruby with solid-gold trim and its shape was that of a fist, sparking Jonathon's curiosity.

"That gemstone that you wear, what does it represent?" he inquired. "I've seen a similar emblem on the armor of your soldiers."

Still walking forward at a slow pace, Eolin turned his head toward Jonathon and responded. "It is the crest of our clan. All of the Great Houses bear a marking symbol of one sort or another."

As Eolin entered the long corridor, the ceiling and walls nearest him radiated a soft white light where he walked, adding to the air of nobility that lingered around him. The glow seemed to be a token of respect on the part of Ixlyo.

"The symbol of House Kashan is a fist of blood, standing for sacrifice and honor. Its origins date back long before the dawn of humanity, before even the Kush'humani dreamt of walking among the stars, back before the Great Houses stood together as one.

"There had been a terrible famine, causing none to be spared from their want for food. Yet hope remained. A new land had been discovered across the beautiful waters of Eden. This land had an abundance of fruits of every kind and unmolested soil that was waiting to be tilled. Many of the Houses wanted to lay claim to the land and preserve it for their own prosperity. And in accordance with tribal law, whichever House reached the new land first could rightfully claim it.

"Many seafaring ships were boarded and set sail in a race of desperation. Illunus'Voldrok, Dominant Patriarch of House

Voldrok, was the first to approach the distant shoreline and he was determined to use the lands selfishly. But Adonhi'Kashan, Dominant Patriarch of House Kashan, followed close behind him. Sensing that the lands would be lost to his rival and his people left to starve, Adonhi'Kashan did something that nobody expected. He unsheathed his blade and severed his own right hand. Then, with all of his remaining strength, he stood at the bow of his ship and tossed his bloody hand onto the shore of the new lands, laying claim before Illunus'Voldrok could take his first step on the precious soil.

"The motives of Adonhi'Kashan were far from selfish. He permitted all of the Houses to benefit from the lands that were rightfully his. His selfless act has stood as a timeless reminder of the sacrifices that we are often asked to make, sacrifices that you too may be asked to make, my young friend."

The tale left quite an impression on Jonathon, adding to the veneration he already had for his newly discovered heritage. It reminded him of the Red Hand of Ulster story that his father had shared of his Irish heritage, strengthening the bond he now felt for Eolin and the Kashanti.

"I'm honored to be part of such a legacy," he said. "I'll wear the crest proudly."

Eolin smiled and bowed his head and eyes gently toward Jonathon, completing the exchange of mutual admiration. He walked with him a little further before stepping beyond the end of the corridor. Jonathon had been led into a circular room with a suspended oval table in the center. It was organically designed and was attached to a series of tentacles hanging from the ceiling.

Two blue-robed Kashanti were standing on either side of the table. Their appearance was similar to that of Eolin, except they were much younger and their snowy white hair was combed straight back and trimmed short. They each pressed their respective palms together, with their fingers pointing toward their chins. And they bowed their heads in reverence to Eolin, all the while keeping their eyes and curiosity focused on Jonathon. They seemed to be as awestruck by him as he was by them.

"*Ehm zil veni*," Eolin greeted, placing a friendly hand on the shoulder of one of the young males. "This is Uruk'Kashan, and over there is Ber'uzul'Kashan. They are both anointed and well trained for the task at hand. Now, let us begin while the Gods are still smiling down upon us."

The table tilted forward.

"Please remove your upper garments," requested Uruk.

Jonathon unfastened and removed his military jacket, feeling a little more vulnerable as he did so. He handed it carefully to Ber'uzul.

"The other garment as well."

Pulling his white T-shirt up over his head, Jonathon passed it along to Ber'uzul, who walked toward the starboard rim of the room. There he placed Jonathon's clothes atop a rounded white pedestal that rested against the wall. The pedestal began to glow and with a flash of fiery light, Jonathon's shirt and military jacket were incinerated, along with the medals and ribbons he so cherished. Turning to face Eolin, Jonathon opened his mouth as if to protest, but he was cut off before he could speak.

"There is no looking back," Eolin admonished. "You must leave behind your past so that you may become whole and embrace your present, your future. It is the only way."

Jonathon nodded. Though he didn't realize it at the time, Eolin was testing him, assessing his thoughts and emotions to determine his willingness to accept and fulfill his destiny. Eolin's expectations for Jonathon were much greater than for the other humans, because Jonathon's purpose and calling were much greater. There was no room for regret. Jonathon had to embrace his new heritage fully if he was to have any chance of convincing his crew and the rest of humanity to accept their destinies and make House Kashan whole again.

"Now, my young friend, it is time."

Stepping in front of the table, Jonathon leaned back against its warm surface. A series of small tentacles quickly wrapped around his body, securing him to the table as it tilted back into a horizontal position.

"You will be put to sleep before the transformation takes place and your heart will stop beating for a time. But fear not. You will not die. We must do this so that your body and mind remain perfectly still. In this way the rebirthing can proceed unhindered and without pain or risk of death to you."

"Uh, right," said Jonathon with a nervous expression that bordered on fear. Trusting them with his well being, even his life, wasn't easy.

"When you awaken, your mind will see clearly."

Turning his gaze upward, Eolin closed his eyes and held the palms of his hands out to the side before uttering a ceremonious statement in his native tongue. *"Humani onlo matray. Kush'humani li'tillae. Kashanti eternus."*

Jonathon heard the translation in his mind. "Defeated no more. Undefeated reborn. Kashanti forever."

Eolin lowered his hands and gave a nod to Uruk, signaling for him to begin the procedure.

Uruk removed two small crystal vials from his robe. One contained a florescent-blue liquid while the other's contents were clear and calm. *"Mortalum un illae,"* he whispered, which translated as "death and life." Holding the glowing-blue container above Jonathon's bare chest, Uruk extended one hand, passing the second container to his companion.

Ber'uzul took the crystalline vial and lowered it to his side. While it was out of view, he hid it within the sleeve of his robe and removed a small crystal vial of his own—one that had been kept secret. Its unusual contents were black and writhing, as if the contained fluid was fighting to escape. He concealed the item in his hand while pressing Jonathon's head to the side. Upon placing one end of the crystal against the base of Jonathon's neck, its liquid contents crawled out and pierced Jonathon's flesh. Ber'uzul smiled sadistically when he saw Jonathon cringe in pain. But the discomfort soon passed as the viscous black material entered his bloodstream. He felt his body becoming warm to the point of numbness and his eyelids were heavy with looming slumber. The slowing, rhythmic thumping of his heart was the last thing Jonathon heard before taking one final breath and becoming limp, as if dead.

Uruk placed the base of his crystal against Jonathon's chest, directly above his heart. And as he removed his hand, the glowing fluid shot into Jonathon's body, after which the vial disintegrated.

Both robed individuals stepped back away from the table and remained in quiet reverence of the transformation.

Jonathon's skin twitched and crawled as his DNA was re-sequenced into that of a Kush'humani. His flesh became fairer and acquired the same subtle blue overtones as Eolin and the others. His hair lightened until it was pure white. But before his genetic rebirth was complete, a black discoloration began forming within his veins, causing a horrified expression to engulf Eolin's face.

"No," he cried. "This cannot be."

Jonathon's eyes popped wide open as he prematurely awakened and became fully conscious of his transformation. He exhaled a blood-curdling scream that caused Ixlyo to shudder. So mighty was its trembling that Eolin and his two assistants fell to the ground. A high-pitched shriek traveled from one end of the living vessel to the other as Ixlyo bonded with Jonathon and empathetically bore the same unbearable pain that coursed through his body. Intense pulses of light flowed through the fleshy membrane of the table, walls, and ceiling, growing more vivid with each passing moment. Jonathon screamed again, as did the ship.

The room became ever brighter as unbridled power flowed through Ixlyo, matching the severity of Jonathon's stinging, burning pain. Jonathon felt as if his internal organs were being ripped apart, and in a way they were. The genetic restructuring was altering every aspect of his physical being, but it wasn't only his body that was changing. The black poison that had been introduced into his bloodstream caused his consciousness to alter, though not in the malicious way that had been intended. His life force teetered on the brink of termination but for a small moment. Then his body began to heal.

The dark discoloration soon weakened and faded, leaving the entirety of Jonathon's eyes glowing with a brilliant white light. His soul had been set free from the physical limitations of his human body. He was beginning to comprehend the universe and to feel his place and significance within it, his connection to all life. It was an incredible, albeit overwhelming experience that left him unable to form any words in either thought or voice that could properly describe it.

With the agony subsiding, Ixlyo lowered the table and released its embracing hold on Jonathon. He stumbled forward, disoriented and holding his head as a chaotic chorus of voices stampeded through his mind. He could hear the thoughts of every living being on the ship and they were growing louder, drowning out his own inner voice. A mounting sense of trepidation was clearly present among the sea of thoughts that belonged to his crew. The ship's unexpected trembling had caused their concerns over their current situation and Jonathon's absence to wax strong, leaving those with the closest emotional connection to Jonathon fearing for his life, and their own lives as well. The host of random thoughts became ever stronger to the point of discomfort. And at that moment, when Jonathon thought he would be driven mad, his mind quieted, leaving only a cold and terrible feeling.

Ber'uzul rose quickly to his feet and tried to depart, but Jonathon had already perceived his thoughts, his dark, murderous thoughts. His piercing eyes zeroed in on Ber'uzul and in a moment of anger he instinctively lashed out with his mind, which was now unbound.

Ber'uzul stopped abruptly, as if he had hit an invisible barrier. His body levitated into the air and was flung across the room, slamming into the back wall in accordance with Jonathon's will.

Having understood the nature of Ber'uzul's treachery, Ixlyo extended a swarm of tentacles from the back wall that surrounded Ber'uzul, restraining him tightly.

All pain and discomfort had vanished from Jonathon's body. The transformation was complete. He had been reborn as a Kush'humani, though with an even more heightened sense of being than had been anticipated.

Uruk helped Eolin to his feet, then stepped back, flush against the wall and fearing that Jonathon might turn on him next. He didn't understand what had gone wrong or why and he trembled at the potency of Jonathon's unrestrained life force.

"By the Gods," Eolin marveled aloud. "You should be dead. No one has ever survived a rebirthing while conscious."

"I'm alive, but no thanks to this one," Jonathon growled, his eyes focused on Ber'uzul. "I've heard his thoughts. Ber'uzul doesn't serve House Kashan. He worships the Dark God and he'd kill us all if given the chance."

The strangling tentacles that surrounded Ber'uzul tightened, making it especially difficult for him to breathe.

"No," Eolin pleaded with tearful eyes and a broken heart. "I took you in as one of my own children," he said, gazing at Ber'uzul. "How is it that you have turned your back on us, on me? How much blood would you have shed to appease him?"

Ber'uzul hissed and his eyes darkened as he established a telepathic link with Drak'Rasha, permitting his master to take control of his mind. Jonathon became enraged when he felt the presence of the great evil that had brought so much suffering and death to his people, human and Kush'humani alike. He marched boldly toward Ber'uzul and, gripping the traitor's throat tightly, he declared, "I'm not afraid of you. Your reign of terror is about to end."

Ber'uzul's face became twisted with unbridled hatred, then with excruciating pain as the Great Betrayer fled from his mind. So forceful and dramatic was the departure that it caused Ber'uzul's brain to hemorrhage. Exhaling his final breath, he fell limp. The tentacles that restrained him retracted back into the wall, discarding his lifeless body onto the floor.

Jonathon's anger subsided and the room returned to its normal state of radiance, save a small glow directly around Eolin. Jonathon's eyes also dimmed until only his striking azure corneas were glowing.

"I beg your forgiveness," pleaded Eolin to Jonathon. "I was blind to the darkness that resided in the heart of Ber'uzul'Kashan. We have dealt with spies in our midst before, but they had always acted swiftly and predictably. None had resided with us so long, nor been so close, as Ber'uzul'Kashan. I do not know when he fell into the shadows, but I weep for his soul."

"How did he manage to hide his intentions?" Jonathon inquired with a hint of frustration in his voice. "Couldn't you read his thoughts?"

"There are ways to train one's mind to block those things that are meant to be safe, to be secret. It is difficult and takes great concentration and training, but it is possible. Ber'uzul'Kashan was gifted and he most likely learned the deceptive art of memory shading before he came into our fold. But you somehow saw through to the truth. He was not able to hide anything from you. I am truly humbled to be in your presence, noble Kashanti."

Eolin bowed his head as a gesture of respect to Jonathon before continuing. Uruk did the same, though he had yet to fully relax.

"You are much more gifted than I had originally thought," Eolin continued. "But I sense that not all of this was due to natural means. I recognized the cursed poison that Ber'uzul'Kashan introduced into your body. It was blood from the Rashok'Tyre. Yet the cleansing agent that genetically purified your body must have altered the vile toxin to such a point as to quicken your mind rather than plunge you into madness. The fact that you were able to use your mind to physically subdue Ber'uzul'Kashan is a testament of that. It is a rare gift indeed to be able to move objects by will alone. Only a handful of Kush'humani have ever been known to achieve such dominion over the physical laws of the universe."

Shifting his eyes, Eolin glanced sorrowfully at Ber'uzul's lifeless body.

"Though my heart grieves for what Ber'uzul'Kashan has done, I am nonetheless overjoyed that you are well and ready to stand at your rightful place within our House. For the first time in my long, weary life I have hope for our people."

"I'll do my best to live up to your expectations," Jonathon replied. "Though I must admit that I'm feeling a little weighed down with all of this."

"Well, that will change. With your body and soul awakened it is now time to awaken your mind. Come, young Kashanti, and we will initiate your education."

"Education?" said Jonathon, looking puzzled. "Do we really have time for that?"

Eolin chucked. "The kind of learning of which I speak is not what you are accustomed to. You shall gain the full knowledge of our people in the twinkling of an eye. But take careful heed. Do *not* mistake knowledge for wisdom. That is a trap in which far too many of our own have fallen."

"I understand."

With the worst part of Jonathon's new beginning now over, he too, like Eolin, was feeling hope return. A daunting task would soon be before him, but he took comfort in the fact that he'd no longer be at the mercy of the enemy. He'd no longer be powerless to fight them.

An incision formed in the portside wall and retracted as Eolin drew near. A small chamber was revealed, granting access to another of the strange teleportation devices.

"What are those?" asked Jonathon. Even though he realized he was only moments away from learning about all of the Kush'humani's amazing technology, he was ever curious and couldn't help but ask more questions.

"They cause a trans-dimensional shift in space, permitting us to move in an instant. Such a means of travel is fatal over great stellar distances, but has proven to be quite efficient when moving between two points on a vessel."

"Fantastic," Jonathon uttered.

"Yes," Eolin chuckled, "I suppose it is."

Stepping up on the platform, he vanished.

Uruk retrieved a meticulously folded royal-blue robe that had been tucked away inside a narrow slit along one edge of the table. He unfolded it and stood behind Jonathon, assisting him as he dressed his body in the finely woven garment. Uruk then bowed his head and motioned for Jonathon to depart.

Stepping up onto the shifter, Jonathon remained still as it hummed to full power. A ring of energy shot up around him and in that instant he was whisked away to a guarded location deep within the belly of Ixlyo.

"The place that we are about to enter is most sacred to us," explained Eolin upon Jonathon's arrival. "So I must ask you to please remain quiet and respect the reverent atmosphere that has been so carefully maintained."

Jonathon nodded and stepped down off the platform, adjusting his robe a little. He was in a small rectangular room with two elite sentinels standing guard a short distance in front of him. They were every bit as majestic and impressive as those that had guarded the way to Eolin's meditation chamber and the meeting that had forever changed Jonathon's life. The sentries bowed their heads as Eolin approached.

An incision formed between them, allowing a soft white light to pierce the opening. Both Eolin and Jonathon stepped through and into a much brighter room. The color immediately faded from their robes until they became pure white, matching the beauty of their surroundings. It was a tranquil scene that reminded Jonathon of the temples he used to visit as a young boy with his father. He was at peace and remained that way even after the opening sealed shut behind him. The prospect of having his mind filled with alien knowledge was much less intimidating than having his body genetically altered, and also less painful, he hoped.

Driven by curiosity, Jonathon cast his eyes round about and studied the room's pyramid-shaped architecture. A pleasant white sparkle emanated from the small interlocking crystals that decorated every inch of the walls, save one tiny diamond-shaped spot in the back. He could no longer hear the echo of his footsteps as he walked, as if the room had deliberately swallowed them in order to maintain the tranquil atmosphere. Glancing down, he observed the strange symbols that were etched into the pearly floor. They were exquisitely drawn and gave him the impression he was seeing the written language of the Kush'humani, though he had no idea what meaning the message conveyed.

Four white-robed figures stood at the far end of the room. They were old, though not quite so old as Eolin. Still, they undoubtedly possessed a great deal of wisdom in their own right. They stood reverently in place with their faces mostly veiled by their hoods and their arms folded inward so that each hand remained concealed within the opposing sleeve. All were of average height, except for one who stood at least a full head taller than the others. A hovering golden slab was partially obscured behind them with a white energy veil that ranged around its perimeter, shielding an unseen object of great significance.

"*Ushun alra nox, valoi uthunaia'ta*," said Eolin, speaking his greeting in a soft voice scarcely louder than a whisper. He also translated the words within Jonathon's mind, leaving no room for misunderstanding. "Peace unto you, my brothers."

Eolin bowed his head in respect to the others and they in turn bowed their heads to him. Then, with Jonathon standing to his right, he spoke to his four robed brethren in plain English, for Jonathon's sake.

"Here stands Jonathon Quinn, purified in form. He has come to have his mind enlightened after the manner of our beloved patriarchs who have walked the same path he now must walk. Shall you grant his request? What say the anointed keepers of the light and knowledge of House Kashan?"

The four elders turned toward one another and whispered for a short time, concluding with a collective nod. Their decision was then conveyed to Eolin by the eldest of their fold. "If it is your wish, then we shall grant his request. Present him at the Circle."

A ring of blue energy faded into view along the floor, slightly off-center from where Jonathon stood. Eolin turned, placed his hands on Jonathon's shoulders, and whispered, "You are about to be given a most rare and precious gift: the full knowledge of our people. It is only given to those who have been predestined to lead our just and righteous House. Each of the life crystals in this room contains a piece of that knowledge. Our language, sciences, religion, philosophies, and all that we have seen and discovered of the known universe will be bestowed upon you. Even our tactics and clever strategies of war shall be yours. But treasured above all else are the previous words of counsel and insight of our leaders. Use their proven wisdom to strengthen your own, noble Kashanti.

"Now, stand here in the center of the Circle of Light and receive what is rightfully yours. And remember, my young friend, that I will always be with you on the long, difficult journeys of your life."

Jonathon smiled appreciatively before Eolin stepped back and away from him. With a sense of nervous excitement fluttering in his stomach, Jonathon positioned himself within the bounds of the gleaming circle, facing the four elders. He glanced up and observed that he was directly under the point of the pyramid. Such positioning was no doubt more than merely symbolic.

Eolin turned around and walked toward the back wall. Once there, he reached into his robe and removed a small diamond-shaped crystal, gazing at his reflection along its smooth, polished surface. Clutching it tightly in his hands, he pressed it in against his chest and closed his eyes while uttering a statement under his breath. "*Ith ogmay pax vail neitray.*" Which translated as, "At last shall I rest."

Opening his eyes again, Eolin placed his cherished crystal inside the matching gap that was directly in front of him. It snapped into place with a faint chiming sound, covering the last vacant spot on the walls. And with a deep, cleansing breath, he turned back around and nodded to the elders.

The writing that had been etched into the floor changed suddenly, shifting the symbols and their meaning. And though they burned with a fiery intensity, Jonathon could feel no heat radiating from them. His attention was then drawn to the crystals along the base of each wall. Their sparkle had increased, producing a dreamy glow that crawled up toward the ceiling. Upon reaching the pointed top, a resplendent glimmer of light burst into view, adding to the radiance of the already lustrous room. Out through the light came a glittery white mist that spiraled and crept toward Jonathon like a ghostly specter. But despite the extraordinary imagery he remained immovable, with his eyes fixed on the approaching apparition and his heart rate rising out of excitement, not fear. He was ready to receive his gift.

The shifting light descended until it swarmed around Jonathon's head. Circling back around, it burst painlessly right through his eyes, causing them to shine with a brilliant white light. He gasped in amazement as his intellect swelled with all of the knowledge that had been promised him. He now knew many intimate details about the Kush'humani and the lives of countless individuals he had never met—thoughts and memories as clear as if they were his own. He understood the Kush'humani technology fully and he gained a broader understanding of their ancient enemy, his enemy. And he also perceived the thoughts of Eolin mixed in with his own.

As quickly as the ordinance had begun it came to an end, returning the room to its natural state of illumination. Realizing what Eolin had done, Jonathon spun around in time to watch him collapse to the ground. He was dead, having surrendered his life during the transfer of knowledge, according to the traditions and customs of his people. But despite the clarity of what had taken place, Jonathon's human instincts kicked in and he ran to Eolin's side and kneeled down, ready to grieve.

One of the elders stepped forward and spoke to Jonathon in the Kush'humani language, which he was now able to understand perfectly. "Do not weep, my Lord. Eolin'Kashan has traveled beyond the veil of life and entered that great rest of those who have gone before him. His life was a righteous one and part of his essence will forever reside within you. Now rise and come stand before your brethren."

"Of course," said Jonathon, now speaking the Kush'humani language himself. Though he was still saddened by the loss of Eolin, he rose to his feet and approached the awaiting elders. He was ready and willing to complete the ceremony, which no longer seemed unusual or alien to him. He felt as if he had always been Kush'humani, as if he had been born to their ways.

One of the elders spoke. "As one patriarch surrenders his life and calling, so too does another rise to take his place. Who now stands before us to be anointed Dominant Patriarch over House Kashan?"

"Here am I," answered Jonathon, speaking the exact words that had been rehearsed by Eolin and countless others before him. "Let the Sacred Archives of House Kashan bear the name of—" He took a moment to decide an appropriate name to call himself—a name that would reflect both his Kush'humani and human heritage. He was proud of both and did not want to completely forsake his human upbringing or the cherished memories of his father. And so, with swelling confidence and a reverent boldness, he spoke his new name. "*Jho'quin'Kashan.*"

The elders nodded in acceptance of his name. "So be it, Jho'quin'Kashan, Dominant Patriarch of all Kashanti born."

Jho'quin dropped to one knee and the elders approached and encircled him. Each retrieved a small crystal vial from inside their robes and held it above Jho'quin's head. Then one of them spoke. "We anoint your head with the purified waters of the sacred pool of Ushun'Ithalae. May it forever keep your mind clean and your thoughts focused on the needs of your righteous followers."

The vials were tilted gently until four individual drops of cool water fell upon Jho'quin's head.

"Now rise, Lord Kashan, and present yourself at the altar."

Jho'quin rose to his feet and walked toward the golden altar that hovered near the far wall. He stopped directly in front of it and stood with a posture and visage that proclaimed the nobility he now fully realized and accepted. Glancing down, his eyes fell upon the markings that were repeated along each side of the altar. They bore a special, prophetic message: *The knowledge and truth of the One shall come forth before the gathering of House Kashan.*

With the four elders standing beside him, two on either side, the oldest of them spoke once again. "Contained on this altar is the sacred life gem of Rael'Kashan. Part of his essence and all of his knowledge have been preserved for the one true heir, preserved by his hands in a moment of great darkness. But from the darkness shall spring forth a light, a shining beacon to our people. Long have the prophecies of our forebears spoken of the day when everything Rael'Kashan stood for, everything he was, would be reborn, to come forth at a time when his wisdom and guidance are needed most, to bring to pass the Great Awakening.

"The cries of our people grow louder each day, calling for those who have been lost from our fold to be gathered under one House, the foundation of which will never be shaken again. The new dawn on Eden approaches. Will you be the one to usher it in?"

The energy field that surrounded the top of the altar faded, revealing a pyramid-shaped crystal that rested on top.

"Place your hand on the life gem and let your soul be judged, as those who have stood here before you have been judged."

Jho'quin placed the palm of his right hand respectfully against the warm surface of the crystal. It instantly glowed and began to vibrate upon recognition of his DNA and bloodline. The elders whispered amongst one another as they witnessed the crystal come to life for the first time since its creation so long ago.

As Jho'quin retracted his hand gently, the writing along the edge of the altar faded and the crystal disintegrated, releasing a sparkling white mist that rose up and pierced straight into his eyes. Rael'Kashan's unique knowledge was added to the collective within Jho'quin's mind.

The elders dropped to their knees beside Jho'quin, bowing at the feet of the one who had been foretold to restore the patriarchal bloodline to its proper lineage, the one in whom they had faith would vanquish their ancient enemy.

"Arise, my brothers," said Jho'quin. "We have much work to do."

Chapter 17
Phoenix Rising

Kate was still in the same spot she had been when Jonathon had last talked with her. She was sitting on the floor with her legs folded in, though she wasn't nearly as comfortable as she looked. A clear crystal bowl rested in her lap, containing a sufficient serving of gelatinous food that had been graciously provided to her and the others. And she had company too. The trio of Chang, Dead Eye, and Parker sat beside her in a semi-circle, yet she seemed scarcely aware of their presence, never looking up except when addressed by name. She simply stared blankly at her spoon while stirring it aimlessly through her untouched food. A look of irritation would cross her face from time to time as she heard the occasional outburst of laughter. Even the pleasant rumbling of conversations that drifted through the air got on her nerves. The atmosphere in the room suggested that everything was perfectly normal and she resented that, feeling at times as if she was the only one concerned about Jonathon.

"Try not to worry about him, Kate," urged Chang, making another vain attempt to cheer her up. "I'm sure he's fine. You should try to eat something, to keep your strength up."

"That's easier said than done," Dead Eye interjected. "This stuff looks like vanilla pudding, but tastes like crap." Sampling another small bite of his food, he cringed and discarded the spoon back into his bowl. "Man, that's nasty."

"I don't think it was intended to be a dessert," Chang opined. "It's probably highly nutritious. They just didn't bother to add any flavor."

"Oh, it's got plenty of flavor, it's just all bad."

Dead Eye's comments brought a smirk to Parker's face. He wholeheartedly agreed with his friend's assessment of their peculiar meal, though other crew members were ingesting it without objection.

A hush fell over the room again, leaving it uncomfortably quiet, except for the echo of approaching footsteps. Glancing up, Kate saw three armored figures approaching. They all had finely-woven blue capes that draped down their backs and swayed with each graceful step. Two of them also had gold-plated shoulder armor and small golden symbols etched above each breast, identifying them as members of the Praeden'Cor, or Guardians of Light. This revered order represented the wisest and most well trained of the Kashanti soldiers, serving as keepers of the peace and protectors of the Kashanti oligarchy. And in times of war they also acted as generals, exercising righteous dominion over all other Kashanti soldiers.

The third individual, who was between the other two, was dressed entirely in golden armor, with a polished pearl faceplate that reflected the expressions of the curious onlookers, all of whom were rising to their feet.

Walking as one, the three approached Kate and her companions. Dead Eye and Chang instinctively inched closer to Kate, not trusting the intentions of the new visitors.

Reaching its right hand up, the middle figure pressed the ornately designed ruby crest that was fixed between its breastplates. As it did so, its armor began to change in a most unusual fashion. To those who didn't understand the Kush'humani technology, it appeared as if the battle suit was melting. Having been constructed out of an innumerable host of highly advanced nano-bots, the Kush'humani armor was able to restructure itself into other forms, as needed or desired by the wearer. The golden glimmer of the once-hardened armor faded and softened into a blue hooded robe, leaving the Kashanti crest as the only remaining constant. The majestic figure then moved its hand up from the ruby clasp and pulled back its hood, revealing its identity.

With a gasp, Kate dropped her crystal bowl, sending it shattering across the floor. A sea of increasingly loud whispers washed through the room as the crew stared in amazement at the alien visage of their once-human leader.

"Don't be alarmed, Kate," counseled Jho'quin calmly, gazing at her with his luminous blue eyes. "I haven't been harmed. In fact, I feel better than I ever have before."

"Admiral," Parker stuttered, his face twisted with curiosity and concern, "what did they do to you?"

"Simply put, they set me free."

"Uh, I hate to point out the obvious here," Dead Eye interjected, "but you don't quite look human any more."

Jho'quin chuckled softly and said, "You're right. My human form has been laid to rest, but I'm still the same person. I'm still your friend."

"Why?" Kate interrupted with an expression that crept toward anger. "Why did you let them do this to you? I told you it was a mistake to go with them, but you wouldn't listen. And now everything's changed."

"You're right, Kate, everything has changed. We have a lot to talk about."

"Obviously," she snapped, folding her arms.

Jho'quin scanned the room and raised his voice to address the crowd. "Everyone please gather around. There's something I need to tell you, but it won't be easy to hear. I ask only that you keep an open mind and trust me as you always used to."

Turning his attention back to Kate, Jho'quin looked warmly into her eyes. *"Trust me,"* he whispered into her mind, bringing a peaceful sensation that coursed through her body. Kate's expression softened a little, but she wouldn't permit herself to relax completely until she had heard the promised explanation of his transformation.

Jho'quin smiled upon sensing her stubbornness. He appreciated her strong will and he had faith that she would believe. In fact, he had no doubts that her destiny was still entwined with his own.

For the next twenty minutes Jho'quin spoke aloud many of the words that Eolin'Kashan had revealed to him. He laid their true origins and heritage before them, bringing a new sense of understanding regarding their conflict and enemy. And he testified of his own experience—the fear, the doubt, and ultimately the decision that had enabled him to rise above his human flesh. His new name was also revealed, along with his title as the head of House Kashan. Then, speaking with power and authority, he shared the unshakable hope he held for the embattled inhabitants of Earth and for the future. He closed his

enlightening speech by offering the crew a choice, the same
choice that had been given him: to ascend to a Kush'humani
existence or to remain human, to remain defeated.

As every man and woman deliberated the startling
revelation internally and amongst their friends and associates,
Jho'quin inconspicuously probed their thoughts, identifying their
concerns, their fears, and addressing them openly as best he
could. He sensed the varying degrees of shock and skepticism,
but he also sensed newfound optimism among many of the crew.
And while it was in his power to force them all to a unanimous
decision, he chose not to do so. Rael'Kashan and his kindred had
been forced to accept a life they did not choose and Jho'quin
didn't want such a travesty to happen again. The freedoms he
held dear as a human were even more precious to him as a
Kush'humani.

"I think the whole idea of this stinks," a particularly
rebellious crewman shouted out from the middle of the group,
causing a gradual parting of the crowd until he had obtained
direct eye contact with Jho'quin. "I mean, come on, Admiral,
what kind of suckers are you trying to play us for? We put our
lives on the line every day fighting for our freedoms, fighting for
the right to live a good life. And now you're telling us the only
way to continue the fight is to become some kind of alien freak.
Well, count me out."

"I'm with him," another crewman added. "I ain't going
along with this fascist plot. Sounds to me like maybe the aliens
have figured out they'll never beat us into submission and this is
their way of wiping out the human race."

"You're joking, right?" a female technician standing beside
the second crewman chimed. "You really think this is some sort
of trick to get us to change sides? Man, you're dumber than you
look."

"Watch your mouth, you little—"

"That's enough," Jho'quin demanded. "I can respect that
everyone's going to have their own opinions regarding this issue,
but fighting with each other about it isn't going to solve
anything. You each need to make the decision for yourselves.
And believe me, I understand what's at stake here. We've all
been raised to believe that our identities and our genetic code are

inseparable. That's simply not true. Being human has been about more than having a particular DNA sequence. It's about what goes on in here and in here," he professed while pointing to his head, then his heart. "It's your decisions, your actions, your character, that define who you are, not your skin and organs."

"Spare us the philosophical crap," the first crewman shot back. "If these aliens here really are the *good guys*, like you claim, then why can't we join up with them and still keep the same bodies we were born with? What are they so afraid of?"

"Yeah," a small chorus of scattered voices called out in agreement.

"As someone once told me," Jho'quin began, "our bodies are merely a tool, and the tools you currently have are genetically incompatible with the organic technology that's used by the Kush'humani. You'd simply be getting in the way, not to mention the fact that you'd be at a *severe* disadvantage without any telepathic capabilities to aid you."

"That's another thing I ain't buying," the second outspoken crewman added. "I mean, talk about tabloid mumbo jumbo and—"

"*There are things in this universe that go far beyond your human understanding,*" Jho'quin said telepathically to the group, removing all doubt about his new abilities. "*You're all being given a rare chance to become so much more than you are, to stop living in limitation and realize your true potential. Whether you choose to take a stand against the oppression that has secretly dominated all of humanity from the beginning is up to you. I won't force you to do anything you don't want to do, but we don't have time to debate this.*"

Speaking out loud once again, he resumed addressing the group. "With each passing moment the survivors on Earth are made to suffer, hunted like animals for the perverse pleasure of our common enemy. A plan has been set in motion that will liberate the Earth and its remaining population. You must decide now if you want to be part of that plan and strike back at the butchers that have slain so many of our friends and loved ones. I will not force you to become Kush'humani, but understand that should you choose to remain in human form, you cannot stay here with the rest of us. And I also can't permit you to return to

Earth. Once liberated, the entire planet will be abandoned as a matter of safety. You'd face certain death by remaining there.

"You should also keep in mind that we have a long road ahead of us. The battle for Earth is only a small piece of the bigger struggle. You *must* be prepared to endure to the end. There's no easy path to follow here.

"As the leader of the Kashanti, I can guarantee you safe passage away from our convoy, if that's your choice. Those who so wish it will be taken to reside among one of our most trusted allies, where you'll live a secluded life out of the prying eyes of our enemies. You won't have all of the freedoms or luxuries you once enjoyed, but you'll still have your life and your human form. The choice is yours. Now choose."

He waited for only a few minutes before pressing them on their decision.

"Those of you who desire, at least for now, to reject my offer of joining House Kashan, come forward." Placing his left hand on the shoulder of one of the guards that stood beside him, Jho'quin continued speaking. "Follow Praeden Zia'uthun'Kashan and he will lead you to one of our transports, which will take you to your new home. And please understand that the offer of joining House Kashan will remain open indefinitely, should you change your mind."

Out of the *Intimidator's* crew of five-hundred strong, just under three-dozen dispersed individuals walked forward, weaving through the crowd. Some of them were stopped by their friends, who pleaded with them to reconsider. Only two were persuaded to change their minds. The rest marched onward, some moving swifter and more determinedly than others were. They walked past Jho'quin, following Zia'uthun as he herded them toward the exit. A few of them glared at their former leader as they moved alongside him, projecting their contempt. They still didn't believe Jho'quin and felt instead that he had sold out, possibly even betrayed his own kind. They departed with great suspicion in their hearts. But the others simply nodded their solemn good-byes, leaving for no other reason than they wanted out of the war, for which Jho'quin gave a nod of respect in return.

"What do we do now, sir?" inquired Chang.

"Let's get right to the point," Dead Eye interjected. "When do we get to play with their cool toys?"

"In due time," Jho'quin chuckled. He then placed his right hand on the shoulder of the remaining guard, who was the most trusted and elite of them all. He served as Master of the Praeden'Cor, as denoted by the unique golden ideogram that decorated his left breastplate. "Please follow Master Praeden Ilian'Kashan. He'll show you the way to the rebirthing chambers. There you will undergo your physical transformation. Your appearance will change, your wounds will be healed, and your illnesses removed. You will truly feel as if you've been reborn.

"In order to ease your transition into the Kashanti society, you'll also receive a basic education on the Kush'humani way of life, as well as instruction in the operation of our technology.

"Many of you will be appointed to serve here on this vessel while others may be spread out among the fleet. But you will all be given tasks that are best suited to your talents, and I expect you all to maintain the same level of excellence you displayed while serving on the *Intimidator*.

"Our time for vengeance is now at hand. The enemies of man and Kush'humani alike are attempting to repeat history, to commit the same atrocities that Rael'Kashan and his kin suffered so long ago. They think they can reshape our destiny, but they couldn't be more wrong. We will reclaim our rightful place among the stars. House Kashan will rise from the ashes, never to fall again. Our name will become a curse and a scourge to our enemies, our presence will strike fear, and our armies will crush everyone that stands in our way. *We will be victorious!*"

The crew cheered on the heels of Jho'quin's speech, feeling more excited than nervous. Slowly they shuffled about and funneled out of the room, conversing about the wonders of the Kush'humani race along the way. Some of the more diehard soldiers in the group even started strategizing about the pending battle and the opportunity to utilize such impressive technology.

Jho'quin smiled appreciatively and nodded his greetings to Murphy and others of his close friends and associates who ambled by. Many of them wanted to stay and chat, but Ilian was broadcasting his thoughts, reminding everyone of the urgency to get the transformations underway. There would be time to visit later.

"Uh, excuse me, sir, but did you say rebirthing chambers?" Dead Eye inquired, his forehead wrinkled with concern. "Because, you know, I've already been born once and the way my mom always talked, it wasn't all that pleasant an experience."

Jho'quin laughed. "You don't have anything to worry about, Lieutenant. I've personally seen to it that nothing will go wrong this time."

"Whoa, wait a minute. What do you mean *this time*? Has something gone wrong in the past? Maybe this isn't—"

"Come on, you coward," Chang prodded, grabbing his friend by the arm and pulling him into the waning sea of people.

Soon Kate and Jho'quin were the only remaining occupants in the room.

"I'm pleased with your decision," said Jho'quin, drawing closer to Kate.

Her arms unfolded and dropped onto her hips. "If you think you're going to get out of marrying me by switching species, you're mistaken."

Jho'quin grinned in amusement. "I wouldn't dream of doing such a thing. Besides, Kashanti law forbids me from remaining in power for long without a companion by my side."

"Oh, really? And how long is that, exactly?"

"Well, if my memory serves me right, it's something like twenty or thirty years. That should give us just enough time to prepare a proper ceremony, don't you think?"

"I see. That shuttle hasn't left yet, has it?"

Jho'quin chuckled and interlocked his arm with Kate's as he escorted her toward the exit. They approached the fleshy tunnel, which began to glow all around Jho'quin, illuminating him as he walked. During his transformation Ixlyo had bonded with him and now showed Jho'quin the same token of respect that had been shown to its previous overseer, Eolin.

They continued walking, but before they got far, Kate let out a startled holler and froze in her tracks. There, staring back at her from the opposing wall, was a molded face. It was at her eye level and mask-like in appearance, without completely distinctive features. To Kate it looked as if someone was on the other side of the wall, pressing his face tightly against the fleshy membrane.

"It's all right," explained Jho'quin. "This is Ixlyo."

"Who?" she replied, unable to take her bulging eyes off the extraordinary image.

"The ship."

"What? Oh...right. You said they were once like us. You know, this is all going to take a lot of getting used to."

Jho'quin smiled in agreement before turning his attention toward Ixlyo's face. Unlike most organic vessels, or star wanderers as they called themselves, Ixlyo still clung tenaciously to its prior Kush'humani form, an existence that had been stolen away countless ages ago. Though Ixlyo was perfectly capable of projecting its thoughts, it chose to speak face to face more often than not.

"Overseer," said Ixlyo, speaking the Kush'humani language in a deep, soothing voice. "My fellow star wanderers have all assembled. We request further counsel."

"Good," Jho'quin replied, speaking Kush'humani as well. "We're almost ready to proceed. Instruct all three strike groups to move to their designated positions and await my orders."

"Very well. We also desire to know if we will be freeing any enslaved star wanderers during this engagement."

"Probably not, my friend. Most of our forces won't have sufficient time to undertake such a task. If they linger too long they'll risk suffering casualties of their own. We will analyze the situation further, however, and if an opportunity does present itself, we won't hesitate to seize it."

"Very well. We respect your decision."

The face retracted back into the wall and vanished.

"What was that all about?" Kate inquired.

"Preparations for the military operation. And if you'll excuse me, I need to meet with the Council of Elders. Just follow this corridor around the corner and down a little ways and you should see the others. Ilian will be waiting for you."

"Okay, but when will I see you again?"

"Soon. Now you'd better get going."

Kate wrapped her arms around Jho'quin's neck and kissed him before departing. He lingered just long enough to watch her disappear around the bend before backtracking a few steps. An incision formed in the wall beside him and stretched from the ceiling to the floor with a soft ripping sound. He stepped through the retracted opening and up onto a trans-dimensional shifter. Then, using a particular telepathic directive, he reconfigured the device to take him to his meditation chamber. With a hum and an upward-shooting ring of light, he was transported to the circular waiting room outside of his chamber.

Stepping off the platform, he marched forward, nodding to the six members of the Praeden'Cor that stood round about. A newly formed incision in the far wall permitted him to enter the room where he had first met with Eolin. It now served as his meditation chamber, where he could conduct all matters concerning House Kashan, and more immediately, matters concerning the war.

The four revered figures comprising the Council of Elders were standing along the back wall, dressed in their unchanging white robes. Their hoods were down, revealing their wrinkled faces and long-flowing white hair. Portions of the wall behind them were glowing softly, demonstrating the respect Ixlyo had for their sacred callings.

Standing on the left was Elengal'Kashan. He was the youngest of the four, yet still drawn with age and wise beyond his years. It was Elengal who had suggested sending all humans who denied their Kush'humani heritage to live with the Brengali, a reclusive race of technology-abstaining humanoids who were even more diverse than the humans whom they had graciously agreed to host. The combination of their mineral-barren planet and unchanging, stone-age lifestyle had made them irrelevant in the eyes of Sa'uluq'Voldrok, which in turn made them valuable allies for the Kashanti. Their world had become a refuge for those who did not wish to be found.

To Elengal's left stood Jho'zul'Kashan, a towering figure who, despite his age, was a commanding presence in his own right. He was known as the "gentle giant," though when crossed his exceptional knowledge of psychic manipulation enabled him to bring pain, even death to his foes without moving a single muscle. In his younger years he had served as Master of the Praeden'Cor, training them in all aspects of defense, including methods to combat the dreaded Ryzonghoul mind assassins that House Voldrok had frequently employed.

Next was Uthur'Kashan. Though not the oldest, his face was tattered and worn well beyond his years. His drooping eyes were overlapped with twin scars—sobering remnants of a chance encounter with a Voldrokian soldier many years ago. The scars could have been healed, but Uthur had chosen to keep them as a testament of the cruelty of his enemies.

Riathol'Kashan, the eldest and wisest of the four, beamed with joy as he saw Jho'quin approach. He was exceedingly pleased with the kind of leader that Jho'quin was and the kind of leader that he knew he could become. He also held a special fondness for Jho'quin—the kind of fondness that a father has for a son. Before Eolin had surrendered his life, he communicated one last thought to Riathol, requesting that he develop such a relationship with the ascendant human, to help make the young ruler's burdens seem light. Riathol was honored to have been given such a request and would have gladly done it even if Eolin hadn't asked.

"We are ready to meet in council my Lord," greeted Riathol with a reverent nod. His three companions bowed their heads as well.

"Good," said Jho'quin. "Please, sit down."

Jho'quin sat in the hanging chair at the head of the room. As he leaned back into the comfortable organic seat, it radiated from the power that coursed through its tiny veins.

Four more chairs tore free from the ceiling and descended into a semicircle pattern in front of Jho'quin, permitting the Council to seat themselves. Ixlyo also joined the group, protruding its face from the starboard wall.

"We are pleased you could join us, Ixlyo," said Jho'quin. "As always, we value your wisdom."

"Thank you, Overseer."

Turning his attention back to the group, Jho'quin opened their discussion. "Everything's proceeding according to plan. As soon as my Humani companions have been reborn, we'll get the fleet underway."

"It is well, my Lord," said Riathol.

Jho'quin nodded. "Tell me, my friend, have you discerned the appropriate callings for our new kin?"

"We have done as you asked, Lord Kashan. We have probed their minds. Your companions will add great strength to our House and they will be ushered into their new callings as soon as is possible."

"If I might interject," Ixlyo spoke up, "Grai'zul, the newest of the star wanderers to join with us, has shown interest in one of the Humani. It desires to have the male who calls himself Dale Hunter serve as its overseer."

"I sensed great things in that one as well," Riathol added. "I have no objections to this request."

"Nor do I," echoed Jho'quin. "When he's ready and his remaining wounds have been tended to, we'll send him to Grai'zul."

"We are pleased with your decision," Ixlyo responded.

"Have the Brengali departed?" asked Jho'quin, turning his attention back to the Council.

"Nearly," Elengal replied. "The last of their guests are boarding as we speak. And I sense that you are troubled by their decision, are you not?"

"I had hoped they'd all believe the truth and stay with us. But I suppose it was too much to ask. I know how demoralizing this conflict has been."

"Do not trouble yourself, my Lord. I have faith they will all change their hearts and minds in time. Some may wait until our enemy has been vanquished before accepting their true heritage, but they will accept it nevertheless."

"I pray that you're right, but what of the survivors on Earth? I suspect there'll be many who will reject the truth as well. Do the Brengali have sufficient means to care for all of our wayward kin?"

"I believe so, or at least they profess such a capability."

"We'll just have to wait and see what unfolds then. Tell me, Uthur, what have you found concerning the Voldrokian devolution chambers?"

"I have studied what information our spies were able to smuggle to us, as you had requested. Most of the towering edifice functions as a biological inhibitor and has been specifically tuned to the Humani genetic code. Such a diabolical device serves only one purpose: to leave all nearby Humani in a paralyzed state, preparatory to wiping their minds clean. We shall have no use for such a mechanism, but the lower part of the chamber does hold promise. It is designed after the fashion of our own enlightenment chambers. And I am quite confident we will be able to modify them to feed knowledge into the mind rather than strip it away.

"I propose that once the planet has been purged of all evil, we gather the surviving Humani near the modified devolution chambers. There are approximately two thousand such devices positioned all around the Earth and if we can make use of them concurrently, it will greatly accelerate the Awakening."

"That's good to hear," Jho'quin said. "And I suspect our enemy has already rounded up many of the survivors, which will accelerate the process even further. But we'll have to move quickly to eradicate their forces, because it wouldn't surprise me if they start executing their captives once they detect our presence."

"It is ironic, is it not," interjected Riathol, "that by choosing to hunt and corral the Humani like animals, rather than subduing them through more efficient means, Sa'uluq'Voldrok has actually made our task easier. Through his blind rage and desire to extend suffering, he has inadvertently laid the foundation for a swift return of House Kashan. His constant favoring of cruelty over wisdom has finally caught up with him."

"Well put, my friend," Jho'quin chuckled, mirroring the amused expressions of his companions. "You've only lived for a brief moment in comparison to our immortal enemy and yet you're far wiser than he could ever dream of becoming."

Riathol bowed his head in appreciation of Jho'quin's compliment and grinned at the fact that it had been given at the expense of his ancient enemy. The Council had often poked fun at Sa'uluq, mostly because he tended to act more like a tantrum-enraged child than the powerful galactic ruler that he was. But they also mocked Sa'uluq as a means of striking out at an enemy that so far had been untouchable by their limited military capabilities.

"Well then," Jho'quin continued, "are we all in agreement about the tasks that are before us?"

The four elders and Ixlyo nodded in response.

"Our soldiers stand ready, Lord Kashan," proclaimed Jho'zul. "They are well trained and long have they waited to strike back at our sworn enemy. They will not fail. House Kashan shall be victorious."

Jho'quin smiled. "I share your sentiments, my friend. House Voldrok will taste bitter defeat for the first time in their protracted and bloody reign of terror. And then others who are oppressed will see that our common enemy can be defeated. They will see that Sa'uluq'Voldrok is not a god, but a mere coward. They will see House Voldrok's power wane. They will see."

"You speak great words of truth, my Lord," said Riathol. "Today will truly be a glorious day."

Chapter 18
The Ties That Bind

Kate was leaning against the suspended table that hung from the center of the circular rebirthing chamber. She had just completed her pleasantly uneventful transformation and become Kush'humani in form. Though she had been at the end of the line, Jho'quin had left specific instructions with Ilian to see to it that Kate was transformed first. He had something special planned for her.

Kate's hands stretched beyond the edges of the royal-blue robe that draped her body. She turned them over and back again, quietly studying their appearance, which was both foreign and familiar. She knew that she was still the same person, yet she felt so different, so much more alive. At the same time, however, she felt isolated. She had yet to be taught in the ways of the Kush'humani. For reasons she was not yet aware of, she had been asked to wait. And so she stood idly by, unaware of exactly how much time had passed, though it didn't seem as if it had been long.

"It is time," said the robed rebirthing master who had been meditating at one end of the room. She smiled pleasantly at Kate and motioned for her to approach.

Kate stood upright and turned around, walking toward the young Kashanti female. An incision formed in the wall beside her, disclosing a trans-dimensional shifter.

"Please, step up. They are waiting for you."

"Who's waiting for me?" Kate inquired, insisting on an answer before she'd take another step.

"Lord Kashan and the Council of Elders."

"Okay, but I don't see how that thing is going to get me there."

"It is irrelevant how the device works. You need only step up on it and it will take you where you need to be. Now please, my lady, step up."

Kate placed one foot on the shifter, then the other. She looked down at the platform for a brief moment before turning around. "It's not doing any—"

A glistening ring of energy shot up around her and in an instant she was transported to a guarded location deep within the belly of Ixlyo. She found herself inside a small rectangular room, with two of the Praeden'Cor standing motionless at the opposite end. As she stepped down off the platform, an incision formed between the guards, permitting a comely light to escape and irradiate the small room. Jho'quin's voice then drifted through her mind, helping her feel more at ease as he beckoned her to meet him in the next room.

Kate walked forward, moving through the parted opening and into the Hilean'Ethaul, which was also known as the Sacred Archives—the room in which Jho'quin had previously received his full knowledge and had been anointed Dominant Patriarch. To those not oriented in the ways of House Kashan, the room could be perceived as nothing more than a gloriously elegant library, full of the comprehensive knowledge and history of the Kashanti.

But to the Kashanti the room was much more. To them, all knowledge and truth was sacred. They believed the minds of their greatest thinkers and wisest leaders to have been touched by Elo'shon, the greatest of all gods. Such people were not only revered as inspired leaders, but also as holy prophets, spreading great words of wisdom and enlightenment. Even now Jho'quin's name had become sacred among the Kashanti, for he had fulfilled the most ancient of their prophecies by ascending to his position as Dominant Patriarch and restoring Rael'Kashan's bloodline. It was forbidden to speak Jho'quin's name except with great reverence.

As Kate's eyes adjusted to the lighting, she noticed Jho'quin standing near the center of the pyramidal room. He was directly behind a golden altar that levitated above the illuminated Circle of Light. The Council of Elders stood beside him. Elengal and Jho'zul were on his left while Uthur and Riathol stood to his right. They were all dressed in pure-white robes with their hoods down so their faces could be plainly seen. And Kate had noticed that her robe too had become white like theirs, adding to the confusion that was mounting in her mind.

"We are pleased to welcome you among us, my lady," greeted Riathol, speaking English for Kate's benefit. "If you will kindly take your place beside this altar we will begin the ceremony."

"I'm sorry," said Kate, speaking in a whisper. "What ceremony are you referring to?"

"Our wedding," Jho'quin replied with a sly grin.

Kate's eyes widened, yet she stood speechless, returning only a steadily increasing smile. The circumstances and location seemed rather unusual to her, far different than she had dreamed. Then again, her life in general had deviated drastically from what she had envisioned, especially in the last few days. But all things considered, nothing really mattered except that she was about to wed the person with whom she wanted to spend the rest of her life.

Jho'quin dropped to both knees and rested his hands palms up on the altar, inviting Kate to join him. She kneeled across from him, taking hold of his hands and giving them a grateful squeeze.

The Council encircled the couple and stood at each corner of the altar. Then, in accordance with the thoughts of Riathol, the inscription on the floor changed to match the ceremonious occasion. The articulate symbols burned brightly, as if on fire. Riathol commenced speaking.

"We are gathered here in the Hilean'Ethaul to join Lord and Lady Kashan in a sacred and eternal union. We, as the Council of Elders and as your brethren and friends, do bear witness to this momentous occasion. You both shall stand as examples to us all, serving as patriarch and matriarch over all Kashanti born."

Uthur continued the ceremony, saying, "The binding of mind, body, and soul between a male and female is a special occurrence, never to be taken lightly. And we would advise you to give strict heed to our words and honor the covenants that you make at this altar. For once this union is sealed, it cannot be undone."

"You shall both become as one," added Jho'zul, "for no Kashanti is truly whole without a companion by their side. You shall be in love inseparable. Even the sting of death shall have no power over your bond. Once you travel beyond the veil of life, you shall enter that great rest together, finding peace and tranquility with one another and those of your ancestors who have gone before you."

"Now, tell us, Jho'quin'Kashan," said Elengal, "what name have you chosen for your mate?"

Jho'quin kept his eyes focused on Kate as he spoke. "Let the Sacred Archives of House Kashan bear the name of Kat'lya'Kashan, Dominant Matriarch over all Kashanti born."

Kate smiled, feeling pleased that he had chosen a name that resembled the one given to her at birth. She too, like him, didn't want to forget her human heritage.

"So be it," Riathol continued. "Then we pronounce you, Jho'quin'Kashan, and you, Kat'lya'Kashan, as our noble Lord and Lady Kashan, heads of our household, unified in body and soul. And we place you under a covenant to cleave unto no other and to honor and respect each other always, as we shall honor and respect you both."

The Council drew closer and each elder took a small crystal vial from inside their robes before Elengal continued speaking.

"We anoint your heads with the purified waters of the sacred pool of Ushun'Ithalae. May it forever strengthen the sacred union that you have heretofore formed."

With a graceful tip of their vials, they each poured a single drop—two falling onto Jho'quin's head at the same time that two drops fell onto Kat'lya's head. After replacing the containers back into their robes, they stepped back and folded their arms so that each hand was inset into the opposing sleeve.

Jho'quin was next in line to speak. "All that I know and all that I am are now yours to share in. Part of my essence shall reside within you forever. And neither the vastness of space nor the darkness of death shall be able to separate me from your side."

On the heels of his words, Jho'quin's eyes shined with a brilliant white light, pouring out a misty vapor that slithered about until it pierced painlessly through Kat'lya's widened, bewildered eyes. The transfer of knowledge was complete. Kat'lya's intellect swelled as she understood her Kush'humani existence fully and all that Jho'quin understood as well. And she felt that portion of him residing inside her bosom, like a constant tender embrace. Tears streamed down her cheeks as an overwhelming sense of joy burned within her. She was at a complete loss for words.

"With the union of your minds complete," said Uthur, now speaking in the Kush'humani tongue, "this ceremony has come to an end, and with it a new beginning for your lives. May the Gods forever smile down upon you."

Though it wasn't part of the traditional ceremony, Jho'quin leaned in and kissed Kat'lya, embracing her as her husband. "I'm sorry we didn't do this sooner," he whispered.

"The past is behind us," she whispered back. "All that matters is that we're together now." She leaned in and kissed him again.

Still holding Kat'lya's hands, Jho'quin rose to his feet, lifting her up in the process. The elders gathered around and embraced Kat'lya themselves, hugging her like fathers would hug their own daughters. She had been welcomed into their fold.

"It's time for us to gather the remainder of our House," proclaimed Jho'quin. "It's time for us to retake the Earth."

Chapter 19
The Great Awakening

There were few life forms in the universe more peculiar than a star wanderer. Though genetically engineered to be spacefaring vessels, they were conscious, autonomous beings that could function well without any crew at all and were even capable of healing themselves. They were one of the most self-sufficient species in the known universe, experiencing neither hunger nor fatigue. Even death had no power over them. Star wanderers were immortal, succumbing only when defeated in battle.

During the dark times in which they had lived as slaves, bound to the will of Sa'uluq'Voldrok and the hive mind that watched over them, the star wanderers had spent their waking moments regretting their very existence. To be telepathically linked with their own kind, yet forbidden to communicate freely, was almost maddening. They spoke only when they had been ordered to do so by their cruel overseers, who referred to them only as *soron'keil*—a name chosen to constantly remind them, even torment them about their origins and purpose. It was a terribly bitter and lonesome existence. But once freed, they developed their own society, patterned after the Kashanti to whom they were indebted for their freedom. The star wanderers took names upon themselves and communed freely with one another. And they placed their trust in one being in particular, a leader who was the oldest and wisest of them all. They called it Father, even though their sexual distinctions had vanished along with their Kush'humani form. But to the Kashanti, the vessel was known as Ixlyo.

Most of the Kashanti residing aboard each vessel served as soldiers to be deployed whenever the need arose, usually for defensive purposes. Others served as healers or in civil and religious callings. And there were some that were simply passengers. Only the overseer and a handful of individuals functioned in the capacity of a crew. The star wanderers had become a home of sorts for the Kashanti nomads. Having led a life that kept them constantly on the run from their enemies, House Kashan had nourished a symbiotic relationship between themselves and the star wanderers.

One of the many beneficial services the living vessels provided to the Kashanti was to serve as both a telepathic shield and an amplifier. The youngest of the Kashanti children and those adults with the weakest psychic abilities could use the unrivaled psychic power of the sentient starships on which they resided to communicate easily with other beings, regardless of the distance that separated them. The star wanderers also warded off attempts by Sa'uluq Voldrok and his minions to intrude into the minds of the Kashanti. Most individuals could train themselves to block unwanted telepathic links, but there were some who were too weak to accomplish this on their own. They had to remain on their vessels at all times or risk having their minds ravaged by their enemies.

Life wasn't easy for the Kashanti, but after having spent several millennia in a defensive mindset, they were about to change their ways. A new offensive would soon begin, ushering in a final civil war that Jho'quin and the Council of Elders hoped would cleanse the galaxy, forever ridding them of their sworn enemy. Open war was nearly upon them.

The star wanderers braced themselves for combat as well, though they took no pleasure in violence. Like their Kashanti allies, they were peaceful at heart, yet their upbringing within House Voldrok had left them well trained for the battles that lay ahead. They would bring justice to their former masters.

Within Ixlyo, final preparations for the pending operation to liberate the Earth were nearing completion. The mood was tense as every able-bodied Kashanti soldier marched through the bowels of Ixlyo, taking up their designated positions and posts. But inside the operations core at the head of the vessel, the atmosphere remained tranquil. The vacant room had yet to be occupied by Jho'quin and his battle council.

A soft tearing sound soon broke the silence as a slit formed near the center of the rear wall. Jho'quin stepped through and into the small circular room, the whole of which was smooth and fleshy. As usual, the portion of Ixlyo nearest Jho'quin radiated upon his arrival, casting a soft light on his majestic blue robe. Kat'lya entered the sterile room soon after and stood by her companion. The area nearest her glowed as well, demonstrating the respect Ixlyo had for Kat'lya and her calling.

They both walked forward as two chunks of tissue tore free from the domed ceiling and descended via a cluster of interwoven tentacles. The organic matter shifted until it resembled a pair of suspended chairs with high-rising backs. They were smooth and curved along the bottom and had been placed relatively close to each other, centered near the back wall.

Jho'quin sat down in the starboard chair and Kat'lya sat beside him. Together they savored the waning moments of peace and quiet, knowing that soon they would be heading down a path from which there would be no turning back.

Jho'quin eventually glanced over at the starboard wall as he sensed three familiar individuals drawing near. A new incision formed, granting them access into the operations core, which symbolized Ixlyo's head.

"I'm pleased that you all accepted your callings to serve with us onboard this star wanderer," greeted Jho'quin, watching the three young Kashanti march to the center of the room.

"We're an inseparable team, Admiral…uh, I mean, Lord Kashan," Dead Eye replied. His hand started up into a military salute out of habit, but he quickly adjusted and brought his fist down and held it against his left breast, signing an appropriate gesture of respect.

Like all of his fellow humans that had been reborn, much of Dead Eye's physical diversity had faded during his rebirthing ceremony. His eyes and skin were indistinguishable from every other Kashanti, and his standard of dress was the traditional blue robe. Even his hair would have been pure white, had he left it alone that is. The genetic transformation he had undergone had caused his hair to grow back at a dramatically accelerated rate, but he had shaved it all off again as soon as he realized it was there. And so far he was the only Kashanti who was bald. It was a small degree of diversity, yet one to which the Kashanti were not accustomed. Diversity was part of being human, and some aspects of humanity would inevitably bleed into Kashanti society. Eolin and the Council of Elders had known the transition would be difficult, full of growing pains. Yet they also saw great potential, a unification of ideas and souls that would transcend both human and Kush'humani flesh, strengthening House Kashan. But only time would tell how difficult the transition would prove to be.

"I see they gave you a new eye," said Kat'lya.

"Yeah. I've got two perfectly good ones now. It feels a little strange having both of them again, but I'm not complaining. They even fixed an annoying kink I had in my back the last couple of days."

"I'm feeling pretty good myself," Chang interjected. "The Kashanti medical technology sure puts our old human knowledge to shame."

"Amen to that," said Dead Eye. "I think life as a Kashanti is going to be a real blast."

Jho'quin chuckled. "I'm glad you're all adjusting well. Now, tell me, what names have you chosen for yourselves?"

Dead Eye was the first to reply. "Adiam'Kashan. Of course, I'm still partial to Dead Eye."

"And you can call me Xiang'Kashan," answered Chang. His racial diversity had been done away with as well, but like Dead Eye, he had chosen to keep his hairstyle the same as when he was human. It was pulled back into a short ponytail.

Parker retracted his hood, revealing a face that was no longer quite so pale or timid. "I've chosen the name of Par'kezul'Kashan."

"Very well," said Jho'quin. "Please take your positions and we'll get under way."

"I can't wait to get back to Earth and kick some Voldrokian butt," Dead Eye uttered to his friends.

"I hear that," echoed Xiang, reaching over in a friendly manner and bumping fists with Dead Eye.

Three more organic wads tore free from the ceiling and descended along the perimeter of the room. They each morphed into chairs that were similar in appearance to the others, but with backs that didn't rise quite as high, suggesting positions of lesser importance. One chair remained suspended along the portside rim, another along the starboard rim, and the third along the far rim. All five chairs faced the center of the room, permitting everyone to easily see and converse with one another, as if sitting in council.

Dead Eye moved to the portside chair and sat down. Due to his natural skill set, he had been appointed to serve as a weapons master. His duties were almost identical to those he had while serving on the *Intimidator*, except that the firepower and technology he now commanded were far superior. The calling was also easier to perform and less stressful than gunnery positions onboard a human warship. All star wanderers had been designed in such a fashion as to leave themselves immune to their own weapons fire, making it impossible to intentionally or accidentally destroy one of their own kind. In fact, some of their weapons had been specifically designed to make use of this trait and magnify their destructive capabilities by bouncing energy from one ship to the next. Yet their genetic makeup was different enough from the living vessels that still served House Voldrok so as to enable them to combat and destroy their enemy.

Xiang sat down in the chair near the starboard wall. He too had been called to serve as a weapons master. Only two such positions were necessary so long as the people who served as weapons masters were well trained. They only had to govern the offensive aspects of combat. Ixlyo would naturally defend itself, managing its own shield strength and defensive weapons fire. That was one area of its operation that it rightfully refused to relinquish to the Kashanti.

Par'kezul sat down in the chair near the front of the room. He would serve as navigator once again, laying out the path that Ixlyo was to follow. But star wanderers would not blindly follow all paths that were given to them. If the navigator was to choose a course that proved too hazardous, the star wanderer would request immediate clarification from its overseer or simply refuse outright.

Kat'lya had also requested to serve in a role, beyond that of her noble position of leadership at Jho'quin's side. The calling she chose was that of sensory master. It was her job to govern all sensory detection and telepathic communications that transpired between vessels, maintaining the unity of the fleet. In effect, she would become the eyes and ears of the operation.

These four individuals, together with Jho'quin, comprised the battle council, which was similar in function to a human command staff. Jho'quin's will reigned supreme, but the others were free to offer their own insights and suggestions rather than be resigned to mindlessly following orders.

As they each leaned back, two thin tentacles stretched out from the headrests of every chair except Jho'quin's. The tentacles attached to the sides of the battle council's heads, near their eyes. This physical connection enabled Ixlyo to establish a clear, uninterrupted telepathic link with each of the individuals, regardless of their own psychic abilities. It quickened their minds and made them one with Ixlyo, helping to ensure a proper focus on the tasks at hand. Due to Jho'quin's unusually advanced psychic powers, however, there was no need for him to physically link with Ixlyo. His mind had already become permanently quickened from the poison that had been introduced into his system during his rebirthing ceremony. He was able to process information at an astonishing rate and his psychic prowess rivaled even Ixlyo's, a truth that no other Kashanti could claim.

The thought-transference tentacles caused a subtle tickling sensation as they burrowed just beneath the skin. Once embedded, they granted dominion over those parts of the vessel that each individual had been chosen to oversee.

"Whoa," said Dead Eye as his eyes became slightly more luminous. "This is weird. I feel like I'm actually part of the ship. I knew what was going to happen here, but nothin' can prepare you for what this is like. This is really cool."

Jho'quin chuckled at the young weapons master's words before turning his attention toward Kat'lya. "Let's get this operation under way. Send in the strike groups."

"With pleasure."

Upon initiating a telepathic link with the other ships, she conveyed the orders, broadcasting her thoughts as if talking through the human communication systems with which she had previously been accustomed. *"Arcana, Gorulan, Alshan, and Uthu'preia, begin your assault against the Voldrokian supply yards near the Boriali asteroid field. Fall back as soon as the enemy responds in force. Remember, this is only a diversion, so we don't want to risk any casualties of our own.*

"Jhe'huth, Ix'uzul, Ai'lin, and Preshan, begin your assault against the spawning pits on Zionis Prime. Destroy the facility if possible, but do not harm any of the fledgling soron'keil."

"If it's safe," Jho'quin interjected, *"and if there are soron'keil in orbit that have yet to be boarded, try to capture a few to bring over to our cause. But do not jeopardize the greater mission. The task at hand is to distract our enemy, inflicting as much damage as possible in the process."*

"Ri'zil, Quix, Draeden, and Val'uzul," continued Kat'lya, *"begin your assault of House Voldrok's military training camp on Tritan. Destroy as much of the facility as possible before their forces respond, then fall back.*

"All remaining forces prepare to follow Ixlyo to Earth."

"We must be swift in the destruction of our enemy," Jho'quin added. *"We cannot let the battle to retake the Earth be drawn into a long engagement or we will fail. As soon as we enter Earth space, all soldiers are to deploy planetside without delay. Hunt down your enemy and eradicate them before they execute any more of our kindred. All star wanderers are ordered to engage the enemy fleet and provide supporting cover for our soldiers. Stay focused and show no mercy to your enemy, for you will receive none. May the Gods be with us all."*

Glancing at each of the determined faces in the room, Jho'quin felt more confident than ever the mission would be a success.

"It's time, my friend," he said aloud.

The mold of Ixlyo's face pressed out from the far wall, to the right of Par'kezul. "I and my fellow star wanderers are with you in strength, Overseer. We shall taste the sweetness of victory together."

As its face withdrew, Ixlyo filled the minds of every person in the room with images of the surrounding space that housed the Kashanti fleet. To each person in the battle council, the room appeared to be vanishing, diminishing to such a point that it seemed as if they were floating in the darkness of space. They could sense each other, but they could no longer see one another or their own bodies unless they made a concerted effort to break their current train of thought. Ixlyo had shared a beautiful panorama of stars and nebulous backdrops, but the view was not necessarily common to everyone. Through navigation of thought, each of them was able to see whatever portion of local space they desired, allowing them to concentrate on their own individual regions and targets. Jho'quin, however, had the power to guide everyone's attentions toward a common view, if such a need arose.

"This is even better than I had imagined it," Dead Eye remarked. "What a rush."

"Xiang," ordered Jho'quin. "Prepare to deploy the screamers on my command."

"Acknowledged."

"What are we waiting for?" inquired Dead Eye.

"For Sa'uluq'Voldrok to attempt the unthinkable. Our strike groups are engaging important targets, but they're also clearly serving as a diversion. Sa'uluq and his warmongers will recognize our strategy for what it is. He'll sense that we're planning to retake Earth and in that moment of paranoia he'll act like the coward he is. He'll deploy a planet killer and that's when we'll move in."

"A planet killer?" Xiang interjected. "That seems a bit extreme."

"Not for someone as ruthless as Sa'uluq'Voldrok. He takes a great deal of pleasure in tormenting us, but he won't dare chance us rebuilding our House. He'll move directly to an endgame scenario as a means of demonstrating and protecting his power. He's done it before to other worlds and he'll do it again. His immortality has made him highly predictable, just one of his many weaknesses."

"But what about his own troops? Won't they be killed as well?"

"Most definitely. I doubt the Great Betrayer will even notify the occupational force of his change in plans. They'll be left to burn with everything else on the planet. He won't hesitate to sacrifice his own people, especially if it means dealing a devastating blow to ours."

"That's brutal," said Dead Eye. "But aren't we taking a big gamble here? I mean, if that planet killer gets through, it's game over."

"I know, but we don't have any other options. We can't simply retake the planet and then hold it indefinitely. Our enemy's too great and we'd be overwhelmed before we could accomplish our goal. No, the Council and I have decided to use Sa'uluq's brutality to our advantage. After intercepting and destroying the planet killer, we'll deploy a ring of Iltilitarian illusion drones around the Earth and make it appear as if Sa'uluq had succeeded in his task. Then we'll hide beneath the cloak and gather our survivors. It'll buy us the time we need to evacuate."

"That's very clever," said Xiang, "but won't they detect us? If I'm not mistaken, those drones are far from foolproof."

"No. The drones we'll be using are significantly more advanced than the ones you're aware of. The Iltilitarian Protectorate has given us a grade of drones similar to what they use to protect their own home world. The psychic shielding is so advanced that unless you know exactly what you're looking for, it's virtually impossible to see through the illusion. And even at that, it would require a great deal of concentration. The Voldrokian warlords will simply see a ravaged, lifeless planet. They'll find evidence of a battle in orbit, of course, but in their arrogance they'll believe their forces were victorious. They won't bother descending to the planet to confirm the situation. It's not their way. The dead will be left to rot and the Voldrokian armada will move out to search for what they believe to be the remnant of our forces."

"The strike groups are reporting heavy resistance," Kat'lya announced. "But they've also inflicted heavy damage. For being nothing more than a distraction, they're certainly doing a fine job of hammering the enemy."

"Excellent," said Jho'quin. "We'll be able to use their success as a tool to convince more of our allies to rise up—"

"The planet killer's been deployed," Kat'lya interrupted, shuddering a bit from the cold tingle in her spine. "I can feel it approaching Earth. I've never felt anything like this before. It's horrible." Her eyes became more luminous as she put all of her concentration into tracking the powerful energy signature of the dreaded weapon—a creation that was referred to by some as the physical embodiment of death itself.

"*All forces move out,*" Jho'quin ordered telepathically. "Deploy the screamers," he instructed to Xiang.

"Screamers launched."

A small circular opening formed along the smooth shimmering hull of Ixlyo's underside, permitting two dozen psychic screamers to drop through and out into the darkness of space. Screamers, as they were more commonly known, earned their name from the fact that they generated a high-frequency shrieking noise that permeated the psychic plane. Anyone unfortunate enough to attempt telepathic communication in the general vicinity of a screamer would be in for a rude awakening, feeling as if someone or something was literally screaming inside their minds, making it impossible to concentrate.

Each of the small devices was comprised of six overlapping magnetic rings that were offset at different angles and rotated independently of one another. They were shiny metallic gray in appearance and spun at a high rate of rotation around a compact, glowing white orb that functioned as the heart of the disruptive piece of technology. Through the guidance and inspiration of Eolin, Kashanti scientists had ingeniously crafted the devices for the sole purpose of blocking all telepathic communication and extrasensory perception within a wide region, sufficient enough to encompass an entire planet when used in combination with each other. The screamers would also temporarily sever the link between oppressed soron'keil and the intrusive hive mind of the Rashok'Tyre. Despite that isolation, however, the enemy vessels would still be genetically bound to the will of their overseers. And due to the physical connection between a vessel and its battle council, they could continue to function without disruption. They would be isolated, yet still dangerous.

The Kashanti, on the other hand, were immune to the screamers' effects, having trained themselves and their star wanderers in the only known way to bypass the potent technology. And even though they'd had the devices in their possession for many years, they had never been tested in battle. Eolin knew it wouldn't take long for his enemies to find a way to counteract the effects and the distinct edge that it would give his own people. He had kept the screamers wrapped in secrecy, reserved for use during a moment of crisis—a time such as the present.

Jho'quin, in his wisdom, had made the decision to deploy the screamers as a means of cutting off the Voldrokian forces on and around the Earth, disrupting their chain of command and preventing them from calling for vital reinforcements. He would use surprise to his advantage and crush his enemies even swifter than they had decimated his own forces when last he stood in view of his home.

As the screamers spun up to full rotation, they became a faint blur and vanished from sight. Several small wormholes popped into view, permitting the screamers to slip into the Solar System and deploy near the Earth.

The remaining sixty star wanderers drew immense power from the quantum singularities that resided deep within their organic frames, pulsating like a vigorous heartbeat. They used that energy and intense concentration to tear through the fabric of space and open a chain of enormous wormholes that ranged around the Earth, encircling the Voldrokian warships that had been plunged into chaos.

With Ixlyo leading the way, the Kashanti fleet began its vengeful assault, surging through the cosmic gateways with unwavering confidence.

"Moving in on an attack vector," Par'kezul announced.

"I don't see the planet killer, but I count five Nova-grade warships and two Suppressor-grade transports," Dead Eye reported. "The weapons stream is charging and as soon as they're in range I'll blow 'em clear out of orbit. There won't be anything left of their ships when I'm through."

On the heels of his enthusiastic statement, the panoramic view of space and the storm-riddled Earth that had been laid before him suddenly vanished. The tentacles that had attached to the sides of his head retracted quickly, leaving him feeling confused and with a mild headache forming from the side effect of such an abrupt termination of the psychic link.

"Hey, what gives?" he squawked.

A bulge of organic tissue stretched down from the ceiling and bent in toward Dead Eye, stopping directly in front of his face. Feeling nervous, he tried to press his body further back into the chair, but it wouldn't budge. In fact, it tilted forward a little. The head of the cylindrical mass morphed into Ixlyo's scowling face. Dead Eye could feel the anger radiating from the powerful being, causing his own heart rate to spike and his eyes to remain wide open.

"Those *ships* are as much a victim of this madness as you are," Ixlyo growled. "Do not take pleasure in shedding the blood of my kin."

"Please forgive his ignorance," Jho'quin intervened calmly. "Adiam meant no harm or disrespect. He's still new to our ways. He's still learning."

"Yeah," Dead Eye began, his voice cracking a little. "I, uh, I'm sorry. I didn't mean it like that."

"Very well," Ixlyo conceded, its face retracting back up into the ceiling. Its thought-transference tentacles were reconnected to Dead Eye, deliberately producing a sharp pinch as they touched the weapons master's flesh. Dead Eye cringed a little, but he didn't dare complain. He just grinned sheepishly at Jho'quin before turning his attention back to the battle.

The Kashanti fleet quickly split in two. The majority of the ships moved into a low orbit around the Earth and prepared to deploy their ground forces. Every able-bodied Kashanti soldier had transferred to those vessels prior to the engagement so the deployment could proceed unhindered while the rest of the fleet dealt with the enemy warships. Once in orbit, the vessels further divided into smaller groups, gathering near the largest collections of human life signs that could be detected. They ignored the disoriented Voldrokian ships that were in the process of breaking orbit, focusing instead on the occupational force that prowled beneath the supernatural storm.

There were a dozen Kashanti transports among the group and each was of a Suppressor-grade design, which meant their primary function was to transport troops and equipment for battle. Though similar in appearance to the enemy's elongated transports, their hulls were much lighter in color and devoid of all sharpened protrusions.

Inside Paraif, the eldest of the transports, approximately two thousand Kashanti soldiers were preparing to disembark. Their directive was to deploy planetside in two waves, the first of which would comprise slightly more than half of those soldiers. They would combine forces with the armored regiments from the other transports and engage their ancient foes in an all-out heavy assault. The second wave would launch soon after, sending an army of elite foot soldiers to secure the Voldrokian concentration camps and their reviled devolution chambers.

The two main levels of Paraif were comprised of spacious spawning chambers that stretched from one side of the vessel to the other and ran almost the full length of the ship. Both chambers were smooth and fleshy, every inch covered in a thin viscous film. Ordinarily, the massive chambers remained empty, but in times of battle they were filled with soldiers.

A chorus of squishing footsteps drifted through the warm, regenerated air as the first wave of Kashanti troops proceeded to position themselves within both chambers. The armor-clad soldiers were forming single-file lines even-spaced along several different rows that spanned the full length of a chamber. Directly above each soldier was a suspended cocoon, hanging from the high-rising ceiling by a series of thick, hollowed-out tentacles. The dusky-blue shells were quite large, measuring over twenty meters in height and approximately twelve meters in diameter near the center. They were also organic in substance, but rough and scaly, unlike the rest of the vessel.

Standing among the Kashanti faithful was Murphy, who now went by the name of Mur'fadeen. He was clean-shaven and of a smaller build, having undergone a painless procedure that removed most of his excess body weight after his rebirthing was complete. The Kashanti healers had also repaired the damage to his spine, returning the former marine to perfect health. Feeling as vigorous as he did when he had first joined the MPF, he was ready and willing to fight alongside his brethren, having longed for such an opportunity since he had been forced to give up the military way of life a few years back.

"Let's get it on," he requested to Paraif.

The bottom of the cocoon cracked open, permitting a small amount of slimy residue to drip out. Two stringy tentacles then plunged through the opening and wrapped securely around Mur'fadeen's shoulders. As they retracted into the cocoon, they pulled him inside and up past the center, after which the shell resealed itself.

All of the other soldiers were lifted into their cocoons as well, leaving behind two dozen blue-robed spawning masters that were spread throughout each chamber, supervising the procedure.

The hollowed tentacles that supported each cocoon shook and pulsated as an organic gel was pumped through them, filling the shells to the point of swelling. As they grew heavy, they sagged until they were mere centimeters away from the floor. And it was only a minute later when the cocoons cracked open, oozing gobs of fluorescent-blue gel that splashed down onto the floor. Separating further, the shells split vertically, allowing each side to extend partway out like a flower in bloom. Hundreds of Enforcer-grade assault units dropped free with a chorus of muffled thuds. The remnant material that had not been used to mold the battle units slid down their exterior, dangling from them like amniotic fluid drips from a newborn baby. The goop along the floor was absorbed back into Paraif to be recycled for later use.

The enforcers were similar in design to the Voldrokian assault units that stalked the dwindling human presence on Earth, yet their appearance was less threatening—to a certain degree— showing no signs of spikes or talons. Shifting patterns of lights glistened along the light-blue fleshy armor of the enforcers as their self-contained power sources activated. Though constructed from organic matter, the assault units themselves were not sentient beings. They were an extension of the Kashanti whom they contained, molded perfectly around their bodies and functioning more like machines than living creatures. The enforcers granted amazing power, protection, and enhanced telepathic communication, but were incapable of operation without a separate life form to complete the symbiotic union.

The remainder of the soldiers emerged from their cocoons embedded within Ravager-grade star fighters, hovering perpendicular to the floor with their four wings closed and dripping residue. They demonstrated the same dancing patterns of light as the enforcers.

Once the battle was over and the soldiers returned to Paraif, all of the star fighters and assault units would break down chemically and return to a gel-like state in order to be dissolved back into the living vessel, restoring its full strength and inner balance. If any of the units failed to return, Paraif could generate new quantities of the moldable gel, but it would take time for the natural process to complete, akin to healing a wound.

All star wanderers were capable of generating star fighters and assault units, but not with the same capacity as the transports. The warships could only manage about two-dozen such creations apiece, as it was not their primary function to spawn significant forces. Likewise, the transports were capable of engaging in battle, though not to a degree that rivaled their warship counterparts.

"All right," said Mur'fadeen, speaking aloud to himself from within his enforcer. "Time to do some major butt kicking."

Several widening incisions formed along the walls and ceiling, providing exit points from Paraif. An invisible energy barrier kept the room's atmosphere safely contained.

Following the lead of his fellow soldiers, Mur'fadeen moved beyond the rim of his cocoon and soared up through one of the openings and out into space, where he started the descent toward his unsuspecting enemies.

With the screamers functioning at full capacity, the occupation force on Earth had become dysfunctional. Not only were they unable to contact each other telepathically, they had also become incapable of sensing dangers beyond their own line of sight, negating a tide-turning portion of their dominance over the humans whom they continued to hunt.

Voldrokian soldiers also weren't known to be great thinkers. They had been trained from their youth to obey orders without question and never act on their own. Within House Voldrok, self-initiative was synonymous with treason. Obedience was strength and Sa'uluq'Voldrok had considered his people to be superior because of their strict obedience. But his pursuit of such absolute power had created a critical weakness the Kashanti didn't hesitate to exploit. The enemy forces were divided, and divided they would fall.

Having obtained optimum firing range, the orbiting star wanderers initiated their bombardment, hurling one energy torpedo after another toward all Voldrokian units within their sights. The planetary assault was under way.

"I've found the planet killer!" Kat'lya announced. "It's in stealth mode. That's why I couldn't see it before, but there's no mistaking its presence. I can feel it strongly now and it's well within our weapons' range."

"Weapons masters," said Jho'quin, "lock onto that abomination and destroy it."

"Roger that," Dead Eye affirmed.

"Wait," Kat'lya cautioned. "It's arming."

"Then let me shoot at it before—"

"No," Jho'quin advised. "If you destroy it now, the blast will take us with it, not to mention fry most of the screamers. We'll have to try a different approach. Stand by to engage the enemy."

"All right," said Dead Eye.

Establishing a telepathic communication with Ilian, Jho'quin conveyed his change in plans. *"Master Praeden, we have a problem. The planet killer has armed itself sooner than anticipated. We can't destroy it from this range. We'll need to secure and redirect it, and quickly."*

"I understand, my Lord," replied Ilian. *"We will send ravagers to deal with it. Perhaps this planet's moon can serve as sufficient enough of a barrier to contain the blast."*

"Excellent suggestion. I'll leave you to your task."

"Do not worry, Lord Kashan. We will not fail you."

Turning toward Kat'lya, Jho'quin said, "Keep the planet killer in your sights and relay its location to Ilian."

Kat'lya nodded before intensifying her concentration, making sure Sa'uluq's evil designs would be sufficiently thwarted.

From out of a hastily expanding incision in Ixlyo's belly dropped a pair of star fighters, one of which had a powerful explosive device fastened to its aft section. The bomb was intended for only one purpose: to bring about the premature detonation of the planet killer. Though still cloaked, Kat'lya had marked House Voldrok's most paramount weapon with a red aura, sharing her extrasensory knowledge of its location with Ilian, who in turn relayed the information to both of the pursuing pilots.

"Engaging the enemy fleet," Par'kezul announced.

Ixlyo and two of its companions, Orogon and Kalail, closed formation and accelerated toward the nearest enemy warship. With shimmering pools of white energy forming along the forward sections of their hulls, the Kashanti vessels delivered the first blow. Six powerful beams lashed out at the Voldrokian target, causing its shields to burn with great intensity. Sorluvol, another of the Kashanti star wanderers, moved in as well and fired a pair of energy beams, overloading the protective force field of its foe. The combined weapons fire tore through the fleshy hull of the besieged vessel, generating a series of rapid explosions as the energy beams ran the full length of the ship.

With its companions keeping up the assault, Ixlyo remorsefully hurled a glistening energy torpedo toward the enemy's position. Upon striking its forward section, it produced a violent explosion that blew the defeated warship apart. Secondary explosions continued to ravage the scattered wreckage, sealing the fates of any remaining survivors. The Kashanti star wanderers grieved in unison as they watched one of their own kind lose its life.

The four remaining Voldrokian warships instinctively moved into a tight formation around the two transports in a maneuver designed to collectively repel their attackers. Due to the effects of the screamers, however, they were still unable to communicate with one another. Coordinating a merger also wasn't an option, leaving them all the more vulnerable.

Orogon moved alongside Kalail and rotated until it was upside down, though its self-contained gravitational field kept its passengers from noticing the change in orientation. Upon achieving a close parallel alignment, both star wanderers merged into a Supernova-grade vessel. Their respective tentacles reached across the companion ship and secured their symmetrical union, permitting energy to flow freely between both vessels as if they were one entity, and to a certain extent they were. Their minds combined and they spoke with one voice, answering by the name of Orogon'Kalail.

Way'ul and Hixum, two more of the Kashanti star wanderers who were advancing on the enemy, moved close together and merged as well, forming Way'ul'Hixum. It moved in alongside Orogon'Kalail as the enemy fleet returned fire.

Unable to coordinate their efforts, the Voldrokian warships lashed out at several targets, diminishing the effectiveness of their attack. The shields around Ixlyo, Sorluvol, and Orogon'Kalail all ignited, but held firm.

"Target the forward-most soron'keil," Jho'quin ordered.

"I'm on it," Dead Eye confirmed.

Jho'quin opened a telepathic link to the ships in formation near Ixlyo and ordered, *"Lock onto my target and fire at will."*

A single energy beam shot from Ixlyo to the targeted vessel, burning against its shields. Pulses of concentrated energy raced down the beam and hammered the Voldrokian warship in a rhythmic pattern.

The other star wanderers joined in as well, striking along the topside of the enemy ship. Its shields were draining fast and out of self-preservation it started to pull back.

Radiant bursts began arcing between the narrow gap that separated the adjoined vessels of Orogon'Kalail. The chaotic exchange of energy surged along the dividing rift, growing more intense until it finally discharged toward the retreating warship. The devastating weapon pierced straight through the enemy's fading shields, shredding a zigzag pattern in the hull before arcing to a nearby vessel. The bolt continued to bounce from one enemy ship to the next, striking all of them in turn. Having accomplished its goal, Orogon'Kalail disengaged the chain-lightning weapon and watched as the enemy fleet scattered from their latest casualty. A blinding spray of light erupted from within their midst as the targeted warship exploded, radiating a fierce shock wave that slammed into its retreating companions, strengthening their desire to flee.

"*Don't let them escape,*" Jho'quin demanded to the fleet. "*Orogon'Kalail and Way'ul'Hixum, target the nearest enemy. Sorluvol, form up with Ixlyo. All other available star wanderers move in and capture the two transports.*"

"Weapons masters, fire a full spread at the target I'm showing you."

"The stream is charged," said Dead Eye, zeroing in on the enemy vessel that had become bathed in a red aura. "Firing now."

Five energy beams and a torpedo burst away from Ixlyo, projecting all of its free energy onto one target. The onslaught of weapons fire broke through the rear shields of the fleeing warship, upon which Sorluvol quickly took advantage. Racing past Ixlyo, it added its arsenal to the fray, searing the flesh of its target. The attack spat a sea of debris out the back end of the enemy vessel, followed by several more blasts that pulsed forward.

Having completed its task, Ixlyo veered toward its next target, bidding Sorluvol to follow. A sprawling explosion illuminated the region behind them as they accelerated away in pursuit of their scattering foe.

In the drama of the moment, Kat'lya found her attention being divided, her concentration disrupted. The visual link she had maintained with the planet killer was broken, causing her to feel as if her heart was sinking into her stomach. Nearly panic stricken, she immediately shut out all other distractions and began a frantic search.

"*I can no longer see it,*" one of the Kashanti fighter pilots advised to the other, and to Ilian. She had almost been within grappling range when its glowing profile vanished.

"*Nor can I,*" replied her companion, who initiated a search for the stealthy weapon himself. But his efforts were proving futile. The planet killer's cloak was too powerful, necessitating a level of concentration and psychic ability that could only come from a star wanderer.

Suddenly, the telltale aura reappeared, popping back into view like a ghostly specter. Kat'lya had found the planet killer once again, but it had altered course and was nearing Earth's upper atmosphere.

"*By the Gods!*" the first Kashanti pilot uttered, his face flush with the realization that the unrivaled weapon was just moments away from committing full genocide.

"*Secure that abomination, now,*" Ilian demanded, his voice ringing clearly through each pilot's thoughts, spurring them to action.

Darting away, they descended on the frigate-sized weapon and straddled both sides in preparation to dock. But as one of the Kashanti drew closer, his ravager trembled fiercely. The planet killer wasn't without its defenses and had lashed out with an invisible, spike-encrusted tentacle that flared the fighter's shields and nearly severed one of its wings.

"*Wait for it to strike again, then fire a controlled burst,*" the other pilot advised, having been assaulted as well. She waited until her ravager trembled once more and then unleashed a few bursts at the unseen threat. A gooey explosion severed the end of the whipping appendage, permitting her to dock. A series of thin tentacles spawned from her fighter's main body, securing the planet killer in a tight web.

Her companion waited anxiously for his chance to follow suit. It came. The defensive pincer lashed out at his fighter and struck with such force that one of the spikes broke through the ravager's shields and punctured the heart of the vessel, materializing in plain view just inches from the Kashanti's startled face. He instinctively discharged a series of energy bursts that shattered the offensive appendage, enabling him to dock, and not a moment too soon. Both vessels began towing the planet killer safely out of Earth's orbit before the loathsome thing could feast on the oxygen-rich atmosphere.

"*Let us head toward that moon, as the Master Praeden has instructed,*" the female pilot advised to her companion. "*We can slingshot around its gravitational pull and jettison this cursed creation along the far side.*"

"*I can see the wisdom in that approach,*" the other pilot answered. "*Let us proceed.*"

"*The planet killer has been secured,*" Ilian reported to Jho'quin, prompting a sigh of relief.

"*Well done,*" Jho'quin replied, though he knew he wouldn't be able to relax fully until he saw the region light up from the weapon's demise.

Orogon'Kalail and Way'ul'Hixum were gaining on their designated target when it suddenly opened a wormhole as a means of escape from the system. Acting without delay, Way'ul'Hixum engaged its chain-lightning weapon, striking the vessel severely as it started to cross the threshold of the cosmic gateway. The energy bolts arced all around the warship, igniting almost every inch of its weakening shields and slowing its escape. But the fatal shot was delivered by Orogon'Kalail, who fired a focused gravity beam directly into the mouth of the wormhole. The gateway destabilized and collapsed around the vessel in a swift blow that severed its forward section like an executioner beheads a criminal. The portion left behind exploded soon after, scattering more detritus throughout the region.

"We're in pursuit of the last Nova-grade warship," Kat'lya reported, her attention shifting to the battle at hand.

"Good," Jho'quin acknowledged before broadcasting a telepathic message. "*All star wanderers stand down and secure the remaining soron'keil.*"

"Ixlyo," said Jho'quin, "disconnect the battle council and attach yourself to that soron'keil. I will add my strength to your own."

"*Thank you for this opportunity, Overseer,*" conveyed Ixlyo telepathically. "*This lone act shall put my mind at ease from the blood that I have spilt this day.*"

The view of space that filled the battle council's mind faded as Ixlyo carefully detached the thought-transference tentacles from their heads. The physical link was severed for the group's own protection, leaving them sitting quietly, waiting and hoping.

Jho'quin's eyes began to shine with a magnificent brightness as he added his own psychic strength to that of Ixlyo.

"What's he doing?" Dead Eye whispered to Kat'lya.

"He's assisting Ixlyo. As you know, capturing an oppressed soron'keil is incredibly dangerous. If something goes wrong, we risk losing one of our own instead of liberating the enemy. Ixlyo's certainly capable of performing this task, but he and Lord Kashan have a special bond and they will support each other, no matter the risk."

Ixlyo and Sorluvol moved up alongside the remaining Voldrokian warship. It fired on Ixlyo, but the desperate attack was repelled, leaving both Kashanti vessels to move into a parallel alignment and straddle their target. They each rotated onto their sides, deflecting further weapons fire in the process. Once perpendicular to their target, they closed the gap and unleashed a swarm of tentacles that attached to the sides of the enemy vessel's dark and shifting hull. With the physical attachment secured, the purging process began.

The screamers had already isolated the Voldrokian vessel from its telepathic link with the hive mind, making the process of liberation notably easier, but still dangerous nonetheless. The Rashok'Tyre's mind-enslaving blood still flowed freely through the repressed soron'keil's veins, presenting a serious threat to any vessels that merged with it. They risked going mad and reverting to a slave state if the poison was allowed to flow uncontrolled through their own systems. It was for this reason that two star wanderers performed the purging operation instead of one, relying on each other to circumvent the poison. But that wasn't the only danger. The full strength and concentration of both star wanderers were required to complete the liberation, leaving themselves without any means of defense. It was a procedure that had resulted in tragedy on more than one occasion, yet it was a noble deed from which no star wanderer or Kashanti would shrink, even at the risk of his own life.

The dark discoloration that danced threateningly across the hull of the secured vessel began to lighten as Ixlyo and Sorluvol transferred the poison into their own bodies. A slithering shadow formed along their bellies as the vile substance spread. Yet through great concentration they forced the acidic liquid to the outer layer of their flesh and sprayed it into space before it could cause any harm.

Two energy pools started forming along the starboard side of the enemy vessel, nearest Ixlyo. Its Voldrokian overseer was determined to retain control.

Ixlyo trembled in pain as the energy beams pierced clear through its hull and upper attachment, inflicting serious damage. It let loose a scream that echoed from one end of its organic frame to the other, giving pause to all Kashanti onboard.

Jho'quin tensed and screamed as well, feeling everything that Ixlyo felt. But his agony soon turned to rage. His thoughts traveled through Ixlyo and into the soron'keil, coursing through the ship until he saw the Voldrokian overseer as clearly as if they were standing face to face. Using all of the strength and determination he could muster, Jho'quin exercised dominion over the bound vessel and caused it to wrap a tentacle around the overseer's throat, strangling him as he sat defiantly in his chair. Jho'quin's righteous anger then turned to the rest of the Voldrokian battle council, who promptly tried to flee. But their attempt proved futile. A plethora of tentacles lashed out at them from all directions, suffocating three while crushing another. In a matter of seconds they were all dead, leaving their soron'keil in a state of confusion.

Jho'quin's eyes dimmed back to normal and he panted in exhaustion, hanging his head low. He felt as if there wasn't a single ounce of strength left in his entire body.

"Are you all right?" asked Kat'lya.

"I'm fine," Jho'quin responded in a voice no louder than a whisper. "I'm...I'm just a little tired."

"A little? I think you've pushed well beyond your limits. You need to conserve your strength and rest. Should I summon a healer?"

"No. I'll be fine."

"It is done," Ixlyo announced with a relieved sigh. The mold of its face pressed out from the far wall and looked straight at Jho'quin. "The poison has passed. The star wanderer has been brought out of the shadows. It now calls itself Ojun'quin out of respect to you, Great One, and it awaits the genetic transformation that I have promised."

"I'll send one of my people to tend to its needs," Jho'quin replied, his voice now a little louder. "We'll see to it the transformation is completed. But what about you, Ixlyo, how serious are your wounds?"

"I will mend properly in time—a day perhaps. Had it not been for your intervention we might not even be here to have this conversation. I am truly astonished at your strength. Never before have I known a Kashanti to exercise such superiority over one of my own. Even now my kindred are whispering your name with great reverence. You have made quite an impression. Well done."

"Thank you, my friend. I'm just glad this stage of the battle is over. I'll dispatch healers to help tend to your wounds and assist you in any way they can."

With a grateful nod, Ixlyo's face blended back into the wall and its attention turned toward the gaping holes that stretched from its belly to its back. They were already being sealed with an energy field, so as to prevent the internal atmosphere from leaking out. But as Ixlyo had indicated, it would take time for the flesh to mend.

"Kat'lya," said Jho'quin, swinging his drooping head her way. "Please dispatch the illusion drones and order the rest of the fleet to descend on Earth and engage the enemy at will. With Earth space secured it won't take long to retake our former home world. Remind them, however, that they must be especially careful to maintain a safe distance beneath the cloak once it has been activated."

"Of course," she replied with a nod.

Jho'quin leaned back into his chair and exhaled a well-deserved breath of relief. His plan had worked, so far at least.

Ixlyo and Sorluvol detached from Ojun'quin. The newly liberated vessel was lighter in color, yet still different from the others. The menacing talons and spikes still remained, but that would change during the genetic re-sequencing that would place its organic frame and energy signature in harmony with its fellow star wanderers.

Having regained its free will, Ojun'quin promptly formed dozens of slit-like openings all around its hull, permitting the atmosphere inside to escape into the vacuum of space. And with that decompression came a steady stream of Voldrokian bodies, some of which were already dead, leaving the remainder to suffocate as they floated helplessly out into the cold darkness. They had all experienced the full vengeance of the vessel they had abused for so long.

The two enemy transports that had been seized by other star wanderers within the Kashanti fleet had also been freed. And with their purging complete, they too jettisoned their occupants, ridding themselves of their vile masters.

With space superiority achieved, all vessels headed planetside, including the three new additions to the fleet. They soared into a low orbit as a momentous explosion erupted from the dark side of the moon, making it appear as if a lunar eclipse was unfolding. The planet killer had been destroyed.

"Whoa!" said Dead Eye, his attention shifting to the lunar scene. "What was that?"

"Sa'uluq's failed attempt to destroy this planet," Kat'lya replied.

"Wicked."

The pyrotechnic display certainly attracted some attention, but the planet killer's premature destruction paled in comparison to the forces that would have been unleashed had it reached its final, oxygen-rich destination. Earth's atmosphere would have ignited, burning away every last molecule of breathable air while reducing all life on the planet to ashes. The Earth itself would have been thrown back into a molten state of existence.

Though Jho'quin had never personally seen the weapon used before, Eolin had witnessed the nightmare it caused and his memories were still fresh in Jho'quin's mind.

"Xiang," Jho'quin called out, sounding more at ease, "redirect the screamers to a low Earth orbit and constrict their range to the planet only. We don't want them creating suspicion for any Voldrokian scouts that might pass this way."

"Understood."

Holding position for a moment, Ixlyo prepared to deploy the array of Iltilitarian illusion drones. From a small incision in its belly launched nearly one hundred of the small diamond-shaped devices, darting away at high speed and encircling the planet. Once in place, they began to separate at their base and each pyramidal half expanded its crystalline sides outward and appeared to vanish, revealing a strange, almost liquid-like interior with a dark copper tone and oscillating boundaries. The "liquid dream" as it was called, sprayed out in a web of laser-thin veins that connected one drone to another while leaving an unsettling illusion in its wake. The masked Earth seemed cloudless and barren, with molten rock and recessed oceans. All signs of life had vanished. It deceptively appeared as if House Voldrok had won.

O'Connor and his squad were on the move near Devil's Tombstone, having reluctantly been forced to pull back after losing a great deal of territory to a reinforced enemy. Though down, they were far from out. Two dozen other squads were converging on their position, gathering within the heavily forested region to discuss plans for a daring multi-pronged offensive that would enable them to outflank the enemy and regain a foothold within south-eastern New York.

"Sir," the sergeant called out, walking a few steps behind O'Connor, "the CCN's finally back online."

"Any word on what caused the communications failure?"

"Looks like it was just a minor computer glitch, nothing to do with the enemy. Hold on...there's a backlog of battle updates coming through."

"Good news, I hope," said the trailing lieutenant as a boisterous clap of thunder rumbled overhead.

"That's odd..." the sergeant mumbled to himself.

"Spit it out, Sergeant," snapped the major, who was leaning over him and expecting immediate compliance.

"A military force of unknown origin appears to be engaging the enemy. Reports are pouring in from all around the planet. They're overpowering and systematically dismantling the aliens like they know their every weakness. It's got some of our troops really spooked."

"Do we have any Black Ops units capable of anything like that?" the lieutenant inquired.

"Negative," O'Connor replied. "We haven't been holding anything back."

"Well, that's the odd thing, sir," the sergeant continued. "From the descriptions that are coming in, these new units don't appear to be human at all. Whoever or whatever they are, the general consensus is they're also alien in origin, possibly a splinter cell."

"Oh, I don't like this," the lieutenant remarked. "Something ain't right here."

"As strange as it sounds," added the major, "we might actually have an ally."

"Possibly," O'Connor replied. "But until we have more information we'll have to consider them hostile as well. Have these new units engaged any of our forces, Sergeant?"

"Uh, it doesn't look like it, sir. Or at least I don't have any reports of any—"

A startling flash of light and a crackling explosion erupted less than twenty meters behind Alpha One, shaking the ground and flinging dirt and tree limbs in all directions.

"Scatter for cover and identify the source of that weapons fire," O'Connor demanded.

"Enemy assault unit at three o'clock, atop that ridge," the major hollered, pointing at the distant alien presence.

As the four marines scattered away from each other, another explosion lit up the region less than five meters from the lieutenant. A sharpened fragment from a shattered tree launched at her with such force that it pierced the armor plating around her left thigh, embedding deep within her muscle tissue. She was knocked off her feet and face planted on the ground. The pain was intense, but she tried to pull herself back up, refusing to utter even the slightest whimper.

"We've got wounded," the major shouted, rushing to her side. He wrapped one hand around the embedded fragment and yanked it from her leg, causing her to flinch.

"Get her up and let's fall back," O'Connor ordered.

"Look up there," the sergeant called out, pointing at the cloud cover directly above the enemy. "Something's happening."

A ring of glistening white lights propagated throughout a wide area of the supernatural thunderheads, causing the winds to die down and the clouds to lighten and disperse. A single ray of sunlight broke through for the first time since the Voldrokian armada had laid siege to the Earth. Then another ray of warming sunlight shone down, followed by another and another. The darkness was finally fading from the surrounding mountains and valley. And then, like an avenging angel descending from heaven, Ixlyo drifted down through the remnants of the storm it had dispersed and unleashed a focused beam at the Voldrokian enforcer, shattering its organic frame. The flame-engulfed wreckage trickled down the ridge to the guarded delight of Alpha One.

"Uh, that thing's getting closer, sirs," the sergeant warned, squinting up at Ixlyo. "I'm thrilled with what it did, but I don't trust whoever's piloting that whacked-out light show."

"I agree," O'Connor replied. "Let's regroup with the other squads."

"*Hold your ground, old friend,*" Jho'quin's voice whispered into O'Connor's mind. He snapped his head around and quickly scanned the surrounding terrain, searching for the source of the voice.

"General, what's wrong?" the major inquired, having noticed the perplexed expression on O'Connor's face.

"Call me crazy, but I'd swear I just heard Admiral Quinn."

"How's that possible? I thought he—"

"*You're among friends now,*" proclaimed Jho'quin, speaking telepathically to the entire squad. "*Lower your weapons and meet me in the clearing to your north. The current conflict will soon be over.*"

"Where's that voice coming from?" asked the lieutenant, feeling concerned despite the peaceful nature of the message.

"I'm officially freaked out now," the sergeant remarked.

"This may be a trick, but if it really is Admiral Quinn we have to speak with him immediately. If he's found a way to secure the enemy's technology…it changes everything."

"Are you sure about this, General?" the major cautioned. "If we head out into the open we'll be easy targets."

"That's an alien warship up there, Major. They could have incinerated half this forest by now if they wanted to. They've shown their hand and now it's time to show ours. We'll move out cautiously, but we are moving out."

"Understood, sir."

The group pressed onward, following O'Connor's lead as Ixlyo descended further and soared gracefully over their heads, gently brushing them with a warm breeze while providing a close up and breathtaking view of its exotic hull. Upon reaching the clearing, it spun around until its forward section faced the edge of the forested ravine. The marines followed the ship into a clearing and moved a few meters out into the open before stopping. As a matter of safety, they simply refused to draw any closer.

Jho'quin sat confidently in his chair within the operations core, keeping a watchful eye on the marines outside. Ixlyo's commanding presence was making O'Connor and his squad more than a little jittery.

"Do what you can to calm their nerves," he said to Kat'lya. "We don't want anyone getting trigger happy."

She nodded and proceeded to use her telepathic abilities to take the edge off the fear and uncertainty that lingered around Alpha One.

"I want the three of you to proceed to Ixlyo's spawning chamber and prepare for battle," Jho'quin ordered, turning his attention toward the rest of the battle council. "Master Praeden Ilian'Kashan has been appointed to serve as High Guardian of Earth. He and his fellow Praeden'Cor will oversee your efforts. Obey their orders and give strict heed to their wisdom. I expect to see all of you back here in once piece when your tasks are complete. And tomorrow, at sunrise, we'll celebrate the commencement of the Great Awakening with a magnificent feast."

"We won't disappoint," Dead Eye promised, pressing his ruby crest. His robe morphed into the standard, silvery battle armor in preparation for combat. He then turned his attention to Ixlyo and made a telepathic request for a weapon. A blob of organic tissue folded up from the right armrest of the chair, completely covering Dead Eye's forearm. As the tissue tore free, it squirmed and shifted until it formed an energy-weapon symbiot, which was similar in appearance to the personal firearms the Voldrokian soldiers had employed while hunting their human prey. It wasn't a life form in and of itself, but rather a telepathically responsive weapon that contained significant power, making the MPF's pulse rifles seem like children's toys. And as with all other spawned creations, the weapon symbiot could later be absorbed back into the star wanderer or re-grown if lost in battle.

"Come on, guys," said Dead Eye, rising to his feet. "Let's get out there and work up an appetite."

Par'kezul and Xiang rose as well, attired for combat in the same manner as Dead Eye. The golden ideogram that decorated their right breastplates was the same among all three, proclaiming their calling as members of the battle council onboard Ixlyo. And as each of them telepathically broadcast their acceptance of the call to battle, two more golden symbols faded in over their left breastplates. The upper symbol identified the praeden that would oversee their combat while the lower symbol identified their brotherhood in arms, or squad. All three Kashanti faithful bowed their heads in respect to Jho'quin and Kat'lya before departing.

"Shall we go greet our old friend?" Jho'quin suggested, activating his golden battle armor.

"Sure," Kat'lya replied with a smile. "It'll be fun to see the expression on his face."

Jho'quin laughed and together with his companion, he walked to the center of the room. Kat'lya pressed her crest and activated her armor as well, covering herself from head to toe in gold plating that was similar to Jho'quin's. As they stood side-by-side, a circular incision ranged around them in the floor. The fleshy segment separated and began to descend. Certain portions of the tissue rose directly in front of Jho'quin and formed an organic railing that ranged halfway around the platform. Both he and Kat'lya grabbed hold of the new railing for support as they descended through Ixlyo and dropped out into the open air. The platform kept them hovering above the clearing while Jho'quin waited for a signal from Ilian, who was securing the area with five other members of the Praeden'Cor.

"*I sense no enemy here, my Lord,*" said Ilian with a projection of thought. "*Nor do I sense any hostility in these Humani, but I urge caution nonetheless.*"

"*Thank you, Master Praeden. Now join me beside the one known as General O'Connor.*"

"*As you wish, Lord Kashan.*"

With a specific sequence of thoughts, Jho'quin caused the platform to glide down toward Alpha One, landing a non-threatening distance away from O'Connor. He stepped down onto the ground and took a second to enjoy the fresh mountain air. Kat'lya stepped down beside him and together they marched up to the anxious marines.

"It's good to see you again, General," Jho'quin hailed, speaking English.

"Jon? Is that you?"

Reaching up with his right hand, Jho'quin pressed in on his crest, causing his faceplate and helmet to retract back around his head and disappear.

"Whoa," said the lieutenant. "What happened to you?"

"That's an interesting story," Jho'quin replied, breaking into smiles. "I'll explain everything in a moment."

"Well I'll be...it is you," O'Connor bellowed with a flabbergasted look on his face. He moved in to give Jho'quin a hug, but Ilian intervened, carefully restraining the general.

"It's all right," Jho'quin advised, speaking to Ilian in the Kush'humani tongue.

Ilian withdrew his hand and returned to his place beside Jho'quin.

O'Connor finished what he had started and grabbed Jho'quin in a firm and friendly hug. "It's good to see you again. I thought we had lost you and your crew. What happened up there?"

"We were taken captive by the enemy for a little while and later rescued by members of the group you see here. They took us in and cared for us."

Kat'lya deactivated her helmet as well, catching O'Connor's attention.

"Lieutenant Hayes?"

"Hello, General. It's nice to see you again." She leaned in and exchanged a hug.

"I'm full of so many questions I don't know where to begin," O'Connor exclaimed.

"Then permit me to clear things up," Jho'quin offered. He spent the next several minutes rehearsing the tale of House Kashan to O'Connor and his squad, summarizing everything that had happened up to that point.

"So you're sayin' we're really like the aliens?" the lieutenant inquired, sounding skeptical.

"That's correct, and you'll have the opportunity to become like us, if you so desire. And that brings me to my first order of business with you, General. We need to gather all remaining survivors and move them toward the large towers that are positioned around the planet."

"I've seen the towers you're speaking of, but I'm not so sure it's a good idea to move anyone near those things. They have an adverse affect on our biology."

"That's an understatement," mumbled the sergeant, shuddering as he recalled the squad's close encounter with an enemy tower and its pain-inducing biological dampening field that had nearly incapacitated him.

"I know," said Jho'quin. "My people are currently in the process of securing and modifying them so that they no longer pose a threat. We plan on using them to transform the willing portions of the population."

"All right. I'll trust your judgment. And I'll spread the word, though I can't guarantee everyone will go along with this. Asking people to undergo genetic alterations isn't the kind of thing that'll be warmly received."

"I understand, and we're prepared to accommodate those who don't want any part of this."

"Well, Sergeant, get word to our soldiers. Explain the situation as best you can and inform them to direct all inquiries to me. Order all squads to assist our new allies in combat, and once an area is secured, they're to sweep through and round up all survivors. Nobody gets left behind."

"Acknowledged, sir."

"We'll have healers standing by to tend to the wounded," Kat'lya added. "And I can have someone look at your leg if you'd like, Lieutenant."

"Thanks, but I'll be fine," the lieutenant replied, tightening the blood-soaked bandage she had wrapped around her thigh. She wasn't quite ready to trust them with her wellbeing until she felt more certain about their intentions. She'd let them prove themselves on the battlefield before making up her mind.

"Once the enemy has been vanquished from Earth," Jho'quin continued, "I'll make a formal announcement to the surviving population and explain everything that's happened, as well as our plans for the future. In particular, I'll disclose our expectations of them in the coming days. They'll have some difficult decisions to make, but hopefully the greater portion will unite behind us. Unfortunately, there's little choice but to press on, no matter how difficult the road ahead of us may seem."

"Speaking of which," interjected the major, "it's going to take decades to recover from this devastation. Every major city is in ruins."

"And they'll remain that way," Jho'quin replied. "We're not staying here."

"What?" the lieutenant exclaimed, hoping that she had misunderstood.

Even the sergeant was taken aback by Jho'quin's comment, snapping his head to full attention and pausing from his duties in order to listen in on the remainder of the conversation.

"As I've told you, our enemy possesses a vast armada. If we rebuild our cities, they'll simply come back and destroy them again. And in that case there wouldn't be any survivors. They have the means to annihilate all life on this planet in the blink of an eye. In fact, the only reason you're still alive right now is because the enemy believes they have done precisely that, thanks to an illusionary projection that's currently enveloping the Earth. But it's an illusion that won't last forever."

"Well that's real friggin' great!" she complained. "So we win the war, but we have to give up our homes in the process."

"We haven't won this war," Jho'quin argued back. "The battle for Earth is nearly over and we *will* be victorious at that, but this is only the beginning."

"He's right," O'Connor interjected with a sigh. "As much as I hate to say it, this planet's become a liability that we can no longer afford. We're better off evacuating, at least for the time being."

"So what now?" the lieutenant grumbled.

"We do as he asked," O'Connor replied. "We get back out there, finish off the remaining hostiles, and tend to the survivors. Is that clear?"

"Perfectly, Boss."

"How can I contact you again, Jon?"

"I'll send four of my best soldiers to accompany you. They'll serve as liaisons between our respective forces, and they'll know how to reach me."

"Excellent. I look forward to visiting with you when this is all over."

"As do I, General. As do I."

"Move out, marines."

Alpha One departed back into the forest, marching with greater confidence than they had experienced since the conflict began. Four of the Praeden'Cor went with them to ensure their safety and the successful completion of their tasks, leaving Ilian and Zia'uthun to remain at Jho'quin's side.

Several slits soon opened along the underside of Ixlyo, permitting a dozen star fighters to drop through and accelerate away from the clearing.

"Looks like the boys are off," Kat'lya reported, sensing the departing presence of Dead Eye, Xiang, and Par'kezul.

"You have done well, Lord Kashan," the familiar voice of Riathol called out from behind Jho'quin. "The Gods are smiling down upon us all."

The Council of Elders had disembarked from Ixlyo and was walking toward their revered leader. They were the only ones not dressed in battle armor. Having taken an oath of non-aggression when first anointed to their callings, they were forbidden to shed any blood, even in self-defense. Their callings were most sacred, and as such, they had abstained from participating in the actions of war, though they gave their counsel freely concerning the matter. One member of the Praeden'Cor served as their escort.

"The scourge of House Voldrok will soon be gone from this world," Riathol continued. "Our victory is at hand, our vengeance begun. The Great Awakening has commenced."

Jho'quin bowed his head in respect to his approaching brethren and produced a smile of satisfaction that crept warmly across his face. "All is well, my friends. All is well."

High above the Earth, within the debris field of the day's battle, a wormhole opened. A lone Voldrokian warship crept into the region and scoured the wreckage, pausing in view of the Earth, which deceptively appeared destroyed. There the vessel lingered but for a moment before departing from whence it came.

Appendix

The following is a compilation of all Kush'humani terms used within this book. Their definitions and appropriate pronunciations are provided for reference. By using this appendix you can return to those passages in the story where the Kush'humani language is used and discern the exact meaning of those statements that weren't explicitly translated.

Prefix/Postfix Listing

Certain prefixes and postfixes can be added to Kush'humani words so as to produce a derivative word or inflected form, though certain exceptions apply (e.g., Praeden is both singular and plural). These affixes are always offset by apostrophes.

'et   *(ĕt)* d or ed (past tense)

         example: krey (kill) and krey'et (killed)

'la   *(lă)* r or er

         example: nox (you) and nox'la (your)

'qui   *(kwī)* ing

         example: jorshu (bring) and jorshu'qui (bringing)

'sa   *(sô)* 's (possessive)

         example: uluqzon (warrior) and uluqzon'sa

         (warrior's)

'ta   *(tə)* s or es (plural)

         example: embatlei (battle) and embatlei'ta (battles)

lash'   *(lôsh)* de

        example: menta (evolution) and lash'menta

        (devolution)

li'   *(lē)* re

        example: tillae (born) and li'tillae (reborn)

Terminology

ablyotum	*(ə-blē-ō-tŭm)* oblivion
abrai	*(ə-brā)* strike or hit
alph'hati	*(ăl-fə-tē)* begin
alra	*(āl-rə)* unto
angelatra	*(ən-jəl-ă-tră)* soul
baylo	*(bā-lō)* yes
chosh	*(kŏsh)* child
con	*(kŏn)* them
cor	*(kôr)* light
deraska	*(dĕ-răs-kə)* depart
dracorum	*(drā-kôr-ŭm)* shadow
drak	*(drôk)* dark
Drak'Rasha	*(drôk-rô-shə)* Dark God
edrox	*(ē-drŏks)* approach
ehm	*(əm)* he
ehmfet	*(əm-fĕt)* she
Elo'shon	*(ē-lō-shŏn)* Name of the King of Gods
embatlei	*(əm-băt-lā)* battle

emla	*(əm-lă)*	male
emlafet	*(əm-lă-fĕt)*	female
enballe	*(ən-bô-lē)*	name
eternus	*(ē-tûr-nəs)*	forever
ethaul	*(ə-thôl)*	archives
ex	*(əks)*	has
folushan	*(fō-lü-shŏn)*	pleasure
gor	*(gōr)*	station
gorgon	*(gōr-gôn)*	power
grabor	*(grə-bôr)*	hand
grasha	*(grə-shə)*	process
grego	*(grā-gō)*	good
gullushui	*(gü-lŭ-shwī)*	prize
haisen	*(hā-zən)*	crime
hem	*(həm)*	him
hes	*(həs)*	his
hesfet	*(həs-fət)*	hers
hilean	*(hĭ-lē-ən)*	sacred
Hilean'Ethaul	*(hĭ-lē-ən ə-thôl)*	The Sacred Archives
Humani	*(hyü-mô-nē)*	The Defeated (or Human)
illae	*(ĭ-lā)*	life
illgrata	*(ĭl-grô-tə)*	fool
ish	*(ĭsh)*	the
ith	*(ĭth)*	at

ithalae	*(ĭth-ô-lā)* isolation
ithca	*(ĭth-kă)* both
jel	*(jĕl)* be
jelai	*(jĕ-lī)* by
jorshu	*(jôr-shoo)* bring
kali	*(kô-lē)* unity
ki	*(kī)* in
killraxun	*(kĭl-rôk-sün)* destruction
krey	*(krā)* kill
Kush'humani	*(kü-shü-mô-nē)* The Undefeated
lay	*(lā)* lesser
Lay'rasha	*(lā-răsh-ə)* lord or lesser god
ledgegon	*(lĕ-jə-gŏn)* knowledge
ledgekor	*(lĕ-jə-kōr)* judge
lenkillra	*(lĕn-kĭl-rə)* scourge
malray	*(môl-rā)* secure
mani	*(mô-nē)* man
matray	*(mô-trā)* more
may	*(mā)* one
menta	*(mĕn-tə)* evolution
mog	*(môg)* first
mortalum	*(mōr-tôl-ŭm)* death
mortalum'quay	*(mōr-tôl-ŭm kwā)* arena or death area
nalak	*(năl-ək)* take
neitray	*(nī-trā)* rest

nixkillrusha	*(nĭks-kĭl-rŭ-shə)* suffer
nox	*(nôks)* you
ogmay	*(ôg-mā)* last
oknala	*(ôk-năl-ə)* open
onlo	*(ôn-lō)* no
orlaban	*(ôr-lă-băn)* world
oshmot	*(ôsh-môt)* under
pa	*(pô)* for
pax	*(păks)* shall
pesh	*(pĕsh)* filthy
peshkal	*(pĕsh-kăl)* prisoner
peshtoy	*(pĕsh-toi)* wretched
praeden	*(prā-dĕn)* guardian or guardians, depending on context
Praeden'Cor	*(prā-dĕn-kôr)* Guardians of Light
preta	*(prā-tă)* before
pur	*(pŭr)* cleanse
quay	*(kwā)* area
ra	*(rô)* to
raituk	*(rā-tŭk)* attack
Rasha	*(rô-shə)* God
reka	*(rā-kə)* until
retamba	*(rā-tôm-bô)* tremble
rotkillrusha	*(rôt-kĭl-rŭ-shə)* torment
saetenta	*(sā-tĕn-tə)* behold

sheloq	*(shā-lôk)* silence
soron'keil	*(sō-rôn-kāl)* generic name given to enslaved star wanderers
tau	*(tou)* that
tillae	*(tĭ-lā)* born
tore	*(tōr)* pod
tox	*(tôks)* this
traden	*(trā-dĕn)* great
trentosh	*(trĕn-tŏsh)* enough
udrokem	*(ü-drō-kəm)* come
uluq	*(ü-lŭk)* prepare
uluqzon	*(ü-lŭk-zŏn)* warrior
un	*(ün)* and
ungali	*(ün-gă-lē)* just
ushun	*(ü-shŭn)* peace
Ushun'Kali	*(ü-shŭn-kô-lē)* Original Kashanti home world. Means "Peace in Unity"
Ushun'Ithalae	*(ü-shŭn-ĭth-ô-lā)* Peace in Isolation
uthun	*(ü-thün)* companion
uthunaia	*(ü-thü-nī-ə)* brother
vail	*(vāl)* I
valoi	*(vă-loi)* my
ven	*(vĕn)* of
veni	*(vĕ-nē)* ready
volun	*(vō-lün)* we
vurloi	*(vûr-loi)* way

wist	*(wĭst)* have
yuke	*(yūk)* curse
zar	*(zăr)* are
zil	*(zĭl)* is